For Beverly
Best Wishes!

LAWFUL
ORDERS

LAWFUL ORDERS

A NOVEL BY

Jonathan P. Tomes

Veterans Press

LEAWOOD, KANSAS

This work is fiction, and any resemblance to actual events or persons,
living or dead, is entirely coincidental. The legal concepts in this fictitious
case are as accurate as possible. As far as military law is concerned, this
court-martial could have happened.

Published by: Veterans Press
5001 College Boulevard, Suite 214
Leawood, Kansas 66211
Phone (913) 327-1181
Fax (913) 327-7997

Printed in the United States of America

10 9 8 7 6 5 4 3 2 1

First Edition

Library of Congress Catalog Card Number: 97-062365

ISBN 1-880483-00-9

*To my fellow combat veterans of
the First Cavalry Division,
especially SGT Thomas Herbst,
to my former students
at the U.S. Army Command and
General Staff College and at
IIT Chicago-Kent College of Law,
and to my running buddies on the
ridgeline and elsewhere.*

ACKNOWLEDGMENTS

This book began with a conversation with my friend Colonel (then Major) Jim Mogridge during which we talked about how we were getting too senior in rank to prosecute or defend soldiers in the Judge Advocate General's Corps, U.S. Army, and how much fun it would have been to have gone up against each other in a court-martial. Jim, thanks for your support.

Many people helped me write this book. Alice McCart, my editor, provided invaluable help with the manuscript. Colonel James Wosepka's unflagging support and confidence in me enabled me—no forced me—to live up to his expectations when I might otherwise have given up on trying to write and publish a novel. Robert Frezza of the U.S. Army Claims Service, an accomplished novelist, taught me a lot about writing fiction—and made me cut down my interminable internal dialogue. Others at the U.S. Army Claims Service, particularly Linda Harrison and John Morton, provided insightful hints on improving the early drafts of the manuscript.

Others who provided valuable assistance and support were Peggy Senko, formerly of Stackpole Books, publisher of my *Servicemember's Legal Guide*, Dan Cragg, author of *A Soldier's Prize*, Tom Carhart, author of *The Offering*, Bill Millar, Mary Cady, Bill Hunt, Lindsay Rupiper, Todd Sanders, Mark McCart, Elizabeth Rogers, and Paul Tomes. Finally, I must acknowledge Professor (Colonel) Michael Spak's sponsorship and the support of Kenda Tomes and Richard Dvorak, who will not let me be less than all I can be.

PROLOGUE

Leadership Reaction Course
Army ROTC Summer Camp
Fort Indiantown Gap, Pennsylvania

J U L Y   1 9 6 8

"Now, listen up, ladies," the Jolly Green Giant roared. The ROTC cadets—all male—immediately fell silent as the Giant, a six-foot-four-inch black major, strode to the front of the bleachers where the cadets were seated.

Cadet James Thomas turned to his short, slim friend from Maine, Cadet Bill Cady, and whispered, "Here it comes."

Jim was right. The first words out of the Giant's mouth were, "Cadet Thomas!"

"Yes, Sir!" Jim bellowed back. He knew from bitter experience that, if he didn't yell loudly enough, the Giant would keep repeating "I can't hear you" until Jim put enough effort into his reply—extra effort that would leave Jim hoarse and out of breath.

"Unless I'm mistaken—which is highly unlikely—you haven't had a chance to be patrol leader yet."

Jim wouldn't have told the Giant he was mistaken even if he had been, but unfortunately, Jim hadn't had his turn at the leadership reaction course yet. "Sir, that's correct, Sir!" he yelled back. With anyone else, that might have been one sir too many, but not with the Jolly Green.

The instructor pointed to a large, acetate-covered map. Framed to the north by long, unbroken mountains shimmering in the haze of the hot afternoon sun, the Giant looked especially large and ominous. "Cadet Thomas, your mission is to take these ladies to this objective—a suspected enemy headquarters—reconnoiter it, and return without being detected by the enemy. Ok, ladies, let's get a move on!" Such concepts as equality of the sexes in the military were several decades in the future

1

at best, and the Jolly Green Giant would neither have cared nor changed his behavior anyway. And anyone who had not served in combat or at least finished airborne or ranger school had not earned a respectful title in the Giant's estimation.

The cadets poured out of the bleachers. As they retrieved their old M-1 rifles from the neat tripods they had stacked them in, Bill said, "You were right, Jim. Your turn in the barrel."

Jim almost smiled. "Yeah, I can't say I'm looking forward to it. But I might as well get it over with." It was the last test Jim had to pass to graduate and get his commission. If he didn't get commissioned, he would owe the Army four years as an enlisted man to repay his ROTC scholarship—tuition, fees, books, and a $50 a month stipend—assuming that, as an enlisted infantryman in Vietnam, he lived that long. The leadership reaction course was a bitch. The last three cadet leaders had flunked. And Jim certainly didn't want to return to the University of Cincinnati as a leadership reject after having won numerous cadet awards, including three Professor of Military Science medals.

"You know, Bill, this has to be the toughest part of summer camp. You can practice with your rifle to make sure you pass marksmanship. But you can't practice for this. How do I know what ungodly crisis they are going to throw at me?"

As he adjusted the straps on his pack, Bill replied, "Yeah, and I hope you have more luck than I did. I passed, but after the Giant chewed me out for twenty minutes, I almost gave up and went home."

An hour later, Jim paused to wipe sweat from his brow, trying unsuccessfully to keep it from streaking down the lenses of his ugly, military-issue glasses with black plastic frames. His short butch haircut didn't slow the perspiration as it ran out from under his heavy helmet. He signaled the patrol to take a break. Salt-crusted stains grew under the armpits of his baggy fatigues as he strained to figure out where on the map they were.

Some of Jim's sweat wasn't due to the heat, however. His nervousness made his sweat both more profuse and less fragrant. "Hey, Bill, how am I doing so far?" he whispered. "Did I screw up the minefield? It seemed like a no-brainer."

"I thought you did ok." Their instructors had taught them to use their bayonets to probe for a path through minefields. Jim had done so and had continued the mission with only one casualty—the cadet the Giant had chosen to act as if he had stepped on a mine and play dead. "You're doing all right," Bill concluded.

"I don't know. The Giant looks pretty pissed off."

"He always looks pissed off!" Jim's friend replied. "I'll never understand why cadets named him 'The Jolly Green Giant.' There's nothing jolly about him. Come on. We'd better get moving, or he'll take points off for too long a break."

"Yeah, mission first, men last."

"That seems to be the point."

The cadets moved out, tailed by their instructor. Jim stole a look at him, but the Giant's face looked neither more nor less disgusted than usual. Ten minutes later, and about a half-mile from their objective, a cadet followed his instructions from the Giant and started yelling hysterically, "I quit! I'm scared! I'm not going to fight!"

"Shut up!" Jim hissed, but the cadet continued to yell hysterically. Afraid the cadet was going to compromise their mission, Jim didn't even think. He just reacted. He took three quick steps toward the screaming cadet, pivoted, and simulated knocking him out with the butt of his rifle. Not surprisingly, the screaming stopped. Even though Jim had not actually hit the cadet, the sight of an M-1 butt coming at him had apparently scared him into silence. The cadet feigned falling down unconscious. Jim ordered, "Leave him. We'll pick him up on the way back if we can. Now let's get going before the enemy finds us."

Once more, the cadets moved out. Again, the Giant's face was impassive. The rest of the patrol passed uneventfully. They found the suspected enemy headquarters. Jim radioed back its location and the details any intelligence officer would be interested in. Then they exfiltrated quietly from the objective area and picked up the hysterical cadet who was still pretending to be dazed at the spot they had left him.

Back at the assembly area, after drinking quarts of tepid water from the olive-drab, canvas lister bags hanging from the trees, the cadets formed up for a critique. Jim still couldn't tell from the Giant's glacially cold expression whether he'd passed or failed.

The major stalked up right in front of them. "Be seated," he thundered. "Everyone but Cadet Thomas."

Oh, shit, Jim thought, here it comes.

The Giant continued, "Well, ladies, how did Cadet Thomas do?" The cadets looked around anxiously, each hoping someone else would volunteer to answer. But the Giant didn't want their opinion. "I'll tell you how he did." Jim closed his eyes briefly, not wanting to hear it. "Take a good look at Cadet Thomas, ladies. For a change, today a cadet acted like a fucking combat leader instead of like a Girl Scout."

Jim blushed furiously, elated, as the Jolly Green Giant continued, "Yes, ladies, he didn't waste time talking. He didn't consult with his subordinates. He didn't call a fucking lawyer or even a chaplain. He didn't worry about the screaming cadet's civil rights. He just knocked the bastard out and carried on with the mission. A few more seconds of his screaming could have compromised the whole company. Remember, mission first. Always! Good job, Cadet Thomas. Get your ass to jump school and ranger school, and we may make a soldier out of you yet. Now get back to the buses, ladies. It's almost time for chow."

As he rode back to his cadet company's dilapidated World War II barracks, Jim smiled, knowing he'd passed summer camp and vowing to be the best combat leader ROTC had ever produced. When they gave him a real combat mission, he'd do it, no matter what. Flushed with pride, he vowed to volunteer for airborne training and ranger school as soon as he got to his first assignment, the Infantry Officer Basic Course at Fort Benning, Georgia, now only two weeks and a commissioning ceremony away.

PART I

THE ACCUSED

I came when my country called.

CHAPTER 1

Near the Song Be River,
North of Saigon,
South Vietnam

JUNE 1970

"Wake up, 1-6! The listening post is on the horn." Lieutenant Jim Thomas felt groggy. He sat up in his hootch and took the radio handset from his RTO. "1-6 here. Go. Over," he whispered.

"1-6, this is 1-1 Alpha. We're getting movement all around us. Request permission to blow our claymores. Over."

"1-1 Alpha, this is 1-6. Don't talk. Just break squelch—once for yes, twice for no. Are you sure it's Charlie? Over."

After a long pause, Lieutenant Thomas, the platoon leader of the first platoon of Alpha Company, First Battalion, Seventh Cavalry, First Cavalry Division (Airmobile), or 1-6, as his men called him, thought he could detect reluctance in the double break in the static. It told him Sergeant Hamm had pressed the push-to-talk button twice—to break squelch. The men on the LP were not certain it was the enemy. How could they be? The night was pitch black. Even if the monsoon clouds had permitted the moon to shine through, the foliage of the triple-canopy jungle wouldn't have. Besides, Hamm was a cherry—a brand new, shake-and-bake sergeant. Sergeants who had not risen from the ranks, but attended Noncommissioned Officer Academy, the course the Army had instituted because of high casualties to provide sergeants quickly to augment those who had followed the normal, several-year progression to sergeant E-5 rank, were known as shake-and-bakes, and anyone new in country was a cherry. So Hamm was twice damned. Worse yet, this was Hamm's first night in charge of a listening post, located outside the perimeter to give early warning of an enemy attack, and he didn't have the experience to tell what were normal night sounds and what were enemy sounds. Although the sergeant outranked the spec four who was squad leader, Lieutenant Thomas had made Hamm assistant squad leader until he could amass some experience. Until that time, the lower ranking troop would be a far better squad leader. Thomas had put Hamm in charge of the listening post to give him some experience. But Jim was now paying for that decision because Hamm's inexperience made him want to fire his claymore mines at the first sounds he heard.

Lieutenant Thomas chewed worriedly on the bottom of his mustache, which was getting way too long. He wondered how he could teach this cherry everything he needed to know in a few minutes without distracting him for too long from the threatening, silent night around the LP. "1-1 Alpha, if you blow your claymores, you won't have any weapons left to use without giving your position away. If you throw your frags in the dark, they could hit a tree and bounce right back on you. The gooks can see the muzzle flashes of your M-16s, so just sit tight. Ok?"

After hearing the single break in the static, the lieutenant wondered what to do next. After all, he didn't have much more experience than Sergeant Hamm. But from having been on a few night ambushes, he knew what it felt like to be isolated from the rest of the company, outside the lines, in the pitch-black night, listening to the alien sounds of the jungle. Even the wind, blowing through the elephant grass or rattling the bamboo stalks against one another, sounded ominous, like Charlie moving nearer, ever nearer. Jim rejected the idea of talking continuously to this scared, eighteen-year-old sergeant because Hamm needed to be listening for the enemy more than he needed reassurance. "Listen, 1-1 Alpha, I'll get you permission to blow your claymores and come in if you're sure that gooks are in front of you. Otherwise, sit tight. Roger?"

"1-6, request permission to come in. Over."

Jim clenched his fist and shook his head in frustration. He wanted to scream at Hamm, but he could only whisper. "Negative, I told you not to talk. Do you want to give your position away? Just break squelch. If you are sure the enemy is in front of you, break squelch three times. I'll stay awake and ask you for a sitrep every fifteen minutes. Break squelch once if you're ok. Over."

As Thomas heard the lone break, he hoped Hamm remembered that "sitrep" meant situation report. He wondered whether learning Vietnamese would be any worse than learning Army jargon and acronyms.

Because sound carries further at night, Jim had ordered the men in his platoon not to talk after dark. He didn't allow them to smoke either. Charlie ruled the night. And even a relatively inexperienced platoon leader like Jim knew enough to want to engage the VC on his own terms, not the enemy's. Any careless sound or light would give away the grunts' night defensive position. Charlie would choose how the battle would be fought. But in his fear, the young sergeant had forgotten how sound carries and had talked too much on the horn.

Lieutenant Thomas eased his slender, six-foot body out of the hootch he and his radio-telephone operator had fashioned out of their rubberized ponchos and sticks. Jim sat quietly on the edge of his foxhole and made sure his M-16 rifle was at his fingertips, but had decided against putting his helmet on over his dirty, brown hair. If he put it on, he'd have a headache from its weight long before dawn. Jim also checked the large pocket on the upper leg of his dirty jungle fatigues to make certain his battery-powered strobe light was handy. The strobe light would be critical if he needed helicopter gunship support. He would have to get down low in his foxhole and activate the bright, flashing light to mark the friendly lines so the gunships wouldn't shoot them up.

Although the Americans had total air superiority, 1-6 didn't find that knowledge particularly comforting. He was afraid some trigger-happy chopper jock might not make a big effort to find out whether a line of green-clad troops humping through the jungle below them were U.S. forces or NVA. Jim did, however, reluctantly admire the NVA for fighting well with no air support. In the previous day's firefight, an NVA soldier had exposed his position to fire three rounds from an obsolete SKS rifle at a jet coming in with a load of napalm—a brave, but ultimately futile, gesture. Jim's men had found the rifle beside the crispy critter. I'd have run like hell rather than shoot at a fast burner looking to dump napalm on my ass, Jim thought. It would be a bitch of a war if the NVA had equal air power, he concluded.

Before coming to Alpha Company, Jim had served in a stateside infantry company for his mandatory six months' troop duty before assignment to Vietnam. His stateside company commander, Captain Carl Morton, had worn a First Cav combat patch on his right shoulder, complementing the Combat Infantry Badge he had proudly worn over his left shirt pocket as he strutted around the company area. Morton brainwashed his new lieutenants about the Cav, but not exactly the way he intended. The captain had regaled all his lieutenants with stories of the Cav's tremendous body-counts, finds of supply caches, and impressive helicopter assaults into enemy-held areas. But the parts of his stories that really enthralled his listeners were his descriptions of the tremendous rear support the division's airmobility provided. They were far more impressed with stories of daily resupply, including mail, cold beer,

Cokes, and frequent hot chow than with any number of victorious fire-fights. In any case, if one of his lieutenants didn't want to serve in the Cav, he didn't dare mention it to Captain Morton.

Jim did want to serve in the Cav, but when his orders to Vietnam came, they did not assign him to a specific unit. Only West Pointers got specific assignments, not mere ROTC graduates. Lieutenant Thomas's orders assigned him to the U.S. Army Transient Detachment, Vietnam, for "further assignment to be determined upon arrival in country," a polite way of saying to whatever unit had the biggest lieutenant casualty list that week.

With his orders to Vietnam in hand, Jim had taken thirty days' leave. All soldiers on orders to Vietnam took a thirty-day leave unless they were insane or gung-ho, even if they had not yet earned thirty days' leave. The theory was that the deceased soldiers wouldn't have to repay any leave if they were killed. Let the Army deduct it from the amount paid to their survivors. Also, like many other newly commissioned offi-cers who knew they were going to Vietnam, Jim had married shortly after becoming a second lieutenant. Although Jim dearly loved his wife, Margaret, he sometimes wondered whether he and others enroute to Vietnam had married out of love, or out of a morbid desire to leave someone behind to mourn them in case they were killed in combat. He spent his thirty-day leave with Meg, trying to cram all the love and joy for the rest of his life into that one short month.

Far too soon, Jim's thirty-day leave had ended, and he had arrived in Vietnam. Jim remembered the U.S. Army replacement battalion in Long Binh as a green daisy-chain of officers going from their billets to the bulletin board, to the officers' club, and back to their billets. The clerks posted the replacements' assignments on the bulletin board. Until you were one of those replacements and saw your name listed under a com-bat division, you could still hope to be a rest-and-relaxation officer in Australia, a club officer in Saigon, or a security platoon leader in Cam Ranh Bay.

One fat little transportation corps lieutenant had told Jim that his stateside assignment officer had guaranteed him that he would end up behind a desk in Saigon. To the chubby lieutenant's chagrin, the trans-portation officer found his name under the heading of an infantry divi-sion. "This just means I'll have to schedule convoys between various elements of the division," he had said. Hope springs eternal, Jim thought.

The realists at the replacement battalion had accepted the inevitabil-ity that the only place they were going to was an infantry unit. But they had had another obsession. They speculated endlessly about which division was most likely to be pulled out and sent home next, hoping for an assignment to the current favorite or, if they were especially gung-ho, hoping for an assignment to a division that was unlikely to be pulled out.

Of course, when U.S. Army Vietnam or USARV (use-er-vee, as everyone called it) announced the actual withdrawals months later, they were rarely the divisions that replacements had thought were good prospects, so those who had managed to worm their way into their favorites were often frustrated. Those who were placed in the withdrawn divisions were also frustrated because the Army let them go home with the division only if they had less than two months left on their one-year tours. Otherwise, they were transferred to other divisions. One formerly 10,000-man "division" went home with only 400 men. The rest of the men in the division, those with two months and one day or more left on their tours, went to other in-country divisions.

Lieutenant Thomas had had several of these men in his platoon for a couple of days and had already decided they were worthless. They were so pissed off at staying behind and so close to finishing their tours that the thought of getting killed or wounded when they were "short" made them nonfunctional.

Although Jim had decided not to try to get into the First Cav, but rather just to go wherever the Army sent him, he had had a momentary rush when he first saw his name under the First Cavalry heading on the bulletin board. Even now, Jim still felt proud whenever he pulled on his fatigues with the big saddle roll on his left shoulder. He knew he would take a lot of shit about his Cav patch. Soldiers in other divisions had a saying about the patch. They said it was "the horse that had never been ridden and the bridge that had never been crossed, and the color, yellow, spoke for itself."

This harassment didn't bother him, however, because he believed they were just jealous. Lieutenant Thomas knew he would always wear his patch proudly. He couldn't wear it on his right shoulder until he left the Cav as a combat veteran, but afterwards, he could always wear the Cav patch on the right sleeve, regardless of which unit he would be assigned to. If the Army ever reassigned Jim to the Cav, he'd be a "Cav sandwich," with a patch on each soldier—the ultimate status symbol.

But Jim could hardly feel as if he had accomplished personal triumph over the Army's assignment system because 90 percent of the replacement infantry lieutenants were going to the Cav. The new skytroopers decided the Cav must have been seeing more contact than the other divisions and must have lost a lot of platoon leaders. All the same, they congratulated themselves on the tremendous support they would have and laughed at the less fortunate officers who would be struggling through dense jungle while the Cav officers rode comfortably to their destinations on helicopters.

How little the naive officers knew. The only advantage of helicopters was that the brass could stick them out in the middle of nowhere faster and have the supply pukes fly over and kick out ammo, water blivets, and C rations. The units that weren't "lucky" enough to have a lot of helicopters went out for only a day or two at a time before returning to a nice firebase with hot chow, cold beer, soft drinks, mail, and other creature comforts.

Jim did luck out in one way, however. Captain Hart, Alpha Company's commander, really had his shit together. Although his company had been in contact with Charlie daily, friendly casualties were light. Only two men had been injured badly enough to be medevaced, and they had returned to the unit quickly. Captain Hart seemed to anticipate what the NVA were going to do and make the right response every time. Like other members of Alpha Company, 1-6 would follow Captain Hart anywhere. But the captain was a strange bird. Even though he was an outstanding combat leader, he was painfully shy. After every firefight, he'd shake hands with every grunt and commend him for his part in the action. Yet he couldn't seem to carry on a simple conversation with his lieutenants. Early on, Jim had decided he preferred Captain Hart's tactical acumen to any social graces he might lack.

After what seemed like hours, Jim determined by the luminous hands of his Army issue watch that fifteen minutes had passed, so he called the LP. "1-1 Alpha, this is 1-6. Give me your bluebird. Over."

Jim was glad he'd remembered to tell Hamm that "bluebird" was the company's code for a situation report—a sitrep. Jim had learned this lesson the hard way. He had taken a radio watch his first night in the field. At 0-dark-thirty, the commander's RTO had called and asked, "How's your bluebird?" Thinking the RTO was smoking pot, Jim had wondered what in the world a bluebird was. He had not endeared himself to his RTO when he had awakened him to ask him to explain bluebird. After learning it was a sitrep, Jim had crawled back to the radio and said his "bluebird" was ok, only to be chewed out for improper radio procedure. His RTO was even less thrilled the second time Jim woke him up, but he told 1-6 that "bluebird volunteer" was the correct response. No wonder the NVA have the courage to attack us, Jim had thought—they must think we're nuts. "Give me your bluebird," he repeated.

Whoever was on the radio out on the LP broke squelch twice. So things weren't ok, Jim thought. But what was wrong? "Do you still have movement? Over."

One break.

"Break once if it is in front of you, twice if it's all around. Over."

Break, break.

"Is it behind you? Over."

Two breaks, no.

"Are you sure it's an enemy probe? Over."

This time the signal was a resounding "yes"—as resounding as a break in static can be.

"1-1 Alpha, wait one. Bad Baron 6, this is 1-6. Over."

The commander's RTO replied, "1-6, this is 6 India. Wait one. I'll get 6. Out."

After a few moments, Captain Hart's disembodied whisper came over the handset. "1-6, this is 6. Go. Over."

"6, 1-6, my lima pappa has been reporting movement for a while. I want to give them permission to blow their claymores and come in when they think they have to. Over."

"1-6, are they sure it's gooks? Over."

"Affirmative, 6. They said they were all around them. Over."

"Ok, when they feel they have to blow their claymores and come in, they can. 6 out."

"1-1 Alpha, this is 1-6. Permission granted. Don't blow your claymores until you are sure you have to. Break squelch four times before you blow them. Break squelch once if you roger. Over."

A single break in static told Lieutenant Thomas that the troops on the listening post had understood the message. Jim thought wistfully of the inflated air mattress in his hootch, but knew he couldn't go back to sleep. Even with someone monitoring the radio, he might not wake up quickly enough to react if the LP came in.

As he sat on the edge of his foxhole and held the radio hand set next to his ear, Jim fell into a reverie, thinking about getting out of the miserable jungle and back to "the world." He had visions of cheeseburgers chased by cold beers and hot showers. Suddenly, four breaks in the constant noise of his radio earphone interrupted his pleasant thoughts.

Oh shit, he thought, they're coming in. He started scrambling towards the foxholes of his platoon members to warn them that the LP was coming in, so they wouldn't blow their buddies away. Suddenly, the roar of the claymores detonating shattered the quiet jungle night. After the roar came a hiss, as each claymore propelled 700 pellets in a

60-degree, 2-meter high, and 50-meter deep arc of destruction. After five eternal minutes, the men from the LP managed to get back within the night defensive perimeter without getting blown away by their anxious buddies. Now safely together again, the men of the first platoon huddled in their foxholes, wide awake, waiting for the enemy's attack.

About an hour later, at 0400, Captain Hart called all four platoon leaders and ordered all of them to get into their foxholes and blow all their claymores. The planners in their freshly pressed jungle fatigues back at battalion headquarters, called this tactic a "reconnaissance by fire." The grunts in the bush called it a mad minute. No matter what anybody called it, it often worked. And it did this time, too.

Alpha Company had caught the NVA coming in—trying to infiltrate the perimeter. Even though the enemy could manage to fire only a few sporadic rounds after the claymores had exploded, Captain Hart called in tube artillery and aerial rocket artillery from cobra gunships to mop up.

The firefight was so one-sided that it quickly attracted several higher ranking commanders who wanted to horn in on the action. The battalion commander, an insecure little lieutenant colonel named McCreary, who loved his macho call-sign, Big Duke 6, was flying overhead in his command and control helicopter, trying to get involved in the firefight just so he could get another Air Medal. He was so desperate for awards that he had been rumored to scratch himself on barbed wire around a firebase right after the NVA had rocketed it, to get another cluster on his Purple Heart.

While flying thousands of feet over the firefight, McCreary called Captain Hart on his radio, "Bad Baron 6, this is Big Duke 6." He always drawled out, "Big Duke," as if he were John Wayne. "Be advised that I'm overhead, but can't find your location." Of course, even if he had been directly overhead, he couldn't have seen anything of the firefight through the jungle canopy except for the cobras working out above it. Captain Hart was too busy to try to placate Duke 6, so he ignored him.

Private Molson, a Canadian grunt who had somehow been drafted while in the United States and who was less than thrilled at being in Vietnam, however, grabbed the radio handset from one of the RTOs and shouted, "Why don't you come down below the fucking clouds and maybe you can find us!" McCreary later ordered a thorough investigation to find out who had made this disrespectful comment, but no one in Alpha Company seemed to have any idea who the culprit could have been, not even the two grunts next to him in his foxhole who had learned it was possible to laugh hysterically during a firefight.

At sunrise, Captain Hart sent the third platoon out to look for bodies. The grunts were startled to find several NVA soldiers, including a senior captain, a lieutenant, a radio-telephone operator, and a medic, all blown away by a claymore only twenty feet from one of the third platoon's foxholes. The RTO was the closest to the claymore. He looked barely human. The captain lay like a rag doll with the stuffing coming out of his head and his limbs sticking out at unnatural angles. The medic's lifeless arm was spread across the lieutenant's mangled torso as if, even in death, he wanted to administer comfort.

Apparently, after the first platoon had detonated its claymores, the NVA decided that 1-6's men were too alert and moved around the perimeter to attack the third platoon's side. Or the movement on the first platoon's side of the perimeter was a diversion. Either way, Captain Hart's mad minute had stopped them before they could launch their attack. The presence of a senior captain indicated that the NVA unit had been at least a reinforced company that had expected to overrun the perimeter. Captain Hart's seeming prescience had again thwarted the enemy—and again with no friendly casualties.

Almost every grunt went to look at the effects of the claymores on the four unnaturally sprawled bodies. Having been the target for a firefight seemed to do away with Christian charity: "This will teach them to fuck with Alpha Company." "Boy, we sure brought scunion on their asses!" "Better you than me, motherfucker!"

Later that morning, Alpha Company's already high morale soared when Captain Hart announced they were being pulled out of the bush to pull perimeter security for the battalion firebase—called "green line duty" for the green line between Charlie's green jungle and the brown dirt of the cleared area around the firebase. It was a reward for kicking Charlie's ass and a rest from humping the boonies. That afternoon, the jubilant skytroopers moved to a pickup zone and were extracted by helicopters for their ride to the firebase.

After a week there of filling sandbags, pulling guard duty, stringing barbed wire, police calls, hauling ammo, police calls, and more police calls, it was time to leave. Although the relative safety of the firebase with its hot chow, its medical attention for jungle rot, immersion foot, and other hazards of the jungle, its daily mail, and its other amenities made the grunts of Company A reluctant to leave, they were also getting more and more restless and bored. But even their unease at returning to the jungle paled next to the shock they felt when they found out that Captain Hart would not be going with the company. Apparently, when the brass had learned that Company A, 1/7th Cavalry, was kicking ass without suffering significant casualties, they decided that its commander must have his act together and should get a job planning operations.

After all, why would the Army want someone who was good at leading soldiers in combat out in the field? That situation would be logical. So when the line of grunts—each hunched over by a heavy pack, four or more canteens, and belts of machine gun ammo—filed out of the fire-base to return to the bush, they were under the command of Captain Mark Armstrong. A cherry.

CHAPTER 2

North of Quan Loi,
South Vietnam

A U G U S T   1 9 7 0

Big Soul, the first platoon sergeant, eased his massive black body down beside Lieutenant Thomas. Alpha Company was taking a break from humping through the jungle. Big Soul had earned his nickname within a few days of joining the first platoon because of his habit of saying, "Praise the Lord," at every opportunity. This frequent outburst, along with his attempts to convert the platoon members, did not make him very popular.

Jim agreed with the troops that the overweight NCO should be more concerned about this world than the next. Although someone once said there were no atheists in foxholes, the lieutenant felt his men needed some physical comforts, like hot chow and a rest, more than they needed their souls saved, especially because Jim felt that his men had paid their dues and that no loving God would fail to welcome them if they died in battle for America. Most of the grunts seemed to agree with 1-6. At least the soldier with "Yea, though I walk through the Valley of the Shadow of Death, I will fear no evil, because I'm the baddest motherfucker in the Valley" printed on his helmet cover seemed to.

Big Soul didn't care much for 1-6, either. Lieutenant Thomas wasn't gung-ho enough to suit the career NCO, not to mention the lieutenant's cavalier attitude towards the platoon members' place in the afterworld. Nevertheless, the E-7 was glad to sit down by the lieutenant and share the good news. While talking to Captain Armstrong's RTO, Big Soul had heard that Big Duke 6 had ordered Alpha Company to move to a new area of operations to work with an armored cavalry regiment, the 11th ACR. Working with the 11th ACR had to be better than pulling night ambushes, as Alpha Company had done for the past six nights. Maybe they would get to ride on the regiment's armored personnel carriers instead of humping the bush. The overweight NCO preferred riding to trying to keep up with young grunts on foot, especially in light of Captain Armstrong's desire to move twice as far each day as his predecessor, Captain Hart, had. This desire had resulted in more than twice as many heat casualties than the company had suffered under Captain Hart's command—unnecessary casualties the already understrength company could ill afford.

Big Soul told Lieutenant Thomas the news about the new AO and said that the commander wanted to see all the platoon leaders ASAP. Jim groaned at the thought of having to report to Captain Armstrong. He had already developed an active dislike for his commander—not without justification. If Armstrong gave a shit about anything but himself and his career, 1-6 had missed it. So had the troops.

Lieutenant Thomas left his relative comfort at the base of a tree he had been leaning against for a little shelter from the incessant rain and joined the group at the company command post. Captain Armstrong nodded as 1-6 approached, but didn't say anything. Jim stifled an urge to snicker at his commander's ridiculous appearance. Captain Armstrong appeared to be imitating a ranger or leader of some other elite unit. Instead of carrying an M-16 rifle like everybody else, he had a CAR-15, a sawed-off version of an M-16. He alone in the company wore camouflage paint on his face. But, then again, tactically, he probably should have tried to camouflage himself because he was the only officer who wore his rank and insignia on his jungle fatigues. All the other officers had sense enough not to wear any rank or to wear enlisted rank so as not to advertise their status to the enemy. His attempt to look like an elite jungle fighter seemed particularly stupid to 1-6 because Armstrong simply looked too young and too green. His face was too round, and his ears stuck out. Even his hair was an indeterminate color—somewhere between unwashed blonde and dirty brown. He looked even less like a tough combat leader when he pulled out a plastic packet of Kleenex, blew his nose, and fastidiously folded the tissue before depositing it in an empty C ration box. Jim made a point out of wiping his nose on his sleeve, an action that left his nose and mustache-covered upper lip even dirtier, considering the grody state of his fatigues. He had been wearing the same fatigues for about a month—a month in which he had slept in the mud, had had Vietnam's red dust blown into the fabric by helicopter blades, had sweat enough to fill up several water blivets, and had carried several of his bleeding troops back out of the line of fire. And it had been three months since 1-6 had seen Kleenex and even longer since he'd seen anyone fold up a used one to discard it.

As soon as all four platoon leaders had arrived, Captain Armstrong detailed the plan for extraction and combat assault into the new AO.

"Ok, we're going to move about one click to the northeast to this clearing," he said, pointing to his acetate-covered map. "Once there, we will link up with Bravo Company, Second of the Fifth, and establish a joint night defensive perimeter with them. Their call sign is Fence Post. The next morning, we will be picked up by slicks for a combat assault. Three-six, you will be first out and LZ control, followed by the CP, 4-6, and 2-6. One-six, you will be last out and PZ control. Any questions? If not, move out." Jim mentally translated this lingo. The third platoon leader would be on the first lift of helicopters and would be in charge of the landing zone. Captain Armstrong would follow with the rest of the command post. Thomas and his platoon would be last, after the fourth platoon and second platoon had left, and he would be in charge of the pickup zone. Being first into a landing zone or being last out were the most dangerous because you didn't have much support if you were hit.

Jim's morale improved considerably after they had linked up with Fence Post and he had seen Bill Cady, now Fence Post 2-6, approaching from his company's sector of the perimeter. Jim and Bill had attended IOBC at Fort Benning together after summer camp. They hadn't seen each other for a couple of months, but the separation felt more like a couple of lifetimes. The two young officers stood there in the steamy jungle and shook hands for a little longer than necessary to maintain a "tough infantry platoon leader" image. What they really wanted to do was hug each other and hang on for dear life, but they did the next best thing and sat down on their helmets and started exchanging war stories. Cady seemed to be the lucky one. Bill had not been in any firefights as yet and had a squared-away commander. Jim allowed that he had not been as lucky—a lot of contact and a doofus commander.

"You know, Bill, Armstrong is a real asshole. My first commander was strac—a lot of contact with only light friendly casualties. And we kicked the gooks' asses. But Armstrong keeps blundering into ambushes where we take casualties for nothing. He's fucking up the troops just so he can seem aggressive to the battalion commander. We've had a dozen cases of heat stroke and heat exhaustion. And he won't listen to anyone. I don't have much experience, either, although I've got more than he does, so I can almost understand why he won't listen to me. But he won't listen to the other platoon leader or to the first sergeant. And First

Sergeant Gore has seen more shit than the rest of us have had nightmares about.

"And I hate the way he screws over the troops. One day, he sat under his hootch while one of the troops, a heat exhaustion casualty, lay not five feet away from him unprotected from the sun until the medic came. And when we get hot chow, Armstrong eats first, followed by the EM, followed by top and the other officers. You'd think that seeing the other officers eat last would tell him something. Half the time, all the hot chow is gone by the time it's our turn. I guess Armstrong wants to make sure he doesn't miss it."

Jim's friend, whose prematurely balding blonde hair belied his otherwise youthful appearance, was silent as Jim continued. Fence Post 2-6 had a lot of empathy and let Jim talk out his frustrations—the same insolvable frustrations other platoon leaders in Vietnam had.

"What really frosts me, though, is getting people killed and wounded for nothing." Jim fell silent for a moment, arms folded over the M-16 on his lap, and looked out over the newly secured perimeter. He frowned. "You know, sometimes, I lie awake nights berating myself for not having the balls to shoot him. It would save lives in the long run. What do you do when your commander gives you a stupid order that might get your men killed for nothing?" One-six sighed.

Bill shook his head, wishing he had the answer. "You've really changed, Thomas."

"How's that?"

"You were so gung-ho in summer camp and IOBC. Always mission first. Now look at you. You've even given up on the regulation haircut. And a Fu Manchu mustache, no less. Next, you'll replace your Army glasses with wire-rims. What gives?"

"I don't know. Maybe the contrast between my first commander, who cared for his troops, and Armstrong, who cares only about his career, woke me up. Maybe part of it is that no one seems to give a shit about the poor grunts out in the bush.

"The final straw was the last time we were back at Quan Loi. We had a couple hours to kill, so I decided to get a haircut. The damn rear echelon MP wouldn't let me in the PX where the barbershop was because my hair was too long. Talk about Catch-22. I was wearing PFC stripes, so I found out a little of what it's like to be an enlisted grunt back in the rear.

"It's hard to know what's right in this place. I always ask myself whether I'll be able to look at myself in the mirror later. Hey, enough of this heavy shit, I've got two beers I've been saving in my pack. The troops seem to prefer warm Coke to warm beer, so I get stuck with them. I'm sure they are piss-warm, but what the hell."

As Fence Post 2-6 picked up his helmet, Jim noticed the words written on it, "Where is Crusader Rabbit now that we need him?" Where indeed?

"Sounds good, Crusader." The two lieutenants passed the rest of the evening talking about more pleasant subjects, like what they'd do when they got back to "the world."

The next morning, after Bravo, 2/5th, had moved out, Captain Armstrong told Lieutenant Thomas to put his men on outposts all around the perimeter in two-man teams to provide security until the helicopters came. He also told 2-6 to put two more teams out in front of his sector of the perimeter.

The wait for the helicopters dragged on for hours. The grunts bitched, concluding that the battalion commander had his head up his ass and didn't have the helicopters ready. Alpha Company had to wait too long. Suddenly, a VC machine gun opened up and killed two men on one of second platoon's outposts. The grunts behind them were pinned down by fire and could not return fire without hitting friendlies on the outpost who might have still been alive. All the second platoon could do was hug the ground as incoming rounds were passing a foot overhead. As shells whizzed over his head, Jim had the irrational thought that he had never hugged his wife as closely as he was hugging the earth. The second platoon leader called in tube artillery and requested cobra gunships. Because 2-6 was new, Jim helped him call in the fire support.

Suddenly, Captain Armstrong came up on the radio, "Bad Baron 1-6, this is 6. Over."

Jim shook his head in exasperation. I don't have time for this shit, he thought, I've got artillery to adjust. But he couldn't ignore his commander. "Six, 1-6. Go. Over."

"Thomas, get your platoon on line and assault the machine gun. Over."

After hearing Armstrong, Jim wished he had ignored his commander. "Six, 1-6. Say again. Over."

"One-six, this is 6. I said, get your platoon on line and assault the machine gun."

"Six, you're coming in garbled. I didn't roger your last transmission. Over."

"One-six, this is 6. Bullshit, Lieutenant, you heard me! Now move out!"

"Six, be advised my platoon is spread out all around the perimeter. I can't get them assembled."

"One-six, move out now or I'll court-martial you!"

To hell with him, Jim thought. I'm not fucking up my platoon for nothing. He obviously doesn't know what the hell is going on. I don't even know where my platoon is! "Six, this is 1-6. Negative. Out."

"Are you disobeying my order, 1-6? Are you a damn coward? Over."

"Affirmative to disobeying the order, 6. Out." Jim dismissed Armstrong and his stupidity from his mind and returned to adjusting artillery.

A few minutes later, cobra helicopters arrived and began pulverizing the area with rockets and miniguns. The machine gun fire slackened and then stopped entirely. The two men on the outpost were dead, but when the grunts made a sweep of the area, they found no dead VC. Not long afterwards, slicks came in to start the extraction. Third platoon left, followed by the company commander, the RTO, the medic, and the artillery forward observer. The two bodies accompanied their buddies of second platoon to the new landing zone on their last combat assault together before helicopters took the two green plastic body bags back to the rear.

The combat assault was uneventful—a "green" LZ. If the enemy had fired on the combat assault, it would have been a "hot" or a "red" LZ. After everyone had landed and the two units had established a two-company night defensive perimeter, Captain Armstrong called his platoon leaders together. He was fuming, red-faced under the green-streaked camouflage paint.

"I called you here to critique your performance in the firefight we just had. Big Duke 6 just chewed me out on the radio for taking casualties without getting a body count. The only reason we didn't annihilate the enemy was because 1-6 disobeyed my order to attack." His voice cracked as he continued raging, "You're a coward, 1-6. I'll deal with you when we get back to the fire support base. I'll court-martial you if it's the last thing I do. I don't give a shit if your platoon loves you, I think you are a damn poor excuse for an officer! You've been frustrating my orders ever since I took command. I'd relieve you now if I had anyone to replace you with. Until I can replace you, I expect you to obey my orders. That goes for all of you. 1-6, get out of my sight!" Lieutenant Thomas opened his mouth to say something, thought fleetingly about flipping the selector switch on his M-16 to rake—full automatic—and shutting up Armstrong permanently, but just shook his head, and then walked away.

When Jim returned to his platoon's portion of the perimeter, his RTO, PFC Darnell, put his arm around the lieutenant's shoulders. The enlisted grapevine was incredibly fast. SP4 Rivera, Jim's most experienced grunt, said, "Thanks, 1-6. We appreciate what you did for us. Don't worry about 6. If he hassles you, we'll all swear the doofus fuck is nuts."

"Thanks, guys." Jim responded with a wan smile. "But forget him for now. Let's improve our perimeter in case Charlie's still around."

The next morning, the company moved out to the east. They moved in three columns, with company headquarters in the middle. The jungle had opened up into a strange area of tall elephant grass and scattered trees. All of a sudden, one of the Kit Carson scouts, a former NVA soldier who had surrendered and agreed to work for the Americans, fired his M-16. None of the grunts could see what he had shot at, but a voice started yelling, "Chieu hoi! Chieu hoi!" This phrase translated loosely to "open hands" and meant that the speaker wanted to rally to the South Vietnamese side and, consequently, have the South Vietnamese government consider him for rehabilitation programs, such as the Kit Carson scout program, rather than be a prisoner of war. A small, scared NVA soldier stood up, with his empty hands above his head. He couldn't have been more than fourteen years old. All he had was a pith helmet, a bag of rice, and a bag of marijuana. The Kit Carson scouts interrogated him and told Captain Armstrong he had come from an NVA regiment that had just come across from Cambodia, but he had gotten separated from his unit and was lost. Armstrong called in a helicopter to extract the prisoner.

While they were waiting for the slick, Lieutenant Thomas joined the CP. "Sir," he began hesitantly, "I think we need to move out. We've been waiting here too long, and if this NVA is around, I'll bet there are more. We may be ambushed if we stay here too long."

Captain Armstrong glared at his first platoon leader. "Lieutenant, you are so deep on my shit list that I don't even want to talk to you. Now get back to your platoon."

"Yes, Sir, but let's at least move out in a different direction and do some zig-zagging."

"Lieutenant, although you don't seem to want to make contact with the enemy, I do. Now get back to your platoon, or I'll relieve you now."

Jim returned to his platoon, his thoughts racing. We're going to get ambushed, somebody's going to get killed for nothing, and that asshole won't listen to me. But if I refuse to move out in the same direction, he'll relieve me. And there's no one else in the platoon who knows how to call in artillery or conduct a firefight. Big Soul's useless in a firefight, and the rest of the troops are too junior. I guess if we're going to walk into an ambush, I'd better be the platoon leader so that someone knows what's going on because 6 sure doesn't.

After close to an hour, the company was able to move out again. After another half hour, Captain Armstrong signaled for a break and called his platoon leaders to his location. He proceeded to chew them all out for not being aggressive enough and for not following his orders with alacrity: "And the next firefight had better not be like the last one. You had better be running around leading your men, and if you get shot, it's your own tough luck."

As if on cue, the NVA chose that moment to spring their ambush. All the officers hit the dirt except for 1-6, who took off running through the impacting rounds to his platoon—and not because of Armstrong's orders. This wasn't one Viet Cong machine gun firing. This was impending death—mortars, machine gun fire, and B-40 rockets, indicating at least a company of main-force North Vietnamese regulars.

When Jim got back to his platoon, he found his men down, firing back at the automatic weapons fire they were taking from their front. Enemy mortar rounds were landing all around first platoon. Chaos. Only a few of the grunts were firing, probably because, as usual, they couldn't see where the enemy was. Jim yelled, "Put your weapons on rake and clear out in front of you." At least some of his men flipped the selector to full automatic and sprayed the area in front of them with the eighteen rounds they had loaded in their M-16 magazines. Although they had twenty-round magazines, experience had taught them that a full load would cause the weapon to jam at the most inopportune time.

After seeing that his men were fighting back, Jim grabbed the radio headset from his RTO and called the artillery forward observer, "6 Mike, this is 1-6. I need some artillery to suppress this machine gun to my front. About 100 meters November Whisky from your position. Over."

"One-six, this is 6 Mike. Be advised that 6 wants the artillery on the mortars. Over."

"Six Mike, fuck 6. Most of the mortar rounds are duds. We're taking casualties from the machine guns. Over."

"One-six, I'll see what I can do. I've got gunships coming. I'll have them make their run to your north. Over."

A sudden scream took 1-6's attention away from the radio. "One-Six, 1-1 Alpha's been hit."

"Get up there, Doc."

Doc Calvin, the platoon medic, grabbed his aid bag and half-ran, half-crawled to the wounded man. Doc was like a split personality. He was scared of everything most of the time. But when someone was wounded, he turned into a tiger and would charge through machine gun fire to give aid. Thomas turned his attention back to getting fire support.

With Doc giving aid, Jim knew he could do nothing for Sergeant Hamm except get the firefight over with quickly. Then, medevac helicopters could get Hamm out and to a hospital.

"Six Mike, this is 1-6. I can hear the cobras, but why aren't they working in front of my platoon? Over."

"One-six, this 6 Mike. Six directed them to suppress the mortars. Over."

Jim snarled, "Six Mike, fuck that shit. I'm losing people here! Get me some ARA now. We need it! The mortars aren't hitting shit! Over."

"One-six, 6 Mike. Roger, pop smoke. ARA call sign is Widowmaker one-niner. Over."

"Six Mike, roger. Smoke out." Thomas popped a purple smoke grenade toward friendly forces for the helicopter gunships. The hissing grenade spread a plume of the distinctive colored smoke, both sweet and acrid-smelling.

"Bad Baron 1-6, this is Widowmaker one-niner rolling in to bring some pee. I see goofy grape smoke. Over."

"Widowmaker one-niner, this is 1-6. Goofy grape, roger. We need fire on the area to our November. Over." The pilot confirmed the color smoke he thought the friendlies had popped because sometimes Charlie popped smoke himself, although they didn't have purple unless they had captured some. By confirming the color that the friendlies popped, the cobra gunship pilots lessened the chance of hitting the wrong troops. The gunship pilots seldom actually saw any troops during a firefight, because both sides would try to stay under cover. In fact, the NVA often tried to hug the U.S. lines close so that the gunships would not fire on them.

The helicopter gunships sprayed the area with their miniguns and rockets. Although it seemed as though no one could possibly survive the devastation the ARA had brought, the NVA machine guns continued to pour rounds into first platoon.

"One-six, this is 6. What's going on? Over."

"Six, 1-6 here, I've got casualties and heavy contact, I need a medevac."

"One-six, this is 6. Who's hurt? What's their condition? What's the enemy doing?"

"This is 1-6. I don't have time. Just get us a medevac. Over." Jim looked around frantically. The cobra gunships were working out too far away. The NVA were between the ARA and Jim's men. Armstrong came up on the horn again.

"One-six, answer my question, I want—"

Jim ignored him. "Break, Break. Widowmaker one-niner this is 1-6. You're too far north. You've got to bring the fire closer. Over."

"One-six, roger. Pop some more smoke. Over."

One-six pulled the pin on another smoke grenade and threw it to mark the right end of his platoon's position and pulled the pin on his last smoke grenade before throwing it to the left.

"One-six, this is Widowmaker one-niner. I see gorpy green. Over."

"Roger, Widowmaker. Bring it in close. Over."

Jim yelled at the top of his lungs, "Get down, first platoon! ARA coming in close."

Just then the jungle foliage erupted as the aerial rocket artillery rounds exploded right in front of the first platoon. The intensity of the NVA fire diminished, but as soon as the cobra gunships completed their pass, the incoming fire picked up again. "One-five, do you have any more smoke? Over," Thomas asked Big Soul.

"Roger, 1-6. Over," Big Soul replied.

"Pop them. The cobras are coming back." Again the popping of smoke, the confirmation of its color, followed by another gunship pass, this time firing their miniguns, the modern versions of Gatling Guns. In a one-second burst, a minigun could put a round in every square yard of a football field. When the miniguns fired, they sounded like a long, explosive belch—braaaaaaap!

"One-six, pop some more smoke! The rounds are getting too close!" one of the first platoon's grunts yelled.

Thomas looked around wildly. None of the grunts he could see had any smoke grenades. "If anyone's got smoke, pop them!" No smoke, only cries.

"Come on, 1-6! We're taking rounds."

Jim scrambled to his feet and ran through the incoming rounds to the third platoon. His platoon was between the third platoon and the enemy, and the third platoon was not involved in the firefight. "Quick, give me some smoke! The ARA's hitting my men!" he blurted out. One of third platoon members shoved four smoke grenades at 1-6. Jim immediately turned and ran back through the elephant grass to his platoon, adrenalin pumping through his system, making him feel almost immortal—what years later would be called a runner's high. He pulled the ring on the smoke grenade as he approached his men. He dove into the platoon CP, rolled over, rose to his knees, and threw the grenade. Just as he released it, he was spun around by an AK-47 round that took him in the chest. He dropped as if poleaxed.

His RTO, PFC Darnell, screamed, "Doc, get over here quick—1-6's been hit! He's fucked up bad." He bent over 1-6, "Hang on, Sir. Doc's on his way."

Lieutenant Thomas coughed, with traces of bloody froth on his lips, and whispered, "Take these smokes and pop them, so we don't get hit by ARA."

Darnell popped more smoke and then turned back to 1-6. Doc scrambled over and began administrating aid. "He's got a sucking chest wound. We've got to medevac him ASAP." Doc worked frantically, slapping a plastic bandage over the wound so Jim could breathe. Darnell told Doc that 1-6 had requested a medevac for 1-1 Alpha. "It's inbound. I overheard 6 India guiding it in. How's 1-1 Alpha?"

"He's dead. I couldn't save him."

By this time, incoming fire was diminishing from the aerial rocket artillery fire, minigun fire, and tube artillery rounds that Armstrong had finally shifted from the suspected mortar site. Big Soul arrived at the platoon CP and called for the company commander on the horn.

"This is 1-5. Over."

"One-five, this is 6 Mike. Go."

"Six Mike. 1-6 is hurt bad. What's the status of the medevac? Over."

"One-five, 6 Mike. It's inbound, over."

"Mike, can we get a chopper in here, or do we need to use a jungle penetrator? Over."

"One-five, 6 Mike. The nearest clearing is five clicks away. Better use the penetrator. Over."

"Roger. Have medevac come in on our yellow smoke. Over."

The medevac slick arrived and hovered overhead. The crew chief lowered a jungle penetrator. The downward wash of the rotor blades blew the elephant grass flat as the helicopter hovered overhead. Doc and Darnell secured the now unconscious Lieutenant Thomas to the jungle penetrator and guided his lolling body as the winch began to pull him up. As they watched 1-6 being hauled up into the open side of the huey, blood dripped down on their upturned faces, mingling with their sweat and tears.

"Will he make it?" Darnell asked Doc.

Doc shook his head. "I don't know—he's shot up pretty bad. He won't be back here. That's for damn sure."

They watched as the medevac Jim had requested for Sergeant Hamm bore him off instead.

PART II

THE INVESTIGATION

Only the dead have seen the end of war.

—PLATO

CHAPTER 3

Division Headquarters,
Eighth Infantry Division
Bad Kreuznach, Germany

NOVEMBER 1984

Major Jim Thomas bounded up the stairs to the second floor of the Eighth Infantry Division headquarters, an old stone building that had been an SS barracks during World War II, called, of all things, "Rose Barracks." A black, two-star general commanded the division, a fact that probably had the SS officers who had preceded him in the building spinning in their graves.

The general was well respected. He had gotten off to a good start the first day he arrived. When a white sergeant first class had failed to salute him, the general had merely said, "Sergeant, if you see a little black son-of-a-bitch wearing two stars, you'd goddam better salute." Everyone saluted after that.

By avoiding too much Wienerschnitzel and Sauerbraten on the German economy and by a lot of running, Jim had kept within five pounds of the weight he had carried while humping the boonies. The mustache he had grown in Vietnam—because all Cav platoon leaders were wearing them—had some gray in it now. At the top of the stairs, he turned right and entered the G-2 shop. "Is it out yet?" he asked Captain Foster, the military intelligence officer who was the division's order of battle specialist.

Foster smiled. "If it is, it hasn't been released to us peons. Don't worry. You'll be on this list," the young captain said sympathetically, knowing that Jim, now assistant G-2, really wanted to be on this Command and General Staff College selection list.

Once an officer made major, no mean feat in itself, selection for an intermediate service school, such as CGSC or the Armed Forces Staff

College, was the next major hurdle in a successful career. Less than 50 percent of all eligible officers would be lucky enough to attend an intermediate service school. Those not selected to attend a resident school would have to take the course by correspondence, or at night with an Army Reserve school unit, if they wanted to be promoted.

Jim poured himself a cup of coffee from the pot in the corner of the office and then decided he might as well get to work or he would worry about the list all day and drive himself crazy. He walked over to the mapboard where Specialist Heinemann was updating the dispositions of the Soviet Group of Forces, Germany.

"The Eighth Guards' Tank Army was seen at this location, Sir," Heinemann said, pointing to the map. Jim grunted, feigning an interest he did not have in the dry details of peacetime intelligence on the day the CGSC list was due out. His thoughts kept returning to whether he would be selected to attend CGSC. Now is the time, he thought, because I'm due to rotate back stateside anyway. I hope my record is good enough.

Captain Foster came back into the office and said, "Sir, Lieutenant Colonel Garnett has called a meeting."

"Now?"

"Yes, Sir."

"Coming."

Jim got up and walked into the G-2's office. As he entered, he noted that everyone was smiling. Lieutenant Colonel Garnett stood up and walked around his desk with his hand extended. "Congratulations, Jim, the Chief of Staff just called and told me you've been selected to attend CGSC."

Flushed and elated, Jim shook hands, first with the G-2 and then with all the other members of the G-2 shop, happily accepting their congratulations. Besides the thrill of being selected for CGSC, Jim was pleased and a little surprised to see how happy his coworkers seemed to be about his good news. Although he got along well with everyone, he and Meg didn't have many friends. They had been almost social outcasts after an incident that had occurred shortly after he had reported in to the Eighth Infantry.

They had gone to dinner at his commander's home. The Thomases were the only couple there who did not have children. Before they had sat down to eat, the men had talked about their work—the only socially acceptable subject of conversation for officers. The women had gossiped. But when both the men and women sat down for dinner, only two topics were fit for discussion. The salad course exhausted the first topic—where to go sightseeing in Europe. During the soup course—split pea—the conversation turned to children. First, the women had discussed their pregnancies. After finishing the soup, they had progressed to their deliveries. Finally, by the time they got to dessert—a chocolate mousse—the conversation had turned to their children's toilet habits. With no children of their own, the Thomases had nothing of substance to add to the diners' parental one-upmanship game.

Throughout the discussion, Jim had sat there seething—rolling his eyes and drinking more beer than he should have, especially because the conversation seemed to depress Meg, who desperately wanted a child. Finally, after Mrs. Williams had commented that her son's doo-doo was yellow and runny, sort of like the split pea soup, Jim could stand it no longer. He stood up, announced, "Yes, and my hamster's turds are little round pellets," and stalked out. Not surprisingly, the Thomases had not been invited out to dinner very often, other than unit functions to which everyone was automatically invited. Although Jim had felt the retort was worth the snub, he'd later had second thoughts because Meg seemed very lonely at times.

Jim had met Meg when they were both students at the University of Cincinnati. The circumstances of their meeting were none too propitious, however. Meg, along with most of her classmates, was against the Vietnam war. Jim, on the other hand, was not only in favor of the war, but actually was in ROTC. He took a lot of harassment from his classmates. They began calling him "General Jim" and defacing his books with such creative epithets as "baby killer" and "fascist." Although the abuse bothered him, it hadn't bothered him enough to make him give up his ROTC scholarship.

Meg hadn't been active in protesting against the war. She thought student protests were futile, and she was pretty wrapped up in her studies. Reading Proust in French and Goethe in German was hard enough without taking time away to engage in sit-ins and protest marches, and academic honors were more important to her than making points with student activists. But one day, she had impulsively joined a crowd protesting in front of the ROTC wing. Rotcy was in the red brick building that housed the Teacher's College, or ding-dong school, as the students who weren't taking teacher's ed called it.

The demonstration had started out peacefully enough. But when one uniformed cadet dared to respond to the obscenities hurled at him, some of the peace-loving protesters had proceeded to beat the shit out of him.

Cadet Major Thomas had been minding his own business in the cadet lounge, drafting a report for the Cadet Brigade Commander, when he heard Dave, his assistant adjutant, yell, "Come on, Jim! We need you!" Dave was a pudgy cadet who would eventually flunk his entrance physical because of a heart problem, thus ending his dream of being an officer. But he had the heart of a lion. Jim had been teaching Dave Korean karate—Tae Kwan Do—in their spare time. So when Dave looked out the window and saw the cadet in trouble, he called on his instructor to help. Jim, not having any idea what he was getting into, followed Dave out the door and found himself in the middle of a small riot. More out of self-preservation than heroism, Jim grabbed the battered cadet and started dragging him into the building. But just as he reached the door, he saw a blur heading for his temple. Hemmed in by the press of bodies, he couldn't duck. So, he instinctively used a circular block with a knife hand to deflect the object. Although he had broken an inch of concrete in karate demonstrations, this time the concrete won. The sharp edge of the cobblestone that a demonstrator had thrown at them shattered two of the fingers on Jim's right hand. So much for the invincibility of the knife hand but at least it had saved his head.

Meg, who had only been yelling at the cadets, had a sudden change of heart as she compared the violent protesters to the two cadets who had come out to pull one of their own from danger. When she saw Jim was hurt she ran to him and helped him into the building, pulling a handkerchief from her purse to stop the bleeding. Because no one else seemed to be doing anything constructive, she then escorted him to the student infirmary, screaming at the peaceniks to get out of the way. Cowed by her resolve, they left the two alone.

The infirmary referred Jim to an orthopedic specialist. Meg stayed with him while the doctor set the bones and prescribed Demoral for the pain. With his right hand splinted, Jim was next to helpless, so she ended up taking him to his apartment and cooking him a meal. Before long, they were dating. She even attended the ROTC award ceremony where the Professor of Military Science had awarded Jim and Dave Military Order of World War Medals for helping the other cadet. Then Jim proposed at the military ball, and she had accepted. Not too long before, Meg would have found it hard to believe she would someday walk out of her church under a saber arch, married to a soldier with a butch haircut, but that's what happened a year later—just after they had graduated and Jim had been commissioned a second lieutenant of infantry.

Jim's reverie ended when Lieutenant Colonel Garnett said, "Here's the list." After confirming that his name was actually on it, Jim looked for a few old friends. He sighed. Bill Cady wasn't on the list. He didn't look at the "A"s. If he had, he would have seen "Armstrong, Mark."

After the last congratulatory handshake, Jim said, "Thanks, everyone, but please excuse me for a minute. I want to call Meg."

Jim returned to his desk and dialed an outside line, cursing silently when he couldn't get one immediately. "Hitler's revenge" was what soldiers assigned to Europe called the military phone system. Finally, he got through to his wife. "Guess what, Honey! I've been selected to attend CGSC!"

Meg's answer was tempered with the realism of having been an Army wife through four previous moves. "Great. But that's in Kansas, isn't it?"

"Fort Leavenworth, Kansas."

"What's at Fort Leavenworth?"

"Well, besides the Command and General Staff College, there are the Combined Arms Center, which puts out combined arms doctrine, and the Disciplinary Barracks." Realizing that those attributes might not have sounded very appealing to her, Jim hastened to add, "It's only for a year, and it's supposed to be a pretty post."

"But it's in Kansas!"

"Yeah, but Kansas City is only about an hour away. There'll be good shopping and some couth there."

"What town is near the fort?"

"Leavenworth, Kansas. It's known as the prison city. Back in the 1800s, Leavenworth had a choice between being a prison center or a transportation center. The town bigwigs chose the prisons, leaving the transportation hub to Kansas City. So Kansas City is a major metropolitan area, and Leavenworth has seven penal institutions within a five-mile radius—including the federal prison, a maximum security state prison, and a women's prison. Most people in Leavenworth work at the post or in a prison. You can always visit Kansas City if Leavenworth bores you."

"How do you know so much about it?" Meg asked.

"Colonel Garnett spent an hour telling me about his student days at CGSC. He even keeps a copy of the yearbook in his office—just like a college yearbook."

"Do you incur a service obligation if you go?"

"Yes, one year."

"I really wish you'd get out instead."

"Look, Meg, we've been over all this before. I know you'd rather settle down and quit moving. And you'd prefer I had a civilian job so that I could be home more often. But CGSC selection means I'm a lock for lieutenant colonel. Then I can retire as an O-5 in only five more years. The only logical thing to do is stay for twenty."

"Knowing you, at twenty, you'll decide to stay for thirty."

"Look, let's not fight over the phone. You may like Kansas."

"Ok." Meg accepted her fate with as much grace as she could muster. "I'm glad you were selected, and even Kansas can't be too bad for a year." She laughed, "Just try to stay out of the Disciplinary Barracks, though!"

C H A P T E R 4

Lieutenant Colonel Paul David smiled as he walked up the sidewalk to 320 Hancock Avenue, Fort Leavenworth, looking for the nameplate that would read, "Major Ken Morgan." As with most Army posts, all quarters on this historic post on the western bank of the Missouri had their occupants' names displayed on the front doors. In 1827, Colonel Henry Leavenworth had founded the post. He had located it near the confluence of the Missouri and Little Platte rivers, which was also the start of the Santa Fe Trail. Leavenworth abandoned his camp a year later, however, because so many of his soldiers had become ill, but in 1829, another unit moved into the remnants of the camp. Since then, Fort Leavenworth has been an active military base.

As he walked, Paul thought, I should have known that asshole Ken would get selected to attend CGSC. I can't escape him. But it will be good to see him again. It's been four years. Paul knocked on the eastern door of the fourplex. Boy, I'm glad I got out of these student quarters when they kept me here on the CGSC faculty to teach law. Ken's petite wife, Elizabeth, opened the door. She smiled when she saw Paul and whispered, "Ken's in the kitchen. Just go in and surprise him."

There was Ken, unpacking kitchen utensils. He was about two inches shorter and ten pounds heavier than Paul. His countenance was kinder and less intense than Paul's—a kindness that soon vanished when he entered a courtroom, however, as some opposing lawyers had learned to their chagrin.

Paul watched for a moment and then said, "I see Beth's got you working, as usual."

"Paulie, you asshole! It's good to see you."

After the obligatory handshaking and back pounding, Ken went to the bar in the living room. "You still a scotch drinker? I don't have any of the swill you used to drink. Do you still drink that frog stuff?"

"Yes, I still drink scotch, and that frog stuff is called Laphroiag, a very fine single malt. But I'll rough it and drink some of your Chivas. I see the first thing you unpacked was your bar."

"Of course. You've got to have your priorities right."

The younger lawyer looked around the quarters as Ken rooted through his fancy wooden bar for a bottle of scotch. Although Paul out-ranked Ken, Paul was younger because he had gone straight into the Army from college. After five years in the infantry, the Army had sent him to law school. Ken, however, had worked for the FBI for a while after law school and entered the Army later. His FBI experience was one of the reasons he was such a dynamic prosecutor. Being aware of the difference between FBI and military police investigations, he always tried to make certain the MPs did not mess up a crime investigation. He had instructed the military police at the posts he served to call him immediately if they had a report of a serious crime. The Army's criminal investigation agents were notorious for messing up big cases. They got so few major crimes that every agent assigned to the post wanted to get involved in every murder, rape, or big robbery, so they could all feel like big city detectives. Consequently, they often stumbled all over each other, destroying evidence at every turn. With Ken on the scene, though, that didn't happen. He'd always take over the investigation and make certain it was done properly—unfortunately for the perpetrator.

Although there were still a few unpacked boxes in the living room, Ken's quarters looked familiar to Paul. After all, any set of government quarters anywhere in the world was much like any other—too small, with a carport instead of a garage at best, and with a small entry foyer—harkening back to the days when officers left their calling cards on a silver tray by the door whenever they visited other officers.

You could almost read the inhabitant's assignment history from his furnishings and decorations. If the officer had been assigned to Europe, for example, you would see beer steins, Delft china trivets, Hummel figurines, and beer deckels—little coasters from gasthauses advertising some small local brewery. If he had served in Korea or Japan, his quarters had black lacquered musical jewelry boxes, dolls in glass boxes, and oriental screens. And, of course, almost every set of quarters would have the ubiquitous paintings and prints from officers' wives' clubs' art auctions used to raise money for the scholarships the clubs awarded. Ken's quarters showed the Vietnam tour—large ceramic elephant planters—and his German service—an ornate "Schrank"—a huge freestanding wooden cupboard used for storage, as few living quarters in Germany had many closets—festooned with beer mugs.

Paul took a sip from the big tumbler of scotch Ken handed him and said, "Welcome to the Command and General Staff College."

Ken removed several boxes stacked on the couch and motioned for Paul to take a seat. "I was surprised to see they kept you here as an instructor. I thought you'd want to be a deputy staff judge advocate after having been a judge for three years."

Paul smiled wryly. "I did, but I got 'sentenced' to stay here close to the Disciplinary Barracks, where you and I sent a few dirtballs when we were prosecuting together at Fort Knox. I had asked for a deputy job, or to teach at the JAG School, but they kept me here anyway. It's not a bad job, though. I get to help assholes like you get through Command and General Staff College."

"What's the course like?"

"The saying that the good news is that you were selected to attend, and the bad news is that you have to attend is true. The course isn't too hard for a JAG. If you can pass your bar exam, you're not going to have any trouble with the tests here. But you have to learn a lot of boring shit that you're never going to need to use. The good thing is not the classes. It's your classmates—other Army officers, not to mention international officers from more than a hundred countries—close to a thousand students altogether."

"What's the course like?"

"It's broken down into core subjects that everyone takes, plus electives. Tactics is the biggest subject, both in terms of importance and hours, followed closely by logistics. Military history, joint and combined operations, and leadership are other major blocks. Naturally, my course—military law, is really the most important, but I haven't managed to convince the commander of that fact yet, so I have only twelve hours of core instruction."

Paul paused to sip his scotch and then continued. "The College divides the student body into sixteen sections, each of which has about sixty students. Each section is divided into four staff groups. You'll do most of your social activities with your staff group, but quite a few with your whole section. You'll have a faculty member as an academic counselor to your staff group—an ACE—Academic Counselor/Evaluator. But enough of this shit. You're not going to have any problems with the class. How did you like deputy at Gordon?"

"I loved it, Paulie. The SJA liked to play golf, so I ran the office while he played."

"How was your caseload? And how were your trial counsel?"

"The caseload was fairly heavy—but nothing like we used to have at Knox. The trial counsel were inexperienced, but they tried hard."

"And you gave them a little guidance now and then, no doubt. You know, I tell stories about you in my law classes. I tell them the story about the Carey case argument. It goes like this: First, I tell them the only evidence you had that Carey was the murderer was bloodstains on his clothing and your forensic evidence that showed only two people out of a thousand had that combination of blood factors. Then I tell them about your very structured, logical argument, followed by the defense smoke-screen when Orton argued, 'Where's the evidence of this? Where's the evidence of that? Why weren't the bloodstains sent to another lab for a second analysis?'

"Then I tell them your rebuttal argument was the shortest but most effective I've ever heard. Picking up Carey's bloodstained pants, you walked over to the president of the court, dropped the pants in front of him, and said, 'Here's your evidence.' Then you picked up Carey's bloodstained shirt, dropped it in front of the next ranking court member, and said, 'Here's your evidence.' Finally, you picked up the tree limb Carey had bludgeoned the victim to death with, put it in front of the third ranking court member, and said, 'And here's your evidence.' Then you whirled, pointed at Carey, and said, 'And there's your murderer!'

"Then I tell them how the jury dove into the deliberation room and returned about a minute later, having convicted Carey of everything he was charged with, even the felony murder/sodomy charge under Article 118(4), of which there was no evidence. We had to disapprove that finding on review. I tell my students you were the best prosecutor I ever saw. The classes love the Carey case story."

"Well, you weren't too bad in court yourself. You were the best at the law—on motion practice—I ever saw."

Paul laughed, "Boy, we're a real mutual admiration society. It's too bad we never got to go head-to-head in court. That would have been some battle."

"Battle, hell—it would have been a war. You know, Paulie, some-times I'm not sure that getting so senior in rank is worth it. We'll never get back into the courtroom. About all we can do is try to help young counsel. And that's only if we get a job supervising trial counsel."

"We might as well face it," Paul laughed. "We're two over-the-hill lawyers dreaming of past courtroom glories."

Ken snorted, "You don't look very over the hill. Are you still running like a madman?"

"I pretty much have to. I'm an ACE for one of the staff groups and have to set an example. I have to take the PT test with them. It does their little infantry, armor, or artillery hearts good to get their asses kicked by an older JAG officer in the two-mile run. I still run a marathon or two a year and a lot of shorter races. Is your back letting you work out?"

"No. I have to substitute the three-mile walk on the PT test. I could get a profile and not take the test, but I'd much rather have my efficiency report show I passed."

"Yeah, as tough as it's getting to get promoted, you don't want some fitness freak on the promotion board dinging you because you have a profile," Paul empathized.

Ken got up, walked over to the window, and looked at the rows of identical quarters with dozens of moving vans. "Well, they are not going to nonselect CGSC graduates unless we screw up. I've got to get a good assignment out of here, though."

"Speaking of getting out of here," Paul said, "if I don't soon get home, I'm going to be in deep kimchee. Let's get together with our wives for dinner after you get settled in. I'll have a party for all the JAG students in a couple of weeks, and we'll have a meeting where I'll fill you guys in on how to study and so forth. If you need any help in the meantime, let me know. Thanks for the scotch, even if it isn't the piss I normally drink."

"My pleasure, Paulie. Damn, it's been good to see you. It's almost worth coming to Leavenworth for a year."

They shook hands again at the door. Paul paused and looked at the lights of the back of the federal prison. "All these prisons here in Leavenworth remind me of criminal trial work. That's where it's at, not this teaching law, important as it is. Seeing you again really makes me realize how much I miss it."

Ken clapped Paul on the back. "Yeah, but those days are over. We might as well get used to it. I'll call you in a day or two, and we'll get together."

Paul walked down the drive to his Toyota, got in, and drove away through the back gate of the post, past the buffalo pen and the federal prison, to his off-post home. Ken went back into the tiny student quarters and started unpacking yet another box sporting cryptic notes and crossed-out addresses from five previous moves.

CHAPTER 5

Eisenhower Auditorium, Bell Hall
U.S. Army Command and General Staff College
Fort Leavenworth, Kansas

A U G U S T   1 9 8 5

An expectant hush lay over Bell Hall's Eisenhower Auditorium as if the enormous room anticipated its thousand seats would soon be filled by a new CGSC class, listening to the opening ceremonies of academic year 1985-86. Although the auditorium was impressive with its theatrical stage, paintings of all the U.S. presidents hanging on the walls, and flags of the Army's combat divisions hanging down from the balcony, every year CGSC students came to call it The Big Bedroom. They called the smaller auditorium, Marshall, The Little Bedroom. The new class would be too uptight to sleep during the opening ceremonies, but in a few weeks, many students would have to struggle to stay awake and listen to each boring guest speaker, especially when the lights dimmed for slide shows. Guest speakers had a nickname, too: guest sleepers.

It seemed to the students that the brass chose guest sleepers more for political reasons than for what they could contribute to the students' learning. One year, for example, the students had had to sit through two interminable hours while some female Department of the Army civilian told them how she had selected the artwork for some military celebration. The students joked that she must have been the Chief of Staff's mistress and was blackmailing him to get an invitation to speak at CGSC so she could get an all-expense-paid trip to the Kansas City area to visit some relatives.

Bell Hall, the home of the U.S. Army Command and General Staff College, is a large, red brick building on a bluff overlooking the Missouri River. This location, among other things, had prompted one student to suggest a school motto, "CGSC—built on a bluff and run that way."

To the north and east of the building are parking lots that are totally inadequate to hold not only the staff and faculty's cars, but also those of all the various students who filled the building at any one time. Besides CGSC, which is in session almost year round, the College is also responsible for several other courses: the Combined Arms and Services Staff School, CAS³—a nine-week staff procedure school that every Army captain must attend; the Pre-Command Course (PCC), for new brigade and battalion commanders; and other functional courses that both students and instructors believed were part of a conspiracy to ensure that the parking problem would never be solved.

The building's shape is almost indescribable. The closest anyone had come to describing it was a "pregnant A," with the bulge of Eisenhower auditorium sticking out to the west. Strange, intimate passageways and tunnels run to and from various wings of the building. In the center is an incongruous open area with canopied picnic tables. Between the legs of the "A," to the north, stands a statue of the lamp of knowledge, the school's symbol. Whenever a guest sleeper is in the building, some of the myriad workers who perform school support functions set out flags around the statue representing every country with an officer in attendance at CGSC. It makes for an impressive display, but unfortunately, seldom helps the quality of the speech.

CGSC had actually begun some weeks earlier. The international officers had come almost two months before the start of the regular course for language training and classes on how to live in the United States, called "Allied Prep, Phase I." The Navy, Marine Corps, and Air Force officers and the Army's professional branch officers, such as doctors, dentists, nurses, chaplains, and lawyers, had joined the foreign officers for Allied Prep, Phase II—an introduction to tactics and logistics. Then, when all the rest of the students had arrived, they had inprocessed and taken a number of diagnostic tests before the formal start of the course. After today's opening ceremony, classes would begin in earnest.

A few students began filing into the auditorium, looking for the seats assigned to them during inprocessing. Each sixty-student section sat together in the auditorium. The entire class was in their seats five minutes early for probably the only time during the course. As the year progressed, they would arrive later and later for any class.

One of the thousand students, Major Mark Armstrong, settled into his seat and introduced himself to the Air Force officer on his right and to the Army officer to his left. He automatically took stock of the Army officer by noting what ribbons he wore on the blouse of his class A uniform. No Vietnam medals—not a combat veteran like I am, he thought.

He turned slightly while talking so that the other major would be sure to notice his Combat Infantry Badge, as well as various Vietnam service medals topped with a Bronze Star with "V" device. He noticed another Army officer—a lawyer, from the branch insignia displayed on his lapel—on the other side of the Air Force officer. He noted that the lawyer's hair was too long. Armstrong still affected the butch haircut he had had ever since Vietnam, a haircut that still made him look too young for his rank.

Major Armstrong felt quite smug sitting there as a new CGSC student. Who would have ever thought, he congratulated himself, that I would end up a CGSC selectee? And even though I did it the hard way—OCS instead of ROTC—and without the benefits of the West Point protective society. I'm sitting here in the top 40 percent. Actually, he had not taken ROTC in college with the hope he wouldn't get drafted and have to go to Vietnam, but he conveniently forgot such a small detail. When he received his draft notice after graduating from Cornell, he had had his uncle, a general officer, pull some strings to get him into OCS so he would avoid serving as an enlisted man.

Suddenly, a voice called out, "Ladies and Gentlemen, the Deputy Commandant." A thousand officers surged to their feet and stood at attention as Major General Treakle strode to the podium on the stage.

Major Armstrong listened intently. He didn't want to miss any hints General Treakle might give on how to best his classmates. Armstrong wanted to win the Marshall Award for the number one student, known as the white briefcase. He felt that if he wasn't number one, he had to be at least an honor graduate—one of the top 20 percent. As he looked around at the competition, he thought, I've got to be better than most of these officers. Why, I'll bet less than a third of them are combat veterans. And, as an infantryman, he knew he had to have an advantage over noncombat arms officers here in the senior tactical school of the Army.

After building all the students up by telling them how great they were to have been selected for CGSC, the general immediately put them back in kindergarten by starting right in on what would get them in trouble: being overweight, failing the physical training test, flunking the writing course, drunken driving, or sleeping with someone else's wife. He hadn't modified his speech for the twenty or so female officers in the class. Apparently, they could sleep with someone else's husband.

The general also warned them about watching their health. "We've lost a student every year for the last four or five years," he said. "Year before last, an Army officer committed suicide, and an African officer died in an automobile accident. Last year, an outstanding officer from

Thailand died of a heart attack. Let's not have anyone die this year." He didn't mention the officers who had been kicked out of CGSC for cheating, or those who had resigned after being caught falsifying their travel payments or household goods claims, or the one who had solicited an undercover military policeman to commit a homosexual act. Just mentioning the deaths put enough of a damper on a welcoming speech without really getting into the darker side of CGSC—the divorces of already shaky marriages from the effects of the stress of studying and trying to keep up with the social whirl, the local black women who preyed on the African allies, and deviant or just plain criminal acts committed by a few bad apples out of a thousand CGSC students.

Mark's attention started to wander now that the general wasn't giving him any hints on how to be the number one student. Suddenly, he stiffened in his seat as his eyes lit on a familiar-looking officer to his right front. It couldn't be, he thought. Is that Jim Thomas? After he was medevaced, we heard he had died. That's the only reason I didn't court-martial him for disobeying my orders. If that's really him, he's done well enough in the Army to be one of the top 40 percent selected to attend resident CGSC. How could a wiseass like him make it this far?

Armstrong couldn't concentrate on the rest of the general's speech as he recalled his humiliation back in Vietnam when Thomas had disobeyed his order to charge the machine gun and how the men had liked and respected Thomas as if he had been the commander. As soon as the speech was over and the class had been released for lunch, Major Armstrong pushed his way past the line of officers trying to leave the auditorium, turned right, walked past classrooms one through six, turned left and went up a small flight of stairs to the Class Director's office. The clerk checked a computer printout. Yes, a Major Jim Thomas was in Section Fifteen. That's him. Armstrong felt a rush of adrenalin. "I'm going to burn him," Armstrong muttered. "Pardon me, Sir?" the clerk asked. "Never mind," Armstrong snapped. "Where's the JAG office?" The clerk showed him on a post map. Vowing to go over there and see a trial counsel the first chance he got, Armstrong forgot all about being an honor graduate.

CHAPTER 6

Office of the Staff Judge Advocate
Building 244
Fort Leavenworth, Kansas

A U G U S T   1 9 8 5

Major Armstrong climbed the stairs to the large, old brick building that housed the office of the post staff judge advocate. Upon entering, Armstrong scanned the directory, saw that the trial counsel were on the second floor, and went upstairs. He paused by the door labeled "Captain Lewis, Trial Counsel." Captain Lewis, a slender brunette dressed in a tailored, Army-green skirt and a pressed blouse, was sitting behind her desk. On the wall behind her were framed diplomas, including a law degree from the University of Texas, and the certificate showing her to be a member of the Texas Bar. Major Armstrong hadn't expected a female lawyer. He noted that the highest military school she had attended was the Judge Advocate General's Basic Course. That was her second strike—she was a fairly young, inexperienced lawyer. "Captain Lewis, I'm Major Armstrong. I called your clerk about preferring court-martial charges."

"Please come in and have a seat, Sir. Whom do you want to prefer charges against, and what is the offense?"

"I want to prefer charges against Major James Thomas. He is in my CGSC class. He was a platoon leader under my command in Vietnam, and he disobeyed my order to assault an enemy position. I want to charge him with disobeying a lawful order."

"Why in the world would you want to charge him now, over a decade later?"

"He was wounded the next day and evacuated. I thought he had died. I didn't know for sure he was alive until I saw him in this CGSC class."

Captain Lewis shook her head. "Well, although anyone subject to the Uniform Code of Military Justice—as you are—can prefer charges against anyone else subject to the UCMJ, I'm not sure it's worth it in this case. But let me check something before we go any further." She picked up the thick, maroon loose-leaf binder called the *Manual for Courts-Martial* and looked through the index. After reading several different sections, she said, "Yes, just as I thought. Article 90 of the UCMJ, disobeying a superior commissioned officer, has a statue of limitations. So does Article 99, misbehavior before the enemy. Thus, it appears to me that the statute of limitations would prevent us from prosecuting him even if the convening authority—here, the post commander, Lieutenant General Lowe—wanted to."

"Isn't there any way to get around the statute of limitations?"

"Well, it is a defense that the accused would have to assert. But if he had even a remotely competent defense counsel, he would use it."

Major Armstrong thought a moment and then continued, his voice rising, "Can't I charge him anyway, so it would at least show him that he can't totally get away with disobeying a superior? Even if we couldn't convict him, charging him would ruin his career."

"No, I can't recommend that," Captain Lewis said calmly. "It's unethical for a lawyer to prosecute a case she knows she cannot win. Although, as I said, you have the right to prefer court-martial charges against any other service member, I am certain the convening authority in a case like this would dismiss the charges barred by the statute of limitations. And I'm not sure he would want to dredge Vietnam up again after all this time, even if we didn't have a statute of limitations problem. After all, the government gave amnesty to draft dodgers and deserters."

His face reddening, Major Armstrong glared at the young captain. "That really sucks. We're not talking about a draft dodger. We're talking about an officer. Do you mean a commissioned officer can disobey an order and get away with it?"

"You don't need to raise your voice, Sir. The best way you could have made sure he didn't get away with it would have been for you to prefer charges and deliver them to your adjutant at the time. That would have tolled—suspended—the statute of limitations. But you didn't, so now you're stuck."

Major Armstrong replied heatedly, "But I thought he was dead."

"Well, perhaps your administrative personnel performed shoddy staff work by not checking on his status," Captain Lewis answered, looking at her watch.

"You don't understand, Captain. This was a war! Things didn't always work according to the regs. All I knew was he had a sucking chest wound and was medevaced. Our medic didn't think he would make it."

"I'm sorry, Sir. But for whatever reason, you didn't prefer charges then, and I can't advise prosecution now. But here's a DD Form 458, Charge Sheet. If you want to prefer charges, I certainly can't stop you. If you do prefer charges, I'll forward them to the convening authority. I'm just advising you that I don't think the convening authority will prosecute them. And that's his call, not yours or mine. You can use the *Manual for Courts-Martial* to get the proper form for the charges, and if you want, I'll swear you to them. But to be honest, when the charges come up here, I'll recommend against pursuing them. And I'm certain my boss, the Chief of Criminal Law, will agree with me. But feel free to check with him."

Major Armstrong took the charge sheet, snapped out a curt, "Thanks for your time, Captain," and stalked out.

Captain Lewis rolled her eyes, looked up, and whispered, "Stay with me on this one, God. I've got a bad feeling I haven't heard the end of it."

CHAPTER 7

Classroom 2
Bell Hall

SEPTEMBER 1985

Ken Morgan and the other students of Section 2, CGSC, tried to pay attention as their P314, Nuclear, Biological, and Chemical Operations, instructor lectured: "Since we assume the enemy will use chemical weapons, our doctrine calls for the use of the mission-oriented protective posture, called MOPP. This doctrine is intended to minimize casualties from chemical, as well as nuclear, warfare while permitting us to accomplish the mission." While the instructor continued, the students stirred restlessly, a few trying unsuccessfully to smother snickers.

Ken Morgan thought, just back up a few more steps. Come on. During the last break, one of the students, an Air Force officer, had taken the protective overgarment, boots, mask, and gloves off the dummy that the instructor had put on the stage to demonstrate MOPP protective gear. Then he had hidden the dummy and donned the protective gear himself. The rest of the class had a hard time avoiding overt laughter as they waited to see what the motionless student standing on the stage would do. The longer the instructor droned on, the greater the nervous tension in the classroom became. Ken glanced around the huge classroom, and his eyes fell on Mark Armstrong across the aisle. He seemed to be the only student who wasn't interested in the gag.

Finally, the instructor backed up to the dummy while talking about how MOPP level one required a soldier to wear the overgarment and carry the rest of the gear. The Air Force officer jumped down from the stage with a mighty roar and grabbed the panic-stricken instructor as the class broke into near-hysterical laughter. The instructor almost shit himself, but pulled himself together long enough to call for another break. Then he rushed for the door.

The students, still laughing, went into the hall. The school did not permit smoking in the classrooms, so the gloomy hallways always looked like foggy London from the cigarette smoke generated during breaks. Talk about a need for MOPP protective gear in a toxic chemical environment. Ken walked out with Armstrong. "Hey, Mark," Ken said, "I'll bet our instructor needed some kind of protective garment other than a gas mask. He looked like he wet his pants! Those Air Force jet jockeys are really wild."

"Yeah, it was pretty funny."

"What's the matter with you? You hardly smiled, and the rest of us were splitting a gut laughing. And you've been moping around for several weeks. Is something the matter?"

"No, nothing's the matter," Mark Armstrong answered quickly. Then he paused, "Well, you're an Army lawyer. Maybe you can give me some advice. Let's go sit somewhere."

"How about the snack bar? We've got twenty minutes."

The two student officers went downstairs to the snack bar, got coffee, and sat in a booth in a secluded corner. "What's bothering you?" Ken asked.

Mark started haltingly and then with a rush told Ken what he had told Captain Lewis and how she had reacted. "She didn't seem to understand anything about combat operations. Of course, that's what we get when we let women into the Army," he smugly concluded.

Ken said, "Well, she's right. The statute of limitations would bar a successful prosecution for misbehavior before the enemy or disobeying an order. But I'm not so certain there isn't another way to prosecute it that isn't barred by the statute of limitations. There is no statute of limitations for mutiny."

"I don't know whether it was a mutiny or not," Mark replied. "What exactly is mutiny?"

"I don't have a copy of the *Manual for Courts-Martial* here, but as I remember, a mutiny involves intending to usurp military authority and disobeying an order in concert with some other person."

"So, in other words, he would have to have been acting with other members of his platoon when he disobeyed my order for it to be mutiny."

"That's right," Ken answered. "Is that what happened?"

"I'm not sure. It had seemed to me that even before the incident, he and others in the company were trying to prevent me from carrying out my mission."

"Well, you may have a valid mutiny charge then, depending on what the evidence shows. If you are convinced he was acting in concert with others when he disobeyed your order, you can swear out charges. But I think you need to think about whether you really want to do so. If you prefer charges and the command investigates them, any dirt on you as a commander would come out. And it may not make you too popular to dredge up all this shit about Vietnam years later. But if you really want to do it, I'll help you draft the charges."

Mark thought for a moment and then said, "You know, Ken, it just galls me that a commissioned officer can disobey an order and get away with it. He was promoted to field grade and even selected to attend this course, after I know he showed cowardice before the enemy. We don't need officers like that. I don't really care if it does make me unpopular. I just want him and others like him to realize that they cannot disobey lawful orders and get away with it. I haven't been able to study properly since I saw him in the class from worrying about what I should do. I think I need to do something." He looked at his watch. "Hey, we'd better get back to class."

Ken nodded as they rose to start back to Classroom 2. "Ok, I can understand that. Tell you what. Write up a detailed statement of what happened, and I'll look it over and give you a more definite answer about whether you have a mutiny charge. Then, you can make a better decision about what to do. Ok?"

"Sounds good. I really appreciate this, Ken. I felt Captain Lewis wasn't really interested in helping me with this. I'll have the statement for you tomorrow."

"Yeah," Ken replied, "Fort Leavenworth's JAG office is just a sleepy little shop where they mostly put out to pasture old colonels who aren't going to make general. They wouldn't have any criminal work to do if they didn't have retrials of prisoners at the disciplinary barracks. They don't get the cream of junior lawyers, either."

They entered the classroom moments before the instructor resumed his rudely interrupted lecture. Ken listened to the instructor and took notes. Mark wrote furiously, but he wasn't taking notes on the lecture. He was drafting a statement.

CHAPTER 8

Office of the Staff Judge Advocate
Building 244
Fort Leavenworth, Kansas

SEPTEMBER 1985

Captain Lewis and her boss, Major Chuck Bailey, the Chief of Criminal Law, stood at the door to the Staff Judge Advocate's office. Chuck was one of the few black attorneys who had made field grade in the Judge Advocate General's Corps. The Corps talked big about equal opportunity and actually did pretty well at recruiting women and minority members. But with a few exceptions, most blacks didn't get promoted to senior grades and didn't get the plum assignments. And it was even worse for women. The Air Force had sent women to CGSC, but not the Army JAG Corps. The JAGC had one token female lieutenant colonel, who was also the token female SJA.

Colonel Ralph Farmer, the post SJA, was sitting behind a big walnut desk flanked on both sides by bookcases full of law books. Instead of the diplomas most Army lawyers had on the walls of their offices, the SJA had signed photographs of the generals he had been legal advisor to. He followed their careers closely, hoping he had allied himself with a future chief of staff whose coattails he might ride to the top of the JAG Corps.

Both junior lawyers hesitated, neither of them wanting to disturb the fifty-year-old colonel with their problem. Colonel Farmer had a tendency to become irritated when anyone brought him a problem, especially if it might hurt his chance of making general—a chance that existed only in his mind. Not only was his career not outstanding, but also his slightly overweight body didn't look like the JAG Corps's image of how a general should look. Because JAG officers were often thought of as wimps by combat arms officers, the JAG brass were extremely conscious of how their leaders looked. Glancing up, Colonel Farmer saw his junior attorneys, flashed his notorious smile, and waved them in. "What can I do for you?"

Captain Lewis looked at Major Bailey. When he nodded, she started in. "Sir, we've got a problem. Several weeks ago, I saw Major Mark Armstrong, a CGSC student. He wanted to prefer charges against a Major Thomas, another CGSC student. It seems Armstrong was Thomas's company commander in Vietnam and Thomas disobeyed one of Armstrong's orders. Apparently, Thomas was wounded and evacuated, and Armstrong, thinking he was dead, did not prefer charges at the time. I told him the statue of limitations would bar prosecution under Article 90, disobedience of a superior commissioned officer, and Article 99, misbehavior before the enemy. He was pretty upset, and now he's preferred charges under Article 94—mutiny. As you know, there is no statue of limitations for mutiny." Captain Lewis handed the charge sheet to Colonel Farmer.

"Did you tell him it was unlikely the convening authority would want to mess around with charges over a decade old, involving an unpopular war that almost everybody would rather forget?"

"Yes, Sir, but he was adamant. He's really serious about wanting to prosecute this guy. I think we should have the convening authority dismiss the charges."

Colonel Farmer asked, "Chuck, what do you think about his?"

"I agree with Captain Lewis, Sir. Besides the cost and the difficulties of proof more than a decade later, I don't know why we would want the potentially adverse publicity that a court-martial for this type of charge would bring. It might be a public relations nightmare."

The SJA thought for a few moments, scratching his thinning hair. Chuck watched his boss. He could almost read the colonel's mind. Now he's thinking about how dredging up these Vietnam-era charges would affect his career and how, if the press gets hold of this, it might make General Lowe, the post commander, look bad.

Finally, Colonel Farmer spoke, "I'm not so sure. I agree with what you said, but I wonder if we aren't exposing the convening authority to some adverse publicity if we just summarily dismiss the charges. I think we might be better off dismissing them after a full investigation. That way, no one could accuse the general of not taking a heinous crime like mutiny during wartime seriously. And if the investigation shows we've got something we can legitimately prosecute, we can decide then what to do. Can you live with that?"

"Yes, Sir."

"Ok, here's what we'll do. Captain Lewis, you call this Major Thomas and read him the charges. Then call the student detachment and the Adjutant General, and make sure they flag him—we don't want him graduating and moving on to his next assignment while this mess is pending. I'll call the Class Director and let him know what's going on. If he agrees, I think the best thing to do is to let Major Thomas continue to attend classes. The investigations may take a long time, so we don't want to put him in pretrial confinement even assuming we could make an argument that he was a flight risk or do anything that will give us any more speedy trial problems than we already have. When you talk to the AG, get the name of a sharp lieutenant colonel to be the Article 32 investigating officer, so I will have a name if the general agrees to conduct an Article 32 investigation. Do you have any problem with Captain Lewis's being the government representative, Chuck?"

"No, Sir."

"Captain, you call this Major Armstrong in and interview him. Get him to give you other possible witnesses' names and any other information you can use to find them. Also, get me both majors' officer record briefs, in case the general has any questions about them. Once you find out when and where this action took place, go to the CGSC library and see whether you can find any histories of the action. According to the charge sheet, the unit was an element of the First Cav. You might also call a trial counsel down at Fort Hood and see whether the Cav has any unit histories that could shed light on the action."

"Yes, Sir."

"Ok, let's move fast on this. I've got to see the general tomorrow, and I'd like to get a decision on the Article 32 from him then. And let's keep this as quiet as possible for now. Anything else?"

"No, Sir," the two young lawyers chorused and left the office.

Colonel Farmer picked up the phone, dialed, and said, "Mary, this is Colonel Farmer. I'm down for a fifteen-minute appointment with the general tomorrow. I think I'm going to need more time. Can you get me an extra fifteen minutes? Thanks a lot. I owe you one." He hung up but sat there staring out the window for a long time before turning back to the stack of papers on his cluttered desk.

The next day after a boring afternoon of classes on personnel management, Major Thomas knocked on Captain Lewis's door. "Captain Lewis, I'm Major Thomas. I had a note to come see you."

"Come in, Major. I have an unpleasant duty here. You have been charged with mutiny. I have to read you the charges." Captain Lewis did not ask him to sit down.

Jim could not speak for a moment. Then he stammered, "Mutiny? What the hell are you talking about? I know I told the Class Director that my staff group wasn't going to wear the MOPP gear all day when we had a soccer game that evening, but we ended up doing it."

"If you'll just listen, Sir, I'll read the charges, and you'll find out." Captain Lewis picked up the DD Form 458 and read, "In that Major James Thomas, then First Lieutenant James Thomas, U.S. Army, with intent to usurp and override lawful military authority, did, at Binh Long Province, Republic of Vietnam, on or about 19 August 1970, refuse, in concert with the members of First Platoon, Alpha Company, First Battalion, Seventh Cavalry, First Cavalry Division, to obey the order of his commander, Major (then Captain) Mark T. Armstrong, to assault the machine gun and did exhort other persons to join him in defiance of Major (then Captain) Mark T. Armstrong."

Without being asked to, Major Thomas sank into a wooden chair across from the trial counsel's desk. He sat for a long moment thinking of the implications of this charge. Could the Army really court-martial him for such a thing more than a decade after it had occurred? Who would want to? What was Meg going to think? A muscle twitched in his cheek until he responded. "Is someone crazy, bringing up this crap after all these years?"

"Major Thomas, I can't discuss the case with you. I'm not a defense counsel, and I may prosecute the case if it goes to trial. You should see a defense counsel downstairs in the Trial Defense Service. I will tell you that Major Mark Armstrong, who is in your CGSC class, preferred the charges himself. Here's a copy of the charge sheet and his statement. I suggest you take them to see a defense counsel."

"Hey, I'm sorry I yelled at you, but this is such a shock. What happens to the charges now?"

The young trial counsel was somewhat sympathetic to Jim's plight, but couldn't help. "Sir, I can't discuss the case with you. Again, I strongly suggest you see a defense counsel."

"Ok, is there anything else?"

"No, Sir. Thanks for coming in."

As he got up to leave, Major Thomas replied with a wan smile, "I wish I could say you're welcome."

He went downstairs and entered the Trial Defense section. The legal clerk at the reception desk asked, "Can I help you, Sir?"

"Yes, I'd like to see a defense counsel. I'm facing court-martial charges," Jim added incredulously.

"Ok, Sir, if you'll have a seat. Captain Wilson is talking to a client right now. He'll see you as soon as he's finished."

"Thank you." Jim sat down and read Major Armstrong's statement, shaking his head. Of all the bullshit, he thought, this is what I get for serving in Vietnam, getting wounded there, writing letters to the parents of my men who got killed with tears running down my cheeks, and putting up with all the other bullshit of that crazy war instead of going to Canada like the damn draft dodgers did.

The clerk interrupted Jim's bitter thoughts. "You can go in now, Sir."

When he entered and saw Captain Wilson, Jim thought, my God, he's young. But the airborne and air assault badges on his battle-dress utility uniform somewhat belied his youthful, clean-cut appearance. Unlike most JAGC officers, he had a butch haircut, cut very close on the sides. White walls and airborne, Jim thought, he can't be all bad. Jim handed the charge sheet and sworn statement to the defense counsel and said, "I'm being charged with a war crime."

Captain Wilson said, "You must be kidding. We haven't been at war for years. Sit down, please." He picked up and read the charge sheet and Armstrong's statement. "Well, if it's any consolation, it's not a war crime. A war crime is killing a noncombatant or something like that. Mutiny is, however, just as serious. But before we go into what happened, I need to explain a number of things to you, ok?"

"Go ahead."

"First, because you are facing a court-martial, the Trial Defense Service will appoint a military attorney to defend you. I will probably be your appointed defense counsel. You also have the right to request military counsel of your own choice, who will be provided at no expense to you if the lawyer you pick is reasonably available. He's not reasonably available if he has other duties that preclude taking your case. You also have the right to have a civilian lawyer of your own choice, at no expense to the government. That rule doesn't mean you necessarily have to pay for one, just that the government won't. If you can get one for free, or if your parents or someone else pays for the civilian attorney, that's fine."

Captain Wilson looked down at his initial interview checklist and continued. "It's very important that you understand the attorney-client privilege. In the military, anything you tell your defense counsel is privileged. That means your defense counsel—whether it's me or another lawyer—cannot tell anyone what you tell us without your permission. The only exception is if you tell me about a crime you intend to commit in the future."

"I think I'm probably in enough trouble without planning to commit any future crimes."

"Right." Wilson didn't seem to appreciate Jim's sarcasm. He'd been in the defense counsel business long enough to know that officers usually made the worst clients, especially those that outranked their lawyer. Unlike low-ranking enlisted men, officer clients would want to run the defense just like they ran the units they commanded. "This privilege is important because it permits you to be entirely frank and honest with your lawyer. My advice to you is only as good as what I know about the facts of the case. If you don't tell me the truth, my advice is worthless. And you don't have to worry about my divulging what you tell me to the prosecutor, your commander, the military police, or anyone else. Ok?"

"Understood," Jim replied tersely.

"Along with that, you must realize you should not talk about the case with anyone. This privilege is only between lawyer and client. Well, excuse me, there is a priest-penitent privilege as well, but unless you really need spiritual comfort, I strongly suggest you discuss the case only with your lawyer."

"I'm not very religious, and I think I need legal help more than spiritual aid right now."

"Good," the young attorney replied. "Look, I don't mean to cut you off, but I've got to be in court in a few minutes. What I want you to do is fill out this questionnaire in as much detail as possible. It will give me the background I need to start working up the case. It's my guess that the convening authority will hold an Article 32 investigation—sort of the military version of a grand jury hearing. You have the right to be present at such an investigation and to have a lawyer represent you. If the general does appoint an Article 32 investigating officer, we'll go over what happens at such a hearing beforehand. I'll call you to come back for a complete interview before anything else happens. In the meantime, I'll scout around and try to find out how serious the command is about this. But remember, don't talk to anyone. If CID agents try to question you, don't waive your rights. Just say you don't want to answer questions and refer them to me. Answering their questions can be very damaging to your case, even if you are as innocent as the driven snow. Here's my card with my duty and home phone number. Any questions?"

"Dozens. But they can probably wait until you call me back over. I'll fill out these forms and wait to hear from you."

"Good. I know it's hard, but try not to worry too much. And most of all, don't talk to anyone about the case."

As Jim left, he thought, don't worry, I'm not going to talk to anyone about this bullshit except a lawyer. Not anyone. But what the hell do I tell Meg?

CHAPTER 9

Post Headquarters
Building 199
Fort Leavenworth, Kansas

SEPTEMBER 1985

Colonel Farmer stirred restlessly as he waited in the plush reception area outside Lieutenant General Lowe's office. Twenty-six years in the service, he thought, and I'm still nervous about seeing a three-star. But if I'm going to make general, I'll need his support. Or maybe I'm just not looking forward to discussing this Thomas case with him.

"You can go in now, Sir," General Lowe's secretary said.

Colonel Farmer nodded his head and said, "Thank you." He gathered up his file folders and entered the general's inner sanctum. General Lowe, a crusty, gray-haired man, was poring over a new AirLand Battle doctrine document.

"Come in, Judge. Sit down." General Lowe said. "What do you have for me today?"

"I've got several actions, Sir. First, I recommend you refer the case of Inmate McBride to a general court-martial. He's the one who assaulted the guard and beat him severely. He is serving a five-year sentence for indecent assault. The Commandant of the Disciplinary Barracks and the Article 32 investigating officer both recommend trial by general court-martial. So do I. We have two eye-witnesses, and the accused confessed. I don't see any problems with the case."

"How's the guard?"

"He's ok. He suffered a broken nose, but it's healing well."

The general initialed the referral sheet. "Ok, Judge, you've got it. What's next?"

"You need to take action on the SP4 Jones case. He is the finance clerk convicted of selling marijuana. The military judge sentenced him to a bad-conduct discharge, confinement at hard labor for two years, total forfeiture of all pay and allowances, and reduction to private E-1. At tab C is a petition for clemency from his defense counsel. The trial had no errors, and there was sufficient evidence to find him guilty beyond a reasonable doubt. I recommend you approve the sentence as adjudged."

After he had read the petition for clemency, he said, "Roger that." As he signed the action, he said, "It seems a little light for a drug sale, but at least the judge gave him a discharge. Anything else?"

"One more action. Sergeant Anthony pled guilty to wrongful appropriation of a military vehicle, AWOL, and ten specifications of bad checks at a BCD special court. The court sentenced him to a BCD and confinement at hard labor for five months. You agreed to suspend any confinement in excess of four months if he pled guilty. His petition for clemency is at tab C. I recommend you approve only so much of the sentence as the pretrial agreement provides for. If you agree, the action is at tab D."

Again the convening authority read the petition for clemency and skimmed over the record of trial and the posttrial review. "Sounds good to me." He signed the action and handed the folders back to the SJA. "Is that all?"

"No, Sir, I've got one more case I need to discuss with you. It seems as if one Major Armstrong, a CGSC student, was the commander of another CGSC student, one Major Thomas, in Vietnam. Thomas allegedly disobeyed Major Armstrong by refusing to assault a machine gun during a firefight, so Armstrong has preferred court-martial charges against Thomas for mutiny."

"Can he do that?"

"Yes, Sir, any person who is subject to the UCMJ can prefer charges against any other person who is subject to it. Of course, as you know, only a convening authority can actually send the charges to a court-martial." Colonel Farmer laid a folder in front of the general. "Sir, here's a folder with the charge sheet, Armstrong's sworn statement, and both officers' record briefs. In addition, one of my trial counsel called the First Cavalry Division historian at Fort Hood and confirmed that an action like the one Armstrong described occurred on that date in that location."

General Lowe took several minutes to read over the materials in the folder. Then he leaned back in his swivel chair, thought a moment, and said, "You know, Judge, although this is a serious crime if it happened, it has been a long time since the Vietnam war, and this Major Thomas appears to have done well since. He even got a valor award and a Purple Heart while he was in Vietnam. I'm not certain that I see a lot of utility in dragging this up now. And I see some potential for bad press. The Army has had enough bad press from that conflict. What do you think?"

Colonel Farmer chose his words carefully before replying, balancing the effect on his career against what he thought the general wanted to hear. "Sir, although I agree with everything you said, I think we need to be careful how we handle this. I think the best thing to do is to fully investigate the allegations. Then, if it looks like it's not worth prosecuting, we can drop it. But after a good investigation, no one can accuse you of not taking a wartime disobedience seriously. I recommend you appoint an Article 32 investigating officer. I got the name of Lieutenant Colonel Glenn from AG. He's a mature infantry officer who will do a good job investigating this charge."

"Well, once again, Judge, you've made a lot of sense. I'll order a 32 investigation and appoint Colonel Glenn. You brief him personally and make sure he handles this thing properly. Do you read me?"

"Yes, Sir." Colonel Farmer got up as the general returned to his papers. That meeting went better than I'd expected, he thought. I hope the investigation goes as well. But he had a disquieting feeling of unease as he walked out of the general's office to return to his own office. I hope it goes half as well, or I may have to retire without making that star.

CHAPTER 10

Office of the Staff Judge Advocate
Building 244
Fort Leavenworth, Kansas

SEPTEMBER 1985

Lieutenant Colonel Daniel Glenn reluctantly entered the legal center. He didn't want to take time out from writing the new light infantry operations manual to investigate some bullshit old charges that some jackass had dredged up from who knew or cared where. Glenn was not happy to give up the little spare time he had, which he spent deer hunting down in the woods along the Missouri River north and east of the post airfield, worrying about getting an investigation done on time. "Hi. I'm Lieutenant Colonel Glenn to see Colonel Farmer."

"Go on in, Sir. He's expecting you," the SJA's secretary replied.

Although he had been prepared to be very irritated with the conversation he was about to have, Glenn was disarmed by Colonel Farmer's smile. But when the staff judge advocate stood up and Glenn noted the colonel's pot belly, he quickly changed his opinion again. Just another out-of-shape old JAGC wimp, he thought. He's probably got some profile to keep from taking the physical training test. I'm not going to give up without a fight. So before Colonel Farmer could say anything, the disgruntled infantry officer launched into his attack to get out of this unwelcome extra duty.

"Sir, before you waste your time briefing me, I must tell you that it's impossible for me to conduct this investigation. I'm far too busy trying to write doctrine. I've got to get a new field manual on light infantry operations out in the next two months, and I've got other pressing duties as well."

There, he thought. We'll just see whether the old buzzard keeps smiling at that.

Colonel Farmer's smile broadened sadistically. I've heard this before, he thought, mentally licking his chops. I'm not wearing these eagles for nothing. "Lieutenant Colonel Glenn," he began, emphasizing the "lieutenant," "the commanding general hand-picked you for this assignment because he thought you had enough experience and maturity to do a good job. Do you really want me to tell him you can't do it?"

Lieutenant Colonel Glenn sputtered, "No, Sir, that won't be necessary. It will take some juggling, and my assistants won't be very happy, but I don't want to let the general down."

Works every time, Colonel Farmer thought, enjoying the power of being the general's lawyer. He always had such fun with the old carrot and stick routine—you were hand-picked and I'll tell the general you can't do the job if you want. "Fine, here's the letter appointing you as the Article 32b Investigating Officer for the case of United States versus Thomas, the charge sheet, and the accuser's sworn statement. And here's a DA Pamphlet 27-17, Guide for the Article 32b Investigating Officer. It will tell you just about everything you need to know about running one of these things. Have you ever been a 32 IO before?"

"Yes, Sir, but it was years ago."

"Well, it hasn't changed much. Now, the general wanted me to brief you personally. This case, as you can see from the charge sheet, is very sensitive. It involves a serious crime, but one that was allegedly committed years ago, during an unfortunate war for our Army. We want a good, thorough investigation, and we want your honest recommendation. The general doesn't have any preconceived ideas about whether these charges are valid, and he wouldn't try to influence your recommendations if he did. But we do want to keep this as low-key as possible. Understand?"

"Yes, Sir."

"Now you've got several duties as the IO. You have to recommend whether or not to try the charge by court-martial and, if so, what level of court. If you recommend against trying the case by court-martial, you may recommend some other disposition, such as administrative action— a discharge, for example. You also need to recommend any necessary changes to the form of the charges. In other words, the charges should accurately reflect the alleged offense. Now, we're not going to leave you out in the cold on making these legal determinations. I've appointed one of my administrative law officers, Major Sherman, as your legal advisor. Captain Lewis will be present as the government representative, and Major Thomas will have a defense counsel, Captain Wilson, with him. Although they may argue some point of law, you must not take their advice. You have to get your legal advice from a disinterested officer, and that's Major Sherman."

The SJA continued, lecturing as if he were a law professor instructing a slow student: "Another important thing to remember is that you run the investigation, not the lawyers. If something comes up that you are not comfortable handling, just call a recess and check with Major Sherman.

"Speed is critical. If the defense wants a delay, make the defense lawyer request it in writing. If the defense counsel can't seem to find an open day where he doesn't have to be in court, schedule the hearing on a Saturday or a Sunday. All of a sudden, he'll magically have an open duty day. You'll need to get Criminal Investigative Division to help you find witnesses. I've called the CID operations officer, and he is primed to help you all he can. If you need anything else, such as travel funds and so forth, just ask. Specialist Porter will be your legal clerk to transcribe the hearings and prepare the report. Now, I suggest you go see Captain Lewis, who has begun the preliminary work of contacting witnesses and gathering evidence. But remember, you can't take any legal advice from her. Any questions?"

Glenn had only one question. "What do I have to tell Major Thomas?"

"It's all spelled out in the procedural guide. It has a script at the back for advising the accused of his rights. Just follow it, and you won't have any trouble. Good luck."

"Ok, Sir. I'll give it my best shot."

Glenn shook Colonel Farmer's outreached hand. What a jerk, Glenn thought. I'd like to rip those eagles off his shoulders and put him in an infantry battalion. He left the SJA's office and went down the hall looking for Captain Lewis's office—for any help he could find to get this investigation over with and get back to his normal, comfortable, sane duties.

CHAPTER 11

Soccer Field
Behind the Post Theater
Fort Leavenworth, Kansas

OCTOBER 1985

"Go, Section 15!" the students' wives yelled from the sideline of the soccer field. Their colorful cheerleading outfits and the blue and red jerseys the players wore were the only bright spots on a dreary, northeastern Kansas October day. The sky was the same color as the slate roofs on the weathered red brick buildings surrounding the soccer field. The grass, which was normally a bright green, was a muddy mess from CGSC fall soccer season games every day of the week and the post's youth league games on Saturdays. Section 15 was playing Section 21 in the semifinals of the CGSC student soccer tournament. Each section had to field a team in every student sport: soccer, basketball, softball, and bowling. Every student had to participate in some sport. The students called this part of the CGSC year "mandatory fun." Munson Army hospital records were a good indicator of what sports the students played: broken ankles, foot injuries, and bruised shins for soccer, more diverse injuries, including broken arms and sprained ankles, from basketball; and spike injuries from softball. The number of injuries was not surprising considering that the students' average age was about thirty-five years old. Many of them had not played competitive sports for years, and they were very competitive "class A" behavior types, or they wouldn't have done well enough to be selected to attend CGSC. The students who were not participating in whatever sport the students were playing were the referees. Not only were most of the referees untrained, but also most of them neither earned nor got much respect from their fellow students, who happened to be the players. Thus, the refs didn't exert much control over the games, thereby resulting in more injuries.

Meg sat on the old wooden bleachers, a little apart from the other wives, watching her husband play. Although she had always enjoyed watching him play in the Army's many sports leagues, this game bore little resemblance to real soccer. Sighing, Meg thought, what am I doing here? Germany was bad enough with Jim in the field all the time. But at least when I watched fussball in Germany, it was real soccer, not this mud-wrestling. And it's worse now with Jim home every night but a million miles away studying. And when he's not studying, he's too uptight about this stupid mutiny charge for us to have any fun together anyway. He never laughs or smiles anymore. I just wish he'd let me help him. Brushing away a tear, Meg turned her attention back to the game. She felt better—and almost smiled—as she saw Jim take a mighty kick at the ball and miss completely. For a moment, he looked like the boyish lieutenant she had married, before Vietnam had made him grow up too soon.

Jim's miss didn't matter much, though. Section 15 was methodically destroying Section 21, even though the latter had more talented players, including a German officer who had played on his country's national military team and a Thai officer who had also played in international competition. But Section 15 had twenty-two good old American thugs who played soccer as if it were tackle football. They would throw in the first wave to beat up on the other team and then throw in a fresh wave of thugs midway through the first half. By the middle of the second half, the international officers had given up and would just get out of the way rather than contest an ungentlemanly 225-pound American madman who was charging the ball. The rest of Section 21's fourteen-man team was exhausted and put up little struggle in the last ten minutes of the game. Section 15 scored three quick goals to take a five-to-one lead with only a few minutes to go.

Lieutenant Colonel Mills, the Academic Counselor Evaluator of Staff Group 15C, cheered from the sidelines. ACEs could play section sports with sections their staff groups were in, but Mills had already seen too many injuries in his three years of ACEing to get out there with the younger officers and risk life and limb, especially when some of the students would love to take out an instructor. He often told his students that when the soccer season was over his student year at CGSC, the first thing he did was get down on his knees and give thanks that he was still in one piece.

When the game was over and the players had finished shaking hands, Mills walked over to Major Thomas. Jim had just popped the tab on a beer he had taken from a cooler brought by some of the nonplaying students. Although he was covered with sweat and mud, Jim grinned happily when his ACE approached. "We really kicked their asses, Sir!"

"Yes, you did. I just hope you guys play as well in the championship next week," Mills replied. "Listen, I need to talk to you."

They walked away from the celebrating section members. "I got a phone call from your defense counsel. He had tried to get you, but apparently, the classroom service people didn't put the message in your box until after you had left for the game. The three-star has appointed an Article 32 Investigating Officer, who needs to see you. In addition, your defense counsel wants to see you before you see the IO. I'm sorry to dump this on you right after your game, but I thought you should know right away."

"I appreciate that, Sir. I'll go over to JAG first thing in the morning. And I appreciate how you've stood behind me through this mess," Jim said.

"Well, all I know is that you've done a fine job as a student and you seem like a fine officer. I'm not very concerned about what might have happened years ago when you were a lieutenant. If you need me for a character witness, let me know. In the meantime, I know it's hard, but just hang in there. How's your wife taking it?"

"Obviously, she's not too happy about it, but she's doing ok. We're both so busy, me with studies and her with the social whirl of a staff group leader's wife, that we haven't had much time to worry about it. It's interesting being accused of something, though. You very quickly learn who your friends are. Some students won't even talk to me for fear they will be contaminated. It's sort of like rats deserting a sinking ship. I've even tutored some of them in tactics, but they don't seem to remember that. Others are uncertain how to treat me. And some have been just great, saying they don't give a damn what bullshit charges have been brought."

Just then the sad, sweet sound of retreat reached their ears from the loudspeakers around the post as the military police performed the five o'clock ritual of lowering the flag in front of Bell Hall. All the military members stood at attention, the families stood up, the cars and the runners stopped on the road by the soccer field, and people got out of their cars and faced in the direction of the big flagpole and the cannon in front of Bell Hall while the music sounded. As if on cue, after the echoes of the last, lingering notes had faded away, the crowd around the soccer field began to disperse, retreating to the warm lights of their quarters in the gathering dusk.

CHAPTER 12

Grant Avenue
Fort Leavenworth, Kansas

NOVEMBER 1985

Lieutenant Colonel Dan Glenn walked down the front steps of his quarters, 512 Grant Avenue, just across from the post library. He was dressed in running gear, Nike shoes, a gray Goretex rainsuit, a painter's hat from last spring's Kaw Valley Levee Run in Lawrence, Kansas, and old brown cotton work gloves. He pressed the button on his running watch and started off easily, at a seven-thirty-a-mile pace, heading north. Two houses down, he jogged in place for a moment until his running buddy, Major Russell Broderick, joined him. Together, they ran to the end of Grant Avenue and turned down past the high, gray stone wall of the Disciplinary Barracks. When they reached the base of the hill, they had two choices. They could turn east and go the easy way around the airfield—a perfectly flat four-mile loop. Or they could turn west and run up the mile-and-a-half-long hill to the top of the ridgeline and make it a six-mile loop back to their quarters. In the irritable mood he was in, Dan made the decision for them. He turned uphill. His pace slackened very little as he ran up the hill, pushing it hard. Russ struggled along, ten feet behind. Neither of them could think about much except their form and their breathing until they got to the top and passed a group of Disciplinary Barracks prisoners dressed in their ugly dark brown prison garb cutting grass along the road. Dan didn't get a warm fuzzy feeling watching them swing their scythes. Yeah, maybe they were trustees, but he knew from his days serving on courts-martial that some of them had been very bad boys. Somehow, he couldn't see Major Thomas swinging a sickle with them for disobeying a stupid order in a war that was long since over.

"What's gotten into you?" Russ asked when his breathing began to return to normal.

"It's this damn 32 investigation. I've finished the hearing, but I still have to make a decision."

"The one you told me about—the disobedience of an order in Vietnam?"

"Yeah, I don't know what to do. The damned defense counsel didn't help me out any. Maybe the accused did disobey an order, but I don't think it was mutiny like the charge says. Why didn't Captain Wilson introduce some evidence to give me something to go on? If he didn't want to deny the offense, why didn't he at least come up with some good character evidence?"

As Dan became more irritated thinking about the case, he picked up the pace, beginning to sweat heavily under his Goretex running suit.

"If he did disobey the order, why isn't it a mutiny?" Russ asked.

Dan thought a moment, then answered. "As I understand it, a mutiny is a bunch of people agreeing to disobey an order. Although, according to their testimony at the 32, his platoon members seem to have supported his attempts to get around other orders the commander had given, I'm not sure they even knew about this one. It seems like a mutiny should be a big, premeditated deal like in *The Caine Mutiny*. Not this spur-of-the-moment thing."

"Sounds good to me."

"I'll tell you something else. His accuser seems like a jerk, while the accused certainly acted properly throughout the hearing. If the crime was so serious, why didn't Armstrong find out for certain whether Thomas died as a result of his wounds? He even signed the paperwork for Thomas to get a medal for the next day's firefight, for God's sake. The whole thing is flakey."

Dan picked up the pace again and flew down the hill at the southern end of the ridgeline. When they reached the bottom of the hill, they turned left again and ran through the national cemetery. The fast pace discouraged conversation. *I wish I knew what the general wanted me to recommend,* Dan thought. *I don't believe the line that slippery SJA gave me about the general's not having any preconceived notions. I knew this damned case was going to be a mess, and I'm stuck right in the middle of it.*

As they reached the northwest corner of the cemetery, Dan saw the gray dome of the Disciplinary Barracks off to the northeast. It seemed to crystalize his thoughts about the case. "You know, Russ," he said, "I can't see a general court-martial—putting a decorated Vietnam vet in the

DB, when so many others went to Canada and got amnesty or deserted and got their discharges upgraded to general or honorable."

"Yeah, you're right. Amnesty was sure a fucked-up decision," Russ replied as they turned east and ran down Doniphan towards home.

"Roger that. I'll draft my report tonight and turn it in. If the general doesn't like it, he can ignore my recommendation." As they stopped in front of Russ's house, Dan checked the running stopwatch on his wrist.

"Forty-three minutes and ten seconds. Not bad for a little over six miles up that bitch of a hill."

"You'll have to run mad more often. But next time you're mad, find some speed demon to run with instead of me. See you at work."

"Ok, thanks for helping me clarify my thoughts."

"Anytime—except running up the ridgeline again."

Dan felt relieved as he entered his quarters. Now that he had made his decision on the case, it was as if a great weight had been lifted from his shoulders. Or from the soles of his running shoes.

C H A P T E R   1 3

Office of the Class Director
U.S. Army Command and General Staff College
Bell Hall, Fort Leavenworth, Kansas

D E C E M B E R   1 9 8 5

Colonel Jerome, the CGSC Class Director, took the Article 32 investigating officer's report out of the shotgun envelope the JAGC office had
sent it over in. Took him long enough, he thought. He quickly skimmed
the first page of the DD Form 457, which merely detailed the procedural
steps of the investigation. The second page was primarily a list of witnesses and evidence that the investigating officer had considered. The
real heart of the report, the recommendations, were usually on the third
page. Blocks 15 and 17 were checked, "No," indicating that the investigating officer had not recommended trial by court-marital.

Colonel Jerome heaved a sigh of relief. As Class Director, he had had
to forward Armstrong's charges through his boss, General Treakle, to
General Lowe, the general court-martial convening authority, because
both the accuser and the accused were CGSC students. Colonel Jerome
leaned back in his swivel chair and turned to the remarks on the fourth
page. No CGSC student had had to face a court-martial in the two-and-
a-half years he had been Class Director, although one had resigned rather
than face court-martial, and Colonel Jerome didn't want any of them to
start now. Besides the administrative burden, prosecuting students was
bad for class morale. He started perusing the stilted form language of the
IO's remarks.

"I received this file at 1300 hours, 30 September 1985. The delay in
completing my investigation was caused by the difficulty in locating witnesses to the thirteen-year-old incident that was the basis of these
charges. After the witnesses were located, the defense requested a week
to prepare their case (written request at inclosure 1).

"Although it appears that the accused did disobey an order, there is insufficient evidence of a mutiny to recommend trying the charge and specification by court-marital, because the included offense of disobeying a superior commissioned officer is barred by the statue of limitations. The accused put on no evidence as to why he might have disobeyed the order. No lives were lost as a result of disobeying the order. Rather, disobeying the order probably saved lives. Considering the length of time since the incident, the difficulty of obtaining evidence, the cost to the government, and the accused's subsequent good duty performance, I recommend that no formal disciplinary action be taken."

Sounds sensible to me, Colonel Jerome thought. Major Thomas was one of the better staff group leaders, and the colonel didn't want to have to replace a good student leader in mid-year. I guess I'd better call him in and tell him the good news. "Specialist Garrett," he called out, "would you have Major Thomas come see me as soon as he's out of class?"

After his tactics class was over at 1500 hours, Jim Thomas approached the Class Director's office. He wondered what it was this time, but after six hours of planning a division attack, he was a little numb. Before he could knock on the door, he heard Colonel Jerome call out, "Come in, Jim. I've got some good news, I think."

"Afternoon, Sir. How's it going?"

"Pretty good. I just received the Article 32 investigating officer's report. He's recommending that the charge be dropped. It's not binding on the convening authority, but I still think it's good news. Congratulations."

"Sounds pretty good to me, Sir."

"Listen, I appreciate the good job you've done as a staff group leader during what must have been a difficult time for you."

"I found it easier to hang in there by keeping busy, Sir."

"Well, regardless, I think you've done well under a lot of pressure. I hope this whole mess dies down quickly now."

"So do I, Sir, so do I. If you'll excuse me, I think I'll go call my wife. And I'd better call my defense counsel and thank him, too."

Jim hurried out of the office, eager to give Meg the good news. Maybe she'd stop telling him how stupid he was for staying in the Army now. No, she wouldn't, he thought, but, God, I'd never had made it this last few weeks without her support. I'll take her to that fancy restaurant in that big old house up on the hill in Leavenworth she's always begging to go to this very evening to celebrate, he concluded, as he fumbled in his Class A uniform pants for change for one of the the pay phones down the hall and around the corner from the Class Director's Office.

Colonel Jerome watched as Major Thomas left. I sure hope we've heard the end of this, he thought, but I won't feel comfortable until the general dismisses the charges. I wonder whether anything could make him ignore the 32 officer's recommendations and still prosecute? Shrugging his shoulders, he turned back to his paperwork, which seemed to breed if he didn't shuffle it quickly and often.

PART III

COURT PERSONNEL

UNITED STATES ARMY
THE CHIEF OF STAFF

6 May 1985

Command action that interferes with lawful military justice requirements is illegal, unfair and destructive to confidence in the military justice system. . . .

Despite repeated emphasis, I continue to receive reports concerning allegations of command actions that may influence illegally the exercise of personal discretion by witnesses, court members, commanders or others acting in their military justice roles. . . .

It is incumbent upon you, together with your legal advisor, to assure that your subordinate commanders understand and adhere to the provisions of Article 37. . . .

JOHN A. WICKHAM, JR.
General, United States Army
Chief of Staff

CHAPTER 14

Headquarters, U.S. Army Training and Doctrine Command
(TRADOC)
Fort Monroe, Virginia

DECEMBER 1985

General Hawkins picked up the letter that was on top of his over-flowing in-box. As the commanding general of the U.S. Army Training and Doctrine Command, he had an in-box that was always overflowing. TRADOC was a huge organization, charged both with developing all the Army's combat and combat support doctrine and with overseeing all training in that doctrine. TRADOC was the parent command of all Army schools except for a few mavericks, such as the Judge Advocate General's School. So as the TRADOC commander, General Hawkins was Lieutenant General Lowe's commander. TRADOC was a prestigious assignment. The TRADOC commander could legitimately hope to become Chief of Staff of the Army. General Hawkins did not hope to be Chief of Staff; he expected to be. His office reflected his preeminent position as the leading contender for Chief of Staff. The walls were covered with framed pictures of the general with the President, the Secretary of Defense, and other high-ranking officials, with plaques from units he had served in and from foreign countries, and with numerous framed awards and diplomas.

The four-star read the letter from Major Armstrong and then reread it with incredulity. He could not believe that an officer could mutiny in combat and no one wanted to do anything about it. What was wrong with that Article 32 investigating officer? And it sure didn't sound like Art Lowe to be soft on such a crime. "Barry," he ordered his aide, "get the JA on the line."

When the aide told him that Colonel Steve Temple, the TRADOC Staff Judge Advocate, was on the phone, the general launched in without any amenities. "Judge, I got a letter here from a Major Armstrong, a

CGSC student, who preferred charges against another student who had led a mutiny against him in Vietnam. This Major Armstrong thought the officer had been killed in action, so he didn't take any action until he found out they were CGSC classmates. An Article 32 investigating officer recommended against court-martial. Can I call up General Lowe and order him to convene a general court-martial?"

"No, Sir, that would be illegal command influence," Colonel Temple replied.

"Do you mean there's nothing I can do about it?"

"No, Sir, I didn't say that. You can withdraw General Lowe's authority to act and order him to forward the case to you with his recommendation for your decision. Then you can refer the case to a court-martial yourself. Just make sure, Sir, that you don't tell General Lowe to recommend a court-marital. That's also illegal command influence. Remember, you don't have to follow his recommendation."

"Airborne, Judge. Can you do this for me through JAGC channels?"

"Yes, Sir. I'll call Leavenworth SJA and tell him that you've withdrawn the CAC commander's authority to act on these charges and that he should forward them to this headquarters."

Colonel Temple hung up the phone only long enough to check his directory and then made an AUTOVON call to the Fort Leavenworth SJA. When Colonel Farmer came on the line, Colonel Temple greeted him warmly. After they had talked about other JAGC officers for a few minutes, speculating on who had the inside chance for the next brigadier general slot to come open and exchanging gossip about who had gotten into trouble, Colonel Temple got down to business. "Listen, Ralph, I've got a situation here that you and your boss aren't going to like. The accuser in that mutiny case you've got down there wrote General Hawkins and got him all stirred up about how no one at Leavenworth was interested in prosecuting a serious crime. I know you and your boss probably have good reasons for not referring it to a court-martial, but General Hawkins wants to look over the case himself."

Colonel Farmer sounded irritated as he launched into a tirade about why it would be better for all concerned if the case died a quick death. It didn't work.

"I know, Ralph, but you've got to realize that, when my four-star gets a burr under his saddle, it's best to humor him. Now he's directed me to notify you that he's withdrawn General Lowe's authority to dispose of the case and that he wants you to forward the case, along with the 32(b) investigation and all recommendations, to him. I know this will piss both you and your boss off, but there's nothing we can do but comply. I promise you I'll take a close look at the case, and if it is really stupid to send it to court, I'll so advise the CG."

"Ok, Steve. You're absolutely right, my three-star isn't going to like it at all. But we'll have to let them fight it out at the general officer level. I'll notify my boss and get the case in the mail to you ASAP."

"Thanks, Ralph, I appreciate your understanding. I'll keep you informed as to what's going on with the case after it gets up here. Bye."

"Bye, Steve." Colonel Farmer hung up the phone and mulled over the situation for a few moments. Damn, he thought, General Lowe is going to be awfully sore at me for recommending no trial now that his boss wants a court-martial. How can I deflect his anger to someone else? It's almost time for him to write my annual efficiency report. Suddenly, the old politician knew how to do it. Military conventional wisdom states that lieutenant colonel is the last rank you make on merit. Full colonel and above depends on politics. And Colonel Farmer was anything but the exception that proves the rule. I'll blame it on Steve, he thought. I'll make it sound as if he pushed taking the case to trial to General Hawkins. Then, if my general does become CG of TRADOC, or even Chief of Staff after General Hawkins retires, I'll have eliminated Steve Temple from the competition for general officer in the JAG Corps. Satisfied with himself, Colonel Farmer picked up the phone to call his general.

CHAPTER 15

Classroom 21
Bell Hall

JANUARY 1986

Major Thomas sat in the back of the CGSC classroom waiting for A955, the military criminal law elective, to begin. The Command and General Staff College curriculum consisted of both required courses and electives. Each student had to take seven electives. In previous years, they had had to take eight, but his year, the students were given one elective credit for the professional reading program. It required them to read ten professional books during the academic year, in addition to any other assigned readings. Thus, unless they wanted to overachieve, this year they had to take only seven electives to get the eight they needed to graduate.

A955 was a popular elective because of its broad appeal to all the students. The tactics electives, such as advanced offensive operations, generally interested only the combat arms officers. The logistics electives not only appealed to some combat arms officers, but also were directly relevant to officers in the combat support branches. But neither tactics nor logistics courses interested some officers—particularly the combat service support officers, such as doctors or dentists. And the Marine and Air Force officers often were less than thrilled about learning about the Army's supply system. But almost all the officers had to deal with the military justice system—a system that differed very little from service to service.

These concerns were not the reason Major Thomas had signed up for the course, however. As an infantry officer, he would normally have loaded up on tactics and logistics courses. But because he was pending a general court-martial, he thought he had better become as familiar with the military justice system as possible.

Right on time, the class started. "I'm Lieutenant Colonel Paul David, the military law instructor. Welcome to A955, Military Law." The six-foot tall, brown-haired instructor paced up and down the walkway between the rows of tables as he introduced himself. "I like to start each class with a humorous military justice story," he continued. "One of my favorites is the 'mummy' case. The mummy case occurred at Fort Sill during the early 1970s, while the Vietnam war was still going on. The mummy was in Artillery AIT when he got orders to Vietnam. He decided that Vietnam was not consistent with his career plans and that he would rather go AWOL and visit Canada. But on a private's pay, he could not afford an extended stay in Canada. So he decided to rob some other trainees to finance his AWOL. Because he was about as good at robbery as he was at soldiering, the authorities quickly apprehended him and charged him with two robberies."

As the class listened raptly, remembering similar problem soldiers they had had in their units, Lieutenant Colonel David continued, "The mummy decided that because he wasn't going to have anything to do with the military because the military was going to send him to Vietnam, he wouldn't have anything to do with the military justice system. At this point, he became 'the mummy.' He refused to do anything. He wouldn't even talk to his defense counsel. But as you all know, the wheels of military justice grind on, and the mummy case continued. The military police would dress the mummy, shave him, and carry him to the courtroom, and sure enough, the mummy appeared before his general court-martial for robbery. Believe it or not, it's not difficult for a military judge to try a mummy. All the judge has to do is exercise the mummy's rights in a way that does not require an affirmative response. For example, if an accused wants a trial by judge alone, he has to sign a request for a judge alone trial and answer questions the judge asks to make certain that he is knowingly and voluntarily giving up his right to a trial by a court composed of members. So all the judge had to do with the mummy was say, 'Private Mummy—I don't remember his actual name—unless you tell me differently, I am going to assume that you want to be tried by a court composed of officer members. Let the record reflect that the accused did not answer. Thus, he obviously wants to be tried by a court composed of officer members.' The military judge entered pleas of not guilty on behalf of the mummy, and the trial continued.

"The jury took a rather dim view of this mummy routine. Their first clue that the mummy was 'mummying' was when they entered the courtroom and the bailiff called out, 'All rise.' Everyone rose, except the mummy. Indeed, he would have had a hard time rising even if he wanted to stop mummying because he was tied to his chair at the defense table. The judge had ordered him tied because he thought that was preferable to the mummy's sliding onto the floor as he had been doing before being tied to the chair. Of course, because the government evidence was overwhelming and the mummy didn't testify that he didn't do it, the court members duly convicted him.

"But he continued to mummy throughout the sentencing phase of the trial. He didn't take the witness stand to say he was sorry, or he wouldn't do it again, or his mother used to kick him with combat boots, or he had found God in the stockade, or any of the other drivel an accused says to avoid jail. Now the maximum sentence for one specification of robbery included a dishonorable discharge, forfeiture of all pay and allowances, reduction to the lowest enlisted grade, and ten years confinement at hard labor. So the jury came back and sentenced the mummy to a dishonorable discharge, forfeiture of all pay and allowances, and confinement at hard labor for twenty years, because he had been convicted of two specifications of robbery. They didn't reduce him to private E-1 only because he was already a private E-1. The president of the court later said that, if the mummy had just acted halfway normal, they would have given him about five years' confinement. But because he wanted to mummy, they'd play along. When the military police carried the mummy out of the courtroom, he finally broke his silence. His first words were, "Duh . . . I think I fucked up!"

The class broke up. As field grade officers, they had had mummies of their own—troops whom they had wished they could put away for twenty years. Lieutenant Colonel David went on, "Now the school brass will get upset at my telling a story like this unless I have a teaching point, so besides informing you never to 'mummy' in a court-martial, I want to point out that this is my goal for this course—to make certain you never have to say what the mummy did when you try to take a military justice action against a wrongdoer."

Major Thomas laughed along with rest of the students, although in the back of his mind was a little sympathy for the mummy. Perhaps, he wouldn't have had this empathy previously, but because he was pending court-martial himself, he didn't find the story as funny as the rest of the class did. I'll damn sure not be a mummy if they try me, he thought. I'll look them in the eye and tell them my side of it.

After the laughter died down again, the CGSC law instructor launched into the requisite explanation of the course. After going over what it would cover, what the texts were, and how he would grade the students, he continued, "I'd like to introduce the JAG students who will be my assistant instructors." Jim didn't pay much attention to the first student David introduced, other than noting vaguely that he was supposed to be an expert in the law of claims. But he became very attentive when the instructor introduced Major Ken Morgan as the best trial attorney in the JAG Corps. David launched into a story about an argument Major Morgan had made in the case of the United States versus Carey. The rest of the class laughed at the punch line, but Jim just sat there expressionless. It came to him in a flash of insight. That's what I need! He's the one I need for my defense counsel. An old, experienced courtroom warhorse. Captain Wilson seems to know what he's doing and is trying hard, but I need someone with a lot of experience for this mess.

Jim opened his notebook and started taking notes as David went on with the class. I've got to understand this stuff, he thought, striving to follow the lecture. First, David explained the sources of the military justice system. "The ultimate source for our separate system of justice is the Constitution," he said. "Article I gives Congress the power to make rules for the government of the land and naval forces." He smiled at the Air Force officers sitting at the front of the room. "They hadn't dreamed of the Air Force when they wrote the Constitution, but because the Air Force came from the Army, Article I allows Congress to regulate the Air Force, too. Congress used its Article I power to enact the Uniform Code of Military Justice, the laws that regulate our conduct as servicemembers. Article II of the Constitution gives the President power over us, as well. It names him Commander in Chief. He uses that power and a delegation of authority from Congress in the Uniform Code to issue the executive order known as the *Manual for Courts-Martial*, which implements the system established by the Code."

As the lecture continued, Jim thought perhaps David would be a good choice for his defense counsel, too. He certainly seems to know this legal garbage. But Jim finally concluded that he needed an expert in courtroom tactics, not an instructor, no matter how well the instructor seemed to know his subject.

Now the instructor was talking about basic principles of the military justice system—about how commanders make the decisions, not lawyers. That's another one of my problems, Jim thought. As best I can tell, the lawyers don't want to take my case to court. Even the Article 32 investigating officer recommended dropping the case. And the commander, the TRADOC commander, can overrule everyone else and prosecute me anyway. Isn't that something?

With a sheer act of will, Major Thomas pulled his attention back to the lecture, which now was about jurisdiction, the power of a court-

marital to decide a case, hoping he could hear some jurisdictional prin-
ciple that would help his case. As he listened intently, he realized no help
was to be had for him there. His case would be decided on what happened in Vietnam, not on what was in some dusty law books. As the class
ended, he felt he understood the military justice system better. But finding out that a trial attorney like Major Morgan was in the class made taking the elective worthwhile, even if he learned nothing more about the
system that he was afraid was going to crush him.

CHAPTER 16

Office of the Staff Judge Advocate
Building 244
Fort Leavenworth, Kansas

J A N U A R Y   1 9 8 6

Captain Lewis nervously smoothed down her skirt as she sat in Colonel Farmer's office, waiting for him to get off the phone. She wasn't comfortable talking to a full colonel without her immediate boss, Major Bailey, with her, but he had told her that, because she was the trial counsel, she could handle the discussion herself. She also was well aware that her chances for getting career status—so that she could stay on active duty past her three-year obligation—hinged on her ability to stay on Colonel Farmer's good side. After he had hung up, he looked at her and said, "What can I do for you?"

"I got a call from one of my friends at TRADOC, Sir," she began. "General Hawkins has referred the Thomas case to a general court-martial and is going to direct that it be tried here."

Colonel Farmer frowned. "I was afraid of that. Does the defense know?"

"I don't know for sure, Sir, but the Trial Defense Service spy system is better than mine. I'd be surprised if Captain Wilson didn't know. One of the defense lawyers at Monroe has probably called him by now."

Colonel Farmer thought for a minute. "Well, you'd better notify him right away. Have you and your boss talked about who would try the case if General Hawkins did refer it to trial?"

"Yes, Sir, we thought I would be the trial counsel, and if necessary, he could be my assistant trial counsel. Even though he outranks me, he doesn't have much trial experience, so he thought I should be the lead counsel—not that I have a lot of experience, either—but I have more than he does."

"Ok, Pam, I'll call the TRADOC SJA and have him get the commander to detail you to try the case. Now, I know you weren't much wilder about trying this mess than I was, but we've received our marching orders, and it's our duty to try the hell out of the case. I expect you to go for a conviction. Can you do that, or do you have some problem aggressively prosecuting this case?"

"Well, as you said, Sir, I don't think we should try the case. But because superior authority has directed us to, I have no ethical problem doing so. And if I try it, I have no intention of losing it."

"Good. I'm going to call the TRADOC SJA right now. You keep me informed about the progress of the case."

"Yes, Sir," Captain Lewis agreed, as she got up to leave. Colonel Farmer looked up the AUTOVON phone number for his counterpart at TRADOC and dialed the access number. As usual, it was busy. The AUTOVON system was like everything in the Army—a product of always contracting with the lowest bidder. Finally, after he had dialed 96 twenty or so times—no redial buttons on the old black Army phones in those days—he heard the dial tone and dialed Colonel Temple's number.

When Steve Temple came on the line, the two staff judge advocates exchanged pleasantries and gossip about the JAG Corps, as usual. Then Colonel Farmer cut off the amenities, "Steve, we need to talk about the Thomas case. I assume that because we are trying it here, my trial counsel will prosecute. If so, General Hawkins needs to detail the counsel and court members. I'll send you a list of potential court members and their officer record briefs, and we've decided that Captain Lewis will be trial counsel."

"Sounds good to me. About Captain Lewis, is he good?"

"She's fairly new, but has done a good job for me so far." Even though Colonel Farmer didn't like women lawyers, he couldn't pass up the chance to hassle a competitor for a JAGC general's star. "As you know, we are not exactly a hotbed of criminal trials here, and none of our counsel are very experienced. But I think she'll do a good job. I may ask the general to detail my Chief of Criminal Law, Major Bailey, as assistant trial counsel. And, of course, Judge Savage is the Chief Circuit Judge, and because he's here, he will probably preside over the case."

"Ok, send me their officer record briefs, as well, and I'll take them into the general together. I had forgotten that you've got hammering Hank Savage out there. He'll probably go into orbit when he gets these charge sheets. I'm not certain I'm wild about having an old fart like him as military judge, but since we can't influence the judiciary's choice of judges, we'll just have to live with it. Listen, I appreciate your attitude—

I know you didn't want to try the case. I wasn't wild about it either, but there is no legal objection to trying the case, and my four-star didn't want to hear my policy objections."

"Yeah, I know how that is," Colonel Farmer replied. "We'll do the best we can with the case. I'll get you the ORBs ASAP. Out here."

"Goodbye, Ralph."

Colonel Farmer hung up the phone and picked up his notebook. Under the heading of "Things to brief the CG on," he added, "Thomas case referred to GCM—to be tried here." I'd be a lot happier if they tried the case at TRADOC, he thought, if indeed it has to be tried at all. The risk-reward ratio doesn't favor trying it here. If we get a conviction, it won't help my career much, and if we lose, there is the potential for disaster. Maybe I'd better call the Judge Advocate General and brief him on this case. That way, if it surfaces at Department of the Army, he'll be pre-briefed. And that way, I can make sure he hears my side of it first.

CHAPTER 17

Headquarters, U.S. Army Training and Doctrine Command
Fort Monroe, Virginia

FEBRUARY 1986

General Hawkins flipped through the prospective court members' officer record briefs that Colonel Farmer had sent from Fort Leavenworth. "What do you think, Judge?" he asked Colonel Temple. "Do we want these members to have any particular qualifications?"

Colonel Temple looked at the four stars adorning the collar of the general's battle-dress uniform. Although TRADOC was the headquarters for writing all Army training and doctrine, General Hawkins always wore his BDUs as if he were going into combat immediately, even though most of his staff worked in class A uniforms. His staff judge advocate chose his words carefully. After all, as a higher level command, TRADOC had few courts-martial, unlike the subordinate units and installations it commanded. Thus, General Hawkins was not as up on the nuances of being a convening authority as many commanders. "The *Manual for Courts-Martial* requires that you choose those members who are best qualified for court duty by reason of age, experience, maturity, and judicial temperament. All those officers probably qualify, but you may want members with combat experience. I think all the court members in the Calley case were combat vets."

"Yeah, you're probably right, Judge. They convicted him, didn't they? And I think I want all ex-commanders. They will understand the main issue in the case—the importance of obeying orders. Can I select all ex-commanders?"

"So long as you do so because they are best qualified. Couldn't you legitimately say that commanders would normally have more experience and maturity than those who had never commanded? You have to have based your decision on those grounds so that if you are accused of stacking the court, you can testify that, instead, you used the manual's guidelines in your selection process."

"Sounds good. That's why I keep you around, Judge, to keep me straight. How many should I select?"

"A general court-martial must have at least five members left after challenges. But there is less chance of an aberrant decision with a larger court. So I'd recommend you select twelve members."

General Hawkins studied each officer record brief for a few moments, putting each of them in one of two piles. When the right-hand pile had twelve records in it, he pushed it across his big desk towards his SJA. "Here, let's go with these."

"Yes, Sir," Colonel Temple replied as he took the records of the court members the general had selected. "Now here's a list of the judge and counsel. You need to detail them also."

The four-star looked at the list. "Ok, looks good. No, wait a minute. Who's this Captain Pamela Lewis? Is she a good prosecutor?"

"Colonel Farmer, the Leavenworth SJA, says she's inexperienced but good—the best he's got."

General Hawkins rubbed the bald spot at the top of his head, although his hair was cut so close you could hardly tell where the bald spot ended. "I don't know. It seems to me we need a really experienced prosecutor. And I'm not sure the court members I selected will be able to relate to a female counsel. Don't you have any good trial counsel here that we could send out there to try the case?"

"No, Sir, I don't have any better trial counsel here than Colonel Farmer does at Leavenworth. As you know, we don't have enough trials here to justify a top-flight prosecutor. But I may have a solution. Perhaps the most experienced prosecutor in the JAG Corps is a student at the Command and General Staff College, Major Ken Morgan. He's tried at least ten murder cases and several hundred general courts-martial. I'm sure that as the TRADOC Commander, you could persuade the CGSC Commandant that Morgan ought to be able to try this case and still graduate from CGSC. After all, he's completed the first term, and Reservists and National Guardsmen get diplomas without staying for the second and third terms. And if necessary, we could see whether the Judge Advocate General would let us keep him a couple of months after graduation."

"Now you're talking, Judge. I want this Major Morgan on the case. I'll tell General Lowe to do whatever's necessary to get him on the case and see that he still graduates from CGSC. Hell, make him an honor graduate. I want him to be able to concentrate on winning the case, not worrying about graduating. But why do we send lawyers to CGSC anyway?"

"Would you want me advising you on the law of war if I didn't understand the AirLand Battle, Sir? Or on procuring new weapons systems if I didn't understand both their prospective use and force modernization? We learn all those things at CGSC."

"Ok, Judge, I give. But it seems a shame to take away good infantry slots and give them to some damn lawyers. Listen, after I get him pried loose and detailed as trial counsel, you talk to this Major Morgan and make sure he understands I want maximum effort on this case. Roger?"

"Yes, Sir."

General Hawkins took another look at the list of lawyers. "What about this judge, Colonel Savage?"

Colonel Temple hesitated a moment. "Well, Sir, it's hard to explain. He's one of our most senior judges. He's pushing thirty years' service, and he has been an 0-6 since the brown shoe Army. He's got a reputation for being very hard on counsel and for dragging cases out. The prosecutors swear he favors the defense, and the defense counsel swear he favors the prosecution. Some of his rulings seem strange, and the lawyers always seem mad at him, and even I was at war with him when I was a trial counsel. But I've got to admit, the appellate courts do not reverse him often. But it is all academic, Sir. You have to detail the judge that the trial judiciary furnishes, and he's the Chief Circuit Judge. He put himself on the case. Said it sounded interesting, unlike the usual, boring, AWOL guilty plea."

"Ok, but you tell me if he screws it up."

"Yes, Sir, but you won't be able to do anything about it. It's illegal command influence to criticize a military judge."

The general shook his head in exasperation. "You know, Judge, sometimes I don't understand this system. I can see not telling court members that it's their duty to convict. They ought to know that anyway, unless it's a really flakey case, and the way we investigate cases, it's a cold day in hell when a flakey case gets to court. But I don't understand why I've got to eat it if a judge is screwed up."

"Sir, the theory is that, if you criticize the judge, you are trying to influence his next decision, which must be an independent decision, uninfluenced by what any commander thinks of him."

"Ok, ok, I don't understand it, but you've done a good job so far of keeping me straight. I don't want to end up splashed all over the *Army Times* for screwing up this case. Anything else?"

"No, Sir."

"Ok, Judge, keep me straight, but get me a conviction."

Colonel Temple saluted and left. The general's last words haunted him as he walked back to his office.

CHAPTER 18

Major Morgan's Quarters, Student Housing
Hancock Avenue
Fort Leavenworth, Kansas

FEBRUARY 1986

Major Morgan struggled to open the door to his part of the fourplex he called home for his CGSC student year. Finally, he gave up and sat his briefcase and armload of books down on the sidewalk in front of the door. He shook the tension out of his arms and shoulders and then opened the door. I don't want to do this training management practical exercise tonight, he thought, as he entered his quarters. Four hours of class on this crap was boring enough. After he had retrieved his study materials and stacked them on the chair just inside the door, he called out, "Elizabeth, I'm home."

"I'll be right down, Dear," she answered.

Ken hung up his jacket and cap. He looked at the gold oak leaves on them, hoping he would get promoted soon. The leaves were getting grungy, and he was too cheap to buy new ones he'd wear for only a couple of months. He walked into the tiny kitchen, took a tumbler from the cupboard, and filled it with ice. Then, he went into the small combination living and dining room—the "livedine," as his two boys called it. The livedine had hardly enough room to turn around in because the furniture they had had in their larger quarters at Fort Gordon filled the smaller students' quarters to overflowing. Ken took a bottle of Chivas Regal from the fancy wooden bar he had bought while stationed in Germany and poured two fingers of the expensive scotch into the tumbler. He didn't usually drink before studying, but he rationalized that the news he'd got today deserved a drink. "Come on down," he called out. "I've got some wild news."

A few minutes later Beth joined him. "A scotch before studying? It must be some news. What is it?"

Ken took a long drink of the smooth, cold scotch. "It's so crazy that I don't know where to start. Remember how Paul David and I were talking about how sad it was that we'd never get back into the courtroom? Well, I'm going to try one more general court-martial."

"That's great, Ken!" Elizabeth said. She was his ardent supporter. Beth had attended every one of her husband's major prosecutions, except those he had tried in Vietnam. She had presided over the spectators, reveling in the reflected glory of her husband's courtroom performances. Ken had come to rely on her assessments as to how the court members were reacting to the evidence.

Ken sat down in one of the overstuffed chairs in the living room portion of the livedine. "I'm not so sure. Let me tell you about it. It seems as if one of the students in the class accused another of disobeying an order to charge a machine gun in Vietnam. But the student charged it as a mutiny, largely because I stupidly ran off my mouth when he asked me how to charge it to get around the statute of limitations. The commanding general here was going to drop it, but the TRADOC commander decided to try it. He felt that the lawyers at the JAG office here were too inexperienced, so he detailed me to try the case."

"Why, that's great, Ken! A four-star picking you to try the case!"

"I don't know, Beth, I've got a funny feeling about his one. I'm not sure how a jury is going to react to a fourteen-year-old charge. And I talked to the victim, Major Armstrong. He's in my CGSC section. You've probably met him. He struck me as kind of a jerk, and I probably planted the idea in his head for the incident being a mutiny instead of just disobeying an order."

"You won't have any problem, Honey. You never do," Beth reassured her husband. "It's not like you to sound negative about a case. This one might be great for your career. Everyone says that General Hawkins is going to be the Chief of Staff someday. If you impress him, you could end up as the Judge Advocate General. And if you do lose, which I doubt seriously, no one could blame you for losing a case that old."

"Well, let's not starting sewing the stars on my uniform just yet. But maybe you're right, and at least I get to go back into the courtroom one more time. I wonder who the defense counsel is? They've got two captains here, but both seem pretty green."

Beth walked behind the chair Ken was sitting in and began to rub his neck. "Do you have a lot of studying to do tonight? I though we might go for a walk together."

"I've got some homework, and I'm going to have to get ahead if I'm going to try this case and still graduate. The Class Director told me not to worry about graduating, but I don't want to take any chances. Where are the boys?"

"They're eating supper next door. I'll get our dinner on the table."

As Beth cheerfully prepared dinner, Ken sat brooding. In a few minutes, she called him to the table. They ate in a companionable silence. Ken's mind was racing—already planning how to prosecute the case. Beth daydreamed she was watching her husband dazzle everyone in the courtroom. Ken dawdled over the food, unwilling to begin studying. Finally, he couldn't put it off any longer and went up to the spare bedroom they had fixed up as his study. He looked disgustedly at the stacks of books and manuals on the hardwood floor before pulling out the training management references. I'll never do this training management shit in a million years, he thought. But I'd better learn it well enough to pass the test. He tried to concentrate on how to manage training in Army units, but somewhere between figuring out training ammunition requirements and the intricacies of planning for transportation, he gave up and pulled out the file the Class Director had given him on the Thomas case. Elizabeth poked her head in once, but when she saw him pouring over witness statements, she recognized that he was working on the case and slipped quietly back out of the room without disturbing him. When their sons came home, she told them to be quiet and finish their homework before going to bed. When she went to bed at eleven-thirty, Ken was still working on the case, with the ice long-since melted in his half-empty glass of scotch.

CHAPTER 19

Bell Hall Snack Bar
Fort Leavenworth, Kansas

FEBRUARY 1986

After picking up a tray, Jim Thomas hesitated. Did he want a nice, healthy salad, or a more appealing, snack bar grossburger? He knew what he wanted, but like many of his classmates, he was trying to watch his cholesterol levels after undergoing the health risk appraisal testing all CGSC students had undergone. Oh, well, he thought, I may be in the Disciplinary Barracks in a couple of months and may not be able to get nice greasy grossburgers. Ever since he had learned that the TRADOC commander had referred his case to a general court-martial, he had experienced wild mood swings, from indifference and fatalism, to pessimism. Why worry about my health anyway? The Army doesn't give a shit about me, so why should I? After putting two of the foil-wrapped burgers on his tray and getting a Coke, he entered the payment line. While standing there, waiting for the obviously new cashier to figure out how to add up another customer's order, he spotted Major Morgan sitting by himself in the dining area. I need to talk to him, he thought. I want him for my defense counsel.

After paying, he walked up to the booth where Morgan sat. "Hi, mind if I sit down?"

Major Morgan looked up and noted the name on Major Thomas's nametag. He seemed to hesitate, but then gestured for Jim to sit down.

Jim introduced himself and immediately blurted out why he wanted to talk to the JAGC officer. "I'm facing a general court-martial, and I want you to be my individually requested defense counsel. Can you do it?"

"No."

Jim was taken aback at the brusqueness of the reply. "Why not?"

"There are several reasons. For one, CGSC students are, by regulation, not reasonably available to act as individual defense counsel. But more importantly, it looks as if I'm going to be detailed to prosecute the case."

Jim sat there stunned. Oh great, he thought, now they've put the lawyer Lieutenant Colonel David called the best prosecutor in the JAG Corps on the case. This snafu is rapidly turning into a nightmare. "Look, Major Morgan, this whole case is bullshit . . . ."

"Wait a minute," Ken interrupted him. "I can't discuss the case with you. It's against legal ethics. I suggest you talk to your defense counsel. Now if you'll excuse me."

"Ok, I get the picture," Jim said bitterly. Then less angrily, he said, "Thanks for the information. It's good to know what I'm up against." He got up, picked up his tray with unopened burgers, and turned to walk away.

Ken watched Jim start to walk away and then called out, "Wait a moment." When Jim turned around, Ken continued, "If I can make one suggestion . . . . If you want a dynamite defense counsel, why don't you consider Lieutenant Colonel David? He's the best I've ever seen on the technical/legal aspects of a court-martial, and he had a great reputation as a defense counsel when I worked with him."

"I just may do that. Thanks for the suggestion." As Jim walked away again, Ken sat there musing. I probably shouldn't have done that. But it would be too easy to prosecute against the inexperienced defense lawyers here. And, damn it, it would be great fun to finally go head to head against Paul. Smiling at himself, Ken turned back to the salad he had been eating.

As he ate, Jim thought about what Major Morgan had said, trying to decide whether he wanted Paul David for his defense counsel. Then he remembered how David had answered a student who had asked him how he could defend a guilty client and look at himself in the mirror after the trial. The instructor had answered by detailing the various theories of defense: how the Constitution, which military lawyers, as well as all other officers, were sworn to uphold, declared that everyone facing a criminal prosecution, not just innocent defendants, had a right to counsel; how he didn't get them off, he just presented their side of the case and the judge or jury found them not guilty; and how it was his duty and how he tried to do it the best he could, just as he did other unpleasant duties the military had assigned him. All those arguments were fine, but what made Jim decide that David would be a good defense counsel for him was the final part of David's answer: "Those are the theories. The reality is simpler. I hate to lose. No matter how much I may hate my client, when I walk into the courtroom and see the other attorney sitting there thinking he wants to kick my ass, I can't abide the thought of giving him that satisfaction. Take your pick. Would you want an idealistic young attorney who believes in your innocence, or would you want a grizzled veteran who hates to lose?"

Now that he had made his decision, Jim climbed the stairs to his section classroom and took the notebook he used for the military law elective out of his briefcase. He had written Lieutenant Colonel David's office room number and phone number in it when David had introduced himself during the first class. Room 220A. David was assigned to the Center for Army Leadership, which was responsible for teaching leadership, military writing, and military law, as well as for writing leadership doctrine. Except for the legal instruction, CAL's classes were so detested by the students that they called CAL the "Center for Army Leadershit." The students all knew that they were born leaders, so why study leadership?

Jim left Section 15 and walked to the other wing of Bell Hall looking for room 220A. When he found it, he entered. Only a tall major puffing on a cigar was in the room. "I'm looking for Lieutenant Colonel David," Jim announced.

"Have a seat. He'll be back in a minute."

Jim sat down and looked at the framed diplomas over David's desk. He found it comforting that the lawyer he wanted for his defense counsel had graduated first in his law school class, as shown by one of the plaques on the wall.

"We call that Paul's love-me wall," the smoke-encircled major quipped. "He says lawyers have to display all their diplomas to intimidate their clients and justify their fees. But we don't buy it, especially because Army lawyers can't charge fees. He just likes to bask in the glory of all his diplomas and awards and licenses."

"What's he really like?" Jim asked.

"No one knows for sure. He's not very outgoing. Yeah, he's a ham in class, but he doesn't socialize much or seem to have many friends. Maybe that's the price he pays for trying to outdo everyone at everything. He's pretty weird though—he reads science fiction and collects fine art. And he doesn't read military books or hunt or fish. But he's no wimp, though. He plays basketball in the over-thirty league and runs marathons. He's not your typical officer or lawyer, that's for sure."

Just as the lanky, cigar-smoking major was leaving the office, David entered. Jim stood up. "Good afternoon, Sir. I'm in your A955 class and would like to talk to you for a minute."

"Fine. Have a seat."

"Sir, I don't know really know how to start, so I'll just dive in. I've been charged with mutiny and am facing a general court-martial for an incident that took place in Vietnam. Captain Wilson has been detailed as my defense counsel, but I'm not certain he has enough experience for a case like this. I want to request you as my individual military counsel."

David got up from behind his desk and closed the door to the office. Sound and gossip traveled faster than flash floods up and down the halls in that building.

"Well, of course, I can't prevent you from requesting me, but I doubt they are going to find me reasonably available. The regulation says that service school instructors are not reasonably available."

Jim rubbed his forehead and then looked David in the eye. "You know, Sir, this run-around is getting old. I'm facing a general court-martial, and the only two lawyers I talk to start off by telling me they can't help me. And now I've got Major Morgan, who you said was the best prosecutor in the Army, trying to put me in jail. He's the one who suggested I consider you for my individual defense counsel."

A thrill shot through Paul as he thought about the chance of going up against Morgan. "That puts a different light on it," he said. "A CGSC student would not normally be detailed as trial counsel, so perhaps that lends support to your request for me as defense counsel. If you still want to, go ahead and request me. If they ask me, I'll tell them I can make the time to act as your lawyer. If they say no, you can ask the judge to rule whether their denial was legal. Ok?"

"Yes, Sir. Thank you! How do I go about requesting you?"

"Just see your detailed defense counsel. He'll type up a request for your signature."

"Ok, Sir. I really appreciate this. About the case . . . ."

"No," Lieutenant Colonel David interrupted, "I don't want to hear about the case until I am detailed as your individual defense counsel. All I'm going to do now is give you the advice I'm sure your lawyer has already given you—keep your mouth shut, and don't talk to anyone except your defense counsel."

"Ok, Sir. Thanks again. I'll see you in class."

"Take care," Lieutenant Colonel David replied, as he turned away towards his Apple 2C and booted it up with a word processing program to update his lesson plans. I must be nuts, he thought, as the disk drive whirred. Why am I trying to take on a court-martial while trying to teach twenty classroom hours a week? Because I can't miss one more chance for courtroom glory, he concluded as he started typing. And anything that gets me out of this office for a few hours would be worth it. I love teaching, but I'm so tired of the rest of the bullshit in this place. Center for Army Leadership, he snorted, I haven't seen any in this place yet. Just a bunch of wimps who love to talk about leadership but would shit if they had to go practice it in a regular unit. With a couple of exceptions, I hope none of them are on Major Thomas's jury.

CHAPTER 20

Office of the Staff Judge Advocate
Building 244
Fort Leavenworth, Kansas

FEBRUARY 1986

Captain Lewis stopped Colonel Farmer as he walked down the corridor toward his office. "Sir, we've got a problem with the Thomas case—well, actually two problems. First, I got a call from the Chief of PPT&O about Major Morgan. The Chief is not wild about leaving Morgan here for a couple of months after graduation. PPT&O was going to assign him as a regional defense counsel, and if Major Morgan stays here, PPT&O has to leave the current regional defense counsel at Lewis there an extra two months, and he was going to take an SJA job. PPT&O wants us to find someone else to prosecute."

"Ok, I'll call Colonel Temple at TRADOC, and if the four-star still wants Morgan, Temple can call the Judge Advocate General, or he can have General Hawkins call TJAG. If that doesn't work, we may have to just cut the orders detailing him and have our boss refuse to cut orders sending him anywhere until after he finishes the case, even if we get a request for orders from OTJAG. What's the second problem?"

"I've got a written request from Major Thomas for an individual defense counsel. Lieutenant Colonel David."

"Good choice. But I don't see it as a problem. Army Regulation 27-10 says that whoever holds the position of CGSC Military Law Instructor is not reasonably available."

Captain Lewis shook her head. "I don't know that I agree, Sir. The regulation also says that Major Morgan wouldn't be available to be an IDC because he is a CGSC student, yet we are detailing him to prosecute. If the defense litigates the denial of Lieutenant Colonel David, they may win—if not at trial, perhaps on appeal. And if the press gets wind of this trial, the Army could get pretty bad publicity for having the most experienced prosecutor in the Army trying the case when we've denied the accused an experienced defense counsel. And the detailed defense counsel, Captain Wilson, is pretty green."

"Yeah, maybe you're right. Have you asked Lieutenant Colonel David whether he believes he is reasonably available?"

"Yes, Sir. David said he would have to request a delay until after the CGSC class graduates in early June. Then he could try the case before the end of June. If he is made available under those terms, he will request a delay in writing, so we won't have any speedy trial problems. The accused is not under any pretrial restraint, so we don't have to worry about bringing him to trial within ninety days or facing dismissal for violation of his speedy trial rights. And Major Morgan is going to need some time to prepare anyway. I called him, and he said June sounded good to him."

"Ok, I'll recommend to the convening authority that Lieutenant Colonel David be found to be reasonably available and be detailed as individual defense counsel. Because you are staying on the case as assistant trial counsel, I suppose we shouldn't request that Captain Wilson be excused. If Major Thomas wants to excuse him, that's his business."

"Sounds good, Sir."

Colonel Farmer turned away and walked down the corridor to his office thinking about the case. Before entering his office, he asked his secretary to get Colonel Temple on the phone. We are nowhere near the trial date, and I'm already sick of this case, he thought, as he waited for the intercom to ring to announce that his call had gone through. I'd like to put Major Thomas under the jail for jeopardizing my chances to make brigadier general, he fumed, and Major Armstrong along with him for bringing this crap up years later.

CHAPTER 21

Trial Defense Service Office
Building 244
Fort Leavenworth, Kansas

FEBRUARY 1986

Captain Wilson handed Lieutenant Colonel David the manila folder containing the case file on the Thomas case. "Here you are, Sir. Everything I've got is in here, including the Article 32 transcript. I'm really glad you're on the case. I was afraid it would be a little much for me. I've defended only fifteen cases, and most of them were guilty pleas. I've moved an extra desk in here for you to use. I know you will do a lot of the work out of your office at Bell Hall, but you'll need a place to work during recesses from the trial. Do you need anything else?"

"Not that I can think of now. It looks as if you've been very thorough," Lieutenant Colonel David replied. "Well, let's get to work. Sam, I hope I don't offend you, but I've got to ask. Did you advise our client of his rights at a general court-martial?"

"Yes, Sir, up to this point. I didn't advise him of the pros and cons of testifying, or of going jury or judge alone. I thought I'd wait until the case was actually referred to trial."

"Good. I'd want to readvise him about those options anyway. By the way—although I started out in the infantry myself and believe in military courtesy, when we are working together on a case such as this one, I think we can dispense with all the 'sirs.' And call me Paul. Ok?"

"Ok, Paul."

Lieutenant Colonel David smiled. "Good. For a moment, I thought we were going to go through that trite 'Ok, Sir—I mean Paul.' I'm going to need a few days to absorb this file. I want to see what I get out of it before you tell me what you think. That way, I'll view it from an unbiased viewpoint. In the meantime, I want the officer record briefs of

Major Thomas, Major Armstrong, and all the court members. I also want the military records of any witnesses who testified in the Article 32 investigation. Also, try to get a national agency check to see whether any of them have any dirt in their backgrounds."

"Sure."

"What time did you tell Major Thomas to be here?"

Sam looked at his watch. "1400 hours. He should be here in a couple of minutes."

"Good." Paul turned his attention to the case file. In a moment, he was so absorbed that his young co-counsel decided not to interrupt him. After calling his national agency contact and leaving a message about the information he needed for Lieutenant Colonel David, Sam turned to the advance sheets of new appellate decisions, thinking he'd better keep up on the current law. Lieutenant Colonel David had a reputation for being a whiz on motion practice—the application of the law to the procedural aspects of a court-martial—and the young attorney didn't want to look if he weren't competent in the law himself. After about ten minutes, Major Thomas appeared at the door. Sam looked up from the cases he was reading and beckoned their client in. Lieutenant Colonel David was so engrossed in the case file that he didn't even notice Major Thomas's entrance. Both junior officers were silent for a few moments while the lieutenant colonel remained absorbed in the case file. Finally, Jim broke the silence. "Are you always so intense when you are working on a case, Sir?"

Paul looked up, reluctantly it seemed. After a moment's pause, he smiled. "Just about." He stood and shook Jim's hand. "Have a seat. Let's get to work."

After Jim took a seat in the now-crowded office, Paul opened a notepad and started in. "Now, Jim, I know Captain Wilson went over a lot of these things, but I want to go over them with you myself. Ok?"

"Sure," Jim replied, "you're the boss, Sir."

"You have two options as to who is going to decide the case. You have an absolute right to have your case decided by a court composed of at least five officers." Paul handed Jim a copy of the court-martial convening order. "General Hawkins has appointed twelve officers whose names you see here as the court members. We can challenge any of them for cause for some type of prejudice. And we have one peremptory challenge. In other words, we can challenge one of them for any reason or no reason, and the military judge will excuse him. Do you know any of these officers or know of any reason why any of them might be disqualified from hearing your case?"

"No, Sir."

"Ok, we'll check further into it. When the trial starts, we can question them to see whether any grounds for challenge exist. Now, two-thirds of the members have to vote to convict before they can find you guilty. If less than two-thirds vote to convict, then they have acquitted you. A court-martial can't have a hung jury on the question of guilt or innocence. If the court finds you guilty, the court also determines your sentence by a two-thirds vote unless it's a sentence to confinement for more than ten years, which requires a three-fourths vote. And a death penalty requires a unanimous vote. However, you can waive your right to a trial by court composed of members and request a trial by military judge alone, unless they referred your case as a capital case, authorizing the death penalty."

Major Thomas looked incredulous. "Don't you know?"

"I can't tell whether they did or not, because, although the referral does not specify that the case is to be tried as noncapital, the pretrial advice to the convening authority didn't tell him that the maximum punishment included the death penalty. The glitch in the referral is unlike Major Morgan's usual handiwork. I suspect either it's one of his pretrial maneuvers, or else they referred it before he was detailed as trial counsel. Colonel Farmer is none too swift and could easily screw up a referral—so don't worry about it—no one's going to sentence you to death for this crap."

Jim didn't look particularly convinced, but Paul kept on, "If the case is noncapital and you do decide to go judge alone, he would determine both your guilt or innocence and, if you are found guilty, an appropriate sentence. You can't have a jury for findings and a judge for sentencing, as the civilian system often does.

"Now it may be a little early, but my initial recommendation is not to waive a jury. What I've learned about the case so far leads me to believe that we want combat arms officers as the fact finders. Judge Savage, name aside, is a fair but tough judge. But he doesn't have any line experience, and we can hope for a phenomenon called "jury nullification" with court members. Simply put, it occurs when a military jury finds that the accused did the act but says, 'So what, I'd have done the same thing myself,' and finds the accused not guilty. A judge won't do that. If Judge Savage finds you did the acts charged, he will convict. If he would have done the same thing himself, that would affect the sentence, but not the findings. Ok?"

Major Thomas sat for a moment, trying to digest what his new lawyer had said. Finally, he said, "Ok, once again, you're the boss, Sir."

"Not in this instance," Lieutenant Colonel David replied. "Although I recommend you choose to have a military jury decide your case, it has to be your decision, not mine. Think about it. You don't need to decide right now.

"There is another important decision you have to make, and that decision is whether to testify. Now, you have an absolute right to remain silent and require the prosecutor to prove you guilty beyond a reasonable doubt. You don't have to present any evidence whatsoever. And you certainly cannot be compelled to testify. In fact, if you do not testify, the military judge must instruct the court members that they cannot draw any inference of guilt from your failure to testify. That's the law. The reality, however, is that officers do not seem to have the right to remain silent. The laws say they do, but a court composed of officers is going to expect a brother officer to get on the witness stand, look them in the eye, and tell them he didn't commit the crime. If he doesn't, it matters little how strongly the judge emphasizes that the law says they cannot hold his failure to testify against him. In some ways, that instruction would just emphasize that he didn't have the balls to look them in the eye and say he didn't do it. They would figure he must have something to hide. Of course, if you testify, the trial counsel will be able to cross-examine you. I think you need to testify—to tell the court what really happened. But again, you think about it."

"Ok, but I can already tell you, after hearing that asshole Armstrong testify at the Article 32 investigation, I want my turn."

Lieutenant Colonel David looked directly at his client. "Before I can advise you to testify, I have to know whether you have any dirt in your background. Anywhere. I want to know every traffic ticket you ever got and any peccadillo and certainly anything more serious. I don't want to be surprised when Major Morgan starts cross-examining you."

Major Thomas returned his lawyer's penetrating stare. "Other than a couple of parking tickets, I got a speeding ticket once. I was on my way home for my thirty-day leave before going to Vietnam and was in a little too much of a hurry to see my wife. That's it. No other hassles with the law." He forced out a strained little laugh and said, "Until now."

"Good. Now I've read the account Sam asked you to write about what happened. I want you to rewrite it for me, but start when you first arrived in Vietnam. I also want a biography. But I want your military service to be detailed. I also want the names and anything you can think of to help us find your past military superiors and any other character witnesses you can think of. And I want copies of all orders you have from your Vietnam service, including awards. If your unit was like mine, a number of people in your unit got their Combat Infantry Badges or Air Medals on one blanket order. We can use them to get the names of potential witnesses from your platoon. Once we get the names, we can get their records from the records center in St. Louis and get homes of record to start finding them. Got all that?" Paul subscribed to the theory that the best way to keep clients under some type of control—and from worrying too much—was to give them something to do.

"Yes, Sir."

"Sam, can you think of anything I've forgotten?"

"No. Not now."

"Ok. I've got to get back to teach my elective. We'll get together again after I've gone over the Article 32 testimony. Remember, Jim, don't talk to anyone about the case but the two of us."

"Ok. Thanks for your help," Jim said as he stood up to leave.

The two lawyers shook hands with their client and watched him walk out of the office. Don't say thanks yet, Paul thought. No one's done any good for you so far.

CHAPTER 22

General Lowe's Quarters
1 Scott Avenue
Fort Leavenworth, Kansas

MARCH 1986

Meg Thomas fumed as she stood in the receiving line waiting to shake Mrs. Lowe's hand. When I told Jim I was willing to play staff group leader's wife and put up with the social whirl, I had no idea it would be this intense, she thought. Every day! If it wasn't a staff group tea, it was a section tea. If neither, then it was a function with the Class Director's wife or an international officers' wives function. They're all so boring. And I can't even get a job because of all this social nonsense. Realizing that getting all worked up was gaining her nothing other than a new worry—whether her deodorant would stand up to the wait—Meg concentrated on the furnishings. Mrs. Lowe apparently didn't go for the oriental or German collectibles many officers wives did, or she had a lot more money. She had apparently decorated the general's quarters in the arts and crafts style with ornate and expensive but slightly schmaltzy decorations all over. Meg felt as if she had somehow found herself back in the thirties, more specifically inside Grant Wood's *American Gothic*. She thought that if she saw one more wall hanging or pillow sham with a goose on it or a "home, sweet home" saying in counted cross-stitch, she'd puke—an act which would make her concern about her deodorant somewhat less important.

Finally, Meg found herself shaking Mrs. Lowe's gloved hand. Unknown to Meg, Mrs. Lowe found these functions as boring as Meg did. But the general's wife also understood how much good she could do for the community by cajoling volunteers for the Red Cross and the Army Community Service activities at these mandatory social events. Mrs. Lowe smiled and said, "Welcome, Mrs. Thompson. So nice to meet you."

Meg ignored the mispronunciation of her name and replied, "Thank you, Ma'am." Perhaps, Meg thought, it's better she doesn't realize I am *the* Mrs. Thomas—wife of the "infamous war criminal" facing court-martial. But you'd think a three-star's wife could read a nametag. Meg had tried to walk past the table where some colonel's wife was writing out last names on stick-on nametags, but hadn't made it. Thus, she wore a stupid-looking nametag perched precariously on her blue silk Liz Claiborne blouse right over her right breast. That sticky stuff had better come off at the cleaners, she thought.

Meg walked into the dining room and took a cup of punch and the requisite (no more, no less) two cookies from the poor woman who was pouring from a large crystal punch bowl with a smile that looked about as brittle as the crystal frozen on her face.

After inching her way through the dozens of other wives standing around, crowding the general's normally spacious quarters, Meg found an empty seat on a lone chair in the living room. She sat down gratefully, relieved at not having to join a group of chattering women. She looked around the room, but didn't see anyone she felt like talking to. The longer Jim's trouble dragged out, the more isolated she felt from the other wives. She couldn't decide whether they were colder or she was simply more withdrawn.

As she tried to deal with the punch cup in one hand and the cookies in the other, she listened to the conversation buzzing around her.

"How can we raise some funds for the scholarship fund? We're several thousand short this year."

"Our quarters are just so small. Why, we still have half our household goods boxed up!"

"Leavenworth is just so provincial. I have to go all the way to Kansas City to find any decent clothes for the children. But I've got to admit that the Nelson Art Gallery is wonderful. What a Chinese art collection!"

"Maggie, Mark, and Izzie looked so cute all dressed up for church at the Post Chapel last Sunday."

"How's your aerobics class going? You look like you've lost a lot of weight."

Meg didn't feel like joining the conversation. But finally, the staff group leader's wife from Section 15 broke her solitude. "Hi, Meg. How nice you look. I like your outfit. And your shoes are really nice. Are they Aigner?"

Meg forced out a smile. "No, Christina, they're just Sears Roebuck specials."

"Well, you could have fooled me. I could have sworn they were Aigner. Your whole outfit looks so—so coordinated. Excuse me, please. I see Colonel Silver's wife is free, and I simply must talk to her about the wives' club bazaar. Talk to you later!"

As Christina bounced away, Meg thought, was that a veiled dig or what? Did I violate the dress code? That's all I need, to mess up the dress code, when Jim said we've got to act normal and not draw any attention to ourselves until the trial is over.

Her thoughts were interrupted when she heard Jim's name. Although she strained to hear, she could pick up only fragments of the conversation over the buzz of conversation in the room.

". . . wonder why they don't have any children. Do you suppose the wound he got when his men shot him after he disobeyed the order . . ."

"Poor thing, she seems to be taking it well, but . . ."

"Mark Armstrong's wife, Susie, says we don't need officers like that in the military. I wonder how Mrs. Thomas can show her face here."

"Hold on, let's wait until the trial is over before we condemn them. She's a nice person. This trial must be horrible for her."

Her face burning, Meg got up and walked out. She shoved her punch cup at the colonel's wife who was still guarding the tea service and stalked out with as much dignity as she could muster. Those bitches, she thought. Jim's men didn't shoot him. And it's none of their business why we haven't had children. God knows, we've tried. Even those damned Army doctors can't tell us why. Maybe it's me. But then again, some civilian specialist thinks maybe Army chemicals or his wound did something to Jim in Vietnam.

Meg got into her Volvo station wagon and drove home, not paying much attention to the speed limit. Fortunately, the MPs must have been hassling teenagers parked up on the ridgeline or something. When she arrived at their quarters, she ran in and threw her arms around Jim. He was studying. Margaret kissed him on the neck and nuzzled his ear. "Come on, Honey, you've been studying for hours. Surely, you need a break. And I need some loving. Let's go to bed," she said, desperately wanting some affection. If not sex, at least some cuddling.

But Jim dashed her hopes. "Can't, Honey. I've got a big test tomorrow, and with all the preparation for the trial, I'm way behind in my studies. This one looks like an all-nighter."

Meg didn't answer. She started to slam their bedroom door shut, but simply closed it quietly before collapsing on the bed and yielding to the tears that had been waiting since she was in the general's living room.

CHAPTER 23

Classroom 15
Bell Hall
Fort Leavenworth, Kansas

MARCH 1986

"Damn, this exercise sucks," Jim said to his table mate, William "Wild Bill" Danford. Bill had picked up his nickname because of his totally irreverent attitude toward CGSC. His most outrageous feat thus far in the CGSC academic year had been placing a piece of masking tape down the middle of his bald head and walking around Bell Hall as a big prick. His instructors agreed with Bill's self-characterization.

"You got that right," Bill replied as he picked up the Middle East Exercise handbook and began plotting Iranian and Soviet unit dispositions on one of the many maps hanging around all of Section 15C's right rear quarter of the classroom. The classroom looked strange—like a hybrid between a one-room schoolhouse and a DTOC (division tactical operations center). The students were trying to simulate fighting a war in Iran from eastern Kansas—a simulation that would bear fruit for many of these officers years later when they moved the operation over one country to the west as Operation Desert Storm.

The Command and General Staff College had three college-wide exercises during the academic year. During most of the year, the four divisions of almost 250 students each would be taking different subjects, normally taught at section or staff group level. But at the end of the first term, right before Christmas break, all the students had to endure the KOREX, the KORean EXercise. Planning this imaginary amphibious operation to cross the Han River Estuary was so tedious and pointless that some students called it the BORE-EX, and a student in one section had had a contest to rename the exercise. The winner was KOrean Training EXercise—KOTEX.

At the end of the second term, CGSC students had to endure the MEEX (Middle East EXercise), and just before graduation, the AFEX (AFrican EXercise). In the MEEX, the students had to plan for an amphibious landing at Bandar Abbas, a port on the Persian Gulf in southern Iran, to block a Soviet thrust towards the gulf from the Trans-Caucasus Military District and Afghanistan. In this wildly fictitious scenario, Iranian moderates (there must be two or three of them) had requested U.S. government assistance in countering the Soviet threat. The exercise was ludicrous because the students were expected to—and with the help of the scenario's controllers did—stop waves of Russian divisions with only three American divisions and a Marine amphibious brigade. Further, the supply problem was unsolvable, but it's easy to ignore the problems of heat, dust, distance, lack of fuel and water, and the like in the Middle East, on a map exercise in a climate-controlled, almost hermetically sealed, classroom high atop the rolling bluffs of the Missouri River.

In an attempt to interject some realism into the MEEX problem this year, the exercise controllers had programmed the Corvus Concept computers that sat in every classroom to wargame the students' actions and print out how the U.S. units had done against the enemy. After all, the college had to find some use for the computers they had spent thousands of dollars to buy. They were so awful that the one and only female instructor at CGSC that year called them user-surly. The students were very upset at the computers because they usually told the student that a much smaller enemy force had wiped them out. Apparently, the controller had programmed the computers with fifty possible scenarios. The computers then matched the student solutions with the closest possible scenario, ignoring any U.S. units that were outside the parameters of the scenario. Thus, a U.S. unit might get credit for less than half its fighting strength. Because the students were supposed to be graded on how well they had planned the battle—translated as how much combat power they got to various objectives—they were close to homicidal when the computers just ignored their units, lowering their grades with every calculation.

"Hey, Jim, the computer is malfunctioning again," Kelvin Chirwa called out in his terribly proper British accent. Kelvin was the staff group's computer guru. Although they didn't have many computers in his native Malawi, a small country in central Africa, he had attended military school in England and was not only more computer literate than many Americans in the staff group, but also more literate, period. He had also signed up for every computer elective the college offered. Jim swore Kelvin could think in binary. In Section 15, they believed in an equal division of labor, which meant that if a staff group member was an expert in a particular area, he did that function for the group. Thus, Section 15 had its designated briefer, its writing team, and its logistics expert. The few students who weren't particularly good at anything did whatever they could to assist, from putting up maps to making briefing charts. As the computer whiz, Kelvin had to fight with the computer during the entire exercise.

"Again or yet?" Jim replied disgustedly. "I'll get a controller. In the meantime, we'd better keep number-crunching by pocket calculator. Otherwise, we'll be here until midnight." He fought his way out of the accordion curtains that were supposed to keep out the noise of the other staff groups. The theory behind these curtains was great, but because the curtains did not go up to the ceiling, the noise just flowed over the top without diminishing in the slightest.

Jim went out into the smoke-filled hallway. The gun metal blue-gray cigarette smoke was so dense from the smokers escaping the boredom of the classroom that the hall looked as if someone had thrown a smoke grenade—probably the closet thing to combat realism in the whole exercise. He spotted his academic counselor evaluator, Lieutenant Colonel Mills, walking down the hallway towards Section 15. ACEs acted as battle staff leaders—glorified monitors—for the exercises. Mills had to play the role of the U.S. corps commander, issuing the commander's guidance to the students, and also had to keep the exercise going if the students revolted or the computer broke down, both likely scenarios in this exercise. Jim stopped him and briefed the fortyish, balding infantry officer on the latest computer problem.

"Ok, I'll go find a computer whiz. All I have to do is look for a line of hacked-off ACEs. Other than the computer, how's it going?"

"Ok, Sir. We'll be ready to brief you on requirement 12 in about twenty minutes. The guys are getting pretty frazzled, though, and I don't think they're going to last much longer."

"Watch it, troop," Mills kidded. "You're caring for your men again. According to your defense lawyer, who called me yesterday to see if I'd be a character witness for you, that's what they're trying to court-martial you for."

"Yes, Sir." Jim grinned. "Some people never learn."

"Seriously, how are things going with you? You hanging in there ok?"

"I'm doing ok. Sometimes, it's hard to concentrate on studying, but because you seem unlikely to allow me to goof off while this hassle continues, I'm hitting the books hard. But I'm worried about Meg. She's not taking this whole thing well. Besides worrying about the trial, I think she's frustrated about this assignment. Like I told you when you asked me whether I was willing to be a staff group leader, with all the social crap of a staff group leader's wife, she can't work. It's also hard to find a good job when you are only going to be in the area for a year—unless, of course, I end up in the Disciplinary Barracks. She's pretty high-strung, and because we don't have any kids, she has lot of time on her hands. She's too well educated to be satisfied with full-time volunteer work. And I think she's mad at me for studying too much and not spending enough time with her. I know I should spend more time with her, but keeping myself busy is the only thing that's keeping me somewhat sane while this mess drags on." Jim was surprised at himself for unloading all of his personal problems on Colonel Mills, but after having worked with his ACE for months, he knew that Mills genuinely cared.

Mills put an arm around Jim's shoulders. "Yeah, it must be rough on both of you. You don't have much choice but to keep busy, and you at least have some control over your fate, what with preparing for the trial with your counsel. But Meg's got a lot of time to brood, without any meaningful work to do.

"You know, the Army really exploits the free labor of spouses and other volunteers. I know it's largely a budget problem, but if the Army really wanted the quality family life it says it does, shouldn't it pay for the programs instead of coercing some volunteer to provide them?"

Jim thought for a moment before responding. "I think I'll plead the Fifth Amendment on that one. I'm in enough trouble without sounding off on the platitudes the generals mouth about all the great things they're doing for family life that never seem to get translated into reality."

"Ok. By the way, how's your defense counsel? Is he as good a lawyer as he is an instructor?"

"Seems to be. I know he's putting in long hours working up the case—on top of his teaching load. He's hard to read, though. I can never tell what he's thinking."

"What do you mean?" the ACE inquired.

"Well, I don't even know whether he thinks I'm innocent or not. I asked him whether he believed I had done the right thing. He said it wasn't his job to decide whether I was innocent or not. That was for the jury. It was his job to represent me. Then I asked him how he could represent me if he didn't believe in me. He said that what he thought was irrelevant. He'd defend me even if he knew I was guilty—and just as vigorously. I suppose that's comforting, but I'd like to be able to think my defense lawyer believed in my innocence. And I'd feel more comfortable if I thought he cared about me more than his win/lose record."

"Yeah, that seems like a pretty cold attitude."

"Yes, Sir. But I'm not really complaining. He certainly seems to know what he's doing. And it's like he said in his law class, would you rather have some idealistic young lawyer who believes in you or a grizzled courtroom veteran who may think you are guilty as hell, but hates to lose?"

"Roger that. All I can say is, hang in there. You've been doing just great. I can't believe the Army is so messed up that this fiasco will turn out badly for you. Well, I'd better go track down some computer whiz so I can get you guys out of here before you mutiny—for real this time."

"Ok, Sir. We'll be ready to brief you when you get back. And I hope you're right about the Army, but I'm not so sure. Sometimes, it seems to eat its young." As Jim walked back into the classroom, he considered that being in the first assault wave into Bandar Abbas and facing a horde of crazed Islamic religious fundamentalists seeking martyrdom would be preferable to walking into the courtroom as the accused. I was never really afraid during a firefight, he thought. Before and after, yes. During, no. No time for it. But I've been afraid throughout this pretrial phase. And if the court-martial is anything like the Article 32 investigation, I'll be afraid in the courtroom, too. I feel like the wheels of military justice are grinding on inexorably, and they're going to roll right over me in the end, just like the 5th Guards Tank Army—or its computer counterpart— is going to roll over us if I don't get my staff group motivated.

CHAPTER 24

Gruber Gymnasium
Building 302
Fort Leavenworth, Kansas

MAY 1986

Captain Lewis backpedaled furiously. Reading the angle of the bounce off the side wall correctly, she sent a wicked passing shot past Major Morgan. He turned to try to return it off the back wall, but stopped abruptly as it died in the back of the racquetball court. "Twenty-one!" Pam shrieked. "I finally beat you!"

"Rather easily, too," Ken replied, after he caught his breath. "I must be getting old."

"Want a rematch?"

"Not on your life. Let's sit down and rest for a few minutes before we go back to the office."

"Ok. I'll go get a couple of Cokes while you rest your old bones."

"Watch it, wise guy! Keep it up and you can face Judge Savage by yourself."

Pam raised her hands in mock surrender. She went to get the Cokes while Ken wiped the sweat from his forehead with his towel and turned the racquetball in to the gym attendant. He took a Coke from Pam with a mumbled thanks as they walked to the bleachers and sat down.

After they had been sitting there a few moments, the young woman couldn't resist any longer and began discussing the Thomas case. "We're getting pretty close to the trial date. We should get a list of motions from the defense pretty soon. I wonder what they'll be. I hope there aren't too many."

"I'm not sure I agree," the more experienced lawyer replied. "When you are facing both Judge Savage and Lieutenant Colonel David, motion practice becomes very tactical. Actually, I'd like to see a lot of motions."

"Why's that?"

"Well, although Judge Savage is very tough on counsel and some-times makes obscure rulings, on the whole he is a good judge for the government. However, if he denies a number of defense motions in a row, I think he subconsciously starts feeling sorry for the defense and is more likely to grant a defense motion. Lieutenant Colonel David has picked up on this, and he will orchestrate his motions so that he loses the ones he expects to lose and saves the ones he really wants to win until Judge Savage has been primed to grant a defense motion. So what we have to do is make certain Judge Savage has some defense motions to grant early on so he doesn't grant the important ones. I call it 'tossing the defense a bone.' For example, I may make a motion in limine to exclude some defense evidence that is clearly admissible just to get the judge to deny our motion. But David will be aware of what I'm trying to do, so it will be an interesting tactical battle."

"They didn't teach us this tactical stuff at the basic course. How did you learn it?"

"In more than five hundred courts-martial. But I'm not all that wor-ried about any motions. What I'm worried about is our star witness, Major Armstrong. Preparing him for both direct and cross-examination will be the key to our case."

"What about cross-examination of the accused—if he testifies?"

"He'll testify. Lieutenant Colonel David knows as well as I do that an officer's right to remain silent is illusory. But his cross-examination is less important than Major Armstrong's. After all, if we don't put on a prima facie case, Judge Savage may grant a motion for a finding of not guilty, and the accused will never need to testify. And just between you and me, Major Armstrong is not a perfect government witness. If he comes across in court as stuffy and arrogant as he seems the rest of the time, then he may just turn the jury off. And without him, we don't have a case. I've been working on his direct examination. I've got him com-ing in after class to start going over his direct testimony. I want you to sit there and play defense counsel—take notes on areas to cross-examine him on. I want to ask him every possible question Lieutenant Colonel David may before he gets on the witness stand."

"Ok. Shall we get back to the office?"

After they had gone to their respective locker rooms to shower and dress, the two lawyers met outside the gym, got into Ken's car, and returned to Captain Lewis's office. Mark Armstrong joined them a short time later. After an exchange of pleasantries, they began work on the case.

Major Morgan started by taking Armstrong into the courtroom and showing him where the judge, the court members, the court reporter, and the counsel would sit and had him sit in the witness chair so that he would be familiar with the layout of the courtroom. "I'll be standing here, but I don't want you looking at me when you answer my questions. Instead, I want you to turn your head and look at the court members. Address your testimony to them, not to me."

Back in the office, Ken continued. "Now, the first rule about testifying in court is to tell the truth. We are going to rehearse both my direct examination of you and the defense counsel's cross-examination. But I don't want to put words into your mouth. Nor do I want you to lie, even if you think your answer hurts your case.

"Second, you must merely answer the question, without elaborating or explaining, again even if it makes you look bad without the explanation. If you are always explaining and qualifying your answers, it makes you look shifty and dishonest. Save your explanations for when I ask you for them. For example, if the defense counsel asks you whether you reported the crime when it occurred, answer 'No,' even if it makes you look stupid. When I get a chance for redirect, I'll ask you to tell the court why you didn't report it at the time if I think they need to know. Ok?"

"Seems simple enough."

"I guarantee it's anything but simple. Even though we rehearse witnesses exhaustively, many still get diarrhea of the mouth and blow their cases. When I read your Article 32 testimony, I noticed you have that tendency. We are going to rehearse it out of you.

"Now, I should hardly have to remind you about your appearance, bearing, and military courtesy in the courtroom. If you want to convict Thomas, you've got to be 'strac.'"

"No problem."

"Now, if you don't hear a question or don't understand it, ask to have it repeated. Feel free to take a moment to think about your answer. Don't blurt out the first thing that comes to your mind. Also, you may have seen a television courtroom drama in which the witness asks, 'Do I have to answer that, your Honor?' I don't want any of that crap from you. I'll do the objecting. You just answer the questions truthfully and succinctly, unless the military judge tells you not to answer. If someone does object, just stop talking until the judge or counsel tells you to continue.

"Now, let's start going over your testimony. After I call you as a witness, the bailiff will get you from the witness waiting room and bring you to the courtroom. Stop in front of the witness chair and face me. I'll ask you to raise your right hand, and I'll administer the witness oath.

Then, I'll ask you to be seated and to state your name, rank, Social Security number, unit, and armed force. Then, the real questions begin. First, I'll ask you . . . ."

Captain Lewis picked up a yellow legal tablet and began to take notes of potential cross-examination areas. It was hard to focus on her notes, however, as she sat mesmerized, watching as the master trial counsel began to weave Major Armstrong's testimony into a coherent, compelling, and damning tale.

CHAPTER 25

Courtroom, Office of the Staff Judge Advocate
Building 244
Fort Leavenworth, Kansas

J U N E   1 9 8 6

Lieutenant Colonel David looked up from the legal pad he was studying as Major Thomas entered the austere courtroom. Even the soft glow of the hardwood maple judge's bench, witness box, and jury box could not offset the effect of the harsh florescent lighting. An American flag behind the judge's bench provided the only color and decorative relief to the drab, stuffy, windowless room. The attorney frowned as he studied Major Thomas's uniform. "Why aren't you wearing your ribbons?" he asked. The only decorations the accused was wearing were his jump wings and Combat Infantry Badge. He was not wearing the three rows of ribbons he was authorized to wear over the left breast pocket of his class A uniform. "I took them off to get my uniform pressed like you told me to, and when I was running behind this morning, I didn't have time to pin nonessential insignia on," Jim replied.

"Listen," Paul began, "the court members are not supposed to decide the case on the basis of your ribbons. But it is extremely important for you to wear every decoration you are entitled to. There's no such thing as a nonessential decoration in a court-martial.

"I heard a lecture about military juries at a defense advocacy course I attended at the JAG school. Military courts, composed as they are of officers, are a type of jury known as 'the authoritarian jury.' The authoritarian model jury tends to believe the first thing it hears, which is the prosecution's opening statement. For that reason, I will make my opening statement right after the trial counsel makes his, instead of waiting until the start of the defense case. I will use every chance I get to present our version of the case to the jury before they start to believe the trial counsel's version. The only way, according to this lecture, of breaking the military jury out of this belief in the first thing they hear is to get them to identify with the other side—in other words, with you. That's why you will wear all your decorations when you are in court. I also want your wife sitting in here looking like a good, supportive, Army officer's wife. Now, the correct decorations aren't too important today because this session is only a preliminary hearing before the judge. But I want you looking sharp with all your decorations when the jury is in here. Clear?"

"Yes, Sir."

Just then, Major Morgan entered, accompanied by Captain Lewis. Like the defense team, they both wore their class A uniforms. Ken's blouse was adorned with two rows of ribbons, showing that he had served in Vietnam, but because he had been a lawyer, he didn't have any combat awards. Pam wore only an Army Achievement Medal in addition to the I-was-alive-in-the-Army basic issue awards. The defense team might not win the case, but they'd win the awards and decorations battle once Jim's ribbons, including combat awards from Vietnam, joined Paul's three rows of ribbons, Combat Infantry Badge, and jump wings. Paul was convinced he may have won some defense cases only because he and his client had more decorations than the trial counsel.

Ken nodded at Paul, then sat down at the trial counsel table. A moment later, Judge Savage swept into the courtroom. The bailiff said loudly, "All rise." The lawyers, the accused, and the few spectators— mostly other lawyers, stood at attention as Judge Savage made his way to the bench. Judge Savage was a full bird colonel, although the spectators couldn't tell his rank because of the black judge's robe he wore over his uniform. He looked like a judge—six-feet-four-inches tall, with a lionlike mane of silver-gray hair. As he sat down, he started the trial, "You may be seated. This Article 39(a) session is called to order."

Right on cue, Major Morgan stood back up and started through the script—the verbiage that begins all U.S. courts-martial: "The court is convened by court-martial convening order number seventeen, Headquarters TRADOC, as amended by court-martial convening orders number nineteen and twenty, copies of which have been furnished the military judge, counsel, and the accused, and to the reporter for inclusion at this point in the record.

"The charges have been properly referred to this court for trial and were served on the accused by Captain Pamela Lewis, the assistant trial counsel, on 21 September 1985.

"The accused and all persons named in the convening orders are present, except the members.

"Maureen Carr has been detailed reporter for this court and has previously been sworn."

Because the trial was by general court-martial, the convening authority had detailed Mrs. Carr to make a verbatim transcript. The attractive blonde spoke into her stenomask as Major Morgan continued with the script. She was quite happy to note that he had a strong, clear voice. The bane of her profession was a mumbling lawyer.

"The legal qualifications and status as to oaths of all members of the prosecution are correctly stated in the convening orders.

"No member of the prosecution has acted as investigating officer, military judge, court member, or as a member of the defense in this case."

As soon as Major Morgan finished, Judge Savage began. Unlike Major Morgan, who had been away from the courtroom for some time, the judge did not read from the script. Instead, he spoke from memory.

"Major Thomas, I am sure Captain Wilson has discussed your rights to counsel with you. However, the law requires me to ensure that you understand your rights.

"You have the right to be represented by Captain Wilson, your detailed defense counsel. He is an attorney and is fully qualified to serve as your defense counsel. His services are provided free of charge by the Trial Defense Service.

"You have the right, however, to request a different military lawyer to represent you. If the person you request is available, he or she would be appointed to represent you free of charge. Do you understand that?"

Jim had stood up as soon as the judge addressed him. Paul had told him to do so whenever the bailiff announced "All rise" and whenever the judge spoke to him. And Jim would have done so anyway, knowing that the judge was a full colonel. "Yes, your Honor."

Judge Savage, who was always courteous to the accused if not to counsel, even if he would ultimately hammer the accused with a life sentence, told Jim that he could remain seated except when asked to stand. As Jim sat down, the judge continued, "If your request for this military lawyer is granted, however, you would not have the right to keep the services of Captain Wilson, your detailed counsel. That is because you are entitled to only one military lawyer. You may ask the convening authority to let you keep your detailed counsel, but the convening authority would not have to grant your request. Do you understand that?"

"Yes, your Honor."

"In addition to the right to request a military lawyer of your own choice, you have the right to be represented by a civilian lawyer. A civilian lawyer would have to be provided by you; he or she would not be at the expense of the government. Do you understand that?"

"Yes, your Honor."

"Do you have any questions about your rights to counsel?"

"No, your Honor."

"Now, I see that you have another military lawyer, Lieutenant Colonel Paul David, at the defense table. Do you want him to represent you?"

"Yes, Sir."

"And has the convening authority agreed to let Captain Wilson remain as your detailed defense counsel?"

Major Morgan stood up. "If I may, your Honor, the convening authority has agreed that the accused may have both an individual counsel, Lieutenant Colonel David, and his detailed defense counsel."

"Thank you, Major Morgan. Is that the defense's understanding?"

Both Captain Wilson and Lieutenant Colonel David nodded. "Yes, your Honor."

"Major Thomas, am I correct that you wish to be represented by Lieutenant Colonel David and Captain Wilson and by no one else?"

"Yes, your Honor."

Judge Savage continued. "Are the qualifications and status as to oaths of the detailed defense counsel correctly stated in the convening orders, and will individual counsel state his legal qualifications?"

Captain Wilson responded first. "My legal qualifications and status as to oaths are correctly stated in the convening orders."

Lieutenant Colonel David stood up. "Your Honor, I am a graduate of an American Bar Association accredited law school, Chicago-Kent College of Law, am a member of the Illinois bar, and am certified to practice before courts-martial."

Captain Wilson took over. "No member of the defense has acted as an accuser, a member of the prosecution, investigating officer, military judge, or member of the court in this case."

Judge Savage nodded. "Has counsel for either side functioned in any disqualifying or inconsistent capacity in the case?"

Both Major Morgan and Lieutenant Colonel David stood up and said, "No, your Honor."

Judge Savage drove right on. "It appears that counsel for both sides have the requisite qualifications and that all personnel of the court required to be present have been sworn except the individual counsel."

Lieutenant Colonel David stood up and raised his right hand. Judge Savage asked, "Do you, Lieutenant Colonel David, swear that you will faithfully perform the duties of individual counsel in the case now in hearing, so help you God?"

"I do."

Judge Savage sat back. Now, it was the trial counsel's turn to continue the formalities. Major Morgan read, "The general nature of the charge in this case is a violation of Article 94, mutiny. The charges were preferred by Major Mark Armstrong, forwarded with recommendations for disposition by Colonel Peter Jerome and Lieutenant General Arthur Lowe, and investigated by Lieutenant Colonel Daniel Glenn. If the military judge is aware of any matter that he believes may be a ground for challenge by either side, he should now state such matter."

"I am aware of no grounds for challenge against me," replied Colonel Savage.

After both sides had said that they had no challenges against the military judge, he continued, "Now, I don't see any instruction on the charge sheet indicating that this case was referred noncapital. Thus, the accused cannot be tried by military judge alone and must be tried by a court composed of not less than five officers."

Lieutenant Colonel David rose and said, "Your Honor, the defense contends, as our motion checklist shows, that the referral was improper, and we do not concede that the case was referred as capital. However, even assuming that the case was referred as capital, the accused does not wish to be tried by military judge alone."

"Very well," the black-robed judge answered. "We can take up your improper referral motion at the appropriate time. The accused may now be arraigned."

Now, it was Major Morgan's turn again. "All parties to the trial have been furnished a copy of the charge. Does the accused desire that it be read?"

Lieutenant Colonel David waived the reading of the charge. The only time he had ever seen a defense lawyer demand that the trial counsel read the charges had backfired badly. The accused was charged with several pages of sex crimes. The inexperienced defense counsel had made the trial counsel, a pretty young female captain, read the sodomy, indecent assault, and indecent exposure language to the court members who, not unsurprisingly, rewarded her for reading them like a trooper, with only a slight blush, and punished both the defense counsel and his client by convicting the accused and imposing the maximum sentence.

The trial counsel continued, "The charges are signed by Major Mark Armstrong, a person subject to the code, as accuser; are properly sworn to before a commissioned officer of the armed forces authorized to administer oaths, and are properly referred to this court for trial by General Carl Hawkins, the convening authority."

The military judge looked at Major Thomas and asked, "Major Thomas, I now ask you, how do you plead? Before receiving your pleas, I advise you that any motions to dismiss any charge or to grant other appropriate relief should be made at this time."

"Your Honor, the defense has several motions we would like to make before entering a plea." Lieutenant Colonel David drew a deep breath before continuing. "First, the defense moves to dismiss the charge and specification for lack of jurisdiction in that the charge was improperly referred to trial because the convening authority was an accuser."

Judge Savage frowned as he asked Major Morgan whether the government opposed the motion. When he learned that the government did, he asked the defense, "Do you have any evidence to present?"

"Yes, your Honor. The defense calls Major Armstrong."

The bailiff left the courtroom to summon Major Armstrong from the witness room. Although he was irritated at having been called as a defense witness on some bullshit motion to get his case thrown out, Major Armstrong strode confidently into the courtroom and, as rehearsed, walked to the witness chair, turned to face Major Morgan, and raised his right hand.

Major Morgan administered the witness oath, "Do you swear or affirm that you will tell the truth, the whole truth, and nothing but the truth in the case now in hearing, so help you God?"

"I do."

"Please be seated. State your name, rank, Social Security number, organization, and armed force."

"Major Mark Armstrong, 474-38-2321, Student Detachment, CGSC, U.S. Army."

"And are you the accuser in this case?"

"Yes, Sir."

Major Morgan turned to the defense table, "Your witness."

Lieutenant Colonel David stood up and said, "Your Honor, Captain Wilson will examine this witness." Captain Wilson approached the witness stand, with a yellow legal tablet in hand. Glancing at his notes, he began the direct examination of the witness.

"Major Armstrong, did you prefer the charge in this case?"

"Yes."

"When did you prefer it?"

"Last fall."

"And this charge involves an alleged mutiny against you, as the commander of the accused, involving the disobedience of an order you gave?"

"That's correct. The accused disobeyed an order I gave him in Vietnam to attack a machine gun."

"Do you know what happened to the charge after you preferred it?"

"They conducted an Article 32 investigation, and the investigating officer recommended that the charge be dismissed."

"Was it dismissed?"

"No."

"Do you know why?"

"I wrote a letter to General Hawkins telling him about the case and that they weren't interested in prosecuting it here."

"Do you know General Hawkins?"

"Yes."

"How do you come to know him?"

"He's my uncle."

"And isn't it true you worked for him as his aide for the first half of your Vietnam tour?"

Major Morgan stood up, "Objection, your Honor. Defense counsel is leading the witness."

Captain Wilson responded before the judge could rule on the objection, "Your Honor, as the accuser, this witness is hostile to the defense. I request permission to treat him as a hostile witness, which would allow the use of leading questions on direct examination."

Judge Savage raised an eyebrow and glared at counsel before ruling. "I'm not sure we need to go through all this rigamarole. I'll simply overrule the objection. You may answer the question, Major."

"Yes, I was General Hawkins's aide."

"No further questions."

Major Morgan began to cross-examine the witness. "Although you are related to General Hawkins, have you ever lived with him?"

"We lived close to each other when I was his aide, but I've never been a member of his household."

"Would you characterize your relationship with him as a close one?"

"Not really. Our relationship was more professional than personal."

"And in this letter, did you refer to your family relationship to try to get him to prosecute this case?"

"No, I simply told him what had happened, that they were not interested in prosecuting it here, and that I thought it set a horrible precedent to allow a crime like this go unpunished."

"No further questions."

The judge looked at the two defense lawyers. "Any redirect?"

"No, your Honor."

"Thank you, Major Armstrong. You are temporarily excused. Please do not discuss your testimony with anyone other than the counsel in this case. If anyone else attempts to discuss your testimony with you, please notify the trial counsel. Does the defense have any further evidence?"

"No, your Honor."

"Does the prosecution have any evidence on this motion?"

Major Morgan stood up. "Yes, your Honor. The government calls General Hawkins."

The whole courtroom stirred as General Hawkins entered, particularly the spectators behind the bar that separated them from the participants—as if they were worried about General Hawkins wondering why they were watching a court-martial instead of doing something more productive in the middle of a workday that ultimately came out of his budget. The four stars on each of the general's shoulders seemed outsized as they glittered under the florescent lights. The general glanced at his watch as he entered the courtroom, apparently either out of irritation at having been kept waiting to testify, or to see how much time he had to waste answering questions. Even the spectators sat up straighter as Major Morgan administered the witness oath and elicited the general's "pedigree"—his name, rank, Social Security number, unit, and armed force—before beginning the direct examination.

"Sir, we appreciate your taking time out of your busy schedule to come over and testify. I know you have to get back to address the Pre-Command Course before returning to Fort Monroe, so we will try to keep your appearance here brief. Would you tell the court how you came to be involved in this case?"

"I received a letter from Major Armstrong, my nephew, complaining that the commander here was not taking this case seriously enough. I talked to my judge advocate, and he told me I could withdraw General Lowe's authority to act in this case and have him forward the case to me for my disposition. After he did so, I reviewed the case and decided to refer it to a general court-martial."

"Why did you refer it to a general court-martial?"

"It was a very serious crime, and I thought that the ends of good order and discipline mandated doing so. If we don't punish misbehavior before the enemy, we are weakening the discipline necessary to win future battles."

"Were you influenced by the fact that the victim was your nephew?"

"The only part that played in my decision was that I'm sure our family relationship induced Major Armstrong to feel free to write me about his problem. I would have done the same thing if I had received such a letter from any other officer."

"No further questions, your Honor."

Lieutenant Colonel David stood up. "I only have a few questions, Sir. First, you are very close to your sister, aren't you?"

"Yes."

"When was the last time you visited with her?"

"She stayed with me over Christmas."

"When she stayed with you, did you discuss her son's career?"

"We may have."

"You are interested in his career, aren't you?"

"Yes."

"And you requested him to be your aide in Vietnam, didn't you?"

"Yes."

"And after he had served as your aide for six months, you made certain he got a company command—the command he had when this incident occurred?"

Again the general's answer was terse. "Yes."

"Now, if I may draw your attention to this charge, you were aware that the Article 32 investigating officer, the CAC commander, his staff judge advocate, and your staff judge advocate all recommended this case be dismissed?"

The general looked at Judge Savage as if wondering why the judge would allow this impudent lawyer to keep asking him questions, but when the judge failed to respond, the general answered with a terse, "Yes."

"And in the face of all these recommendations to the contrary, you still referred the case to trial?"

"Yes."

"Does what Major Thomas did bother you personally?"

"It bothered me professionally."

"Isn't it true that you were bothered personally by this alleged affront to your nephew's command—a command you selected him for and wanted him to succeed in?"

General Hawkins glowered at the defense counsel as he answered, "As I said, it bothered me professionally, not personally."

"And you expect this court to believe that you weren't influenced in this decision by the family tie—the fact that the victim was not only your nephew, but also your ex-aide?"

"I don't know what I expect this court to believe, Colonel." Moments earlier, Paul would not have believed that the word "colonel" could sound lower than the word "private," but he believed it now.

"No further questions." Paul sat down and whispered to Captain Lewis, "Somehow, I don't think I improved my chances to make full colonel by that cross-examination." The captain whispered back, "No, but I liked it."

Major Morgan began to conduct a redirect examination of the four-star witness. "Sir, once more, why did you refer the case to trial?"

"Because the needs of discipline in today's Army require us to take firm, effective action against officers who flout military authority."

"And why didn't you follow the advice of the investigating officer and the judge advocates?"

"My SJA informed me there was no legal objection to my referring the case to trial, and I decided I understood the needs of good order and discipline better than the investigating officers and the lawyers did."

"Thank you, Sir. No further questions."

"Does the defense have any further questions?" Judge Savage inquired. Upon seeing that the defense did not and that neither side objected to excusing the witness permanently, the judge thanked General Hawkins and excused him. Normally, he liked to question witnesses himself, to stretch out the trial so that he would have more in-court hours than any other military judge. He was not, however, about to question a four-star unnecessarily. Upon learning that neither side had any further evidence to present, the military judge asked for their arguments on the motion to dismiss.

Because he had made the motion, Lieutenant Colonel David argued first. "Your Honor, the evidence shows not only that Major Armstrong is the nephew of the convening authority here, but also that he worked for General Hawkins as his aide. Indeed, the general even got Major Armstrong his company command—the very command that Major Armstrong alleges Major Thomas threatened. Of course, General Hawkins would want his nephew to be successful in the command he arranged for him. But he would have us believe that he referred the case to trial only to enforce discipline. This statement is patently unbelievable in light of the general's close ties to his sister, his interest in her son's career, all the recommendations not to refer the case to trial, and the fact that the victim was his nephew—a nephew whose military career he had tried to improve on two occasions—first by getting him a job as his aide and then by getting him a company command.

"Paragraph 5b(2) of the *Manual for Courts-Martial* prohibits a convening authority from referring charges to a court he has convened if he is an accuser in the case. An accuser is one who has a personal interest in the case's outcome rather than only an official interest. Although the defense has not found a case that states explicitly that if the convening authority's nephew is the victim, he is an accuser, a reading of a number of cases together compels the conclusion that General Hawkins is an accuser here.

"A seminal case, *United States v. Gordon*, 1 C.M.A. 255, 2 C.M.R. 161, a 1952 case, establishes the test to use to determine this issue: if the convening authority is so closely connected to the offense that a reasonable person would conclude that he had a personal interest, he is an accuser.

"The *Gordon* case and *United States v. Crews*, 49 C.M.R. 502, a 1974 Coast Guard Court of Military Review case, establish that if the convening authority is a victim of the offense, he is an accuser.

"In *United States v. Moseley*, 2 C.M.R. 263 (A.B.R. 1951), this disqualification was extended to the situation in which the convening authority or his family was the victim.

"In *United States v. Marsh*, a convening authority became the accuser when he referred a case in which the accused disobeyed an order he had given. The language of that case is especially applicable here: 'It is clear from the facts in this record that the accused violated a direct order of General Hodge and that the latter had a personal interest in seeing his orders were obeyed. Militiary discipline and order is based upon obedience to superiors, and every commander jealously, but rightly, requires compliance and frowns on disobedience. For that and other reasons we cannot say that the superior officer would be entirely impartial in selecting a court to try a given case where the accused was charged with willful disobedience of the order.'

"The defense contends, your Honor, that you cannot say that General Hawkins would be entirely impartial in selecting this court, where the accused is alleged to have mutinied against his nephew, in light of his interest in his nephew's career and his close family ties to the victim's mother. The defense respectfully prays you to grant the defense motion and dismiss the charge."

Lieutenant Colonel David sat down as Major Morgan got up to argue. "Your Honor, General Hawkins testified truthfully as to his relationship with Major Armstrong and his mother. He didn't try to hide it or even to hide his interest in the major's career. On the contrary, he was very open and frank with this court. And now the defense would have you believe that General Hawkins is lying when he says he had a professional, as opposed to a personal, interest. He testified that he had a legitimate reason for referring the case to trial, to enforce discipline. Such a reason is an entirely proper official, as opposed to a personal, interest. The defense evidence is insufficient to overcome the presumption of regularity inherent in a convening authority's actions. Unlike the cases the defense cited, the convening authority was not a close relation to the victim, nor the victim himself. The victims in *Moseley*—a larceny and housebreaking case— were the convening authority himself and members of his immediate family. The relationship is too remote here to make the convening authority an accuser.

"Nor did General Hawkins issue the order that the accused is charged with disobeying, as in the *Marsh* case. The defense is grasping at straws. The connections here are simply too tenuous to warrant ruling against the convening authority, and the government requests you deny the defense motion."

Judge Savage stared up at the ceiling for a moment and then said, "I want to read the cases and deliberate on this motion. We'll be in recess."

The bailiff's, "All rise," resounded in the quiet courtroom. Everyone rose as the judge left by his personal door leading to his judge's chambers.

CHAPTER 26

Military Judge's Chambers
Office of the Staff Judge Advocate
Building 244, Fort Leavenworth, Kansas

JUNE 1986

Judge Savage took off his black judge's robe, hung it up on the Army issue oak coatrack in the corner of his office, and sat down behind his large desk. As a full bird colonel and the Chief Judge of the Judicial Circuit, his office was as big as the staff judge advocate's. He glanced at his watch, noting that it was 0945 hours. I'll deliberate on this motion for about twenty minutes, he thought. Before becoming a military judge, he had attended the military judges' course at the JAG School on the campus of the University of Virginia in Charlottesville. One of the things the instructors had taught him was the importance of giving the appearance of deliberate justice. They had suggested that a judge retire to his chambers when deciding guilt or innocence, the sentence, or a serious motion—even if he had already made up his mind. Leaving the courtroom for a time, they said, gave the appearance that a judge was taking care to deliberate about something as important as the outcome of a court-martial. One of his instructors had said, "I don't care if you read a comic book while you are back in your chambers. But go in there and close the door and make it look like you are seriously considering the issue." Judge Savage was very conscious of the reputation of the military judiciary and had always followed this guidance.

I don't believe this convening authority is disqualified because he is an accuser, he thought. And if I find that he was, that's the same as saying he's a liar. But maybe I'll read the cases just to make sure. Savage walked over to his bookshelves, picked out the volumes of the Court-Martial Reports and the Military Justice Reporter that the lawyers had cited, and began reading.

While Judge Savage read, Major Morgan and Captain Lewis remained at the prosecution table in the courtroom. "I'm worried about this motion," Pam said. "Do you think Judge Savage will grant it?"

"Not a chance," Ken replied. "Lieutenant Colonel David doesn't even want it granted. If the judge grants it, all we have to do is kick the case up to DA. DA can refer the case to trial or send it to another command, such as FORSCOM, for disposition. David only made this motion for two reasons: The primary one was to show the judge that no one besides General Hawkins thought the case should go to court and start getting him mad at the government, so the defense will win some motion that David really wants to win down the road. But he is also following an old defense rule—if the convening authority wants to try a questionable case—such as a very old charge like this one, he's going to pay the price, such as by having to come all the way here to Leavenworth to testify. It's called putting the government through the hoops."

"What are we going to do about it?"

"Pretty soon, it will be time to toss the defense a bone. That's why the referral doesn't show that the case is to be tried as noncapital, even though the pretrial advice told General Hawkins the maximum punishment is life imprisonment. Lieutenant Colonel David will move to limit the punishment to life imprisonment, and after the appropriate protest, we'll roll over and allow the judge to toss the defense its bone. The accused is never going to get sentenced to death, anyway. I'm not even certain I could argue for the death sentence even if we get a conviction. Enough of this. Let's go get some coffee."

Twenty-five minutes later, the bailiff summoned all the parties back to the courtroom. After having told everyone to be seated, Savage called the court to order.

"All parties to the trial who were present when the court recessed are again present," Major Morgan said. One of the duties of the trial counsel is to "protect the record." Thus, Major Morgan had to say who was present in the courtroom after every recess ended, so the record of trial would reflect the parties' attendance.

Judge Savage looked at the notes he had made while deciding the defense motion. Sometimes, he would comment on the points in favor of each side's position, bouncing from side to side, keeping the lawyers guessing as to how he would rule. But in a case of this magnitude, he played it straight and came right out with his ruling. "In regards to the defense motion to dismiss for improper referral, the court finds that General Hawkins acted in an official capacity rather than in a personal one when he referred this case to trial. His family relationship with the accused was too remote to make the general a victim. Nor did he have any personal interest in, or knowledge of the order the accused is alleged to have violated to form the basis of the mutiny charge. Consequently, the defense motion is denied. Does the defense have any other motions?"

"Yes, your Honor," Lieutenant Colonel David replied. Paul moved to dismiss the charge and specification because his rights to a speedy trial and to due process of law were violated by the years of delay in bringing the charge to trial. Before he got very far in his argument, however, Judge Savage interrupted. "Yes, Colonel David, we all know that it's been a long time, but your client hasn't been in pretrial confinement. So where's the prejudice?"

Paul quickly segued to the prejudice part of his argument. "Your Honor, the extreme delay makes it impossible for the accused to defend himself because many members of Major Thomas's platoon are long since out of the Army and we have not been able to locate them to testify in his behalf. Thus, the accused has suffered specific prejudice—the loss of witnesses—on top of the general prejudice one suffers by facing stale charges."

Judge Savage looked at the prosecution team. "Well, Major Morgan?"

Captain Lewis responded. Ken had tasked her with arguing this motion so he could concentrate on the more important aspects of the case. He knew Judge Savage wasn't about to dismiss the case on speedy trial grounds when the accused was not confined and the prejudice suffered by the accused was so nebulous. Pam wasn't so certain, so she argued vehemently. "Your Honor, the prosecution's accountability for speedy trial did not begin until charges were preferred, which occurred less than ten months ago. And a good part of the ten months was delay the defense had requested, bringing the total period for which the government was liable to less than 120 days. Further, the accused had not been in pretrial confinement, which would have triggered the rule requiring the government to try him within ninety days, excluding periods of defense delay. Thus, the government has violated neither the accused's Sixth Amendment right to a speedy trial nor any of the more stringent military speedy trial rules. Further, your Honor, under the Sixth Amendment, delay alone is insufficient to cause a violation of one's speedy trial right. The delay must prejudice the accused before it violates his speedy trial right. And with all due respect to Colonel David, the defense's inability to locate witnesses that may or may not testify favorably to the defense does not amount to specific prejudice. It's just speculation and conjecture that these witnesses would help the defense. They might, in fact, help the prosecution."

"Any final words, defense?"

Paul responded, realizing that Judge Savage used such a general query rather than a more focused question when he had already made up his mind. He decided to focus on due process because it didn't look as if the judge was buying the speedy trial argument. "Your Honor, even if the government had not violated Major Thomas's Sixth Amendment right to a speedy trial or his military speedy trial rights, which we contend it did, the excessive delay violated his Fifth Amendment right to due process of law. The Due Process Clause's language, 'Nor shall any person be deprived of life, liberty, or property without due process of law,' means that the defense must have the opportunity to call witnesses and present evidence in a criminal prosecution and that the years of delay prevented the defense from doing so. It's one thing, your Honor, when the defense fails to locate witnesses and find out exactly what they would testify to within months after the preferral of charges. It's quite another when over a decade has elapsed. The normal rules requiring the defense to be able to identify what missing witnesses will testify to ought not to apply when the delay is that long. Your Honor, both constitutional and military due process, as well as the right to a speedy trial, are violated by the extreme delay in bringing Major Thomas to trial."

Pam, not realizing that she had already won, stood up. Judge Savage asked, "Do you have something else, counsel?" which should have clued her in that she didn't need to say anymore. But she had not faced Judge Savage often enough to be confident that she could read him properly and didn't want to miss out on any of her part of the trial. "Your Honor, the government was equally hampered in locating witnesses, and we all know that delay usually favors the defense. No violation of the accused's due process rights justifying dismissal of the charges has occurred, and your Honor certainly has the power to deal with any evidentiary or procedural problem that may arise during the course of the trial."

Again, Judge Savage retired to his chambers, deliberated, returned to the courtroom, and said, "The defense's inability to say, with any degree of certainty, what the unlocated, potential witnesses would testify to, show they have not suffered any prejudice by the delay. Motion denied."

After a few more unimportant motions, which Judge Savage did not even retire to his chamber to deliberate upon, but instead denied from the bench, Lieutenant Colonel David announced, "The defense has no further motions to present, your Honor."

Ken and Pam looked at each other in consternation. Why wasn't the defense moving to limit the punishment to life imprisonment, rather than death, as the pretrial advice had stated?

"What's going on?" Pam whispered.

Suddenly, Ken realized what the defense tactic was. "He's not allowing Judge Savage to toss him a bone. He's betting his client will never get the death sentence even if convicted," Ken informed his young assistant.

Ken rose and said, "Your Honor, the defense earlier stated there was a defect with referral or the pretrial advice as to the maximum punishment. Does the defense intend to waive any such defects?"

Paul stood up, "Your Honor, the defense waives any defect as to the enumeration of the maximum punishment in the pretrial advice. Hence, although we still contend the referral was improper because the convening authority was an accuser, we agree that in all other respects the case was properly referred. We do, however, contend that the military procedure for imposing the death penalty is unconstitutional, but suggest deferring any such motion until the sentencing phase to avoid wasting the court's time, because the accused may not be convicted of a crime carrying the death penalty."

"Very well," Judge Savage agreed. "Are you prepared to plead?"

"Yes, your Honor. The accused pleads, to the charge and specifications: Not guilty."

"Thank you. Are there any other matters to take up before bringing in the court members?"

The lawyers went over the "flier"—the extract of the charge sheet that the trial counsel would present to the court members. Upon learning that the defense had no objection to the flier, the judge approved it. After a few minor evidentiary matters, Major Morgan stood up. "Your Honor, the accused is not under any form of pretrial restraint. The government would ask you to inform him that since he has been arraigned, the trial can continue without him if he voluntarily absents himself."

The judge did so and asked the accused whether he understood.

"Don't worry, your Honor, if I'm alive, I'll be here," Major Thomas promised.

Because neither side had any other matters to take up, Judge Savage put the court in recess until the following Monday morning, when the trial would begin in earnest.

As Ken walked out of the courtroom, he didn't know whether to be relieved that he had gotten past Paul David's specialty, the motions, so easily. He was now on his home turf, the presentation of the facts of the case to the jury, but the stocky major was worried about what new tactic Lieutenant Colonel David was up to.

CHAPTER 27

Kansas State University Natatorium
Manhattan, Kansas

JUNE 1986

For the first time in an athletic event, Paul David felt totally out of place. These triathletes looked fit. Paul was an experienced runner with a dozen marathons and many shorter races to his credit and had also played basketball in the recreational leagues on whatever Army post he happened to be assigned to, so he thought of himself as an athlete. At road races, Paul felt like an elite runner if he wore one of his marathon T-shirts and his $75 running shoes. But here, with his marathon T-shirt, borrowed ten-speed bike, and running shoes, Paul felt vastly inferior to the tanned, muscular triathletes with their $500 racing bikes with toe clips, racing helmets with rear-view mirrors, different shoes for biking and running, and other exotic paraphernalia.

Paul had entered the Taxi Triathlon for his first try at a triathlon for a number of reasons: to show the combat arms officers at CGSC that Army lawyers were hard-core, to give him an emotional outlet from the Thomas court-martial, and to compensate for not having run a marathon that spring. Paul tried to run two marathons a year—one marathon in the fall and one in the spring. But because of a stupid decision he had made to play in two basketball leagues—in the over-thirty league and in the student league with his staff group—his forty-year-old knees were too battered to run the miles necessary to train for a marathon. As Paul considered the reasons he was standing in this long line of triathletes waiting to check in, trying to convince himself not to chicken out, he remembered how it had felt to play six basketball games in five nights. But having moved to Indiana at age eleven, he loved basketball, even though he was anything but a star player. He had played so much during his tenure as military judge that, whenever anyone had asked his clerk where he was, the clerk had only to say, "Court." After all, if Judge David wasn't in the courtroom, he was on the basketball or racquetball court— or running from one court to the next.

Finally, Paul found himself at the front of the check-in line. A prepubescent, but heavily made-up girl wearing a baseball cap, with the bill jauntily tilted sideways, wrote his race number, 256, on both arms and both thighs. Paul knew many of the competitors would wear their T-shirts and shorts for several days after the triathlon to show off the indelible race number. Looking at the other competitors made Paul wish he had had time to train properly. But in preparing for the Thomas trial and finishing up his teaching schedule, he had managed only to bike twice and to swim three times. He had figured a marathoner could gut out a 500-meter swim in a pool, no less, a fifteen-and-a-half-mile bike, and a five-kilometer run even without training.

The first event, the swim, consisted of swimming up and back in the far left lane, ducking under the lane rope, doing the same thing in each of seven lanes, and then getting out, running a few feet, and doing it all over again in the second pool. The officials started a swimmer when the swimmer seeded just before him had reached the far end of the first lane.

After more than an hour had passed since the first swimmer had started, Paul finally got into the water. As a first-time triathlete, he was seeded 256th out of 265. Although he took off at what seemed to be a fast crawl, the two women seeded just behind him passed him before he had completed two laps. With what remained of his ego totally deflated, Paul gave up on the crawl and started a survival breaststroke. Other than hitting his head on the lane ropes every time he had to duck under them, and swallowing half the water in the pool every time his head bobbed up to take a breath—just in time to receive a splash in the face from other swimmers in the lane—Paul managed to complete the first pool with no major problems.

His confidence partially restored by having half of the swim done, Paul leapt into the second pool. Not fun. The first pool had been heated to 85 degrees. The second pool was not. Paul quickly discovered he could swim without breathing and without having a heart beat. He managed about two laps without either and even managed to breaststroke past a couple of swimmers who had apparently frozen.

On the last lap, Paul returned to the crawl, so he would look good going past the spectator seating. A kick in the head from a swimmer who wanted to look even better ended the crawl, so Paul ignominiously dog-paddled the last few yards. Then he heaved himself out of the pool only to sink back into the water because his sodden running shorts had refused to exit the water with him. It was a real feat for Paul to leave the pool using one hand to pull himself out and the other to hold up his shorts, while still trying to look like a stud triathlete. He didn't quite manage all that, but at least he avoided indecent exposure. Good thing the court members aren't watching, he thought, or I'd have no credibility whatsoever.

After setting the all-time record for slowest transition, Paul appeared to be the last competitor to start the bike course. The top-seeded athletes were finishing the bike event and starting on the run as Paul wobbled out onto the bike course.

His two training rides had not prepared him for the sheer terror of going down a steep hill on a ten-speed bike. With teeth clenched and trying not to brake completely, he hung on for dear life and eased down the hill. But the course was four loops, so before he knew it, Paul was at the top of the cliff again. After Paul had passed one biker and dozens had passed him, Paul's embarrassment overcame his fear, and he kept his hand off the brakes for the remaining three descents and flew downhill.

With a tremendous feeling of relief, the tired lawyer finally pulled back into the transition area. Thank God, he thought, I've finally made it to the run—the one thing I know I can do. He dropped the bike and took off at a dead run. Unfortunately, only his upper body moved—his legs seemed to be paralyzed—and he barely avoided a sprawl in front of the experienced triathletes who, having already finished, were gathering up their gear.

Arms pumping furiously and legs wobbling, Paul lurched onto the running course and completed the first mile at about the pace he usually did the last mile of a marathon—and with no better form. By the second mile, however, he had loosened up enough to run more smoothly. Because he didn't have to concentrate on what he was doing any more in order to avoid drowning or having a bike accident, his thoughts turned to the court-martial.

I'm on Morgan's turf now—the facts of the case, he thought. Too bad this case doesn't have any of the legal issues I'm really good at, like jurisdiction or search and seizure. There's no physical evidence to contest the admissibility of, no bad search, no bad chain of custody, no flakey procedures. Just the testimony of the participants in the incident. And they're not snitches with drug convictions on their records to impeach them with. Yeah, Armstrong is an asshole, but you can't say, "Major Armstrong, isn't true that you're an asshole?" the way you could say, "Isn't it true you've been convicted for perjury?"

If I can't get the mutiny charge thrown out, he thought, I've got to turn this into a referendum on the Vietnam war and try to get the jury to conclude that they would have done the same thing under the same circumstances and let Thomas go. If I don't, he's going to have the same feeling when they announce the findings as I did when I jumped into the unheated pool. And I don't want to lose. Losing to Morgan would be worse than finishing dead last in this triathlon, Paul thought, as he saw the finish line off in the distance. With new motivation, he sped up, picked off a couple of runners ahead of him, and charged across the finish line like a veteran triathlete.

CHAPTER 28

Courtroom, Office of the Staff Judge Advocate
Building 244
Fort Leavenworth, Kansas

J U N E 1 9 8 6

At nine o'clock the following Monday morning, Judge Savage entered the courtroom. "Major Morgan," he began, "are the court members ready?"

"Yes, your Honor."

"Get them."

Major Morgan signaled to the bailiff, who knocked on the door to the jury deliberation room. The ten court members filed into the courtroom, led by the junior member. They, along with the counsel, the accused, and the witnesses, were dressed in their class A uniforms with all their ribbons and badges. Before the court members were called, they had arranged themselves as instructed by the trial counsel so that they would be seated alternately to the right and left of the president of the court, according to rank with the junior members on the ends.

"All rise," the bailiff ordered. Everyone in the courtroom stood except Judge Savage. Besides some of the procedural differences, courts-martial differed from civilian courts by requiring everyone to stand when the jury entered or exited, as well as when the judge did— probably a throwback to the days when courts-martial did not have a judge, as such, and the president of the court presided over the proceedings.

When the court members were all in place, standing behind their chairs in the jury box, Judge Savage opened the day's session, "The court will come to order. You may be seated."

Again Major Morgan went through the verbiage, announcing which orders convened the court. After stating that the accused, the military judge, and the counsel were present, he read the names of the court members, "COL Richard T. Parkhill, COL Robert L. Harrison, COL Orlin P. Nesbit, LTC Robertson I. Fletcher, LTC George M. Brokaw, LTC William O. Penders, MAJ Timothy A. Brantley, MAJ Lloyd G. Erickson, MAJ Steve R. Campbell, and MAJ Carlton H. Walker.

"LTC Maxwell O. Daniel and MAJ Ellis W. Royal are absent and have been excused by the convening authority." Before the assembly of the court, the convening authority may excuse court members without giving any reason. After assembly, he could not excuse court members without showing good cause, such as illness or urgent military necessity. Lieutenant Colonel Daniel had wanted to go on leave, and Major Royal had gone on temporary duty to observe training at the National Training Center at Fort Irwin, California—both activities apparently more important to the convening authority than court-martial duty.

Major Morgan continued. "The prosecution is ready to proceed with the trial in the case of the United States against Major James Thomas, who is present in court.

"The members of the court will now be sworn. All persons please rise."

Again, everyone except the military judge rose. The trial counsel administered the oath. "Do you . . . .," he started and then read the names of all ten court members, "swear or affirm you will faithfully perform your duties as a member of this court, that you will faithfully and impartially try, according to the evidence, your conscience, and the laws applicable to trials by courts-martial, the case of the accused now before this court, and that you will not disclose or discover the vote or opinion of any particular member of the court upon the findings or sentence unless required to do so in the due course of law, so help you God?"

The court members chorused, "I do."

Judge Savage told the court members to be seated and announced that the court was assembled. Then, he began to give the court members their preliminary instructions, again from memory. "Members of the Court, it is appropriate for me to give you some preliminary instructions. It is my duty to ensure that this trial is conducted in a fair and orderly manner. I will rule upon objections and instruct you on the law. You must follow my instructions on the law and may not consult any other source as to the law unless it is admitted into evidence. This rule applies throughout the trial, including closed sessions and recesses. Any questions you have must be asked of me in open court.

"As court members, it is your duty to hear the evidence and determine the guilt or innocence of this accused and, if you find him guilty, to adjudge an appropriate sentence. Under the law, the accused is presumed innocent of the offense you see on the flier before you. The government has the burden of proving the accused's guilt beyond a reasonable doubt. The fact that charges have been preferred against the accused and referred to this court for trial does not permit any inference of guilt. You must make your own determination as to the guilt or innocence of the accused based solely upon the evidence presented here in court and the instructions I will give you. Because you cannot properly reach your determination until all the evidence has been presented and I have instructed you on the law, it is of vital importance that you keep an open mind until all the evidence and instructions have been presented to you."

As boring as these instructions were for the few spectators in the courtroom for this preliminary part of the trial, they were too cowed by the judge's reputation for jumping all over spectators who disrupted the proceedings to fidget. So they tried to look attentive as the judge continued:

"In a few minutes, counsel will ask you questions and exercise challenges. With regard to challenges, if you know of any matter that you feel might affect your impartiality to sit as a panel member in this case, you must disclose the matter when asked to do so. Bear in mind that any statement you make should be made in general terms so as not to disqualify other panel members who hear the statement."

Judge Savage continued for five more minutes. He detailed the grounds for challenge—such as already having an opinion as to the accused's guilt or innocence or having a preconceived idea as to what would be an appropriate punishment if the accused were to be convicted. Next, he informed the court members that, if they had questions for a witness, after the lawyers had finished, the members could write their questions out so that the judge could make certain the questions were unobjectionable. He cautioned the members that, although they might question witnesses, they could not become advocates for either the prosecution or the defense. He also instructed them not to discuss the case with anyone, not even among themselves, during a recess. Then he concluded by saying, "Each of you has an equal voice and vote with the other members in discussing and deciding all issues submitted to you. The senior member's vote counts as one, the same as the junior member's. However, in addition to the duties of the other members, the senior member acts as the presiding officer during the closed session deliberations, and he will speak for the panel in announcing the results."

Judge Savage's voice rose as he stressed courtroom decorum. He was famous for allowing no levity whatsoever in his courtroom. "The appearance and demeanor of all parties to the trial should reflect the seriousness with which the trial is viewed. Careful attention to all that occurs is required by all parties. Are there any questions over these preliminary matters? Apparently not. You may proceed, Major Morgan."

Major Morgan stood up. "The general nature of the charge is a violation of Article 94, mutiny. The charges were preferred by Major Mark Armstrong, forwarded with recommendations for disposition by Colonel Peter Jerome and Lieutenant General Arthur Lowe, and investigated by Lieutenant Colonel Daniel Glenn.

"The record of this case discloses no grounds for challenge. If any member of the court is aware of any matters that he believes may be a ground for challenge by either side, he should now so state. Let the record reflect that no member has responded."

While the preliminaries of the trial continued, Major Armstrong sat in the witness waiting room waiting for Major Morgan to call him to testify. He had tried to read some of the old magazines scattered around the bleak room, adorned only with a few faded prints of soldiers in Revolutionary War uniforms. He was too nervous to concentrate on the out-of-date articles, however. Instead, his thoughts kept returning to his upcoming testimony. Major Morgan had told him that his testimony was the key to the case, and he didn't want to blow it. As he tried to remember all of Morgan's instructions on how to conduct himself during cross-examination, he felt the first stirrings of doubt about the wisdom of having brought the charges. But he deliberately suppressed them, thinking instead of how 1-6 had continually embarrassed him during the war.

His mind went back to the early days of his command of Alpha Company. He remembered coming back to the brigade base camp at Quan Loi to pull green line duty. The brigade commander had invited all the officers of Alpha Company to supper. Armstrong had overheard Thomas make a sarcastic comment to the other platoon leaders about the "largess of the liege lord allowing the poor grunts to come to dinner at the manor house." Thomas always had to show off how well read he was, Armstrong thought. And he had to embarrass me during that meal.

The meal had been sumptuous by grunt standards, with rare roast beef and all the trimmings, served on china with silver place settings. Compared to the bush, the colonel's air-conditioned trailer, white linen, and soft glow of candles was like another world to the platoon leaders. It had not impressed Armstrong much, however, accustomed as he was to Brigadier General Hawkins's mess.

The meal had started out well with Mark, as commander, seated to the brigade commander's right. Unfortunately, however, Thomas was seated next to the colonel on his left. The other platoon leaders were to Thomas's left. The brigade commander's staff had been exiled to the far end of the table so the colonel could show how close he was to his troops.

Armstrong still, these many years later, fumed as he thought about how the brigade commander had ignored him to talk to Thomas—just because Thomas had been in the firefights off LZ Stone with Captain Hart. So what if Alpha Company had kicked ass then without taking any significant casualties? He knew he could've done even better than Hart if 1-6 and the other platoon leaders had been more aggressive.

Thomas was always showing me up, he thought. The very first time I chewed him out, he just toyed with his Combat Infantry Badge while staring pointedly at my bare chest. I don't care whether the defense counsel does tear me up on cross-examination, Armstrong concluded. It will be worth it to ruin that smart-ass's career.

Meanwhile, Major Morgan had began the voir dire procedure, the questioning of the court members to determine whether any grounds for challenge existed.

"Good morning, Mr. President, Members of the Court. I am Major Ken Morgan, the trial counsel in this case. At the prosecution table is Captain Pamela Lewis, the assistant trial counsel. It is our duty to represent the government in this case."

Smoothly, Ken introduced the defense as if they represented the accused as a direct result of the prosecution's generosity, "The accused is represented by Lieutenant Colonel Paul David and Captain Samuel Wilson."

Ken emphasized "lieutenant colonel" as if the accused were so guilty he had to have a high-ranking officer to represent him and, at the same time, cast the prosecution in the underdog's role. Major Morgan would refer to Major Thomas as "the accused" whenever possible, while the defense would call him by his name and rank, both to humanize him and to maintain his dignity.

"I have just a few questions for you," Major Morgan continued. He did not want to alienate the court members by asking them too many questions about their fitness to sit on the court-martial. He would let the defense do that.

"As you can see from the flier, the charge involves an alleged mutiny in Vietnam. Do any of you have any knowledge of this incident?" When there was no response, he protected the record. "Let the record reflect a negative response from all court members."

His questions continued, none of them eliciting a positive response.

"Do any of you know the accused?"

"Do any of you know the accuser, Major Mark Armstrong?"

"Do any of you know any of the following potential government witnesses—Lieutenant Colonel (Ret.) Roger McCreary; First Sergeant Alonzo Tabler; Mr. Danny Ellis, previously a specialist fourth class?" No response. Major Morgan continued.

"Now this alleged mutiny involves the accused's disobeying, in concert with members of his platoon, a command to get his platoon on line and assault a machine gun. The government expects the military judge will instruct you that a command is lawful if reasonably necessary to safeguard and protect the morale, discipline, and usefulness of the members of a command and is directly related to the maintenance of good order in the services. Are there any of you who could not follow this instruction if given by the military judge?" Ken did not expect any court member to admit he couldn't follow the judge's instructions. He asked this question to begin indoctrinating the court members with the government theory of the case.

"Do any of you have a preconceived idea of what an appropriate sentence would be if the accused were to be convicted of mutiny?" Once again, silence met his question.

"If the military judge informed you that the maximum punishment included death or confinement for life and dismissal from the service, is there any court member who could not vote for such a sentence if, after hearing both the prosecution and the defense evidence, it was warranted? Apparently not. Thank you, Mr. President, Members of the Court. No further questions, your Honor."

"Defense?" Judge Savage asked.

Lieutenant Colonel David rose and walked up close to the court members. His approach was a calculated act to give the members a moment to notice his Combat Infantry Badge, his jump wings, and his ten ribbons—including a Silver Star for gallantry in action. He was well aware that one of his few advantages over the more experienced prosecutor was his combat experience, which would give him instant credibility with the court members. It helped that there were two Silver Star wearers at the defense table—the accused and his lead counsel—and none at the prosecution table.

"Thank you, your Honor. As the trial counsel pointed out, I am Lieutenant Colonel David, my assistant is Captain Samuel Wilson, and we have the duty to represent Major James Thomas. I have a few more questions than the prosecutor did. It is not my intent to embarrass any of you by asking these questions. Rather, it is my duty to ensure that my client gets a completely impartial court.

"Now I'm certain you all heard his Honor inform you that neither the fact that charges were preferred against Major Thomas nor the fact that they were referred to this court-martial warrants any inference of guilt. Do any of you think the accused is more likely to be guilty than not because this case has been investigated and referred to this court? Gentlemen, I'll ask you to speak up or to shake or nod your head."

Paul looked each member in the eye, in turn, until they either said, "No," or shook their head.

"Let the record reflect each court member shook his head, 'No.' Thank you." Paul did not believe in letting the members avoid responding orally. He wanted them to commit to a position.

Most military court members believed that any accused soldier was probably guilty because the military did not prosecute anyone unless it had thoroughly investigated the case and the case had been reviewed by both commanders and military lawyers. The court members also knew, if they admitted the accused was probably guilty, the defense would challenge them off of the court. But Lieutenant Colonel David knew that, if he could get the court members to think about it, they would bend so far backwards trying to ignore their preconceptions and be fair that this belief could actually help the defense. He also wanted them to participate in his defense of Major Thomas by not allowing them to sit in mute condemnation.

"Now, the defense expects the military judge will instruct you that you cannot convict Major Thomas unless the prosection proves him guilty beyond a reasonable doubt. If you have a reasonable doubt, how will you vote?"

After a moment's silence, the members answered, "Not guilty."

"Thank you. See, that wasn't so hard, was it?" He smiled and continued, "Have any of you been a victim of disobedience of an order you gave? Let the record reflect that Lieutenant Colonel William Penders and Major Tim Brantley answered in the affirmative. Colonel Penders, was there anything about that incident that might affect your sitting on this case?"

"No."

"Was it during combat?"

"No, it was a run-of-the-mill garrison disobedience. I gave the soldier an Article 15."

"Major Brantley?"

"My situation was much the same, and no, it wouldn't affect me in this case."

"I see from your uniforms that all of you served in Vietnam. Did any of you have any incidents in Vietnam, such as soldiers refusing to go to the field or problems with your junior leaders that might affect your deliberations on this case? Colonel Nesbit?"

"Yes, I had to counsel some of my junior officers about not being aggressive enough."

"Thank you. Any others? Apparently not."

"Now, it is the defense position that, after you have heard all the evidence, you will find Major Thomas not guilty. You already told Major Morgan you could impose death or life imprisonment and dismissal if appropriate. However, although I am not conceding guilt by any stretch of the imagination, I must ask, if you find Major Thomas guilty, do any of you believe that any of those penalties are mandated just by the nature of the offense?" When several of the court members hesitated, with confused looks on their faces and their eyes glazing over, Paul realized he was falling into his habit of using too much legalese. So he tried again, "In other words, if you convict the accused, do you feel that you must sentence him to any particular punishment just because the crime is mutiny?" This time, the court members responded quickly. "Let the record reflect that all court members shook their heads, 'No.' Thank you very much, Mr. President, Members of the Court. No further questions, your Honor."

Major Morgan rose to his feet. "The government has no further questions, your Honor, and has no challenges." He smiled at the court members as if to say he had the utmost faith in them and would not dream of challenging them off the court. If they were challenged off, it was because the defense thought they would be unfair.

Paul was having none of it, though. "May we approach the bench, your Honor?"

Judge Savage frowned, knowing full well the game both lawyers were playing, but he beckoned them to approach the bench. He knew the defense didn't want to challenge a member in front of the other members and the trial counsel wanted to make the defense do so. "I suppose you want an out-of-court hearing?" he asked Lieutenant Colonel David.

"Yes, your Honor. Colonel Nesbit stated that he had had to counsel some of his officers about their aggressiveness in combat. I would like to ask him more questions about that, out of the presence of the other members."

Without giving Major Morgan a chance to respond, the judge motioned the lawyers back to their seats. "Mr. President, Members of the

Court, we are going to excuse all of you except Colonel Nesbit for a few moments. You may wait in the deliberation room."

After all the other jurors had retired from the courtroom, Lieutenant Colonel David began to question the colonel sitting by himself in the jury box.

"Sir, you indicated that you had had some problems with your subordinates' lack of aggressiveness in Vietnam. Were you a commander then?"

"Yes. I had some problems both as a company commander on my first tour and as a battalion commander on my second tour."

"What was the nature of these problems?"

"When I was a company commander, I had to relieve one of my platoon leaders for not aggressively seeking contact with the enemy. And I took over from a battalion commander who was not making his company commanders actively seek out the enemy. Instead, he'd just let them blunder around until they were ambushed, instead of making contact on our terms. I had to shake things up a little when I took over the battalion from him."

"If you heard testimony that Major Thomas's commander thought he had not acted aggressively enough, would these experiences you had affect your ability to evaluate such testimony?"

"Well, I don't think much of officers who don't want to close with and destroy the enemy. One of the reasons we lost the war in Vietnam was that we were too passive. If we had really taken the war to the communists, we would have won."

"Thank you. Government."

Major Morgan got up to "rehabilitate" the court member, to ask him questions to show that these experiences did not disqualify him from sitting on the panel. "Sir, if the military judge so instructed you, could you put those experiences out of your mind and decide this case solely on the evidence you hear?"

"I think so."

"Are there situations where a defensive posture is better than aggressively attacking?"

"Not often, but sometimes."

"Wouldn't you wait to judge whether an officer was aggressive enough until you learned what the tactical situation was?"

"Yes."

"And although you correctly evaluated the need for your subordinates to become more aggressive, would you concede that another commander might be wrong in a particular tactical situation?"

"Certainly."

"Do you feel you can fairly and impartially decide the case?"

"Yes. If I didn't, I would have said so when the judge asked."

"Thank you."

Judge Savage looked down at the colonel from his elevated bench. "Do I understand that you can lay aside these experiences and decide this case solely on the evidence presented and my instructions on the law?"

"Yes, your Honor."

"Thank you. That will be all, Colonel. If you will join the other court members in the deliberation room, we'll call the court back shortly."

After Colonel Nesbit had left, Judge Savage asked the defense whether they had any challenges for cause.

Lieutenant Colonel David replied, "Yes, your Honor. The defense challenges Colonel Nesbit."

"Grounds?" the Judge asked.

"Your Honor, Colonel Nesbit had problems similar to those of the accuser, Major Armstrong, in Vietnam and didn't think much of officers who weren't aggressive. Even though Major Morgan did a good job of trying to rehabilitate him, the defense contends that Colonel Nesbit cannot be impartial, no matter how hard he tries."

The military judge asked Major Morgan whether the government contested the challenge. The trial counsel did, stating that the court member had unequivocally answered that he could put his experiences aside and decide the case only on the evidence and the judge's instructions. Ken wanted the full colonel to remain on the court because, as the president, he would exercise considerable control over the other members, notwithstanding the judge's instruction that no member could use superiority in rank to control the independence of the other members.

Judge Savage thought for a few moments and then ruled: "Although I'm not certain the colonel would be unable to put aside his experiences, the law compels military judges to be liberal in granting challenges for cause to ensure that both sides get an impartial court. I'll sustain the defense challenge. Does the government wish to exercise its peremptory challenge?"

Both sides in a court-martial get one peremptory challenge, which allows them to excuse a court member for any reason or for no reason. Ken consulted briefly with his assistant and then answered, "No, your Honor."

Nine members favored the government because a two-thirds majority, or six, could convict in a court-martial. Morgan knew that if the panel had ten members, the government would have to convince seven out of ten, or 70 percent, that the accused was guilty to get a conviction. If they convinced only six, the court would have to find the accused not guilty.

Judge Savage looked at the defense counsel.

"Your Honor, the defense challenges Colonel Parkhill peremptorily." Eight members was a better number for the defense because the prosecution would have to convince six out of eight, or 80 percent, instead of six out of nine, that the accused was guilty to get a conviction.

"Very well. Reseat the court members, trial counsel, and get them back in here," the judge ordered, recessing the court. Whenever court members were excused, the remaining court members had to reseat themselves alternately to the right and left of the president according to rank. The trial counsel usually helped them do this in the deliberation room before they re-entered the courtroom to avoid an unseemly game of musical chairs—especially in Judge Savage's courtroom.

Captain Lewis went to the jury room, told the two colonels they were excused, and told Colonel Harrison he was now the president. As they returned to the courtroom, she said, "All rise."

After telling everyone to be seated and calling the court to order, the judge usurped the trial counsel's duty and announced that all parties to the trial who were present when the court recessed were again present, along with the court members—except for Colonels Nesbit and Parkhill, who had been excused and would take no further part in the proceedings. Finally, he stated, "Members of the Court, at an earlier session, the accused was arraigned and entered a plea of not guilty to the charge and specification before you."

He asked the lawyers, "Do both counsel intend to make opening statements at this time?" When they both indicated affirmatively, he suggested the court take an early lunch so that they could return and then make their opening arguments and continue uninterrupted with the first witness. When no one objected to this procedure, he put the court in recess, again cautioning court members not to discuss the case with anyone else or among themselves. Court members had been known to talk to witnesses during recesses. They might have noble motives, such as to learn everything they could to help them decide the case, but they could also hear inadmissible evidence that way. Hence, the prohibition. Then, the bailiff called, "All rise." Everyone stood as the judge and the court members filed out of the courtroom. The spectators, now able to comment without running afoul of Judge Savage, talked excitedly. After the recess, this legal battle would begin.

PART IV

THE FACTS

But for the inferior to assume to determine the question of the lawfulness of an order given him by a superior would of itself, as a general rule, amount to insubordination, and such an assumption carried into practice would subvert military discipline. Where the order is apparently regular and lawful on its face, he is not to go behind it to satisfy himself that his superior had proceeded with authority, but is to obey it according to its terms, the only exception recognized to the rule of obedience being cases of orders so manifestly beyond the legal power or discretion of the commander as to admit of no rational doubt of their unlawfulness . . . .

—Winthrop, Military Law and Precedents (2d ed., 1896)

CHAPTER 29

Courtroom, Office of the Staff Judge Advocate
Building 244
Fort Leavenworth, Kansas

J U N E   1 9 8 6

"All rise."

"Be seated," Judge Savage said a nanosecond after the bailiff's order, freezing everyone in the courtroom halfway out of their seats for a second until they sank back down into them. As was his practice, he preempted the government's duty of accounting for the parties to the trial, "Let the record reflect that all parties to the trial who were present when the court last recessed are again present, including the court members. Does the government have an opening argument?"

"Yes, your Honor," Major Morgan replied.

Again, the experienced attorney stood and regarded the jury with a faint smile on his lips. "Mr. President, Members of the Court," he began, "the facts of this case will be fairly simple. The government does not have any scientific evidence—no laboratory report, no expert witnesses, nor fancy charts. What we do have is the simple, straightforward testimony of several witnesses. Those witnesses, including Major, then Captain Armstrong, the victim of this mutiny, will testify that, from the very moment Major Armstrong took command of Company A, First Battalion, Seventh Cavalry, First Cavalry Division, the accused resisted his authority. Not only the company commander, Major Armstrong, but also the accused's own platoon sergeant will testify that the accused resisted, circumvented, and disobeyed his commander's lawful orders. The members of the accused's platoon, the first platoon, supported and assisted the accused in this pattern of resistance to the lawful authority of their commander. The accused's platoon sergeant, Sergeant First Class Tabler, will testify that the accused was too friendly with the junior enlisted men in his platoon and that they worked together to frustrate the commander's orders.

"The situation came to a head in August 1970, when the company was in a perimeter waiting to be extracted for a combat assault into another area of operations. To maintain good all-around security while waiting for the helicopters, Major Armstrong ordered the accused to place the members of his platoon in two-man observation posts around the perimeter. Because the first platoon was somewhat understrength, he also had the second platoon leader put two OPs out. An enemy machine gun opened fire on one of the second platoon OPs. Major Armstrong got on the radio and ordered the accused to get his platoon on line and charge the machine gun. The accused first pretended he couldn't understand the order and then simply disobeyed it. He actually had the gall to answer, 'Affirmative,' when his commander asked him whether he was disobeying a direct order. The accused was supported in this mutinous act by the junior enlisted members of his platoon.

"Now, you may, quite legitimately, wonder why it took until now to bring this incident to trial. Major Armstrong will testify that, the very next day, the accused was wounded and medevaced. Through an erroneous report, Major Armstrong believed that the accused was dead and that, with a new platoon leader to replace him, Major Armstrong didn't need to take any action concerning the incident. He felt it would further harm the accused's family if they found out he had died pending charges for mutiny.

"The government contends that the case is very simple and that, after you have heard all the evidence, you will conclude beyond a reasonable doubt that, in concert with the junior enlisted men in his platoon, the accused refused to obey the lawful order of Major Armstrong to 'charge the machine gun.' And that's mutiny. Thank you."

As Major Morgan sat down, Judge Savage asked the defense whether they wanted to make an opening statement or reserve it until the opening of the defense case. As he had told Jim Thomas, Lieutenant Colonel David was not about to let the opportunity pass to try to prevent the court members from believing the first thing they heard, the prosecution's opening statement.

Paul walked confidently up to the podium, turned it slightly to better face the court members, and began. "Mr. President, Members of the Court, this case is not going to be as simple as the trial counsel would have you believe. Contrary to what he told you the evidence would show, the defense contends that both the government's own evidence and the defense evidence will show that Major Jim Thomas was a very good platoon leader, indeed, the recipient of a Silver Star for heroism, that Major Armstrong was a very poor commander and was out of touch with the tactical situation when he gave the order to charge the machine gun, that there was no concert of action with the members of his platoon or anyone else to disobey the order, and that, although strictly speaking, Major Thomas disobeyed the order, he did so because it was impossible to obey. He could not even contact the members of his platoon, spread out in two-man outposts—most of whom did not have radios—much less get them organized to attack the machine gun. Instead, he took the proper tactical actions, calling in both tube and aerial rocket artillery— actions that resulted in the suppression of the enemy fire with no further friendly casualties. The defense expects the military judge will instruct you that inability to comply with an order is a valid defense to disobedi- ence of an order and that, if the accused could not obey the order, he was not trying to mutiny.

"Consequently, Mr. President, Members of the Court, the defense is confident that, when you have heard all the evidence, you will find Major Thomas not guilty of the charge and specification. Thank you." As Major Morgan had done, Lieutenant Colonel David spoke in the third person because it was against military legal ethics for a counsel to express his own opinion before a court-martial.

"Call your first witness, Major Morgan," Judge Savage said.

The court members sat up a little more attentively and picked up the pencils set before them on the jury bench alongside tablets for them to take notes.

"The government calls Major Armstrong."

The court members craned their necks, anxious for their first glimpse of the victim of this alleged mutiny. Major Armstrong entered the court- room and strode confidently to the witness stand. As instructed by the trial counsel, he looked sharp. He had gotten a very short haircut the day before, and his freshly pressed uniform looked very good with its glit- tering badges and multicolored ribbons.

Because Major Armstrong had already testified, Major Morgan could have simply asked him whether he was the same Major Armstrong who had previously testified and reminded him that he was still under oath. But the trial counsel went through the whole routine again because he wanted the court members to see his witness take the oath.

"Please raise your right hand. Do you swear or affirm that the evi- dence you are about to give in the case now in hearing is the truth, the whole truth, and nothing but the truth, so help you God?"

"I do," Major Armstrong replied in a loud, clear voice.

"Please state your name, rank, Social Security number, organization, and armed force."

"Mark Armstrong, Major, 312-56-3109, Student Detachment, Command and General Staff College, U.S. Army."

Then, Ken began his direct examination, "Major Armstrong, would you please explain the circumstance of your taking command of Company A, First of the Seventh Cavalry?"

As the trial counsel had coached him, Major Armstrong didn't answer the trial counsel. Instead, he looked at the court members as he answered the question, "I arrived in Vietnam in January 1970. For the first six months of my tour, I was an aide to then Brigadier General, now General Hawkins, my uncle."

"Objection, your Honor!" Lieutenant Colonel David exploded. "The reference to the witness's family relationship interjects what amounts to illegal command influence. It is nothing more than a blatant attempt to influence the court members to believe this witness solely because his uncle is a four-star general. The defense moves for a mistrial."

"Approach the bench, counsel," Judge Savage ordered with a far less than pleased look on his face. All four counsel and the accused gathered around the judge's bench, playing a quick game of tag to avoid being the one closest to Judge Savage. Ken lost and found himself right under the judge's patrician nose. At courts-martial, the accused was always allowed to accompany his defense counsel to bench-side conferences so that he could be certain nothing adverse to his case was taking place without his knowledge.

"What's the government's position on this matter?" the military judge asked Major Morgan.

"Your Honor, the government did not elicit this testimony. The witness apparently volunteered it on his own. The government contends, however, that any inference that the court members might give extra credence to the witness's testimony because his uncle is a general is speculative. Even assuming the worst, any potential harm can be cured by an instruction from your Honor."

"May I be heard, your Honor?" When the military judge looked at him, Lieutenant Colonel David argued that his testimony emphasized the danger he had pointed out in his motion to have the convening authority disqualified as the accuser and that the only remedy was a mistrial followed by a re-referral by a different convening authority.

Although Judge Savage agreed with Major Morgan, ruling that the harm was too speculative and denying the defense motion for a mistrial, out of what he called an excess of caution, he instructed the jury to disregard the family connection between the witness and General Hawkins. He also counseled the trial counsel to control his witness, or if there were any more references to General Hawkins, he might just grant the defense motion.

Major Morgan resumed his direct examination of the witness. "What job did you have after your first six months?"

"I was given command of Alpha Company, First Battalion, Seventh Cavalry, First Cavalry Division, in late June of 1970, replacing Captain Hart."

"Who was the battalion commander?"

"Lieutenant Colonel McCreary."

"And what, if anything, did he tell you about Alpha Company?"

"He told me it was basically a good company, but that, in his opinion, Captain Hart had not been aggressive enough in patrolling, which was why the enemy had ambushed the company so often. He suggested I move further and faster than Captain Hart had and meet the enemy on my terms instead of his."

"Did you encounter any problems when you took command?"

"Nothing major at first, but it was a difficult assumption of command. Captain Hart had been very popular, and the troops seemed to resent me. And they certainly did not like it when I pushed them to cover more ground and set out more night ambushes."

"Do you know the accused in this case? If so, please point to him and state his name."

Major Armstrong looked the accused in the eye, pointed at him, and said, "Major James Thomas." The eyes of the court members all followed Armstrong's accusing finger. Jim did not flinch, however. He just stared back as if daring Armstrong to take his best shot.

"Let the record reflect that the witness correctly identified the accused. How did you come to know him?"

"When I took over Alpha Company, he was the first platoon leader."

"What kind of platoon leader was the accused?"

"Technically, he was not too bad. He knew his stuff. But he was too close to his men, and he was not aggressive enough."

"Could you give the court members an example of this lack of aggression?"

"Yes, we had a mission to patrol the rocket belt north of Quan Loi. I had each platoon work separately so we could cover as much ground as possible to deny the enemy the ability to set up rockets. The company would come together every four days for resupply. The command post and I would go with one of the platoons for four days and then rotate to another. When I went with the first platoon, I noticed the accused wasn't aggressive. He didn't travel as far or as fast as the other platoon leaders and didn't search as aggressively for the enemy. He almost never set out night ambushes unless I told him to.

"One time, I got a report of a suspected enemy regiment to the north of the rocket belt. His platoon was the closest, so I ordered him to move to the reported location and try to locate the regiment. He made it only about three clicks north and apparently quit looking. I didn't hear from him until the next morning."

Lieutenant Colonel David again rose to his feet. "Objection, your Honor. This testimony is both uncharged misconduct and irrelevant."

Major Morgan responded, "Your Honor, this testimony is necessary. It informs the court members of the background for the mutiny, and because mutiny requires proof of an intent to usurp lawful authority, the government may attempt to show that intent by circumstantial evidence such as this."

"Overruled."

"Thank you, your Honor," Ken continued. "Now, Major Armstrong, did this passive resistance to your command worsen?"

"Objection!" Again Paul stood up. "Your Honor, the trial counsel is putting words into the witness's mouth. No one has said a word about passive resistance. All we have so far, at most, is a lack of aggression in the witness's opinion."

"Sustained. The court members will disregard the trial counsel's reference to passive resistance. Rephrase the question, Major Morgan."

"Yes, your Honor. Did the first platoon actively frustrate your orders?"

"Yes. By carefully monitoring their radio conversations and by talking to their platoon sergeant, Sergeant First Class Tabler, who was loyal to me, I learned that the accused would report that he was on a night ambush when, in reality, he was in a night defensive perimeter. The enlisted men, with the exception of the platoon sergeant, supported him in this subterfuge, and in fact, his RTO and several others made some of these false reports."

"Then what happened?"

"In mid-August 1970, while we were still north of Quan Loi, the battalion commander, Lieutenant Colonel McCreary, called me up on the radio and told me to go to a clearing a few kilometers away to be extracted the next morning by helicopter for a combat assault into another area. I briefed my junior leaders, and we moved out. When we reached the pickup zone, I ordered Lieutenant Thomas to put his men out in two-man teams around the perimeter to provide early warning of an enemy attack. Because his platoon was somewhat understrength, I also told the second platoon leader to put two listening posts out."

The court members seemed to sit up even a little straighter and listen even more attentively as the testimony got to the heart of the mutiny charge.

"Apparently, there was a problem getting the helicopters, and we had a long wait. I was talking to the battalion commander on the radio when I heard a machine gun open up on the eastern side of the perimeter. From monitoring the radio, I concluded that one of the listening posts belonging to the second platoon had been hit, and no one was returning fire for fear of hitting the two men on the outpost. Consequently, I ordered the accused to get his platoon on line and charge the machine gun. Once they went past the outpost, they could fire without worrying about hitting their own men."

Both defense counsel furiously scribbled notes to assist them in cross-examining the witness as Major Morgan continued.

"Was that the only reason for giving the order?"

Major Armstrong continued as if he were giving a tactics lesson to a class of new lieutenants. "No, I was also following the battalion commander's instruction to be aggressive. When you are trapped in a killing zone, you can't just stay in it and die. You have to attempt to close with and destroy the enemy."

"How did you communicate the order?"

"I called Lieutenant Thomas up on the radio."

"Did he answer?"

"I don't remember whether he answered initially or his RTO answered and then put him on the horn. But I gave the order directly to Thomas."

"What was the order?"

"I told him to get his platoon on line and charge the machine gun."

"Did he respond?"

"Yes, he asked me to repeat what I had said, and after I did, he said I was coming in garbled. I told him he had heard me and he had to obey my order. Then he said, 'Negative.' I asked him whether he was disobeying my order, and he said that he was."

"Did the order require immediate compliance?"

"Yes."

"Did the accused ever obey it?"

"No."

"Then, what happened?"

"Pretty soon, the machine gun fire slackened off. The artillery I had called in must have driven the gooks off. I was about to call a medevac for the two men on the listening post, but when I learned they were dead, I decided to evacuate them on the slicks that were going to extract us. I called battalion and reported the results of the firefight and that we were ready to be extracted."

"By slicks do you mean helicopters?"

"Yes."

"Did anyone assist the accused in this disobedience?"

"His RTO assisted, and no one in his platoon followed my orders."

"How did his RTO assist?"

"He ignored my continued attempts to get 1-6—the accused—back on the horn to get him to comply with my order."

"Did you take any action as a result of this incident?"

"After the combat assault, I called all the platoon leaders together and read them the riot act. I told them the reason we didn't find any enemy KIA was that 1-6 had disobeyed my order to charge the machine gun. I told him he was a coward and I would deal with him when we got back to the firebase."

"Did he respond?"

"No, he didn't say anything."

"Why didn't you relieve him?"

"His platoon sergeant was fairly new and inexperienced, and I wanted to wait until the battalion commander could replace 1-6 before relieving him and bringing charges."

"What happened next?"

"The next day, we were in another firefight, and the accused was seriously wounded. I believe he was shot in the chest—a sucking chest wound. After we medevaced him, I got a report that he had died. Obviously, he didn't, but at the time, we all thought he had. He never came back to the battalion. Consequently, I didn't bother drawing up court-martial charges. I didn't want his surviving family to think he was a coward."

"Lying son of a bitch—he didn't want what happened during that firefight to come out! He didn't give a shit about my family!" Jim whispered in Paul's ear.

"Shut up and write down anything you want to say to me on that yellow legal tablet in front of you so that I can concentrate on the witness's testimony," Paul snarled. Several of his friends, family, colleagues, clients, and opposing counsel had noted over the years that whenever

Paul was focused on a trial, all sense of civility left him and returned only after the trial was over. He usually left a lot of tears and hurt feelings in his wake, and he could never really understand why those closest to him thought his behavior was anything other than perfectly normal during a trial.

"When did you prefer charges?"

"After coming to attend CGSC and discovering that he was a fellow student."

"Now, at the time you gave this command, what rank were you?"

"I was a captain."

"And what rank was the accused?"

"He was a first lieutenant."

"And you were not only superior to him in rank, but also his commander?"

"Yes."

"And once more, why did you give the order to charge the machine gun?"

"To close with and destroy the enemy, which was our mission, and to prevent any further unnecessary casualties. I thought it was the best way to quickly suppress the machine gun fire."

"Thank you. No further questions. Defense?" Major Morgan sat down, pleased with the way the direct examination of his most important witness had gone.

"He did well, didn't he, Sir?" Captain Lewis whispered to the lead counsel for the government.

"So far, but let's not congratulate ourselves until we see how he does on cross," Ken replied.

Paul David got up from the defense table, his yellow legal tablet in hand. He walked up to the witness stand and stood there for a minute looking at the witness. Major Armstrong returned his gaze for a moment, then began to shift nervously on the witness chair, apparently having misplaced his resolve to stand up to the defense counsel. He pulled a tissue out of a small pack of Kleenex, unfolded it, wiped his nose, and neatly refolded the tissue. Then, Lieutenant Colonel David began the cross examination, just before the court members could conclude that he was trying to intimidate the witness.

He started off somewhat innocuously. "Major Armstrong, was this your first tour in Vietnam?"

"Yes." Even though Major Morgan had warned him to call the lieutenant colonel defense counsel, "Sir," Mark balked at dignifying his opponent's lawyer with the customary title of respect. Lieutenant Colonel David noted the absence of "Sir," but thought that, if he corrected it, he would look like the heavy to the court members, but that, if the subtle disrespect continued, it would show the jury that Major Armstrong was lacking in at least one attribute of a good officer. You didn't have to mean it, but you had to call a superior officer, "Sir," even if that superior officer were a mere Army lawyer.

"And you were an aide for the first half of your tour?"

"Yes."

"So when you took over as commander of Alpha Company, you had no combat experience?"

"That's correct."

"You had never served as a platoon leader in combat?"

"No."

"Had you been a company commander in CONUS?"

"No."

"What about your platoon leaders—how experienced were they?"

"The second platoon leader was the least experienced. He had very little time as a platoon leader. The third platoon leader had close to six months, and Lieutenant Thomas, under two months. The weapons platoon leader was an experienced noncommissioned officer."

"What about your first sergeant?"

"He had about five months in country."

"Isn't it true that he had had combat experience in World War II and Korea and was on his third tour with the First Cav in Vietnam?"

"Yes."

"And isn't it true that on the first day you spent in the field with Alpha Company, you announced that, while you were commander, the company would hump at least three times as far as under the previous commander, Captain Hart?"

"Yes."

"And you changed the formation the unit used to move through the jungle so that all three platoons cut their way through the jungle in parallel files?"

"Yes."

"And did you consult with any of these officers or NCOs whom you have admitted were more experienced than you were before making these changes?"

"No."

"In fact, didn't your first sergeant tell you that was too far to hump in the heat and humidity?"

"I don't remember."

Lieutenant Colonel David looked down at his notes for a moment and then continued. "Now, you testified that Major Thomas didn't set out ambushes when you thought he should."

Although his client had been a lieutenant at that time, Paul called him by his higher current rank to give the accused more status before the members, just as the trial counsel had with his witness.

"What did you do to correct this alleged deficiency?"

"I started spending more time with his platoon to make certain he carried out my instructions."

"And did he?"

"When I was with his platoon, he did."

"So after this alleged incident of frustrating your orders by reporting he was on an ambush when he was really in a night defensive perimeter, you spent some time with his platoon and had no problems during that time?"

"I suppose."

"Yes or no, Major?"

"Yes."

"Did you formally counsel him?"

"No."

"So all you did to stop this alleged resistance to your authority was to spend more time with his platoon?"

"Yes."

"And two of the other platoons were led by more experienced platoon leaders than Major Thomas was?"

"Yes."

"And were you with his platoon when this machine gun opened up while you were waiting to be extracted?"

"The company was all back together. We had reassembled to be picked up for the combat assault."

"So after these apparently minor problems some time earlier, which were not even serious enough to relieve Major Thomas, and after he had apparently quit this so-called resistance to your authority, he all of a sudden disobeyed this order to charge the machine gun?"

Major Armstrong wanted to elaborate, but he remembered Ken's persistent admonitions to just answer, "Yes," or "No," so as not to look evasive. "Yes."

"Let me draw your attention to that incident. You testified that, when you arrived at the pickup zone, you had Major Thomas put his platoon in two-man outposts outside the perimeter. Did he object to doing that?"

"Yes."

"Do you remember what his objection was?"

"He said he wouldn't have any platoon integrity or effective means of controlling his men."

"But you ordered him to do so anyway?"

"Yes."

"But even though he had tactical objections to your order, he obeyed it?"

"He obeyed that order."

"And you put out two more listening posts from the second platoon?"

"Yes."

"Why?"

"As I said before, because the first platoon was somewhat under-strength."

"How many troops were in the first platoon?"

"Approximately fourteen, including the platoon leader and platoon sergeant."

"How many would there have been if the platoon had been full-strength?"

"Close to forty."

"And how many radios did the first platoon have?"

"Two. The platoon leader had one, and the platoon sergeant had one."

"So with fourteen men, leaving out the platoon command post and the two RTOs, the first platoon could put out five listening posts. And unless they took the platoon leader's radio, only one of them would have had a radio?"

"Yes."

Paul noticed Armstrong was starting to worry the Kleenex he was still holding in his left hand. Good, he thought. I hope the members of the panel notice it, too. "Now, am I correct that the attack was on the east side of the perimeter?"

"Yes."

"Where was your command post?"

"We were located on the southwest side of the perimeter."

"Did you move toward the contact?"

"No."

"So based only on what you heard on the radio, you ordered the accused to charge a machine gun?"

"Yes. I'm sure you remember from your Vietnam service that you often can't see very much during a firefight, considering the dense foliage, and you have to rely on reports. My job was to control the whole company, not just one platoon."

Major Morgan whispered to Captain Lewis, "Oh, no, he's starting to lose it."

Paul didn't rise to the bait, he merely continued in the same level voice, "Now, because the attack was initially against one of the second platoon listening posts, wouldn't it be correct to say that Major Thomas's men were located all around the perimeter except for where the contact was taking place?"

"I suppose you could say that."

"Yet this allegedly unaggressive platoon leader was where the contact was taking place?"

"I suppose—yes."

"And how exactly was he supposed to get his platoon assembled, with no radio contact with them, with the noise and confusion of a fire-fight going on, and with them scattered around the rest of the perimeter in two-man LPs?"

Major Armstrong was beginning to show his irritation. His voice rose, almost cracking. "I don't know—but he didn't even try. He refused to even try. He disobeyed my order."

Lieutenant Colonel David looked at the court members. Good, he thought, they don't look so impressed with Major Armstrong now. "Isn't it true that he told you his platoon was spread around the perimeter and he couldn't assemble them?"

"I don't remember."

"Are you sure?"

Heatedly, Major Armstrong almost shouted, "I said I don't remember!"

"So after he allegedly disobeyed this order, you counseled him and told him you would take care of him when you got back to the firebase?"

"Yes."

"You didn't relieve him then?"

"No."

"Why not?"

Major Armstrong looked at Ken Morgan, but when Ken didn't react, the witness answered, "As I said, I didn't have anyone experienced enough to take his place."

"Wasn't his platoon sergeant a sergeant first class? And didn't you testify that not only was he loyal to you, but also he had told you about practices of Major Thomas that he objected to?"

"Yes, but—"

"Just answer the question, please. Now, the next day, didn't Major Thomas warn you that you were about to be ambushed if you continued to move in the same direction?"

"I don't remember."

"And during that firefight, didn't he save a lot of American lives by keeping smoke out so they wouldn't be hit by friendly cobra gunships?"

"Yes."

"And when one of his troops put him in for a Silver Star, you endorsed it, recommending approval?"

Again, the witness looked at the trial counsel and again got no help from that quarter. "Yes, I thought it would be an appropriate posthumous award."

"Did you write an efficiency report on Major Thomas?"

"Yes."

"Did you mention this alleged mutiny or lack of aggressiveness?"

"I don't remember. No, I don't think so. Again, I saw no reason to brand a deceased officer as a coward."

"And you never reported this alleged mutiny to anyone until recently?"

"That's correct."

"And you testified that was because you didn't want to hurt his survivors?"

"Yes."

"Isn't it true that the real reason you didn't report it was because you lost control of the situation during the firefight and had no idea what to do and it's only now, sixteen years later, when most of the witnesses are gone or don't remember how you screwed up as a commander that you've got the courage to bring this mess up?"

"Objection, your Honor!" Both Major Morgan and Captain Lewis stood up.

"Withdraw the question, your Honor," Lieutenant Colonel David responded.

"The jury will disregard the question," the judge ordered.

Like hell, they will, Ken and Pam thought.

Lieutenant Colonel David started in again, "Now, you testified that you gave this order to enable your troops to bring fire on the enemy without hitting the men on the outpost?"

Major Armstrong appeared to relax at this seemingly less dangerous line of questioning. "That's correct."

"So you were concerned with killing the enemy?"

"Yes," the witness replied sarcastically, "after all, that was our mission."

"And how had you done at this mission during the time you had been commander?"

"I don't understand the question."

"How many enemy had you killed?"

"I don't remember."

"Isn't it true that Lieutenant Colonel McCreary had chewed you out because you had been in contact a number of times, had taken a lot of casualties, and had not yet produced a body count?"

"The gooks would carry their dead and wounded away. It was hard to tell whether you had a body count or not."

"Answer the question, Major. Didn't the battalion commander chew you out for not having a body count? After all, your predecessor had produced large body counts with few casualties."

"He may have talked to me about body counts, but I don't remember being chewed out for not producing one."

"Major Armstrong, isn't the real reason you gave this order to charge the machine gun that it was a knee-jerk reaction to another enemy contact—a contact in which you desperately needed a body count to get Lieutenant Colonel McCreary off your back?"

The veins in Armstrong's neck bulged, "No, that's not true! That's a lie!"

"A contact in which you were going to get a body count no matter how many of the first platoon's soldiers you had to kill to get it?"

"No, I was trying to save the men on the outpost and prevent further casualties." Major Armstrong glowered at Paul. The tissue in his hand had disintegrated into a shredded, sweaty wad.

"But a minute ago, you testified that you gave the order so as to kill the enemy. Now, it's to save the men on the outpost. Which was it?"

"Both."

"Now, did this alleged disobedience result in any further American casualties?"

"No, but it didn't get us any enemy body count, either."

"So let me see if I understand your testimony. You're saying that Major Thomas cowardly disobeyed your order when he was at the scene of the fighting and you weren't, that your order would have required him to locate all his men around all the portions of the perimeter without radios except where he was located, that you didn't relieve him for disobeying, and that his cowardly nature was belied by his winning the Silver Star the very next day, an award that you signed off on?"

"It wasn't like you're making it sound."

Rather than force the witness to answer, Lieutenant Colonel David sat down as if he were washing his hands of the witness. "No further questions, your Honor."

Ken got up to try to rehabilitate his witness. "Why did you make the changes involving the distances you humped and the formation you used without consulting your officers or first sergeant?"

"I knew Captain Hart was very popular, and I felt it was important for me to come in and take charge in a firm manner. I didn't want the men to think they could push me around."

"Why did you have the first platoon set out the outposts after hearing the accused's objections?"

"I felt that early warning of any enemy movement was more important than platoon integrity. That way, the other platoons had platoon integrity and could react if necessary."

"You told Lieutenant Colonel David that you didn't move toward the contact. Why not?"

"I didn't know whether the initial contact was a diversion or the main attack, and I thought I would stay where I was centrally located and could monitor the entire situation."

"Why didn't you feel you could replace the accused with Sergeant First Class Tabler?"

"Even though he was an experienced NCO, he was fairly new in the company and did not have a lot of combat experience. I thought I could last a few days until we got back to the firebase and I could get a replacement for Lieutenant Thomas from the battalion commander."

"Now, the defense counsel asked about whether Lieutenant Thomas had objected to putting out two-man outposts around the perimeter, and you said you didn't remember his doing so. Is that correct?"

"If he pointed out any objections, I don't remember them. If he did object, and I don't remember him doing so, he must not have made any sense. I might have given him other instructions if he had made a valid tactical objection. But as I testified before, I thought the best thing to do was to assault out of the killing zone and try to suppress the machine gun—that's what they taught us to do in Ranger School when ambushed. He didn't really discuss it or offer an alternative. He simply disobeyed me."

"No further redirect, your Honor."

Judge Savage looked at the defense table. "Recross?"

"No, your Honor." Lieutenant Colonel David shook his head, as if it were futile to spend any more time with this lying witness.

Then the military judge asked, "Questions by any member of the court?"

Lieutenant Colonel Penders raised his hand.

"Please write your question out," Judge Savage instructed him.

When the colonel had finished, Major Morgan took the question to the reporter to have it marked as an appellate exhibit, read it, showed it to Lieutenant Colonel David, and then handed it to the military judge. "No objection, your Honor."

The defense also had no objection, so the judge asked the witness Lieutenant Colonel Pender's question, "If the other platoons could react because they had platoon integrity, why didn't you order one of the other platoons to charge the machine gun?"

"I heard 1-6 on the horn and knew he was right at the scene of the action and could take action."

Judge Savage asked Lieutenant Colonel Penders whether that response answered his question. When the court member indicated that it had, the judge asked whether counsel for either side had any questions based on Lieutenant Colonel Pender's question. Lieutenant Colonel David did.

"Isn't it true that you ordered Major Thomas to attack because you had developed some respect for him while accompanying his platoon and thought he was the right leader to handle the situation?"

"I thought he could handle the mission," Major Armstrong answered lamely.

"If there are no further questions, I'll excuse this witness temporarily," Judge Savage stated. When no one indicated that he had another question, the judge turned towards the witness, "Major, you are temporarily excused. Do not discuss your testimony with anyone except the counsel for either side. If anyone attempts to discuss your testimony with you, you must forbid them to and report the attempt to the trial counsel."

After Major Armstrong nodded his understanding of the instructions and left, Judge Savage looked at his watch. "In view of the late hour, court will be in recess until 0900 tomorrow morning."

"All rise," the bailiff said.

Everyone stood up as the judge and the court members filed out.

Major Armstrong was waiting outside the courtroom. "How did I do?" he asked Major Morgan as soon as he came out of the courtroom.

"About as I had expected," Ken answered and walked away.

CHAPTER 30

Student Housing
Oregon Village
Fort Leavenworth, Kansas

JUNE 1986

Margaret Thomas looked out the window. Jim's car still wasn't in sight. I've got to hurry, she thought, running her hand through her long brown hair, because he'll be home soon. As she stirred the spicy Thai chili-fried rice Jim loved so much in the battered wok that had accompanied them all over the world, her eyes fell on the silver-framed photograph on top of the stove. It showed her standing alongside Jim in front of the Eiffel Tower. She smiled ruefully as she remembered the trip they had taken to Paris during Jim's tour in Germany. It had been fantastic, she thought, but it couldn't compensate for all the time he had spent in the field, leaving me alone in the temporary quarters we had had to live in for fourteen months while waiting for permanent quarters. And nothing can compensate for the hell we've been going through here. I was dumb enough to think this year would be a rest from the endless round of field training problems and mandatory social functions. Some improvement—studying and a court-martial. And my foolish husband won't cut his losses and get out.

She stirred the rice viciously, still wondering why she was cooking Jim's favorite meal when she really wanted to take him by his epaulets and shake some sense into him. She was so absorbed in stirring the rice as if she were grinding everyone involved in the court-martial into dust, that she started when she heard the door shut. Jim was home.

"Meg, why weren't you at the trial after lunch? You know Colonel David said it would help the case for the court members to see you there every session," Jim said from the small entry foyer. He took a deep, appreciative sniff. "Hey, what's the chili-fried rice for? Is it a hint I should flee the country and go to Thailand?"

"Just a minute, Jim. I've got to keep stirring or it will burn. You know wok cooking—high heat and very little oil."

Jim decided not to press Meg about her absence. "Yeah, talk about high heat—you should have been at the trial," Jim gushed. "I'm glad I requested Colonel David. He really tore Armstrong up on cross-examination. One of the court members even asked a very penetrating question. I feel a lot better about the case than I did this morning." He smiled at Meg as he walked into the kitchen.

"Jim, I wish I could feel good about it. I just know they are going to hammer you in the end. You've said yourself that your career is ruined even if you are found not guilty."

"That was before. Everyone I talked to today said that, after Armstrong's testimony, I've got a real good chance of beating this thing. Look, I know it has been hard on you, but it will all be over soon."

"Listen, I know I should have been there today. I'll go tomorrow. But I'm sick of this trial—watching the lawyers playing games with your life—talking about you like a piece of meat, as if you weren't even there, as if you were just another file folder in a steel gray government file cabinet. You had a chance to get out and avoid this trial if you had accepted the resignation instead of court-martial your defense counsel told you about. Is it too late to take the resignation instead of the trial?"

"Resignation in lieu of court-martial."

Meg smacked the wooden spatula on the side of the wok and sent rice and bits of Thai chilies all over the stove and counter. "Come on, Jim. Don't play word games with me. We've both been making compromises for your career for years. I asked you to get out rather than go through this trial crap. You could work for my dad, or I'll support us until you find something else. Why put yourself through this mess any longer when you can't win?"

Jim held up his hands as if in surrender. "Listen, Meg, I can beat this stupid charge."

"If it were just this stupid trial, maybe I wouldn't care so much. But it's the whole thing—the Army. I'm tired of being an Army wife. I'm sick of the way all our so-called friends have treated us like pariahs since this trial started. And even if you are found innocent, I don't want to go to another dreary Army post and sit at home while you go to the field. Are you going to resign?" Meg demanded.

"No, I can't."

"If I had any sense, I'd leave you. But I love you too much. I'll support you throughout this trial." Meg smiled in spite of the tears streaking black mascara down both of her cheeks. "But I want you to promise me one thing."

"What's that?"

"After this trial is over, however it turns out, we have to sit down and talk about what we are going to do with rest of our lives together. And I'm adamant about it. Ok?"

Jim opened his mouth to argue but then shut it and just nodded. He leaned over the small table crammed into the tiny kitchen, took Meg's face into his hands, and kissed her. "I don't deserve you," he said.

"No, you don't," Meg agreed, as she put her hands on his cheeks and used her long slender fingers to wipe his tears and smooth his mustache. "Come on and eat your dinner. If I'm going to have to do without you if they throw you into jail, at least we're going to have some fun first."

After they finished the spicy rice, washing it down with copious drinks of Anchor Steam beer and ice water, Meg couldn't help focusing on the needlepoint she had hung on the wall by the telephone. She had made it from a kit she'd bought at the little gift shop at the post museum soon after their arrival. Although it was her one arts and crafts decoration, she doubted she'd find its twin in General Lowe's quarters. Now she wished they had followed its guidance:

Auntie Em.

Hate you.

Hate Kansas.

Taking the dog.

Dorothy.

CHAPTER 31

Courtroom, Office of the Staff Judge Advocate
Building 244
Fort Leavenworth, Kansas

JUNE 1986

Paul looked up from his case notes as Major and Mrs. Thomas entered the courtroom. "You look like hell," Paul said. "What's the matter?"

"Meg and I partied last night. I guess I drank too much. I didn't want to think about this crummy trial for one night."

Partying may be premature, Paul thought. For a moment, he resented Jim's partying while he was working on the case, but then good sense reasserted itself, and he remembered the pressure Jim and his wife were under. "A party sounds like a good idea." Paul made it a point to turn around and smile reassuringly at Meg, who had taken a seat in the back corner of the courtroom. She didn't smile back.

Jim replied, "Well, let's make it a preparatory celebration—let's win this case."

Paul didn't answer. He just nodded and went back to reviewing his notes.

Just before 0900 hours, Ken and Pam entered. Ken winked at Paul and then assumed a serious expression as Judge Savage poked his head out of his chamber and asked whether the court members were ready. "Yes, your Honor," Ken answered.

"Let's get started on time for a change, then."

After the court members had entered and Major Morgan had gone through the preliminaries, he called his next witness. "The government calls Master Sergeant, Retired, Alonzo Tabler."

The big, black, retired NCO entered the courtroom. Even in his civilian suit, Tabler looked like an NCO. He wore a miniature Bronze Star ribbon in the lapel of his expensive suit. He was heavy while on active duty, but after five years' retirement, he carried close to 250 pounds on his six-foot, two-inch frame. "Now, you see where we got the 'Big' part of 'Big Soul,' don't you?" Jim wrote on the yellow legal pad and pushed it toward to his defense counsel.

Major Morgan swore the witness in.

Instead of responding, "I do," Mr. Tabler, said, "So help me, God," in a loud, clear voice.

The trial counsel began his questioning. "Would you state your name, address, and Social Security number for the record?"

"Alonzo Tabler, 20 Ridge Avenue, Detroit, Michigan. 312-99-3109."

"Mr. Tabler, were you ever in the Army?"

"Yes. I retired as a Master Sergeant, E-8, after twenty-four years."

"And what is your current occupation?"

"I own my own McDonald's franchise," the retired sergeant answered proudly.

"Do you know the accused in the case?"

"Yes."

"Would you please point to him and state his name?"

SFC Tabler extended a big finger in the accused's direction as if he were the Pope designating a heretic. "Lieutenant—I mean Major— Thomas."

"Let the record reflect the witness pointed to the accused. How did you come to know him?"

"I was his platoon sergeant in Vietnam."

"And when was that?"

"I joined Alpha Company, First of the Seventh, in July of 1970. The CO—Captain Armstrong—assigned me to the first platoon."

"What shape was the first platoon in when you took over as platoon sergeant?"

"It was in pretty bad shape. The acting platoon sergeant was a SP4, even though there were two sergeant E-5s in the platoon. There wasn't much discipline."

"What do you mean by 'there wasn't much discipline?'"

"The men were very dirty, their hair was too long, they didn't shave, and they were almost totally lacking in military courtesy."

"What did the accused do about this situation?"

"Nothing. He had a Fu Manchu mustache himself, and his hair hung down to his shoulders—strictly against regulations."

"What did the enlisted men call the accused?"

"1-6."

"Did they ever call him 'Sir' or 'Lieutenant?'"

"Not that I heard."

"Who was the company commander at this time?"

"Captain Mark Armstrong."

"What was the platoon's feeling about Major Armstrong?"

"He was very unpopular. He tried to enforce discipline, and tight discipline in the field didn't sit well with the junior enlisted men."

"How did this unpopularity manifest itself?"

"They put a price on his head."

The older court members flinched at Mr. Tabler's answer. It brought back one of the worst memories of the Vietnam war, the fraggings of unpopular officers.

"They put a price on his head—what does that mean?"

"It means that if one of the men killed him, the others would pay a bounty to the killer. The idea was that if they got rid of Captain Armstrong, 1-6 would become the commander."

"How much was the price?"

"Not much—one hundred dollars."

"Did the accused know about the price on Major Armstrong's head?"

"Yes."

"What did he do about it?"

"Nothing." Several of the court members frowned at this revelation. An officer who did nothing to prevent a fragging?

Major Morgan gave the witness an incredulous look. "Do you mean he didn't try to discourage them?"

"That's correct."

"In other words, the members of the first platoon wanted to get rid of their commander and replace him with their platoon leader?"

"Objection, your Honor!" Lieutenant Colonel David interjected. "Counsel is leading the witness."

"Withdraw the question," Major Morgan countered. That's payback for the last question you asked Major Armstrong, he thought.

"Do you remember the name of the accused's RTO?"

"His name was Darnell. I don't remember his first name. I think he was a private first class—maybe a spec 4."

"What was his relationship to the accused?"

"They were pretty friendly."

"Did he ever do anything to help the accused get around Major Armstrong's orders?"

"Sometimes, he would give misleading reports over the radio."

"What kinds of reports?"

"That the platoon was moving when in fact we were taking a break. Captain Armstrong didn't like breaks, so when 1-6 was working separately, he would report he was moving when we were just sitting there."

"And PFC Darnell helped him do this?"

"Yes, the RTO often talked for the platoon leader—relaying his conversations."

"Now, do you remember the firefight where two members of the second platoon were killed while you were waiting to be extracted to go to work with the armored cavalry?"

"Yes."

"What formation was the company in?"

"We had set up a perimeter. Our platoon—first platoon—was spread out in two-man outposts."

"And where were you?"

"I was at the western end of the perimeter. 1-6 had told me to stay there with my radio so that we would have some control over the OPs at that end. 1-6 was on the east side of the perimeter."

"What happened while you were waiting there?"

"A machine gun opened up on the east side of the perimeter. No one knew what was going on. We didn't know whether it was just a probe and we were going to get hit elsewhere or whether it was the main attack. I continued to monitor the horn. After a while, I heard Captain Armstrong tell 1-6 to assemble the first platoon and attack the machine gun."

"What did the accused do?"

"First, he said he couldn't understand Captain Armstrong. Then, when Captain Armstrong told him . . . ." The witness looked at the military judge and said, "He used bad language, your Honor. I don't want to repeat it." One of the other witnesses had told Mr. Tabler about Judge Savage's reputation for jumping all over witnesses who used foul language in his court.

Judge Savage reassured the nervous witness. "If you are repeating what someone else said, I'm not going to hold you in contempt. Answer the question."

Mr. Tabler looked relieved. "Yes, your Honor. Captain Armstrong said, 'Bullshit. You understood me. Move out,' or words to that effect."

"Did the accused answer?"

"He said, 'Negative.'"

"Meaning that he wouldn't obey the order?"

Lieutenant Colonel David made a show of rising wearily to his feet. "Objection, your Honor. The witness cannot know what Major Thomas meant."

"I'll rephrase the question," Major Morgan interposed. "Mr. Tabler, after this response, did the accused appear to do anything to comply with the order?"

"No."

"Did he call you on the radio and tell you to start assembling the members of your platoon?"

"No."

"Because you were on the west side of the perimeter and the firefight was on the east side, could you have gone out to the OPs and brought them in?"

"Absolutely."

"Did any of the other members of the platoon help the accused disobey this order?"

"I heard Captain Armstrong trying to get 1-6 back on the radio. But his RTO said the lieutenant was too busy and he couldn't come to the radio."

"So to the best of your knowledge, the accused said he was not going to obey the order and never took any steps to assemble the first platoon and charge the machine gun?"

"That's right."

"No further questions. Thank you, Mr. Tabler."

The witness started to get to his feet. Lieutenant Colonel David smiled at him. It was not a friendly smile. "Not so fast, Master Sergeant, I have a few questions."

The retired NCO sat back down heavily and waited for the first defense question.

"You testified that you didn't think Major Thomas's platoon was disciplined enough because they were dirty and unshaven and their hair was too long. Were their weapons clean?"

"Yes."

"Did Major Thomas make them take their malaria pills?"

"Yes."

"Did the platoon observe noise and light discipline at night?"

"Yes, Sir." Without thinking of it, the witness began adding "Sir" to his answers. It was becoming obvious to him that the defense counsel remembered what he must have learned in Vietnam judging from the decorations on his chest. When Tabler had retired, he thought he was done calling people, "Sir." Selling fast food had debased him of that thought rapidly. But he was beginning to feel like a master sergeant again as he remembered his combat tours.

"This was your first time in the field with an infantry platoon?"

"Yes, Sir."

"Now, if strict military courtesy were observed—saluting and all— wouldn't these military courtesies have identified the leaders for snipers?"

"I suppose so."

"And did the troops in the other platoons call their platoon leaders 'Sir,' or did they also call them by their radio call sign?"

"Usually by their call sign."

"Now, you testified that Lieutenant Thomas had long hair and a long mustache. I believe you called it a Fu Manchu. Did you have a barber with you in the field?"

"No, Sir."

"How was the water supply?"

"The men humped four to six canteens. We had to drink a lot in the heat and humidity."

"And isn't it true that you didn't have much spare water for shaving?"

"I shaved. Sir."

"Answer the question, please, Master Sergeant."

"No, we didn't have much spare water."

"So the only signs of this alleged lack of discipline were physical appearance and a lack of military courtesy?"

"Yes, Sir."

"Now, you stated that Lieutenant Thomas didn't discourage the men from putting a price on the commander's head. Did he encourage them?"

"Not that I remember. If he did, I didn't hear it. If I had, I would have told the CO."

"Did you tell Captain Armstrong about the price on his head?"

"No, he already knew about it."

"How did you know he knew about it?"

"Whenever he went outside the perimeter to take a shit, he took Six-India with him. Six-India was very popular, and the CO knew that no one would shoot or frag him if Six-India was right next to him." The court members, aware of Judge Savage's reputation, suppressed smiles, but a few of the spectators tittered at the thought of the prim-looking major taking an enlisted man with him to perform such an intimate bodily function.

Judge Savage glared at the witness. "Mr. Tabler, if you use language like that again in my courtroom, I'll hold you in contempt." With his voice rising, he continued, "And if I hear anymore laughter, I'll clear the court. Is that understood?"

Chastened, the witness said, "Yes, your Honor. Sorry, your Honor."

Lieutenant Colonel David continued. "By Six-India, do you mean his radio operator?"

"Yes, Sir."

"Now, you said that Captain Armstrong was not very popular with the troops. You weren't either, were you?"

"No, Sir. Like Captain Armstrong, I tried to enforce discipline."

"Didn't the troops call you, 'Big Soul?'"

"Yes."

"Why?"

"I supposed it was because I was religious."

"Isn't it true that you were more concerned about spreading your gospel than just about anything else?"

"Not everything else. But I thought, praise the Lord, it was important that young troops who could get killed at any time accept Christ as their Savior."

"What did you think of this formation with your platoon spread out all around the perimeter in two-man outposts?"

"I thought it was a little unusual. Normally, each platoon put out its own outposts in front of its sector. But I figured Six—Captain Armstrong—knew what he was doing."

"Do you know why 1-6 was too busy to come to the radio when Captain Armstrong kept calling him?"

"No, Sir."

"Could it have been because he was engaged in a firefight?"

"I guess so, Sir."

"So for all you know, the RTO was telling the truth when he said that 1-6 was too busy to talk to the commander on the phone?"

"Maybe, Sir."

"At the time of this incident, did you think that the first platoon was engaged in a mutiny?"

"Objection, your Honor. Whether the witness thought this was a mutiny or not is irrelevant," Major Morgan stated.

Lieutenant Colonel David responded quickly. "Your Honor, you overruled my objection to Major Armstrong's testimony about uncharged misconduct, stating it was admissible as circumstantial evidence of intent to usurp lawful authority. This testimony is similar. If the witness did not think a mutiny was taking place, that is circumstantial evidence that there was no intent to usurp lawful authority."

Judge Savage, realizing that he was stuck, agreed with the defense. He did, however, counsel the jury that they could consider the witness's answer as evidence only on the question of whether the members of the platoon had the intent to usurp Major Armstrong's authority. They would still have to determine whether a mutiny had in fact occurred.

"Answer the question, Mr. Tabler," Lieutenant Colonel David prompted.

"Could you repeat it, Sir?"

"Did you ever think they were engaged in a mutiny?"

"No, Sir."

"In fact, of the first platoon, only you, Lieutenant Thomas, his RTO—Darnell—and perhaps your RTO even knew about this order?"

"Yes, Sir."

"And if you had thought a mutiny was taking place, I take it you would have taken some strong action to quell it?"

"Absolutely, Sir."

"Thank you, Master Sergeant."

After quickly comparing the notes Captain Lewis had taken on the cross-examination to his own, Ken began again.

"Why did you think PFC Darnell was trying to keep Captain Armstrong from talking to the accused?"

"Because of the false reports he had been giving about his platoon's activities, the price on Captain Armstrong's head, and his close relationship with Lieutenant Thomas."

"Now, even if the other members of the platoon were unaware that the accused took this particular order to disobey, I take it they would have supported the accused because of their dislike for Captain Armstrong?"

"Yes, Sir."

"And because you were not in contact with every outpost, is it possible that some members of the platoon assisted the accused in disobeying this order?"

"Yes, Sir."

"And at least one person, the RTO, assisted the accused in the conversation that terminated in the flagrant disobedience of the commander's order?"

"Yes, Sir."

"If you had been the platoon leader, would you have obeyed the order?"

"Roger that, Sir."

"No more questions, your Honor."

After looking at the defense table and seeing Lieutenant Colonel David shake his head, signifying no recross, Judge Savage asked,

"Questions by any member of the court? Apparently not." He excused the witness, who rose ponderously and strode out of the courtroom without looking at Major Thomas.

"Your Honor, the government calls Mr. Tyrone Henderson."

Mr. Henderson entered the courtroom. Like the previous witness, he wore a coat and tie. Tyrone was a black man in his late thirties. He smiled at the court members, showing a gold tooth, as he sat in the witness chair. After taking the oath and giving his name, address, and Social Security number, he identified the accused.

"How did you know the accused?"

"I was Six's—Captain Armstrong's RTO while Lieutenant Thomas was 1-6—da first platoon leader."

"I'd like to draw your attention to a firefight north of Quan Loi in mid-August 1970. Do you remember it?"

"Yes."

After a few more questions setting the stage, Major Morgan asked the witness whether he had heard Major Armstrong give any orders to the first platoon.

"I hear Six order 1-6 to get his men together and charge da machine gun."

"What response, if any, did Major Armstrong get?"

"1-6 wuzn't about to do it."

"Is that what he said?"

"Yes. When Six ax was he disobeyin,' 1-6 answer, 'Affirmative.'"

"Did Six keep trying to get Lieutenant Thomas to obey the order?"

"Six keep tryin' to get 1-6 back on da radio, but 1-6 India, he say 1-6 wuz busy."

"Who was 1-6 India?"

The witness looked at Major Morgan as if he were stupid, but answered the question. "1-6's RTO."

"No further questions. Your witness, Colonel David."

"What, if anything, was Captain Armstrong doing during this firefight, Mr. Henderson?"

"Sir, he was hidin' under a tree."

Lieutenant Colonel David quickly followed up on the revelation—a revelation that was not a surprise to him because of the preparation he had done for the cross-examination. "What do you mean, he was hiding under a tree?"

"When we hear da machine gun go off, he dive under a tree. I didn't hear no rounds comin' our way, so I jus' sat der. Da cap'n didn't do nothin' for a long time, so finally, I crawl under da tree with him, bringin' da radio. Den, he snatch da handset and start yellin' for 1-6 to charge da machine gun."

"Did he ask any questions to find out the situation before giving this order?"

"No, Sir. He jus' snatch da handset and start yellin.'"

"Didn't you hear Lieutenant Thomas tell Captain Armstrong that he couldn't obey the order?"

"I don't 'member he say nothin' like dat."

"Are you sure he didn't?"

"No, Sir. He might could have. I jus' don't remember. It wuz a long time ago."

"Yes, it was a long time ago, Mr. Henderson. No further questions."

"What should we do?" Pam Lewis asked the trial counsel.

But Ken just stood up and asked, "Now, you had a lot more combat experience than Major Armstrong did at this time, didn't you?"

"E'rybody did, Sir."

"And you could say he was almost a 'cherry' at this point, couldn't you?"

"Yeah, he be a cherry. Sir."

"And for any court members not familiar with the term, what was a 'cherry' in Vietnam?"

"Anybody who ain't been in no firefights. Sometimes, a newbie in country."

"And wasn't it typical for a 'cherry' to get under cover at the sound of incoming when a more experienced grunt would realize it was not impacting close enough to be dangerous?"

"Yes, Sir."

After he had sat down, Pam wrote Ken a note, "I'm impressed, you really saved that one—how did you know to ask those questions?" Ken did not answer. He just put a finger in front of his lips for silence as Lieutenant Colonel David got up again.

"At any time during the firefight, did Captain Armstrong get out from under the tree and try to find out what was going on?"

"No, Sir. He jus' laid der yellin' on da radio."

"Thank you. No further questions."

Major Steve Campbell raised his hand. Everyone looked at the jury box as he held out a piece of paper on which he had written out a question he wanted to ask the witness. After showing it to all parties to the trial, Major Morgan objected, contending it was irrelevant.

Before the defense could even argue, Judge Savage overruled the objection and asked the question, "Mr. Henderson, did Captain Armstrong take you with him whenever he went outside the perimeter?"

"Yes, indeed, Judge."

"Do you know why?"

"I dunno. I guess I was suppose' to watch for gooks whilst he took a whiz."

Judge Savage frowned, but decided he couldn't chew out the witness when he had asked the question and no spectator had laughed. He looked at Major Campbell. "I think that's all we need to pursue on this matter."

Major Morgan stood up. "Your Honor, the government rests."

C H A P T E R   3 2

Deputy Commandant's Office
U.S. Army Command and General Staff College
Bell Hall, Fort Leavenworth, Kansas

J U N E   1 9 8 6

Major General Treakle picked up the phone. Colonel Farmer had returned the Deputy Commandant's call.

"Hello, Judge. Thanks for calling me back so quickly. Listen, I got a call from General Hawkins's chief of staff. The general is really concerned about how this case is going. It sounds as if the defense is doing too well. I want to get Lieutenant Colonel David to back off. Can I counsel him about being overzealous? I don't want to get in trouble for illegal command influence."

Colonel Farmer smiled before answering. He had felt the Deputy Commandant had not been paying enough attention to legal matters and hence to the SJA. Thus, the portly lawyer was gratified to have the Deputy Commandant ask him for advice. I've got to do this right, he thought. If I do, I'll have one more general beholden to me.

"First of all, Sir, I totally sympathize with General Hawkins," Colonel Farmer began, conveniently forgetting that he had not wanted the court-martial to take place. "But command influence is a tricky area. A two-star in Germany watched his career come to a screeching halt because some of his subordinates interpreted his remarks as attempts to prevent witnesses from testifying for the defense. We don't want anything like that to happen to you. But I'm sure we can find a way to do what you want without risk to your career.

"Colonel Zimmer works for you as the Director of the Center for Army Leadership and is Lieutenant Colonel David's rater, isn't he?"

"That's right."

"Perhaps, in his capacity as an expert on leadership doctrine, he could talk to Lieutenant Colonel David about the dangerous precedent a 'not guilty' finding would set. That way, you would not be involved. And Lieutenant Colonel David is bright enough to get the message. If he doesn't, Colonel Zimmer can damn him with faint praise on his efficiency report. David could successfully appeal a really bad efficiency report because the law says you cannot lower a defense lawyer's report card because of the zeal with which he defends his client. In these days of inflated efficiency reports, however, anything less than a '1' in judgment, coupled with a senior rater potential evaluation in the third or fourth block, would kill his chances for promotion."

"Sounds good. I'll do that. Out here."

"Goodbye, Sir."

After hanging up, Major General Treakle pushed the button on the squawk box that connected him immediately and directly—no secretaries and no hold buttons—to any colonel's office in Bell Hall.

"Colonel Zimmer speaking."

"Treakle here. Come see me."

"Yes, Sir."

While he waited for Colonel Zimmer to fly directly out of his office and down a flight of stairs to the ground floor and walk about 20 yards to enter the Deputy Commandant's office at the northeast corner of the building, the general looked around his plush office at the gifts from CGSC students from other nations. Whenever he took a break from meetings or paperwork, he liked to feast his eyes on some of the valuable mementos, like the gold and jade crown from Korea and the silver scimitar from Saudi Arabia. His favorite, however, was a simple stone lamp from Carthage. It reminded him of the Punic Wars, his favorite period of military history. Commanding was easier than, he thought. If somebody screwed up, you just ordered his execution. He remembered Sun Tzu's story in *The Art of War* in which a subordinate had disobeyed an order and attacked before he was supposed to, thereby winning a great victory. His superior had first commended the subordinate for his bravery and then beheaded him for disobeying the order. They didn't worry about command influence back then, the general concluded.

Colonel Zimmer knocked on the door, entered, and saluted. Treakle didn't require his department directors to salute when they entered his office, but Zimmer was enough of a sycophant that he was not about to miss any chance to impress the general with his military courtesy. The general invited the director to be seated and then asked him to discuss the leadership implications of the Thomas case with Lieutenant Colonel

David. Zimmer, accurately reading where the general was coming from, quickly jumped on the bandwagon and agreed to point out the problems of a "not guilty" verdict to the defense counsel in the strongest possible terms.

"Make sure you don't order him not to defend his client," the general continued. "We don't want to commit illegal command influence."

"Yes, Sir. I'll be careful."

"Good. By the way, since I've got you here, let's discuss the writing course. I got the ACCESS survey results for Division C, and writing has bombed as usual. And the student comments are devastating. The students call one of your civilians "the Pillsbury dough boy" because he is so overweight and doofus, and your branch chief isn't much thinner. One comment said that no professional officer could give any credibility to such doofus-looking instructors. The only instructor any of the students seemed to remotely tolerate was that token woman we got rid of right after the College got its civilian graduate school accreditation for the next ten years. Can't you do any better than that? I know it's hard to shape up a civilian, but can't you at least shape up that fat lieutenant colonel? I want you to get together with your writing instructors and the Director of Academic Operations and figure out some way to improve the writing course ASAP. It sucks that military law gets rave reviews and important courses like leadership and writing take it in the ear. How about getting right on that?"

"Yes, Sir."

"That's all." The general abruptly turned away so that his subordinate couldn't salute.

That's enough, Zimmer thought, as he returned to his office, faced with what he thought were two impossible missions: to improve the writing course and to somehow cause Lieutenant Colonel David to ease off without jeopardizing the general's career or, more importantly, his own.

CHAPTER 33

Barbershop
Bell Hall
Fort Leavenworth, Kansas

J U N E   1 9 8 6

Lieutenant Colonel David entered the barbershop in the basement of Bell Hall. Although the post had two other barbershops, the thousand student officers, plus the staff and faculty, of the Command and General Staff College easily supported the two-man shop.

"Morning, Judge." One of the barbers looked up as Paul took his number from the dispenser and took a seat. Although most JAGC officers were not judges, most officers called Army lawyers, "Judge." And the usage had spread to the two Bell Hall barbers, both retired noncommissioned officers. Calling him "Judge" certainly didn't hurt the size of the tip Paul left, especially because he had been a judge and would cheerfully have given up teaching to return to the bench. Paul liked the crusty old retirees, and they seemed to like to talk to him. They didn't impress easily. They had cut the hair of several chiefs of staff and many four-star generals and later their sons and daughters, and mere field grade officers like Lieutenant Colonel David were a dime a dozen. But maybe because Paul always tipped a dollar, or because he was always willing to give them a legal analysis of current news stories, they not only were friendlier to him than to most customers, but also took more care with his haircut. Of course, he tipped well after hearing their stories of butchering the haircut of an officer who not only tipped poorly, but also gave them a hard time.

Paul opened his briefcase and took out his notes on the Thomas case. He reviewed the testimony of the government witnesses, highlighting important points for the motion he intended to make when court resumed. In a few moments, however, one of the barbers called his number, and he reluctantly put his notes away and got into the barber chair. "Just trim the hair and mustache, please."

"Sure, Judge. Keepin' busy?"

"Busier than usual for June. After graduation, I normally take a couple weeks' leave before the next CGSC class comes in. But I'm involved in a court-martial, and it looks like no leave this June."

"Yeah, I wondered why you were in your uniform. Most of the faculty is on leave. What case are you involved with?"

"I'm defending an officer charged with mutiny in Vietnam."

"You're defending—I thought you used to be a judge."

"I was. But you know the Army, you've got to keep rotating jobs if you want to get promoted. The accused was in my military law elective and requested me for his defense counsel."

"You gonna win?"

"I don't know, but I should find out shortly. I may even know today."

They fell silent, and the barber turned his attention to the hair on the back of Paul's neck. Paul began thinking about the case again. Boy, he thought, this case is just like being a full-time defense counsel all over again. I never could think about much else besides the case during a trial. I even had a dream about it last night. I hope the reality is better than the dream. I'd better win this motion, or the bad dream may become a reality.

Ken probably wondered why I lost a few motions and then entered my client's plea without ever making a winning motion. He is aware of my tactic of making motions to set up later winners. But I never before made motions to set up a winner—well, I hope it's a winner—after the government rested its case. My motion for a finding of not guilty has got to be a winner.

Well, even if I lose this motion, or even the whole case and the court members do find him guilty, they can't be too hard on him after hearing Armstrong and the other government witnesses testify. After all, which is worse—disobeying a stupid command in order to take proper defensive tactics or hiding under a tree? But even though that jackass Armstrong may have shot himself down by bringing up this stupid charge, at best, Jim's suffered almost a year's mental anguish pending this court-martial. And the worst is unthinkable.

"How's that, Judge?" the barber said, holding up a mirror for his customer to inspect the haircut.

"Looks good."

After the barber had gone through the ritual of brushing him off and ceremoniously ringing up the charge on the antique cash register, Paul handed him a $5 bill and told him to keep the change. A haircut cost only $3.90 in Fort Leavenworth's barbershops. And the haircuts were even cheaper at the Disciplinary Barracks barbershop, but you assumed a certain risk allowing a convict to cut your hair—and shave the back of your neck—especially if you were a military lawyer. That risk doubled for a military lawyer who had been a military judge and sentenced some of them to learn the barbering trade at the Disciplinary Barracks.

"Why, thank you, Judge," the barber said. He always acted surprised when David gave him a dollar because most officers tipped only a quarter or fifty cents.

Paul gathered up his briefcase and glanced at his watch. Almost time to go to court. With any luck at all, I'll earn my money today, he thought. I've got to win this motion and get Jim off the hook. Maybe if I can win this thing today, he can save his career and go on with the rest of his life.

When Paul went up to his office to get his hat, he found a note that his boss's boss, Colonel Zimmer wanted to see him. As required by the Army's rating scheme, Paul's immediate supervisor rated his duty performance. Colonel Zimmer, David's senior rater, compared David to other officers in what was called a "senior rater profile." If David wanted to be promoted, he needed his senior rater to rate him in the top block— as the best out of 100 officers. Hence, David, like many officers, felt that he really worked for his senior rater instead of his immediate supervisor. I don't have time to listen to whatever Zimmer is going to spout off now, Paul thought, but he went across the hall and poked his head into the director's office. It seemed as if everytime Paul was summoned to one of his military superior's offices, he got stuck teaching some other nonlegal subject, like effective writing.

"Come on in, Paul," Colonel Zimmer said with a friendly smile on his face. Paul was not taken in. Although he had worked for Colonel Zimmer for only a few weeks since the previous director had left, Zimmer's reputation for steamrolling over people to get ahead in his career had preceded him. The director gestured to one of the chairs around the conference table in front of his desk. "I wanted to talk to you about this Thomas case."

"Yes, Sir," Paul replied, wondering what Colonel Zimmer could possibly care about his client's court-martial.

The colonel toyed with the simulated bayonet letter opener on his desk for a moment and then began. "Have you thought about the implications to our mission here at the Center for Army Leadership if you win this case?"

"No, Sir." Uh-oh, here it comes, Paul thought. I don't want to hear this.

"Well, you know if you win this thing and your client is found 'not guilty,' it is going to set a horrible leadership example."

Paul just stared at his senior rater, hoping he wasn't going to hear what he thought he was going to hear.

Colonel Zimmer continued. "We just can't send out a message from the Center that soldiers can disobey orders in combat, get some slick lawyer to defend them, and get away with it. Now, I think you should think very hard about what you are going to do in this case. Do you read me?"

"Yes, Sir." Paul thought about giving his senior rater a lecture on illegal command influence, but didn't, realizing he might as well lecture the twelve-foot thick wall of the Disciplinary Barracks as try to make Colonel Zimmer see the error of his ways. "Is there anything else?"

"No. Just remember how a 'not guilty' finding will make the Center look. Is there anything we can do for you?"

"No, Sir." Not a thing. Not a blessed thing.

CHAPTER 34

Courtroom
Office of the Staff Judge Advocate
Building 244, Fort Leavenworth, Kansas

J U N E   1 9 8 6

Before Judge Savage could order the bailiff to get the court members, Lieutenant Colonel David stood up. "Your Honor, might we have an out-of-court hearing so that I can make a motion?"

"Your Honor," Major Morgan responded, "the court members are ready, and we don't want to keep them waiting."

One of Judge Savage's pet peeves was keeping court members waiting, but he couldn't very well deny the defense the opportunity to make just about any motion it could come up with, although he could certainly deny it. "What motion do you intend to make, Colonel David? Is it one we can defer until later so we don't keep the court members waiting?"

"Your Honor, the defense has a motion for a finding of not guilty, and as you know, if you denied such a motion in the presence of the court members, it would prejudice the defense."

"Very well, court will come to order. Let the record reflect that all parties who were present when the court recessed are again present except the court members. At the request of the defense, we are having this session to consider a motion for a finding of not guilty. The government objected to having this out-of-court hearing, but I ruled that it should be conducted out of the presence of the court members." Judge Savage, having protected the record, looked expectantly at the defense. Before the defense could begin, however, Major Morgan said that now the government knew the substance of the motion, the government withdrew any objection to litigating it outside the presence of the court members.

"Thank you, Major Morgan," Lieutenant Colonel David began. "Your Honor, the defense moves for a finding of not guilty to the charged offense, mutiny, contending that there is no evidence whatsoever of several elements of mutiny. Although the defense concedes for the sake of this motion that there is some evidence that the accused refused to obey Major—then Captain—Armstrong's order to charge the machine gun, there is no evidence that he did so in concert with anyone, and there is no evidence that he did so in pursuance of a common intent with anyone else to usurp and override lawful military authority."

"Oh shit," Captain Lewis whispered to Major Morgan. She was too concerned to remember to write a note. "This is the motion Colonel David was leading up to. We're in trouble."

Major Morgan silenced her with a wave of his hand. "Not necessarily."

"Does the government resist this motion?" Judge Savage asked.

"We do, your Honor," Major Morgan answered. "First, as your Honor knows, it is inappropriate to grant such a motion when there is a lesser included offense. Here, we have the lesser included offense of disobedience of a lawful command. Second, the government contends that there is evidence, along with justifiable inferences from that evidence, that establishes every essential element of a mutiny."

"What does the defense say about the included offense?" the military judge asked.

"Your Honor, the defense admits that disobedience of a lawful command is an included offense of a mutiny. In this case, however, the included offense is barred by the statute of limitations. Second, we would move for a partial finding of not guilty. In other words, we would move for a finding of not guilty as to mutiny, but leave the offense of disobeying a lawful command for resolution."

"Your Honor, may the government be heard?"

"Go ahead, Major Morgan."

"Your Honor, because the included offense is barred by the statute of limitations, if you grant this motion, you are, in effect, acquitting the accused entirely."

"Your Honor," Lieutenant Colonel David countered, "if I may draw your attention to several cases. First, the case of *United States v. Spearman,* 48 CMR 405, a 1974 Army Court of Military Review case, states that, when a motion for a finding of not guilty is denied, the accused still has the remedy of making a motion for appropriate relief, asking the judge to instruct the court that its consideration is limited to the included offense. Second, in *United States v. Cooper*, 16 USCMA 390, 37 CMR 10, a 1966 Court of Military Appeals case, the court ruled that it was prejudicial error to fail to instruct on an included offense, even when that included offense was barred by the statute of limitations. Taken together, these cases mean that unless your Honor finds that the government has introduced evidence in each and every element of the offense of mutiny, you must either grant the motion for a partial finding of not guilty or, in the alternative, instruct the court members that they may find the accused guilty only of the included offense of disobedience of a lawful command."

"I'll want to read those cases," Judge Savage informed the counsel, having written the case cites down so that he could look them up in the old burgundy colored law books lining the walls of his chambers. "In the meantime, I would like to hear the positions of both sides as to whether the evidence and all permissible inferences I may draw there-from establish the elements of concerted action and intent to usurp military authority."

"If it please the Court," Major Morgan argued first, "Major Armstrong, the accused's commander, testified that the accused failed to locate an enemy regiment he was ordered to find and apparently quit looking, that the accused reported he was in an ambush site when he was really in a night defensive perimeter, and that the accused was too close to his men. From this circumstantial evidence, your Honor may infer intent to usurp lawful authority when coupled with his disobedience of the order to charge the machine gun. Major Armstrong also testified that the accused's radio operator wouldn't get the accused back on the radio when he wanted to try again to get him to comply with the order.

"The accused's own platoon sergeant, Sergeant First Class Tabler, testified that the accused's platoon was undisciplined, that Major Armstrong was unpopular and the accused was very popular, that the enlisted men had put a price on Major Armstrong's head, which the accused had done nothing to discourage, that the accused's RTO, Darnell, would give misleading reports, and that Darnell wouldn't get the accused back on the radio when Major Armstrong wanted to try again to get him to charge the machine gun. Finally, Major Armstrong's RTO, Tyrone Henderson, heard the accused's disobedience and his RTO's refusal to get him back on the phone. All of this evidence, taken together, establishes that at least the accused and his RTO, if not other members of the platoon, had the intent to, and acted together to, usurp the com-mander's lawful authority. The evidence and all permissible inferences establish every element of the offense of mutiny. Thus, the government respectfully prays that you deny the defense motion."

Lieutenant Colonel David rose for his turn. "Your Honor, first of all, Major Armstrong testified that when he accompanied the platoon, he had no problems with Major Thomas, that he had quit this alleged passive resistance, if in fact it had even existed, before the machine gun opened up, and that, even though Major Thomas disagreed with the tactical decision to split up his platoon into multiple outposts, he had complied with the order. In fact, your Honor, assuming that then-Lieutenant Thomas disobeyed the order, doesn't the evidence show that his alleged disobedience was because he had no way to comply with the order with his platoon scattered all around the perimeter except where the contact was taking place, with no radio communication with the listening posts? If this incident was really a mutiny, would the commander have recommended approval of a Silver Star? The defense would point out that after this alleged mutiny, the accused made no attempt to take over from Major Armstrong. Quite the contrary, he and his troops followed orders well enough for him to be awarded the Silver Star for an action that took place on the very next day.

"The defense would also point out that, although Mr. Tabler felt the platoon was undisciplined, as if this somehow makes them mutinous, he testified that their weapons were clean, that they took their malaria pills, and that they maintained noise and light discipline at night, better indications of combat discipline than haircuts or cleanliness. And he said there was a price on Major Armstrong's head. He never said that anyone in the first platoon put the price on the commander's head. He said that the commander's unpopularity with the enlisted men was manifested by the fact that 'they' put a price on his head. He never said who 'they' were. What enlisted men are we talking about? It could have been the second platoon or even the company's rear contingent for all we know.

"As to this alleged failure by the RTO to put Lieutenant Thomas on the radio, Mr. Tabler admitted that, in the middle of a firefight, the lieutenant could have been too busy to come to the radio. So for all we know, the RTO could have been telling the truth. Who else could have acted in concert with Thomas when he disobeyed the order? Mr. Tabler stated that, of the first platoon, only he, his RTO, and the accused's RTO even knew of the order. Finally, Mr. Tabler, the accused's own platoon sergeant, testified that he didn't think the platoon was mutinying at any time. And he certainly did not have the intent to mutiny. Mr. Henderson's testimony doesn't help the prosecution at all. He even testified that Captain Armstrong was hiding under a tree during the entire firefight.

"Your Honor, the government even misstated the standard you are to apply when ruling on this motion. *United States v. Tobin,* 17 USCMA 625, 38 CMR 423, a 1968 Court of Military Appeals case, established the standard to use for ruling on motions for a finding of not guilty. If there is any substantial evidence before the court that, together with all justifiable inferences to be drawn therefrom, reasonably tends to establish every essential element of this offense, the motion should not be granted. But here we don't have any substantial evidence, and the inferences the trial counsel would have you draw are anything but justifiable."

Paul paused and looked down at his notes, before continuing, "At best, your Honor, the government's evidence shows that the accused may have disobeyed an order because he thought the tactical situation required another course of action and because of the difficulty of rounding up his spread-out platoon, without radio communications, in the middle of a firefight. The defense respectfully submits that your Honor should grant the defense motion."

"If counsel have nothing further, we will be in recess," Judge Savage intoned and swept out of the courtroom before the bailiff, who had nearly fallen asleep during the legal argument, could rouse himself.

After the judge had gone into his chambers, Major Thomas and the defense team gathered up their papers and left the courtroom. Trial counsel just sat there. "How's he going to rule, Ken?" Pam asked.

"I don't know," he replied as the two finally got up to leave the courtroom. "I just don't know."

CHAPTER 3 5

Military Judge's Chambers
Office of the Staff Judge Advocate
Building 244, Fort Leavenworth, Kansas

J U N E   1 9 8 6

Judge Savage sat down at his desk. Well, I won't have to time myself or work a crossword puzzle to take an appropriate length of time to decide this motion, he thought. This motion is a tough one. He picked out the law books from his shelves and began reading the cases the attorneys had cited during their arguments. But he found it difficult to concentrate on the cases. This ruling would be easier, he thought, if my granting the defense motion wouldn't effectively terminate the government's case. No judge lightly took a case away from the jury by granting a motion for a finding of not guilty. But I don't think I can let that influence my decision, he said to himself. I'm going to have to put that out of my mind and simply decide whether there is any evidence on each and every element of the charged mutiny. Then, if there isn't, I'll have to figure out whether I must deny the motion because there is an included offense, even though it is barred by the statute of limitations. Having figured out a methodology to solve the problem, the judge turned back to the law books.

In the wing of the building on the other side of the courtroom, Major Morgan and Captain Lewis sat in her office talking about the case.

"I don't see what more we could have done to prove a mutiny," Pam said. "I don't even believe there was one myself. Although I do believe the accused disobeyed his commander, I think Major Armstrong made this mutiny up to get around the statute of limitations."

"Yeah," Ken responded, "and I'm afraid it's my fault. I'm the one who told him there was no statute of limitations on mutiny. But I never thought he'd dream up a mutiny. I still thought the incident was a mutiny until Paul finished with his cross-examination of the government witnesses. They sure changed their tune from when we questioned them."

"What do we do now?"

"I think we should wait and see how the judge rules. If he grants the defense motion, we've got no problem. If he doesn't, then I think we have to seriously consider going to the convening authority and asking him to withdraw the mutiny charge. If we lose the disobedience on the statute of limitations, so be it."

"General Hawkins isn't going to like it," Pam thought out loud.

"I know. And I'd hate to lose this case. But I'd hate it more if I won it when the accused wasn't really guilty of mutiny. If General Hawkins doesn't like it, tough. We gave it our best shot."

Downstairs in the Trial Defense Service offices, Captain Wilson also had questions for the more experienced lawyer. "I still don't understand why you didn't move to dismiss the charges because of illegal command influence. Wasn't Colonel Zimmer's comment that you should think very hard about what you were doing in this case illegal command influence? I think I know you too well to believe it's because you are afraid of what Zimmer will do to your career."

"It was arguably command influence," Paul replied. "But I'm not going to move to dismiss for illegal command influence for several reasons. First, it's my word against Zimmer's, and Judge Savage isn't likely to rule for me against another full colonel.

"Second, if I move for dismissal, I'll have to disqualify myself from the case. You know as well as I do that I'd have to testify as to what Colonel Zimmer said to even have a prayer of winning such a motion. And once I became a witness, I could no longer participate as Jim's lawyer. I discussed it with Jim, and he said he'd rather have me on the case than make a motion that I think would be nothing more than a lot of sound and fury, signifying nothing.

"Third, under the recent command influence cases, we're not going to win a motion to dismiss unless we show prejudice. Remember the peyote platoon case? The case where a commander in Europe had a mass arrest in front of the whole division artillery unit, stripped all the suspects of their unit insignia, and put them all into a special 'peyote platoon.' The Army Court of Military Review found no prejudice and upheld the conviction, although they did cut the accused some slack on sentencing. That was a lot worse than what we have here. What's the harm here? I'm not going to defend Jim with less zeal. In fact, I want to win more than ever after Zimmer's idiotic remarks.

"Fourth, I'll have to rely on the provision in the Uniform Code that states that no one may lower the efficiency rating of a servicemember because of the zeal with which he defended a client.

"Finally, I don't think enough of Zimmer to worry about what he says. In fact, if I have to lose this case to get promoted, to hell with the promotion. Retiring at twenty years as a light colonel and going to practice law is fine with me. After twenty years, they'll pay me half my salary if I retire. I'd be working for the other half if I stayed in the Army."

A half hour later, the bailiff summoned the attorneys and the accused back to the courtroom. The judge was ready to announce his ruling. After the preliminaries, Judge Savage looked down at a legal tablet on which he had outlined his thoughts. He started speaking in a firm, measured voice.

"It is the ruling of this court that the government has presented no credible evidence that, even assuming that the accused intended to usurp Major Armstrong's authority, he acted in concert with anyone else. Thus, if there were no included offense, I would grant the motion for a finding of not guilty. However, there is an included offense, disobedience of a command. Yes, it is barred by the statute of limitations, but nevertheless, until the accused asserts the statute, the included offense is viable. I will, therefore, grant so much of the defense motion as requested that I instruct the court members that their consideration is limited to the included offense of disobedience of a command."

Lieutenant Colonel David turned to Major Thomas and his assistant defense counsel with a big grin. "We've won," he whispered. Captain Wilson smiled back. In their euphoria, they failed to notice the grim expression in their client's eyes.

"Major Thomas," Judge Savage continued, "the law requires that I advise you of your right to assert the statute of limitations. If you do, you cannot be convicted of or punished for the included offense of disobedience of a superior commissioned officer. Do you understand?"

"Yes, your Honor."

"And do you want to assert the statute of limitations?"

"No, your Honor."

The spectators gasped as one. During the recess, a legal clerk in the audience had explained to the other spectators the effect of the judge's ruling and of the importance of the statute of limitations.

Judge Savage was too shocked at the accused's answer to admonish the spectators. He frowned at the accused. "Do I understand you don't want to assert the statute of limitations—in other words, you want this trial to continue on the included offense of disobedience of Major Armstrong's order to charge the machine gun?"

"That's correct, your Honor."

Lieutenant Colonel David stood up. "May we have a recess so I may consult with my client, your Honor?"

"You most certainly can. We'll be in recess." Before the bailiff could even call out, "All rise," Judge Savage was almost out of the courtroom, shaking his head in disbelief as he disappeared into his chambers.

CHAPTER 36

Trial Defense Service Office
Office of the Staff Judge Advocate
Building 244, Fort Leavenworth, Kansas

JUNE 1986

Lieutenant Colonel David slammed the door. "Just what the hell do you think you are doing?" he yelled at Jim. "We had the case won! Have you lost your mind?" He paced up and down the tiny office as he ranted.

Jim sat there quietly, waiting for Paul's tirade to subside. Finally, he spoke—so softly that the two defense lawyers had to strain to hear. "I know what I'm doing. I know I can't be convicted if I use the statute of limitations. But I don't want to win on a technicality. I want to be vindicated."

"You want what?" Paul bellowed. "I think you want to be convicted. You must have some martyr complex! You didn't have any objection to my making the motion to dismiss because the convening authority was the accuser."

Captain Wilson expected Jim to get mad at this, but Jim continued to sit there calmly. Almost without emotion, Jim said, "I don't need to be analyzed. I'm the accused, and it is my decision whether to invoke the statute of limitations. And I'm not going to invoke it. And I didn't object to your making the motion to disqualify the convening authority because you told me the judge wouldn't grant it, and if he did, they'd just get another convening authority to refer the case to trial."

Paul sat down and stared at Jim, so Sam took over. "Paul's right, you know. Regardless of what you think, you can still be convicted of disobeying an order. This case can go either way. That the order was stupid isn't a defense. Just like it's not a defense that Armstrong is a jerk. Yes, we may get jury nullification—a yes-he-disobeyed-an-order-but-we'd-have-done-the-same-thing not guilty finding. But they are just as likely to convict you. And although we don't think the case was really referred capital, if we are wrong, you could be sentenced to death. At best, if you are convicted, you can still be sentenced to dismissal or confinement."

"I know all of that. Look, Vietnam cost me a lot of pain and time spent in the hospital. Not to mention the lives of some of my friends. All I have left is whatever remains of my career. And that's gone, too, if I'm always the officer who beat a mutiny or disobedience charge on a technicality. I don't want a tactical victory in court. I want a total, moral victory—not this half-assed victory. It's like Vietnam—we won the tactical victories and lost the war because, for whatever reasons, we bailed out. Well, I'm not bailing out. I want to tell the court what really happened and let them decide. If I lose the case, I don't have much left anyway."

Both attorneys tried for some time to change Jim's mind, but he was adamant. Finally, he lost a little his of almost unnatural calm. "Listen, stop hassling me! You just want to win this case so you can beat Morgan. Well, I don't care whether you beat him or not. I want to be vindicated."

Paul snarled, "Look, I'm not worried about competing with Morgan. I'm worried about you. If you are convicted, I can go home. Hell, losing would probably improve my chances for promotion. But you may go to jail. I can get over losing. Can you? I can always rationalize it by telling myself you wouldn't let me win anyway. Don't you realize this isn't about winning or losing anymore? Vietnam should have taught you that. This is about survival. Your survival."

All three officers just sat there thinking for a while. Jim finally got up and walked over to Paul. He took him by the shoulders, silver oak leaves and all, and said, "Ok, I'm a suicidal jerk, and you're right about everything you said. I'm sorry, but none of that matters because I'm your client, and this is my call. And you are too good an attorney to quit on me now. So let's just pretend there is no statute of limitations anyway and go win this thing."

Paul just stood there for an uncertain moment. Then, almost reluctantly, he smiled. "Ok, you're nuts, but so are Sam and I. What the hell. I didn't really want to win this case the easy way anyhow. If you want to go down in flames, I'll make certain the prosecution has to work hard. Sam, you go tell the bailiff we are ready whenever the judge is. Jim, let's go over your testimony one more time."

Upstairs, in the prosecution offices, Ken Morgan and Pam Lewis sat stunned by the unexpected developments. "Well, at least we don't have to worry about asking General Hawkins to drop the mutiny charge," Pam said with a forced laugh.

"Some consolation," Ken replied without joining in the laughter.

"What are we going to do if he continues to refuse to invoke the statute of limitations?"

"If we continue with the disobedience charge, we'll have to ask the judge to make certain he waives it both as to findings and to sentence. I can't see continuing just to get a conviction and then have him assert it to prevent us from sentencing him. But I'm still tempted to ask the convening authority to let us withdraw the included offense. What do we really have to gain now?"

Pam had no answer, so Ken got up and walked to the door. "I'm going to go talk to Colonel Farmer and see what he thinks about having the convening authority withdraw the charge."

Twenty minutes later, Ken returned. "That was a total waste of time," he began. "General Hawkins, quite predictably, didn't want to hear anything about quitting this important prosecution. I think he was about ready to court-martial me for losing the mutiny. So as long as the accused is dumb enough to want to continue, we'll be hanging in there."

As he gathered up the case file, he tried to think of a good reason for continuing with the case. If there is a reason, he thought, it must be an obscure one. When I was a CGSC student, my low-intensity combat instructors called the Vietnam war ambiguous combat because you didn't know who the enemy was. I think this case is rapidly becoming ambiguous combat, too.

PART V

THE VERDICT

Regard your soldiers as your children and they will follow you into the deepest valleys: look on them as your beloved sons, and they will stand by you even unto death.

—Sun Tzu, *The Art of War*

CHAPTER 37

Courtroom
Office of the Staff Judge Advocate
Building 244, Fort Leavenworth, Kansas

JUNE 1986

"Court will come to order," Judge Savage said wearily, sinking into his large, throne-like chair.

"All parties to the trial who were present when the court recessed are again present," Major Morgan announced. "The court members are absent."

"You asked for a recess, Colonel David," the judge began. "Are you ready to proceed?"

"Yes, your Honor. I have conferred with my client and ascertained that he knows what he is doing and wants to continue with the trial rather than invoke the statute of limitations."

"Is that correct, Major Thomas?"

"Yes, your Honor."

"Your Honor, may I interrupt?" Major Morgan asked deferentially.

"I suppose," the judge growled.

"Your Honor, the government requests that you make certain this refusal to invoke the statute of limitations is permanent. The government sees no reason to finish this case, get a conviction, and then have the accused assert the statute of limitations to prevent any punishment."

"That sounds reasonable. Defense?"

"Your Honor, against the advice of counsel, Major Thomas agrees to totally waive his right to invoke the statute of limitations. He understands that by refusing to invoke it now he cannot later invoke it in the event he is convicted."

"Do you agree, Major Thomas?"

"Yes, your Honor."

"Do you understand that if you waive the statute of limitations, you not only may be convicted of disobeying a lawful command, but also may be punished by the death penalty or confinement for life and a dismissal and total forfeitures of all pay and allowances?"

"Yes, I do, your Honor."

"Are you making this decision of your own free will?"

"Yes, your Honor."

"Did anyone force you to make this decision or promise you any benefit if you waived the statute of limitations?"

"No, your Honor."

Judge Savage thought for a moment and then asked, "Are you certain your client is competent to make such a decision, Colonel David? You must admit it's a little strange to waive a perfectly good defense to a charge carrying the death penalty."

"There is no doubt my client is competent, your Honor. He is knowingly and intelligently making this decision."

"Very well. I find the accused made a knowing and voluntary waiver of his right to assert the statute of limitations to the offense of disobedience of a command both for findings and sentence. Are you satisfied, Major Morgan?"

"Yes, your Honor."

"Is there anything else to take up before we get the court members in here?"

"No, your Honor," both lead attorneys chorused.

Lieutenant Colonel David added, "The defense is ready to proceed with the defense case."

"Get the court members," Judge Savage ordered.

After the members had filed in and the trial counsel had accounted for their presence for the record, Judge Savage turned towards the jury box and instructed the court members. "Mr. President, Members of the Court, I have granted a defense motion for a partial finding of not guilty. Consequently, you may not convict the accused of mutiny. Your consideration in this case is now limited to the lesser included offense of disobedience of a lawful command. I will advise you of the elements of that offense at the appropriate time. Finally, you are not to take my granting a finding of not guilty as to the mutiny charge as any indication on my part whether the accused is guilty of the lesser included offense. You must determine that for yourselves after hearing all of the evidence in the case and receiving my instructions. Are there any questions?

The court members looked somewhat taken aback, but were unwilling to risk Judge Savage's displeasure by asking any questions. They adopted a wait-and-see attitude, hoping that if they waited and listened, they would find out what had happened.

"Defense?"

"Thank you, your Honor. The defense calls Major Thomas."

Calling the accused first was the result of two tactical decisions. First, whether the accused should testify at all. Although military law certainly requires that the court members not hold an accused's failure to testify against him, as a practical matter, when the accused is an officer, he'd damn well better take the oath, look them in the eye, and tell them he wasn't guilty—law books and judge's instructions notwithstanding. The more difficult decision for the defense was when to have him testify. Paul usually put strong witnesses on last, after laying the groundwork for their testimony with the other defense evidence. And he had certainly thought that Jim would be a good witness, at least until Jim's not so lucid decision to forego the statute of limitations defense. So Paul decided to call Jim first so that if he didn't do well, the last thing the court members would hear would be strong witnesses supporting Jim rather than Jim decomposing under the prosecution's cross-examination.

Even though the accused was a defense witness, the trial counsel swears all witnesses in a court-martial. Thus, Major Morgan swore in the accused and then asked the standard questions for the record.

"State your name, rank, Social Security number, organization, and armed force."

"James Thomas, Major, 312-64-3109, Student Detachment, CGSC, U.S. Army."

"And are you the accused in this case?"

"Yes, Sir." Unlike Major Armstrong, Jim called the opposing counsel "Sir," even though they both held the same rank.

"Your witness." As he had earlier in the trial, so that jurors would think the defense counsel represented the accused as a result of his generosity, Ken turned over the accused to the defense as if the accused were testifying as a result of Ken's personal efforts to ensure that the court members heard everything there was to hear about the case.

"Thank you, Major Morgan." Even though Paul knew what Ken was doing, he wasn't going to fall into the trap of appearing to resent the trial counsel's assistance.

"Major Thomas, how did you get your commission?"

"I was a Distinguished Military Graduate from ROTC, so I got a Regular Army commission after graduation from the University of Cincinnati."

"What assignment did you have before going to Vietnam?"

"I graduated from Infantry Officer Basic Course, Airborne School, and Jungle Warfare School. Then, I served in the 4/31st Infantry at Fort Sill for six months before getting orders to Vietnam."

"What unit were you assigned to in Vietnam?"

"Company A, 1/7th Cavalry, First Cavalry Division."

"When did you join Company A?"

"Late May of 1970."

"Where was the company when you joined it?"

"Off LZ Stone near the Song Be River north of Saigon."

"And who was the commander?"

"Captain Hart."

"What kind of commander was he?"

"He was an excellent commander. He seemed almost psychic. He always anticipated what the enemy was going to do and took the right countermeasures. In my first ten days in the field, we were in contact every day—four times with a reinforced NVA company. And we didn't take a single casualty bad enough to need a medevac. One day, they got so close we found an NVA senior captain, a lieutenant, a medic, and a radio operator dead right outside one of our foxholes. They got that close, and we didn't take a single casualty because Captain Hart had us blow our claymores just before they started their assault."

"How was the unit's morale at this time?"

"It was great. We were kicking Charlie's tail and not suffering any significant casualties. Everyone really thought Captain Hart had his . . . was doing a great job." Major Thomas stole a look at Judge Savage, but the judge didn't react to the cut-off "shit together." However, an accused testifying in his own defense in a court-martial carrying such a severe sentence would have to actually use a lot worse language than that before Judge Savage would risk prejudicing his case by chewing him out.

"How long did you serve under Captain Hart?"

"Unfortunately, when the higher ups got word about how well Alpha Company was doing, they decided Captain Hart should be pulled up to a job planning operations, so they yanked him out and made him the battalion S-3."

"How did this transfer affect the company?"

"We were all sorry to see Captain Hart go, although we were glad for him. He was much safer in a rear job. The enlisted men were particularly crushed that we'd lost such a good—and lucky—commander."

"Who replaced Captain Hart?"

"Captain Mark Armstrong."

"Describe the first meeting you had with him."

"I met him about a day before we left the firebase to go back to the bush. We talked for a few moments. Then, he mentioned that he needed his patches sewn on some jungle fatigues. I told him we normally didn't wear our rank out in the bush. The troops all knew who we were. Why advertise that we were leaders to enemy snipers? But he insisted he had to wear a proper uniform. So I offered to have his patches sewn on for him. When I got them back from the Vietnamese tailor, he just threw them down on the ground and said, 'I can't wear these. They've got "gook" sewing on them.' I wanted to point out that we didn't have any French seamstresses on the firebase or within fifty clicks, for all I knew, but I kept my mouth shut."

"Objection, your Honor," Major Morgan interrupted. "This line of questioning is totally irrelevant. Major Armstrong isn't on trial here."

Wanna bet, Paul thought before responding. "Your Honor, you permitted the trial counsel to bring out a lot of uncharged misconduct on the part of Major Thomas. This testimony both impeaches Major Armstrong and is necessary to show the circumstances leading to this alleged disobedience. Finally, we would offer it to show bias on the part of Major Armstrong under Military Rule of Evidence 608."

Major Morgan countered, "Your Honor, even assuming the evidence has some relevance, under Military Rule of Evidence 403, you should exclude the evidence because its probative value is outweighed by the danger of unfair prejudice, confusion, and waste of time."

Judge Savage overruled the prosecution objection, without giving any reason. Major Morgan grimaced, but sat down.

"Now, Major Thomas," Lieutenant Colonel David continued, "how did things go when you left the firebase with your new commander?"

"Not well, Sir. Captain Armstrong had some theory that the reason we were in so much contact was that we weren't moving far enough or fast enough. So we would hump ten to fifteen clicks a day and stop so late we didn't have time to set up a good NDP. Or we would have to set up a night ambush. He also changed the formation so that the three rifle platoons were cutting their way through the jungle in parallel files. This tripled the work load."

"What do you mean by NDP?"

"Night defensive perimeter."

"And what, if anything, was the problem with moving ten to fifteen kilometers and setting up late?"

"Well, ten to fifteen kilometers may not sound like much, but when you are carrying 75 to 100 pounds—including four to six canteens of water, and hacking your way through thick jungle in 100 degree heat and high humidity, it's a killer. And Captain—Major—Armstrong wouldn't let us stop for a break very often. Every time I'd call him on the radio and ask for a break, he'd reply, 'Drive on.' One day, we had ten men evacuated for heat exhaustion. By the time we stopped at the end of the day, it was too dark to set out our claymores properly or dig good fox-holes. Sometimes, we were on night ambush for three or four days in a row."

Paul kept looking at the court members out of the corner of his eye during this testimony. He noted with satisfaction that several of them were nodding in apparent agreement at the recitation of humping 75 to 100 pounds through the bush in 100 degree heat and high humidity—something no one who had done it ever forgot.

"How did the night ambushes and long humps affect the troops?"

"Morale really went down. The troops were really tired. We were already understrength but kept losing more men to heat injuries. And the commander's plan for making contact on our terms and not the enemy's seemed to backfire. Unlike our contacts under Captain Hart's command, we were making a lot of light contact and suffering casualties with nothing to show for it. We were used to kicking butt, and getting ours kicked instead increased the frustration level."

"We heard testimony about a price on the commander's head. What, if anything, did you know about it?"

"I heard some troops talking about it, but I didn't worry about it too much. They were just blowing off steam."

"Did anyone ever actually try to kill the commander?"

"No, Sir."

"Major Armstrong testified that one day he sent you ten kilometers to the north to check on a report of an NVA unit and you only went two kilometers before quitting. What happened?"

"He sent us out at about 1630. We humped for a couple of hours and came to a marshy area just as it was starting to get dark. We were unable to find a way through the marshy area, and I called it quits when one of my men almost drowned. We were out of radio range, so we could not have contacted anyone if we had found NVA. We couldn't have requested artillery support or medevac. The next day, I had to order my RTO to climb a tree with a long whip antenna before we could raise anyone. We finally contacted a helicopter that had been sent up to look for us. Battalion thought we had been wiped out. Anyway, when it got dark, I just had the men set up a perimeter. The next day, I asked 6—Captain Armstrong—if he wanted me to continue trying to move to the north. He said it was too late."

"Was it unusual to be out of radio control?"

"We had a lot of trouble with our radios. It was hard to get resupplied with batteries, so when they wore out, commo was poor." Major Thomas spoke bitterly, "We couldn't get resupplied batteries, but when we went back to the rear, the rear echelon types had them connected up in parallel to run their stereos and refrigerators."

Paul moved right up to the witness chair as if to dramatize the testimony to come. "Now, let me draw your attention to the day you received this order to charge the machine gun. Tell the court members what happened."

"Yes, Sir." Major Thomas shifted in the witness chair so that he was looking directly at the court members. They appeared to be waiting expectantly for his version of the firefight. "Earlier in the day, Captain Armstrong had called all the platoon leaders together and told us we were going to be extracted. We were going to move about a kilometer to the north where there was a clearing big enough for the helicopters to pick us up. I was PZ control. I don't know whether it was my turn or whether Six was just sticking it to me. Being PZ control meant my platoon would be the last one out—responsible for security of the pickup zone. It made you nervous to be the last few troops left on the ground especially when you had had a firefight there recently. Anyway, when we got to the PZ, Six—Captain Armstrong—told me to put my platoon all around the perimeter of the PZ in two-man outposts. He told 2-6 to put out two teams in front of his sector because my platoon was down to twelve men. I told him that wasn't a good idea because I wouldn't have any control over my men if they were spread out that thin. Normally, each platoon put out listening posts in front of its section of the perimeter. He said to do it anyway, so I did. I told my platoon sergeant to take one radio and go to the west side of the perimeter, and I went to the east, close to the two outposts from the second platoon. That way I'd at least have our two radios near as many of the outposts as possible, and I wanted to be near the second platoon leader."

"Why did you want to be near the second platoon leader?"

"Lieutenant Olgin, the previous second platoon leader, had gotten a rear job a few days earlier, and the new platoon leader was a staff sergeant. He had asked me to help him until he got his feet on the ground."

"Please continue."

"We had a long wait for the choppers. Suddenly, a machine gun opened up on one of the second platoon's outposts. Initially, we all just hit the ground. We couldn't fire back because the outpost was between us and the enemy. 2-6—Sergeant Dimitroff—got on the radio and requested tube artillery and gunships. I decided I couldn't just stay there and do nothing, so a couple of the enlisted men from the second platoon and I went out to see whether we could help the men on the outpost."

"Were you still taking fire at this time?"

"Yes, Sir."

"So you exposed yourself to enemy fire to go out to the outpost?"

"Yes, Sir. But when we got out there, we discovered the two men on the outpost were dead. We left them there for the time being and returned to the perimeter so we could tell 2-6 his platoon could fire out without worrying about hitting the guys on the LP. By this time, Dimitroff had artillery coming in, so he started adjusting it closer to the machine gun's location now that he didn't have to worry about hitting the LP."

"Did you receive a call on the radio from the commander?"

"Yes, at about this time, he called and ordered me to get my platoon on line and assault the machine gun."

"What did you do?"

"First, I asked him to repeat the order. I couldn't believe he was serious. I thought he understood that I didn't have any control over my platoon because they were spread out all around the perimeter, everywhere but the sector where the firefight was going on. He repeated it, but I still couldn't believe it, so I said something about not understanding. He said that I understood him and that I should move out. I tried to explain that my platoon was all spread out and I couldn't assemble them. He didn't want to hear it and repeated the order. I said, 'Negative,' and got back to assisting the second platoon leader adjust the artillery and keep his troops firing suppressive fires."

"Why did you tell him, 'Negative?'"

"I had no way of complying with the order. I had no idea where my outposts were, and it would have taken a lot of time to get them together. Once we started firing suppressive fires, the enemy machine gunfire wasn't accurate, and as long as we stayed down, we weren't taking any more casualties. If I had been able to round my platoon up, I would have taken a lot of casualties for nothing. The cobras arrived about that time, and between them and the tube artillery, the machine gun stopped firing."

"Did you ever round your platoon up?"

"Yes, after the machine gun quit firing, I started rounding my platoon up. Eventually, we made a sweep out to see whether we could find any dead VC and to recover the friendly KIAs."

"How long did it take to round up your platoon?"

"Sir, it's hard to estimate time during and right after a firefight. Minutes can seem like hours and vice versa. To the best of my knowledge, it was twenty to thirty minutes before I found them all and got them back together."

"And how long did the firefight last?"

"Again, it's hard to say for sure, but certainly less than fifteen minutes. We were close enough to Quan Loi that it didn't take the cobras long to get on station."

"Tell the Court what happened after the firefight ended."

"Shortly after it ended, the helicopters came to extract us. We had carried the two bodies close to the clearing so that we could get them onto the helicopters. Captain Armstrong walked up, looked at the bodies, and said, 'Well, it's a hardship tour.' I had to restrain one of the second platoon members from assaulting him. Then the helicopters arrived, and we made a combat assault into the new AO—area of operations—without incident. After we got our NDP set up, the other platoon leaders came over to talk about the firefight. We all agreed that our mistake was having the two-man observation posts out in front of our perimeter with no communication so that we could not fire to our front without hitting them and having them so undermanned that one burst from a weapon could wipe out the whole OP. The commander's RTO joined us and told us that Captain Armstrong had distinguished himself by hiding under a fallen tree during the entire firefight and telling his RTO to get more men to protect the company command post. Of course, . . ."

"Objection, your Honor," Major Morgan interrupted. "Hearsay."

"Your Honor," Lieutenant Colonel David replied, "the defense withdraws the question. We have the RTO present to testify."

"The court will disregard that portion of Major Thomas's testimony concerning what the RTO said," Judge Savage instructed.

"What happened then?"

"Captain Armstrong called all the platoon leaders together for a critique. He announced that the reason we had not annihilated the attacking force was that I had not been ready to react with my platoon and had disobeyed his order. He said I was a coward and he would deal with me later. I tried to point out to him that there was no way I could get my men together because he had ordered me to put them in two-man outposts. He said he had not told me to do that—that, if I had even gotten such an order, it must have come from the first sergeant.

"Later that day, I asked him whether I could put the enlisted men who had gone out under fire to try to get the wounded in for Bronze Stars. He said we had to determine appropriate criteria for awards and we couldn't give them out for nothing. Because he hadn't seen the action, he couldn't recommend approval of the awards, he said."

Ken, with a weary look on his face, rose to object. "Your Honor, I fail to see the relevance of whether the commander put troops in for awards or not."

Judge Savage frowned at the defense counsel and spoke in a gruff tone, "So do I, Major Morgan. Move on to something relevant, Colonel David."

"Yes, your Honor. What happened the next day?"

"The next day, we got into another firefight, and I was wounded and medevaced."

"No further questions." Lieutenant Colonel David looked over at Major Morgan and said, "Your witness."

Major Morgan had already decided he was going to treat the accused respectfully to avoid alienating the court members, in case they sympathized with the witness. "Major Thomas," he began, "am I correct that you were disappointed when Captain Armstrong replaced Captain Hart?"

"Yes, Sir."

"You weren't very happy about Captain Armstrong's assumption of command, were you?"

"I wasn't happy about losing Captain Hart, but I was neutral about Captain Armstrong at first."

"Later on, you did develop some strong negative feelings about him, didn't you?"

"Yes, Sir."

"How would you describe the troops' attitude toward him?"

"They hated him."

"And according to your testimony, they were very tired and frustrated from humping so far with little sleep?"

"Yes, Sir."

"Now, let me get this straight, Major Thomas, even though the troops were tired and frustrated from all this humping and lack of sleep, and even though they were frustrated by making contact and suffering casualties without hurting the enemy, and even though they hated the commander, you didn't do anything about these threats to frag him because you felt the troops were just blowing off steam?"

"That's correct."

"And isn't it correct that you had a number of techniques you used to frustrate other orders before you disobeyed the order to charge the machine gun?" Ken had worded the question so that if the accused answered it, he admitted that he disobeyed the order. Major Thomas, however, didn't fall into the trap. Paul had prepared him well.

"I don't understand the question, Sir."

Ken smiled to let the witness know he appreciated his astute recognition of the trap. "Let me be more specific. Isn't it true you developed a code with the members of your platoon for breaks? When someone in your platoon called you on the radio and asked to take a break, didn't you say, 'Drive on!' if you approved the request?"

"Yes, Sir." Even though he wanted to add an explanation, Jim followed Paul's direction to just answer, "Yes" or "No," without explaining, even if it made him look bad, because adding qualifiers and explanations would make him look deceptive. He repeated Jim's phrase, "the shortest truthful answer," to himself between questions to help him avoid unnecessary running off at the mouth.

"And this response was to mislead Captain Armstrong into thinking you were continuing to march, when you really had stopped for a rest, wasn't it?"

"Yes, Sir."

"And sometimes you would switch radio frequencies so you could talk to other platoon leaders without Captain Armstrong hearing?"

"Yes, Sir."

"So before this firefight at the pickup zone, you had been deceiving Captain Armstrong and frustrating his wishes?"

"I suppose, Sir."

"Yes or no, Major."

Major Thomas hesitated for only a moment and then looked Major Morgan in the eyes. "Yes, Sir."

"During the firefight at the pickup zone, you heard Captain Armstrong give you the order to charge the machine gun?"

"Yes, Sir."

"And you knew it was Captain Armstrong?"

"Yes, Sir."

"And he was your superior commissioned officer and commander at that time?"

"Yes, Sir."

"Did you think that the order was illegal?"

"No, Sir."

"Would it be correct to say then that you received a lawful command from a superior commissioned officer?"

"Yes, Sir."

"And did you get your platoon on line and charge the machine gun?"

"No, Sir."

"In fact, didn't you refuse, over the radio, to obey the order?"

"Yes, Sir."

"Did you ever attempt to comply with the order?"

"No, Sir."

"Let me see if I have this straight—you received a lawful command from a superior commissioned officer and not only did not comply or even attempt to comply, but also actually disobeyed by telling Major Armstrong that you wouldn't obey it. Is that correct?"

"Objection, your Honor." Lieutenant Colonel David interjected before the witness could answer. "The question goes to the ultimate issue." Because it was the court members' job to determine whether the accused was guilty, witnesses were not permitted to answer questions that were too close to the ultimate issue—guilt or innocence.

"Withdraw the question, your Honor." Major Morgan couldn't have cared less what the accused answered or even whether he answered. He just wanted the court members to think about the question and the obvious, but unstated, answer. "No further questions, your Honor."

"Redirect?" the judge inquired.

"Why did you develop this technique of saying 'drive on' when you wanted to take a break?" Lieutenant Colonel David rose and walked over close to the jury box to question his witness.

"Because Captain Armstrong would never grant a request to take a break, and if he overheard me say to take a break on the radio, he would punish me for it by putting my platoon on night ambush. And we already had too many soldiers medevaced for heat injuries. My platoon was down to less than half its authorized strength, and I felt we had to take some breaks in the heat and humidity if we were going to remain combat effective. One time, we were on night ambush for six straight nights while members of the other platoons got to sleep, except when they were on guard duty. With the heat, my platoon couldn't continue without an occasional break, so we developed this code, 'drive on,' to get a short break without being punished for wanting to rest."

"Now, one more time, could you have obeyed the order to get your platoon on line and charge the machine gun?"

"I don't see how, Sir."

Lieutenant Colonel David looked down at the yellow legal pad he had written his redirect notes on. Even though he had other areas he could have explored further, he decided the risk-reward ratio would become unfavorable if he continued. "No further questions."

Major Morgan stood up. "I have only a few questions on recross, your Honor. Major Thomas, did you ever try to obey the order?"

"No, Sir, I couldn't obey it."

"But you didn't even try?"

"No, Sir."

"And isn't it a fact that you said, 'Negative,' thereby refusing to obey the order, before you even checked with your platoon sergeant to see whether he could round up any of the men in your platoon?"

"Yes, Sir."

"No further questions, your Honor."

Judge Savage looked up from his notes. "Questions by any Members of the Court?"

Major Brantley raised his hand. Ken walked over and took the paper upon which the question was written from the court member, had the court reporter mark it as an appellate exhibit, showed it to Lieutenant Colonel David, and then handed it to the judge. "The government has no objection, your Honor."

"Neither does the defense," Lieutenant Colonel David said.

Judge Savage read the question aloud, "Major Thomas, how big was the open area where the helicopters were to land?"

"It was pretty big. Two helicopters could easily get in at the same time. Almost as big as a football field."

"Was the company right at the edge of the field?"

"No, your Honor. We were into the treeline a ways. Maybe twenty meters into the foliage."

"How much further in were the outposts?"

"They were fifty to seventy meters outside the perimeter."

"Does that answer your question, Major Brantley?"

"Yes, your Honor."

"Any questions engendered by the court's question?"

"No, your Honor," both counsel replied.

"Thank you for testifying, Major Thomas," the military judge excused the witness. "You may return to your seat."

"Your Honor, the defense calls Mr. Tyrone Henderson," Lieutenant Colonel David announced.

Mr. Henderson came into the courtroom again. He had an irritated look on his face. He was less than thrilled at having to remain at Fort Leavenworth after having testified the first time, even though the government was paying his expenses and a daily allowance.

"Are you the same Mr. Tyrone Henderson who previously testified in this case?" Major Morgan asked.

"Yes, Sir."

"You are reminded that you are still under oath. Your witness, Lieutenant Colonel David."

"Thank you. Mr. Henderson, I believe you testified that you were Captain Armstrong's RTO?"

"That's right."

"And you testified that, during the firefight, Captain Armstrong was hiding under a tree?"

"Yes, Sir."

"And we heard you testify that he 'snatched' the headset and told 1-6 to charge the machine gun. Did he give you any orders?"

"Yeah, he tol' me to get some men to protect da command post."

"And did you?"

"No."

"Why not?"

"I could see there was nothin' to protect it from, Sir. The rounds weren't hittin' anywhere near us. Stead, I called battalion to report da contact."

"Had Captain Armstrong ever reported to battalion or asked for support?"

"No, Sir. He jus' yelled for 1-6 to charge da machine gun and for us to get round da command post to protect him."

"No further questions."

As Lieutenant Colonel David sat down, Major Morgan conferred briefly with Major Lewis and then shook his head when Judge Savage asked whether he had any cross-examination.

"The defense calls Mr. Richard Rivera."

Richard Rivera, who had been Specialist Fourth Class Rivera—an eleven bravo, light weapons infantryman—entered the courtroom. He had been Lieutenant Thomas's acting platoon sergeant before Big Soul's arrival and a squad leader afterwards. Even when he had been a grunt, somehow everyone could tell he had come from California. His laid-back California look had not changed although, when he was in the Army, he had not had the long hair and full beard he now sported. Jim could tell by looking at him that he was more content now as a professor of economics at UCLA than he had been as an infantryman. He had been a good one though, Jim thought, as he remembered how Rivera had squared him away when he was a cherry.

Rivera responded to the defense questions by detailing how he had come to Alpha, First of the Seventh Cavalry, how he had worked for

Lieutenant Thomas, and how Armstrong had taken unnecessary casualties as commander because he wouldn't listen to anyone.

"Now, Mr. Rivera," Paul continued, "where were you during the firefight on the PZ when a couple of the second platoon members got killed by the VC machine gun—the day before 1-6 got medevaced?"

"I was on the next outpost to the left of the one that got hit." The witness had not used "Sir" very frequently when he was a nineteen-year-old draftee. He was damn sure not going to call any officer "Sir" now that he was a full professor at UCLA and, in his mind, the equivalent of any general he had ever heard of. He might force himself to call a big contributor to the university "Sir," but that was about it.

"How did you come to be there?"

"The CO had told 1-6 to put us out in two-man outposts all around the perimeter. 1-6 and I both thought it was stupid, but 6 insisted, so we did it."

"Were you aware that Captain Armstrong had ordered 1-6 to get his platoon on line and charge the machine gun?"

"Yes."

"How did you learn of it?"

"I overheard Armstrong chew him out after the firefight."

"Did you know of it at the time?"

"No."

"Why not?"

"Well, my OP didn't have a radio. The machine gun fire was too intense for 1-6 to go running around trying to round us up. I doubt that 1-6 even knew exactly where we were because all of us were in front of different platoon sectors."

"Could you have heard him if he had yelled?"

"Not from where he was. Not with all the noise of the VC machine gun—it sounded like a .30 caliber—and incoming artillery."

"Assuming that Lieutenant Thomas disobeyed the order, did he do so out of fear?"

"No way. He had been out under fire trying to pull back the casualties."

"How did you know that?"

"I saw him go off to my right."

"Was the machine gun firing then?"

"Yes."

"Thank you. No further questions."

Major Morgan sat there for a moment, then slowly rose to his feet. "Mr. Rivera. What was the highest rank you achieved while you were in Vietnam?"

"Specialist Fourth Class."

"The same pay grade as a corporal, but without the noncommissioned officer status, right?"

"Yeah, I guess."

"And what training had you had before coming to Vietnam?"

"Basic and AIT."

"Advanced Individual Training—that's where they teach you the basic skills of your military occupational specialty, isn't it?"

"Yes, Major." The witness made the word "Major" sound as if it should be followed by the word "nuisance." But he wanted to help, not hurt, his old platoon leader, so he reined in his irritation.

"Did they teach leadership or platoon or company level tactics in AIT?"

"No."

"Did you have any diplomas from any advanced military schools?"

"No."

"Do you know what military schooling Captain Armstrong had?"

"Not exactly."

"Would it surprise you to learn that he had been through the infantry officer's basic course and Ranger School at Fort Benning?"

"No. He was always trying to act like a ranger—a snake eater."

"Just answer the question without editorializing, please."

"Ok." Rivera was too laid back to be bothered by the admonition.

"So with only basic and AIT and with only the rank of a spec four, you're going to presume to say not only that a captain's tactical decisions were stupid, but also that the order was impossible to obey?"

"Yes."

"Now, you had a lot of respect for the accused, didn't you?"

"If by 'the accused,' you mean 1-6, yes."

"And you were quite close to him—closer perhaps than the norm for the Army?"

"I don't know what the 'norm' for the Army was. We were in a lot of deep shit together and worked together as a team." Although the defense lawyers had briefed him about Judge Savage's reaction to bad language in the courtroom, Richard Rivera wasn't worried about some old military judge now that he had been a civilian for years. "Lieutenant Thomas wasn't hung up on all that rank nonsense. He was almost one of the guys, but he didn't hesitate to jack us up when we needed it."

"Isn't it true that when you were back in the rear, he'd take his rank off and go to the enlisted club with you and some others in the platoon?"

"He didn't take his rank off because he never wore it in the bush. But yes, we did take him to the enlisted club."

"He became a friend of yours, didn't he?"

"Yes."

"And isn't it true that you talked to some of the men in the platoon about lying if Captain Armstrong tried to hassle 1-6? Didn't you say that everyone should swear that Captain Armstrong never gave the order?"

"Yes, I did."

"So you'd have lied for him then?"

"Yes. In a heartbeat, just like I'd have tried to rescue him if he were wounded and needed help."

"And if you'd have lied for him then, would you be willing to lie for him now?"

"I would, but I'm not."

"Just answer 'Yes' or 'No.' Would you lie for him?"

"Yes."

Lieutenant Colonel David rose to begin his redirect examination. "Mr. Rivera. Although you apparently have so much loyalty that you would be willing to lie for him, did you today?"

"No."

"Now, the trial counsel made a big deal of your lack of military schooling. You had some other qualifications, didn't you?"

"Yes."

"Even though you weren't an NCO, you had held down an E-7 slot as platoon sergeant for several months?"

"That's correct."

"And did you learn anything about platoon tactics during that time?"

"I'd be dead now, if I hadn't."

"And what, if any, awards did you get while you were with Alpha Company?"

"Five Bronze Stars with 'V' device for valor."

"And although you didn't get any diplomas, you earned a blue and silver badge consisting of a rifle surrounded by a wreath that you can't get in any classroom, didn't you?"

"Yes."

"And tell the court members what award that was." As if they didn't know.

"A Combat Infantry Badge."

"No further questions."

Not to be undone, Ken decided to recross. He had saved something to recross with in case Paul managed to rehabilitate his witness. It was risky, because if Paul hadn't asked any more questions, he wouldn't have been able to show the jury this evidence. But knowing how aggressive Paul was, it was a pretty good gamble. "Mr. Rivera, didn't you talk to my assistant, Captain Lewis, yesterday?"

"Yes."

"And didn't you tell her you didn't know whether the accused could have obeyed the order or not?"

"I may have—yes."

"But all of a sudden, you're sure he couldn't have obeyed it."

"Emphatically. He couldn't have obeyed it."

"But yesterday, you said you weren't sure he could have?"

"Yes."

Ken paused for a moment, then continued. "Which time were you lying?"

Both Lieutenant Colonel David and Captain Wilson jumped up. "Objection!"

"Withdraw the question, your Honor." Ken sat down, satisfied that this witness wasn't going to help the defense much.

Rivera smiled and flashed a "V" signal with his fingers as he passed by. Jim didn't know whether it meant victory or peace. Probably the latter.

Lieutenant Colonel David called three officers whom Major Thomas had worked for as witnesses for the defense. They testified as to his good military character and that they would believe him under oath. Major Morgan's cross-examination was perfunctory. He only cross-examined these witnesses at all so as not to give the court members the impression that the prosecution agreed with the testimony and to show that they didn't know what his character was like when he was a young lieutenant in Vietnam. Ken saw no point in reinforcing the good things the witnesses had to say about the accused by cross-examining them extensively. After the last defense witness had testified, the defense concluded its case.

"Your Honor, the defense rests."

Judge Savage nodded and then looked at Major Morgan. "Does the government have any rebuttal?"

"May we have a moment, your Honor?"

"Very well."

Ken turned to Pam and whispered, "We can call Lieutenant Colonel McCreary to rebut the accused's testimony. But he seems to have been as flakey a battalion commander as Armstrong was a company commander. I'm tempted to cut our losses. If the court members decide the whole leadership of the 1/7th was screwed up, we may get jury nullification. They'll decide he disobeyed the order, but not care and find him not guilty, anyway. I think we'd better skip the rebuttal." Pam nodded in agreement. Ken stood up. "Your Honor, the government has no rebuttal."

Judge Savage then looked at the court members. "Mr. President, Members of the Court, are there any witnesses you want called or recalled?"

Colonel Harrison looked up and down the jury box at the other members. When none of them signified they wanted a witness called or recalled, he said, "No, your Honor."

"Very well. Looking at the hour, I believe it would be appropriate to recess until tomorrow morning. The counsel and I have to go over the instructions on the law we will give you. Remember, do not discuss the case among yourselves or with anyone else. Court will be in recess."

"All rise," the bailiff ordered, as Judge Savage and the court members filed out, leaving the counsel, the accused, and the spectators sitting there thinking that this sixteen-year-old controversy would be resolved the next morning. Or would it?

CHAPTER 38

Courtroom
Office of the Staff Judge Advocate
Building 244, Fort Leavenworth, Kansas

J U N E   1 9 8 6

At 0700 the bailiff entered the courtroom to make sure everything was ready for the trial to continue. He placed a new yellow legal pad and two sharpened pencils for each court member in front of their chairs. Then, he put a pitcher filled with ice water and a glass on the little stand behind the judge's bench so the judge could wet his throat during the reading of the instructions to the jury.

As the bailiff scurried around lining up all the chairs in the courtroom, the first spectators started to file in. Even though the court would not come to order for a half hour or more, the spectators came early to be sure to get a seat for the lawyers' final arguments. Major Morgan's reputation guaranteed him an audience in any case, and the local interest in this case was running at a fever pitch. Surprisingly, the press coverage had been minimal—probably because Fort Leavenworth was hardly a hotbed of military news and because *The Leavenworth Times* never printed anything controversial. Leavenworth had a higher crime rate than Kansas City, but you'd never know it by reading the local paper. Apparently, the national news services were unaware of the story.

All the spectator seats were filled before the first participant in the courtroom drama entered. Right at 0900, Major Morgan and his assistant, Captain Lewis, entered. He smiled and nodded at the spectators as he pushed through the swinging door of the rail that divided the spectator section from the courtroom proper. His wife, Elizabeth, seemed to swell with pride at the stir his entrance caused. "Are the court members all here?" Ken asked the bailiff. They were. There was nothing left to do now until the court came to order. Ken looked relaxed and confident as he sat waiting.

Five minutes later, the defense team and the accused came in. Unlike Major Morgan, Lieutenant Colonel David looked tired. As was usual for him, he had gotten little sleep, and as usual, he had an upset stomach before the start of the climactic portion of the trial. He nodded at Ken, then sat down, and started looking at the outline he had made of his final argument. He had hardly begun, however, when everybody had to rise for Judge Savage's entrance, followed immediately by that of the court members.

After Major Morgan had accounted for all the parties, Judge Savage asked whether counsel were prepared to argue. They were.

Because the trial counsel had the burden of proof, Major Morgan got to argue both before and after the defense. Sometimes, he would waive the opening argument and only rebut the defense argument, but not in a case like this one. He was not about to pass up a chance to convince the court members. If he argued well enough, he might convince them so thoroughly that they would make up their minds to convict before even hearing the defense argument.

Ken walked up to the podium, carrying only a three-by-five card on which he had written a few notes. Without even looking at the card, he began his argument.

"Mr. President, Members of the Court, the government would like to thank you for your attention during this case. This case is really simple. There is very little dispute between the government and the defense as to what happened on the pickup zone during the firefight. Both Major Armstrong and the accused testified that Major Armstrong was the accused's superior commissioned officer, that he gave a lawful order to charge the machine gun, that the accused heard the order, that the accused said, 'Negative,' meaning he would not obey the order, and that the accused never attempted to obey the order.

"The only thing the prosecution evidence and the defense evidence disagree on is whether the accused could have obeyed the order. But even though the defense contends that the accused could not have obeyed the order, the accused never even tried to obey it. He just said, 'Negative.' Perhaps, you could find that he could not have obeyed the order if he had attempted to gather the members of this platoon together as the first step towards charging the machine gun. But he never did that. He never did anything but say, 'Negative.'

"And are you surprised that he refused? By his own testimony, he disliked Captain Armstrong and had frustrated his orders all along. The accused's earlier actions indicated that, no matter what the order was, he was going to disobey it. In fact, he was just waiting for a chance to flout Captain Armstrong's authority. We don't know for certain what his motive for doing so was, whether it was misguided loyalty to his troops—troops he was too close to—or simply that he disliked Captain Armstrong. But we do know that he didn't do anything to warn Captain Armstrong about the price on his head. Nor did he ever bother to try to put a stop to the troops' plot to kill Captain Armstrong. All these actions and derelictions on the accused's part indicate that he didn't disobey the order because he thought it was impossible to obey. Rather, he disobeyed it as part of a cold, calculated design to frustrate Captain Armstrong's lawful authority.

"Of course, although the government has the burden of proving each and every element of this offense beyond a reasonable doubt, the government is not required to prove the accused's motive for disobeying the order. And if the order was a lawful one, as the government contends it was, it does not matter what the motive for disobeying it was. Perhaps, the accused had a noble motive for disobeying the order. But do we really want to set a precedent for a case in which a soldier can legally disobey the order of a superior just because he has a noble motive for doing so? If the accused has some unselfish motive for committing this crime, then his reason for disobeying is a proper consideration in arriving at an appropriate sentence. But it is your duty to convict him if the government has proven his guilt beyond a reasonable doubt. And we have.

"And how can you have any doubt? Indeed, you have enough evidence just from the defense case to convict the accused. Although it may not be pleasant to convict the accused so many years after the Vietnam War, the alternative—setting a precedent that an officer may disobey the lawful order of his commander in combat—is far worse. Thus, the government asks you to do your duty and return a finding of guilty as to the charge and specification. Thank you."

"Defense," Judge Savage nodded at the defense table, signifying that they could begin their argument.

"Thank you, your Honor." Lieutenant Colonel David walked over to the podium, carrying the yellow legal pad on which he had outlined his argument. The bright overhead lights made his Combat Infantry Badge and jump wings shine as he drew a deep breath before beginning. "Mr. President, Members of the Court, the defense would like to thank you for your attention during this trial. Unfortunately, this case is nowhere near as simple as the trial counsel would have you believe. First, the defense does not agree with the prosecution that the order was lawful. The defense expects that the military judge will instruct you that an order is lawful if given for a valid military purpose. Now, although we admit that killing the enemy is a valid military purpose, we submit that, if Captain Armstrong's purpose for giving the order was nothing more than to get the credit for a body count, regardless of how many American lives it cost, it was not a valid military purpose. You've been in combat. Although some military objectives are worth taking many casualties for, this enemy contact was not one of them. The two members of the outpost were already dead. The machine gun could not depress enough to hit any other members of Alpha Company, and both tube and aerial rocket artillery were incoming and would eventually suppress the machine gun fire. How many lives would you have sacrificed to kill the handful of enemy troops manning that machine gun? Two more? Ten more? Twenty more? At some point, charging a machine gun becomes stupidity. Another Gallipoli. Another Charge of the Light Brigade. Another commander out for only his own glory at the expense of his men. No, the defense does not agree that the order was lawful."

Lieutenant Colonel David continued, growing more impassioned as he continued to argue. "The wrong officer is on trial here. Major Armstrong should be charged with dereliction of duty for having given such an order while hiding under a tree and without at least calling someone on the radio to find out what orders were necessary if he couldn't work up the courage to move to the area where his troops were in contact. He didn't call the ARA, the tube artillery, or the medevac. His RTO called his higher headquarters. All he could do, without making any attempt to find out the tactical situation, was 'snatch' the radio headphone and order 1-6 to charge the machine gun. Captain Medina said he didn't know what Lieutenant Calley was doing at My Lai 4. Captain Armstrong wouldn't have either. But Captain Armstrong was luckier than Captain Medina. He had a platoon leader who did the right things while his commander stuck his head in the sand. A platoon leader who took prompt, effective actions to suppress the machine gun without suffering any further casualties.

"The trial counsel is right about one thing. We do disagree on whether Major Thomas could have obeyed the order. How was he supposed to obey it? Was he supposed to abandon the second platoon leader, who, although inexperienced, was astute enough to ask 1-6 to help him? Notice that 2-6—Sergeant Dimitroff—didn't ask the commander, or one of the other platoon leaders for help. No, he asked 1-6. Was 1-6 supposed to go running around the perimeter gathering up his men to accomplish this idiotic mission? None of the LPs had radios. Who was going to adjust the artillery fire while he did this? If the attack was a feint, who was going to provide early warning with the outposts withdrawn if Major Thomas did manage to get them together? You've heard the size of the LZ. How, in the thick foliage—twenty-five to thirty meters into the jungle, outside a perimeter bigger than a football field, was 1-6 supposed to round up his troops during a firefight—a firefight that lasted less than fifteen minutes? And remember, 1-6—against his objection—had no platoon integrity. Major Thomas was unable to comply with the order. And remember, he tried to explain his inability to comply to Captain Armstrong, who wouldn't listen.

"The trial counsel made a big deal about the fact that the accused not only said that he wasn't obeying the order, but also never tried to comply with it. But neither of those contentions is relevant if he could not comply with the order. And which would you have preferred he do— make a futile attempt to round his platoon up, or take prompt, effective measures to suppress the machine gun fire without suffering any other American casualties?

"You know, it's really easy for the trial counsel to criticize Major Thomas here in this climate-controlled courtroom over a decade later. It's not so easy to make the right decision in combat, when you are in deep shit and your men are wounded and dying, after humping day after day through the bush, after getting very little sleep, after drinking too little lukewarm water flavored by decontamination tablets, and after all-day bouts of diarrhea." Paul looked at Judge Savage when he said 'deep shit' as if to challenge him to interrupt and admonish him, but Judge Savage merely stared back impassively. "Yes, it's really easy for some lawyer to be critical now. But it wasn't so easy at the time."

Lieutenant Colonel David walked out from behind the podium and stood right before the jury box, standing so close that he forced the court members to look at his Combat Infantry Badge and Vietnam combat ribbons. He looked each court member in the eye, almost challenging them.

"Mr. President, Members of the Court, more is at stake here than Major Thomas's career. Yes, obedience of orders is critical, especially during combat. And we certainly don't want enlisted men questioning orders during combat. But do we want to send out a message to our young officers that they have to take unnecessary casualties in a situation such as this one where they are on the scene and know the tactical situation and the commander isn't on the scene and doesn't know the situation and issues a stupid order?

"AirLand Battle doctrine calls for initiative on the part of junior leaders who are separated from their commanders. Major Thomas was just as effectively separated as if Captain Armstrong had not been in the AO, and the order couldn't have been any more stupid if Captain Armstrong had been asked to come up with the dumbest order he could give in the current situation. Another tenet of AirLand Battle doctrine is to preserve the fighting force. 1-6 did that.

"More than fifteen years later, do we want to condone the body-count-at-any-cost mentality that led to so many of our problems in Vietnam? The defense contends not and asks you not only to find this fine officer 'not guilty' of the charge, but also to honor him for fighting under adverse conditions, with little or no support, thereby saving American lives."

As Lieutenant Colonel David sat down, Captain Wilson reached over to shake his hand. "Great job, Sir," he whispered. Paul smiled ruefully. He knew that with the trial counsel having the last word, all his eloquence could well be for nothing.

Major Morgan got up to begin his rebuttal argument. "Mr. President, Members of the Court, the defense did a good job of blowing smoke. A smoke screen to obscure the real issues in this case. He's attempting to put the Vietnam war, the body-count mentality, Major Armstrong, and everybody but his client on trial. Why is he doing that? Because, if you can't defend your client, you attack everybody else. And he can't defend his client because his client admitted to each and every element of this offense.

"Major Armstrong testified that he had a valid military purpose for this order—to get the members of the first platoon out in front of the listening post so they could fire at the enemy without worrying about hitting the friendly troops. When you listen to the judge's instructions on the lawfulness of orders, you will notice that nowhere will he say that a lawful order has to be the best possible order—the best possible tactical decision.

"As to the accused's alleged inability to obey the order, why couldn't he have ordered his platoon sergeant to round up the members of the first platoon and bring them to his location? That way he could have continued to call in artillery if necessary and would have been able to attack the machine gun aggressively. In fact, didn't he ultimately get his platoon together and make a sweep to see whether there was a body count? That sweep to recover the friendly casualties and see whether there were any enemy bodies proves he could have complied with the order.

"As to this alleged attempt to discuss whether he could comply with the order, we only have the accused's word for it. The RTO, Mr. Tabler, didn't remember any such conversation."

Ken paused for a moment, until every court member was looking at him. "The defense tried to make your decision some type of referendum on how the Vietnam War was conducted, or whether we should permit junior leaders some flexibility in following their superiors' orders under AirLand Battle doctrine. But you do not need to decide those things in this case. All you have to decide is whether the accused disobeyed the lawful command of his superior commissioned officer, Captain Armstrong. And he did. Do you want to send out a message that subordinates may disobey orders to close with and destroy the enemy during combat because they don't agree with the orders? If you want to set that precedent, find him not guilty! But you will do your duty, unpleasant as it may be, and convict him because the evidence says he is guilty and because you have served in combat and know the importance of both aggressively attacking the enemy and of following orders without question or hesitation. Do your duty."

There was a hush in the courtroom as Major Morgan sat down. Finally, Judge Savage broke the silence and began to instruct the court members on the law they would follow in deciding the case. Both Lieutenant Colonel David and Major Morgan had told their assistants to follow the judge's instructions carefully to make certain they were not objectionable. Both lead counsel were worn out after their emotional arguments and knew they would not be able to concentrate fully on the instructions.

Judge Savage instructed the court members on the presumption of innocence, that the prosecution had the burden of proving the accused guilty beyond a reasonable doubt, of the elements, or facts, that the government had to prove to convict the accused of disobedience of a lawful command of a superior commissioned officer, of what constituted the defense of inability to obey the order, and of various evidentiary matters, such as credibility of witnesses and circumstantial evidence.

Then, he instructed the court members on the lawfulness of orders. "To be lawful, the order must relate to specific military duty and be one that a superior was authorized under the circumstances to give the accused. The order must require the accused to do or cease doing a particular thing either at once or at a future time. An order is lawful if reasonably necessary to safeguard and protect morale, discipline, and usefulness of members of a command and is directly connected with the maintenance of good order in the services. An order is illegal if it is unrelated to military duty or its sole purpose is to accomplish some private end or it is arbitrary and unreasonable." The President of the court scribbled notes furiously as if he would violate a lawful order himself if he missed anything.

Finally, after having instructed the court members that the influence of superiority in rank could not be used in any manner to control the independence of the other members, he gave the procedural instructions on voting. He explained that, because there were eight members, six would have to vote "guilty" to convict the accused, that, if fewer than six voted "guilty," the vote would result in an acquittal, and that courts-martial had no "hung juries" on guilt or innocence.

After ascertaining that none of the court members had any questions on the instructions, Judge Savage reminded them they could not talk to anyone else while in their closed session deliberations. If they wanted a break, they had to come into open court and ask the judge for a recess.

"Do counsel for either side have any objection to the instructions as given or requests for additional instructions?" Judge Savage asked.

"Government does not, your Honor."

"Nor does the defense, your Honor."

"Very well, the court is closed," Judge Savage announced as he banged his gavel to signify the start of the court's deliberations.

As the bailiff called, "All rise," the court members filed into the deliberation room. The bailiff closed the door behind them and then pulled a chair up to guard it until they announced that they had reached a verdict. Everyone else left the courtroom, speculating what the jury would do behind the closed, guarded door.

CHAPTER 39

Trial Defense Service Office
Office of the Staff Judge Advocate
Building 244, Fort Leavenworth, Kansas

J U N E   1 9 8 6

Light streamed in through the high windows as the two defense counsel and their client entered Sam's office. "What do you think?" Sam asked Paul.

"There's no telling. I gave up trying to predict juries years ago. But let's not waste this time in case they do convict. Let's go over our extenuation and mitigation one more time. I go crazy waiting for juries unless I keep busy."

Jim, who had just sat down in the corner, raised his head and said, "I don't want to rehearse the sentencing phase. You can't think they're going to convict me."

"Listen, Jim, I told you back when you made this idiotic move to waive the statute of limitations that you could be convicted. Now, you made us continue with this trial, so let me do my job. We're going to prepare for the worst. I hope you're not convicted, but if you are, we want to get the lightest sentence possible."

"If I'm convicted, I don't really care what sentence I get."

"It's easy to say that now, but regardless, we're going over the sentencing phase."

"Wait a minute," Jim said. "Tell me about what happens if I get sentenced to confinement at hard labor."

"Ok. First, the term is 'confinement' now, not 'confinement at hard labor.' You've seen the prisoners mowing lawns and bagging groceries in the commissary? It's not really breaking rocks. But it's still not pleasant.

"Not all enlisted Army prisoners come to the Disciplinary Barracks—the DB. Generally, they have to have at least a two-year sentence for the DB. If they get less than six months, they stay at local stockades. Between six months and two years, they go to the Army Correctional Activity at Fort Riley. But all Army officer prisoners qualify for the Disciplinary Barracks.

"Officers have two rights that enlisted prisoners don't: the right to be confined separately and the right to do work commensurate with their grade. The right to be confined separately doesn't mean it's any better. The cells are identical—just in a different wing of the prison. There aren't many jobs that are suitable for officers. Working in the library and teaching inmate classes are about the only officer-type jobs. Consequently, most officers waive their right to work only at officer-type jobs so they can work in the print shop or the upholstery shop to have something to do to kill time. But they never waive their right to be billeted separately from the enlisted prisoners. Enlisted prisoners don't like officers. However, if the officer is sentenced to be dismissed, after all his appeals are over, the convening authority will order the sentence executed, and he loses his officer status. At that point, the prison administration will transfer him into the general population. Enough of this, let's go over your testimony so that we can avoid a sentence of confinement."

While the defense team went over Jim Thomas's testimony, Ken Morgan returned to the courtroom, apparently to gather up the law books he had left on the prosecution table. After stacking them up neatly, he sat down, however, and stared at the closed door to the deliberations room, wishing he knew what was going on in there. Suddenly, he heard shouting behind the door, but try as he might, he could not make out what they were saying. It's probably a good sign, he thought. At least some of them must want to convict or they wouldn't be arguing. He wanted to go close to the door and try to hear better, but knew that would be improper because the jury deliberations were supposed to be secret. Besides, the bailiff was starting to eye him suspiciously. So he gathered up his law books and walked out.

As he walked down the hall, Colonel Farmer stopped him. "How is it going, Ken? Are you going to get a conviction?"

"I don't know, Sir. It's up to the court members."

"Well, I hope you do. We don't need dirtbags like that in the officer corps."

Ken just nodded and walked away. Armstrong was the dirtbag, not Thomas, he had decided. This case is the first time I've ever had mixed feelings about convicting someone, he thought. It's too bad the only time Paul and I got to go head to head it had to be a case like this one.

Behind closed doors, in the small deliberation room, the President of the Court, Colonel Harrison, who had remained silent during the court members' arguments until now, finally spoke, "Look, we all know he's guilty, let's just vote and quit this meaningless discussion."

"It's not that easy, Sir," Lieutenant Colonel Fletcher replied. "Yes, he disobeyed a lawful order, but I'd have disobeyed it, too."

"Then you'd be as guilty as he is!"

Major Campbell broke in, seeing the argument was about to get heated again. "It seems to me that if we believe beyond a reasonable doubt that he disobeyed the order, it's our duty to convict. If we would have done the same thing, then we cut him some slack on sentencing. If the order was legal, but stupid, that's an extenuating circumstance that justifies a lighter sentence."

"We all know it was a stupid order," Fletcher said.

"Yeah, but that's irrelevant. It's a cop-out—a compromise to agree to convict but give a light sentence if we are not sure," Lieutenant Colonel Penders, who had also been silent up to now, interjected. "I say we have to decide whether the prosecution proved his guilt or not, and if he did, we convict. It's that simple."

"For such a hot-shot prosecutor, he certainly didn't put on much evidence. Why didn't he call the battalion commander?" Major Walker asked.

"Because the whole battalion was probably as screwed up as the company was," Fletcher said bitterly.

"Yes, but that's still no excuse for disobeying an order in combat," Colonel Harrison said, "Let's vote."

Major Walker, who had already torn a sheet from his yellow legal pad into smaller pieces, passed the ballots to the other members. Colonel Harrison directed the other members to write "guilty" or "not guilty" and reminded them that everyone must vote. After each member wrote his decision down, they folded the ballots and handed them to Major Walker, the junior member, who had the duty to collect and count the votes. He shuffled them so that no one would know whose vote he was reading and then began announcing the votes. Colonel Harrison wrote "Guilty" and "Not Guilty" in two columns on the blackboard and prepared to tally the votes under them.

"Guilty."

"Guilty."

"Not Guilty."

"Guilty."

"Not Guilty."

"Guilty."

"Guilty."

Major Walker paused before opening the last ballot, "This is it—the deciding vote. If it's a guilty vote, we have two-thirds, and it's a conviction. If not, it's an acquittal."

"Just get on with it," Colonel Harrison growled.

While the court deliberated, Judge Savage went to his chambers and started to read over a record of trial he had to authenticate. No record of trial was official until a military judge signed it, affirming that it was an accurate transcript of the trial. Several records had stacked up in Judge Savage's office during the Thomas trial. But even though he had been involved in hundreds of trials and should have been able to turn his attention to authenticating these records, his thoughts kept returning to the Thomas case. He wondered what the members would do in this one. Right after the court closed, Captain Wilson had tried to find out whether Judge Savage would have convicted or not, but Judge Savage followed his usual practice and said, "I never say what I would have done in a jury trial. And I don't even know. I listen to the evidence differently when I'm presiding over a jury case. I listen for instructional issues and objectionable matters, not to decide guilt or innocence."

Sam, like most Army lawyers, felt that waiting for court members to reach a verdict was the hardest part of a trial. It's bad enough waiting for military judges, but judges are far more predictable than military juries. While a court-martial is in session, the lawyers feel as if they have some control over the outcome of the case. But once court members retire behind closed doors to deliberate, anything can happen. And because the members' deliberations are secret, it is unlikely that anyone will ever know whether the court members do something improper.

Although no less an expert than F. Lee Bailey has said that military juries are, on the whole, as fair as or fairer than their civilian counterparts, both the trial and the defense counsel always worry about the aberrant jury that might ignore the evidence or the law and reach an improper verdict. Court members are far more likely than judges to ignore the facts and decide the case on some extraneous factor, such as sympathy, identification with the accused, or dislike of the victim, or because of some strange military reasoning, such as the boys-will-be-boys rule or the mere-WAC rule. The boys-will-be-boys rule is a military lawyer's shorthand phrase for the situation in which a military jury finds a thug not guilty of a knifing or other aggression on the theory that we trained him to be a killer, so what if he practices in the barracks. The mere-WAC rule is even more horrendous. It refers to the belief of some military court members that a WAC can't be raped on the sick reasoning that no chaste woman would become an enlisted soldier. Fortunately, in the mid-1980s, both rules seemed to be dying out—albeit too slowly. Nevertheless, for these and similar reasons, trial attorneys worry more while court members are deliberating than while judges are.

Even with many courts-martial under their belts, Paul and Ken were not immune from the tension of waiting for a jury verdict. Paul compensated by working—preparing for the sentencing phase even while hoping desperately that a sentencing phase would be unnecessary. Ken, being much more experienced, was more pragmatic—he'd done his best, and he'd either win or not. Thus, he suppressed his concern over winning the case and thought about his golf game. The two assistant counsel hadn't yet learned how to avoid worrying themselves unduly during the court's deliberations. Sam tried unsuccessfully to concentrate on Paul's attempts to better prepare for the sentencing phase of the trial. Pam was even less able to stop worrying about the outcome because she didn't have anything to occupy herself with, while her mentor just sat there daydreaming—apparently gripping an imaginary golf club in his hands. Pam wished she could go to the gym and beat the hell out of a racquetball instead of just sitting there.

If lawyers are nervous while a jury deliberates, defendants are in spades. Some accused soldiers think courts-martial are big jokes until the court members begin their deliberations. Then reality sets in. It isn't funny anymore when an accused realizes that his whole future depends on what a group of officers decide behind closed doors.

Jim had not taken the trial as a big joke—not for a moment. But even though he did not see how the court could convict him, he had enough respect for Paul David to accept his view that a conviction was possible. He would not have been human if he hadn't been worried about the outcome. His decision to waive the statute of limitations, which seemed so right at the time, now looked more and more stupid every extra minute the court members deliberated. And those minutes seemed like years behind bars now.

After the members had reached their verdict, they knocked on the door to let the bailiff know. The bailiff first notified the judge and then, acting on the judge's instructions, notified the trial and the defense counsel. Within minutes, all parties had returned to the courtroom. Both Lieutenant Colonel David and Major Morgan tried to read the court members' expressions to get some clue as to what they had decided.

Some military lawyers think that if the court members look at the accused, they have found him not guilty. Some of the members looked at Major Thomas while other's didn't—an inconclusive signal at best.

"Court will come to order," Judge Savage began.

"All parties to the trial who were present when the court closed are again present," Major Morgan continued.

"Has the court reached a verdict?" Judge Savage inquired.

"We have, your Honor."

"Bailiff, would you get the findings worksheet from the President of the Court and, without looking at it, bring it to me," the judge directed.

After the bailiff had done so, Judge Savage looked over the findings worksheet—the paper on which the jury recorded its decision—to see whether there were any defects in its form. If there were, he had to correct them before the verdict was announced. Thus, he always looked over both findings and sentence worksheets before allowing the President to announce the court's decision. As always, he kept his face impassive—so no one could guess what the verdict was or speculate as to whether he agreed with it. "I see no defects in form. You may announce the findings. Accused and counsel please rise."

As the bailiff handed the worksheet back to the President, Lieutenant Colonel David, Captain Wilson, and Major Thomas all rose. The Army had dispensed with the practice of saluting the President of the Court years ago, but the accused and his lawyers still had to stand for the court's decision.

Colonel Harrison stood up and began to read the court's decision. Major Thomas stood stiffly at attention, looking directly at the President. "Major Thomas, it is my duty as President of this court to inform you. . . ."

All the lawyers reacted to the word "inform," which told them what the court had decided, because the other decision would have resulted in the word "advise."

" . . . that this court finds you of the charge and specification, guilty."

The spectators gasped—all but Major Armstrong, who broke out into a big grin—but a stern glance from Judge Savage was enough to bring quiet to the courtroom. Jim stood there stony faced, fighting back the tears by mentally chanting, "I will not cry," a thought that didn't work for Meg in the back of the courtroom. Jim sat down when Paul tugged at his sleeve. "Thank you, Mr. President, Members of the Court," Judge Savage began, reasserting control over the proceedings. "We have some preliminary matters to go over concerning sentencing. Why don't you reconvene at 1300 hours. Court will be in recess."

"All rise" resounded as the members filed out.

Pam grabbed Ken's hand and shook it vigorously. "Congratulations, Sir," she said, "I didn't think we could win it."

Ken smiled wryly as he accepted her congratulations. "We didn't."

"Sorry, Jim," Paul said. He wanted to console Jim, but looking at the expression in Jim's normally hazel eyes, which seemed to have changed to a steely gray, and the rigid set of his jaw, Paul decided to keep quiet for now.

Meg was trying to get to Jim but stopped when Judge Savage called the court back to order so that he could inform the accused of his rights during sentencing out of the presence of the court members. The most important part of these rights were the accused's rights either to remain silent or to testify. If the accused wanted to testify, he could either testify under oath, in which case the trial counsel could cross-examine him, or make an unsworn statement. The trial counsel could offer evidence to rebut an unsworn statement, but could not cross-examine the accused. Major Thomas, still stony-faced, told the military judge that he understood his rights during the sentencing portion of the trial. Just as in the guilt or innocence phase, however, as a practical matter, an officer accused had to take the stand to testify under oath regardless of the fact that the judge would inform the court members they should draw no adverse inference from his failure to testify under oath.

Paul then moved to limit the maximum punishment to life imprisonment. Even though the charge sheet did not contain the language that the charge was referred as noncapital, Paul pointed out that the pretrial advice that the convening authority relied on stated that the maximum punishment was life imprisonment. When asked whether he opposed the motion, Ken Morgan did not, doubting that the court was going to sentence the accused to substantial confinement, much less impose the death penalty. The lawyers devoted the remainder of the session to admitting various documents to inform the court members about the character of Major Thomas's service, a proceeding that seemed a lot less important to Meg than letting her take Jim away so she could try to console him.

Sometimes, accused soldiers who become convicted soldiers thereby become flight risks justifying confinement awaiting sentencing. Often, trial counsel will seek to put a convicted accused in confinement after the guilty verdict on the theory that they now know that they face lengthy jail time and they may be very tempted to opt out of the sentencing phase of the trial. But Ken refused to believe that the court members would sentence Jim to lengthy confinement, so he decided that no reason existed to confine him for what would probably only be one night in the detention cell at the military police station on post. Nor did he want to face Paul if he tried to confine Major Thomas. So he watched as Meg walked through the swinging gate from the spectator area into the courtroom proper, took Jim's arm, and pulled him away from his lawyers. "You can have him later," she said, "He's mine now."

PART VI

THE SENTENCE

Do not stand at my grave and weep;
I am not there, I do not sleep.
I am a thousand winds that blow,
I am a diamond glint on snow,
I am the sunlight on ripened grain,
I am the autumn rain,
When you awake in the morning hush,
I am the swift, uplifting rush
Of birds circling in flight.
I am the stars that shine at night.
So do not stand at my grave and cry;
I am not there—I did not die.

—Poem written by an unknown member of the 4th Infantry
Division shortly before he was killed in action in the Central
Highlands of Vietnam. Reprinted by permission of *Army
Magazine.*

CHAPTER 40

Trial Defense Service Office
Office of the Staff Judge Advocate
Building 244, Fort Leavenworth, Kansas

JUNE 1986

Promptly at 1300 hours, the court reconvened. The court members seemed more relaxed as they sat in the jury box, now that they had made the tough decision that the accused was guilty. Apparently, they did not realize that deciding on an appropriate sentence was often tougher than deciding guilt or innocence.

The sentencing procedure began with the assistant trial counsel, Pam Lewis, reading the data concerning the accused's service from the first page of the charge sheet, such as his unit, his years of service, and that he had neither prior convictions by court-martial nor records of nonjudicial punishment under Article 15 of the Uniform Code of Military Justice. Pam then handed the President of the Court the accused's Form 2-1, which detailed the highlights of his military service, from his assignments to his awards and decorations.

"The government has one witness, your Honor," Major Morgan said before calling Colonel Zimmer.

After the preliminaries, he asked Colonel Zimmer what his duty position was.

"I'm director of the Center for Army Leadership."

"And what do your duties as director entail?"

"I'm responsible for overseeing our missions of writing leadership doctrine for the Army and for teaching leadership at CGSC and monitoring the instruction at other service schools."

"Would it be correct to say you are one of the Army's experts on current leadership doctrine?"

"Objection!" Lieutenant Colonel David interjected, "The defense does not see the relevance of this testimony. Nor do we see a need for expert testimony. Finally, although the government gave us notice that they would call this witness in aggravation, they did not notify us that he was to testify as an expert."

"Your Honor, the government is offering evidence of the accused's lack of rehabilitative potential as permitted by the *Manual for Court-Martial,* and we are not attempting to qualify the witness as an expert, merely to show his background," Major Morgan answered.

"Very well, objection overruled. You may answer the question, Colonel."

"Yes, your Honor." Colonel Zimmer tried unsuccessfully to appear modest. "I suppose I am one of the Army's experts."

"Do you know the accused?"

"Yes, that's Major Thomas sitting over there," the stocky colonel said, pointing to the defense table.

"How do you know him?"

"I observed him participate in some leadership classes. They were small group classes where the students had to participate, and I was able to listen to his leadership philosophy."

"What did you think of his performance in the leadership classes?"

"I was not impressed. He seemed to think that leadership instruction was worthless. He said the only way to learn leadership was out in the field with real leaders and real soldiers, not in a classroom. And he seemed far too concerned with taking care of the troops. Although I'm all for taking care of the troops, the mission must come first."

Paul involuntarily shook his head. If Colonel Zimmer ever took care of his troops, it was to enhance his chances of making general and for no other reason.

"Are you aware he has been convicted of disobeying the lawful command of his company commander to charge a machine gun during combat in Vietnam?"

"Yes, Major Morgan."

"Based on your observation of his classroom performance and the fact that he has been convicted today, do you have an opinion as to whether he can be rehabilitated to be a productive officer for the Army?"

"Yes, I do. I don't think he has any future in the Army."

"Thank you, no further questions."

Lieutenant Colonel David sat there for a moment, thinking. Well, here goes what's left of my career, he thought, cross-examining my senior rater after he has already tried to talk me out of winning the case.

"Sir, I have only a few questions. First, Lieutenant Colonel Kelly was Major Thomas's actual leadership instructor, wasn't he?"

"Yes."

"And he is one of the best officers and instructors you have in the Center for Army Leadership, isn't he?"

"I suppose."

"And isn't it true that he awarded Major Thomas an 'A' in the leadership course?"

"I believe so."

"And as a director, you sit on academic boards, don't you?"

"Yes."

"Did you vote against the College's designation of Major Thomas as an honor graduate?"

"No, but that was before this conviction."

Lieutenant Colonel David's next question came out more sarcastically than he had intended. "Now, Sir, his leadership skills must really have been awful for him to have gotten an 'A' in leadership and be designated an honor graduate, right?"

Before Colonel Zimmer could answer, Judge Savage, anxious to protect another full colonel, growled, "You are perilously close to contempt, Lieutenant Colonel David."

You don't know how much contempt I have, your Honor, Paul thought, but responded simply, "Sorry, your Honor. Withdraw the question." The jury got the point anyway, he thought, and if they didn't, there isn't much more I can do about it.

Paul continued, "Isn't it true that you are my senior rater?"

"Yes."

The courtroom had barely finished its first gasp as Lieutenant Colonel David asked his next question. "And, Sir, isn't it true that yesterday morning, while this trial was going on, you tried to convince me not to defend my client?"

"Objection!" Major Morgan jumped to his feet, forgetting the customary, "Your Honor." "May we approach the bench?" After all four lawyers and Major Thomas had edged up to the judge's bench, still not one of them wanting to be up close and personal with the judge, Ken continued. "This line of questioning is irrelevant. Or is the defense trying to raise command influence? If so, they should have raised it before entering a plea."

"Your Honor," Paul interjected, "this evidence is relevant to show bias on the part of the witness. We do not have a command influence motion. It is our belief that the witness was not acting for the command to try to influence the defense not to do its duty to defend the accused to the best of our ability, but rather was doing so out of a misguided notion of what a finding of not guilty would do to leadership in the Army."

Judge Savage thought for a moment. "I'm not sure I see the difference, but if you are sure this discussion between you and Colonel Zimmer did not amount to command influence or prejudice the defense case, I suppose we can let the matter rest insofar as this trial is concerned. I will say for the record that, if this is less than your best defense, I'm sure the government wouldn't want to see your best effort. However, Major Morgan, you will investigate this allegation and, if it is true, report Colonel Zimmer's actions to the convening authority. I will not permit even the appearance of illegal command influence in my court. And I'll permit the cross-examination because it may show bias on the part of the witness. Clear?"

"Yes, your Honor," both lead counsel said.

After all but Lieutenant Colonel David had returned to their seats, Judge Savage said, "You may answer the question, Colonel."

Colonel Zimmer shot Paul a look of pure disgust. "I don't remember the question," he said, stalling.

"Didn't you call me into your office to attempt to convince me not to defend my client to the best of my ability because of some imagined danger to Army leadership if he was found not guilty?"

"I did have a conversation with you about the case, but I was only trying to point out that it would be a bad precedent for Army leadership if an individual could disobey an order in combat and get away with it. I certainly wasn't trying to influence you not to defend your client."

Lieutenant Colonel David took a deep breath and continued. "Sir, didn't you say to me, and I quote, 'We just can't send out a message from the Center that soldiers can disobey orders in combat and get some slick lawyer to defend them and get away with it. Now, I think you should think very hard about what you are going to do in this case. Do you read me?' Isn't that what you told me?"

"Well, I might have said something like that, but I was just trying to point out the dangers to leadership."

"Isn't it true that the only thing you were worried about was that the 'slick lawyer' worked for you and that it might reflect badly on you and your hopes for a star?"

Colonel Zimmer sputtered, red-faced. "No, of course not! I resent your implications!"

I'm not implying anything, Paul thought. I'm saying it on this verbatim record. My career's shot now anyway, so I may as well continue. "Isn't it true you are biased against my client because you are afraid that my zeal will make it look as if you can't control one of your officers and make him toe the party line?"

"Objection!" Major Morgan almost shouted. "Counsel is badgering the witness."

Judge Savage was not quite so sympathetic to the witness as he had been earlier, but before he could decide how to rule on the objection, the defense counsel withdrew the question and announced that he had no further questions. Major Morgan announced that the government had no further matters to present on sentencing as Colonel Zimmer stalked out of the courtroom. Sam whispered as Paul sat down, "You really tore him up. That took guts to cross-examine your senior rater that way." Guts, yes—brains, no, Paul thought.

"Defense?" Judge Savage asked.

"Thank you, your Honor," Paul responded. "The defense calls Lieutenant Colonel Mills." After the witness had been sworn in and had answered the preliminaries, Lieutenant Colonel David elicited that the witness was Major Thomas's academic counselor. Lieutenant Colonel Mills testified that, even though Major Thomas had had all the pressures of preparing for the court-martial and being one of the best staff group leaders at CGSC, he had still maintained the highest standards of physical fitness and academic excellence. Indeed, he had been an honor graduate of CGSC. Lieutenant Colonel Mills also said that, despite the conviction, he would serve with him at any time, including in combat. Major Morgan's cross-examination was limited to bringing out that the witness had known the accused for only a year and only in an academic, rather than a tactical, environment.

Next, the defense called Colonel Jerome, the CGSC Class Director. He testified not only that Major Thomas was one of the most outstanding officers in the CGSC class, but also that he was one of the most outstanding officers he had known anywhere.

Next, Paul called Lieutenant Colonel Kelly, Major Thomas's leadership instructor, to rebut Colonel Zimmer's testimony. This witness praised Jim's performance in leadership instruction and his demonstrated leadership ability.

The next to the last defense witness was Lieutenant Colonel Garnett, Jim's boss before CGSC. He also testified that Jim was one of the most outstanding officers he had ever known and that he would serve in combat with him anywhere. Major Morgan did not cross-examine any of these witnesses, not wanting to reinforce the good things they had to say about the accused.

Lieutenant Colonel David saved the accused for last and elected to have him make a sworn statement. When called, Jim took the stand. His military appearance was impeccable, except that he had chosen not to wear his ribbons. Instead, his Combat Infantry Badge was pinned in solitary splendor above his jump wings.

"Major Thomas," he began, still using the formal address of name and rank. Some defense counsel would call their clients by their first name during sentencing in an attempt to humanize them. But Paul believed that court members, especially senior officers, preferred the militarily correct use of one's rank. "When and how did you get your commission?" Even though Paul had gone through some of these questions when Jim had testified earlier, he wanted to go over them again so that the court members would have a fresh version to consider in sentencing.

"I graduated from the University of Cincinnati in 1968 and was commissioned a Regular Army second lieutenant of infantry as an ROTC distinguished military graduate."

"Would you briefly highlight your military career for the court members?"

"Yes, Sir. After Infantry Officer Basic, Airborne School, and Ranger School, I went to Fort Sill, where I served in the infantry battalion in support of the Artillery School for the mandatory six months' troop duty before going to Vietnam. Then, I served in the First Cavalry Division in Vietnam until I was wounded. After I got out of the hospital, I commanded a basic training company at Fort Knox and then attended the Infantry Officer Advanced course at Fort Benning. I taught in the tactics department there after graduation. My next assignment was as a company commander again, with the Eighth Infantry Division in Mainz, Germany, followed by a tour in the Eighth Division's G-2 slot before being selected for CGSC."

"You were an honor graduate at both Infantry Officer Advanced Course and CGSC, weren't you?"

"Yes, Sir."

"Major Thomas, are you married?"

"Yes, Sir. That's my wife, Meg, in the courtroom."

"How has this court-martial affected your wife?"

Jim paused for a moment, looking down. With tears in his eyes, he answered, "It's been rough on her. But I've got to give Meg credit. She's stuck by me." Although he faced the jury, his eyes sought out Meg in the back of the courtroom.

"Do you have any children?"

"No, we couldn't."

"Of course, you understand that you were convicted of disobeying the order to 'charge the machine gun,' and that you could be dismissed from the Army—the officer version of a dishonorable discharge—and sentenced to confinement?"

"Yes, Sir."

"Do you want to remain in the Army?"

"I don't want to be dismissed. I'm willing to accept whatever punishment the court feels appropriate, but would rather go to jail than be dismissed."

"Are you sorry that you disobeyed the order?"

"I'm sorry that the situation arose and for all the trouble it's caused."

"Is there anything else you'd like to tell the court members?"

"No, Sir."

"Your witness, Major Morgan."

Ken got up. He hadn't even made any notes to use in cross-examination. "Now, let me see if I understood what you said. When Lieutenant Colonel David asked you whether you were sorry that you disobeyed the order, you said you were sorry that the situation arose and for the trouble it had caused. But you didn't say that you were sorry for disobeying the order, did you?"

"No, I didn't."

"You aren't sorry, are you?"

"No, Sir."

"You haven't learned anything from this trial, have you? You would disobey the order again, wouldn't you?"

In a low, measured voice, Jim replied, "I've learned a lot from this trial, but yes, I would disobey the order again in the same circumstances."

"Thank you, Major. No further questions."

Lieutenant Colonel David walked up to the witness stand to begin his redirect examination. "Major Thomas, why would you disobey the order again in the same circumstances, even after having been convicted here?"

Major Thomas looked around the packed courtroom, his eyes coming to rest on the court members. "Because, regardless of what you do to me here, I kept soldiers from dying needlessly. I know the leadership doctrine of those who preach leadership doctrine from their ivory towers but would do anything to avoid an assignment where they would have to practice what they preach—those people in the Center for Army Leadership, who say, 'Mission first.' But without the men, you can't do the mission. And no good platoon leader in Vietnam sacrificed his men so that Armstrong or some other careerist superior officer could get a meaningless body count. I'll risk my life and even the lives of the men I command—but not just for someone else's glory."

"Thank you, no further questions. Your Honor, the defense requests permission to hand defense exhibits F through RR to the President of the Court."

"Permission granted. Is there any recross, Major Morgan?"

Ken thought for a moment, then responded, "No, your Honor."

"Questions by any member of the court? Apparently not."

After Lieutenant Colonel David had handed the President of the Court the previously admitted letters of commendation, efficiency reports, citations for Major Thomas's awards, and other laudatory documents, he said, "Your Honor, the defense rests."

"The government has no rebuttal, your Honor," Major Morgan announced.

After the court members had indicated that there were no witnesses they wanted called or recalled, Judge Savage asked the counsel whether they were ready to argue. They were.

"Open or close?" Judge Savage asked Lieutenant Colonel David. Although the prosecution got to argue first and last on findings, Judge Savage permitted the defense the choice of arguing first or last on sentencing. Any smart defense counsel wanted the last word.

"Close, your Honor."

When Judge Savage nodded that he could begin, Major Morgan got up to argue. He had thought about merely saying, "The government trusts you will impose an appropriate sentence," but he was too good an advocate to quit at that, so he said, "Mr. President, Members of the Court, although you have already made a difficult decision in this case, the decision you have to make now will be more difficult. Previously, you had to decide only whether he had committed this crime. But now you have many things to evaluate in arriving at an appropriate sentence. You have to balance the seriousness of the crime against the accused's admittedly sterling military record.

"The government expects the military judge will instruct you that you should consider the needs of good order and discipline, the welfare of society, and the needs of the accused in arriving at an appropriate sentence.

"Let's take the first factor—the needs of good order and discipline. Yes, a conviction does send out a message that you cannot disobey the lawful order of a superior officer. But that conviction is meaningless without an appropriate sentence—a sentence that will send out the message that disobeying orders in combat has a real price.

"The same consideration applies to the welfare of our military society. Our military society is based on discipline—the prompt and unquestioning obedience of lawful orders. And while discipline begins with good leadership, when that does not work, we have the Uniform Code of Military Justice to enforce discipline. The seriousness with which our military society views disobedience of orders during combat is illustrated by the maximum punishment for such an offense—the death penalty. Although this case was not referred capital and thus you may not impose the death penalty, the alternate maximum—life imprisonment—also shows the seriousness of this crime in our military society.

"What about the needs of the accused? Yes, he has a great record, including a valor award and a Purple Heart. And yes, he has already been punished by being convicted. But note—he still hasn't learned anything. He told you that, even after this conviction, he would disobey the order again in similar circumstances. Thus, his sentence must be one that will impress on him that disobedience of lawful orders, no matter how noble the motive, is wrong.

"Consequently, the government contends that you should dismiss the accused from the service. Thank you."

Lieutenant Colonel David rose for what he felt would be the most important and, almost certainly, the last argument he would make as an Army lawyer. For probably the only time, he had not outlined his argument beforehand. He had thought about the argument for hours and had started to outline it. But Paul finally decided to just go with his feelings. He wanted the court members to decide his client's sentence with their hearts, not their heads. He left the podium and walked right up to the railing separating the court members from the rest of the courtroom and began to argue in a soft voice, unlike the loud, forceful voice he usually used. "Mr. President, Members of the Court, it's very easy for the trial counsel to say that Major Thomas hasn't learned anything because, under the same conditions, he would disobey the order again. Instead, I suggest that it's the government, not Major Thomas, and officers like Major Armstrong and Colonel Zimmer, who haven't learned anything. They haven't learned, as Major Thomas instinctively knew from the start, that you don't waste lives only to enhance your career, only to get a meaningless body count so that you can impress your commander, or only to attempt to show you are in command of a firefight when, in actuality, you are hiding under a tree two hundred meters to the rear."

Lieutenant Colonel David's voice began to rise. "Major Thomas was honest with you. He testified that he disobeyed the order and that under the same circumstances he would do it again. Apparently, you disagreed with the defense's contention that he was unable to obey the order. But you have to respect an officer who makes a difficult decision and is prepared to take the consequences. How easy it would have been for Major Thomas to have said, 'I've learned my lesson, and I'll never disobey an order like that again.' But he still cares enough for the lives of American soldiers that, even after having been convicted and even facing possible life imprisonment, he would still protect them and face the consequences. And he had the courage to tell you he would do so even knowing you could dismiss him from the service and imprison him."

Paul's voice rose even more. "You know, it's easy for Colonel Zimmer to sit up there in the ivory tower of the Center for Army Leadership and pontificate on what leaders should be, know, and do. It's not quite so easy in the terrible chaos of a firefight, after you've already taken friendly KIA, and knowing not only that your commander is incompetent, but also that you have little or no support for the war at home.

"In his classic books on war, S. L. A. Marshall noted that men in combat don't fight for their country or for some noble cause, but that they fight instead for the men in their fire teams, their squads, and their platoons. Major Armstrong never was a platoon leader. He became a company commander without ever having served at a level where there is a bond stronger than friendship, stronger than marriage, and, as witnessed by the next day's action in which Major Thomas earned a Silver Star and suffered a grievous wound to protect his platoon, stronger than life itself. And remember, he did accomplish the mission that day—suppressing the enemy fire without taking any unnecessary casualties. He didn't disobey the order out of fear—he had already been out under fire to try to pull back the men on the outpost who were the casualties of the machine gun.

"I'm not going to dwell on how sterling Major Thomas's career has been. You have the pile of defense exhibits in front of you, and you have heard the testimony of the officers he has served under. They don't think he should be dismissed or go to jail. They would serve with him again. Give them, and the Army, that privilege.

Paul looked at the court members, who sat there like stones. I wish I could read them, he thought. What will get through to them? He continued, more passionately, trying to convince them by the force of his will. "When you deliberate on an appropriate sentence, the defense would ask you to also consider the draft evaders who got amnesty, the deserters who were given discharges in lieu of court-martial, and the traitors who collaborated with the North Vietnamese and increased the suffering of our POWs and yet are free today to enjoy the benefits of American citizenship. Major Thomas came when his country called. Are you going to dismiss and/or incarcerate this officer who earned a Silver Star and a Purple Heart, among other decorations, when those 'men,' and I use the word loosely, walked?

"How many of you have been to the Vietnam memorial? Pretty awesome, isn't it? Well, the next time you see it, remember that there, but for Major Thomas's willingness to put his career on the line and do what he thought was right, would be several more names. And there are far too many on the wall now. How many of those honored dead shouldn't be there? How many should still be alive? How many died because somebody wanted to be promoted, whatever the cost? Your sentence in this case should cry, 'Enough!' The prosecution and Colonel Zimmer want you to send out a message that you don't disobey orders in combat. You've done that by finding my client guilty. Now it's time to send out another message—don't sacrifice American lives for nothing!"

More quietly, Paul said, "The Vietnam War has been over for years. And that war has taken enough casualties. Major Thomas is one of them. Now, he has a federal conviction for the rest of his life. Is he going to get promoted with that on his records? No way. And this conviction is on top of the pain of the sucking chest wound he got in Vietnam. He has been punished enough. The defense contends that the only appropriate sentence for Major Thomas is no punishment. We've all been punished enough. Let it rest."

Paul returned to his seat and sat down heavily. He stole a look at the court members, but they remained impassive. Oh well, he thought, it's like the title of Santoli's book on Vietnam, *Everything We Had*. I gave this case everything I had, just like Jim gave everything he had north of the Song Be River many years ago.

After a moment's silence, Judge Savage began instructing the court members on sentencing. He informed them that the maximum punishment was dismissal, confinement for life, and total forfeiture of all pay and allowances. He also discussed several lesser punishments, such as a reprimand, and concluded the instruction on possible punishments by saying, "Finally, if you wish, you may sentence the accused to no punishment." Paul mentally crossed his fingers as the judge gave that particular portion of the instructions. Then, the judge gave the procedural instructions. Unlike voting on findings, the court members continued to vote on an appropriate sentence until three-fourths of them agreed if the sentence was to confinement of ten years or more, or two-thirds agreed for any lesser sentence. Each member who wanted to could propose a sentence, and the members voted on them in order, beginning with the lightest. As soon as the requisite majority agreed with a proposal, that was the sentence. Judge Savage concluded by saying, "You should select the sentence that best serves the ends of good order and discipline in the military, the welfare of our society, and the needs of this accused." After making sure that the court members understood the instructions and that the lawyers had no objections to them, the judge closed the court. The court members filed into the deliberation room for the last time. Again, everyone but the bailiff left the courtroom, leaving it strangely empty in the gathering dusk.

CHAPTER 41

Trial Defense Service Office
Office of the Staff Judge Advocate
Building 244, Fort Leavenworth, Kansas

J U N E   1 9 8 6

While the court members deliberated on the sentence, the two defense counsel rehashed the sentencing phase of the trial. Paul was convinced he had blown it—that his argument was too emotional for the conservative court members who had, after all, convicted his client of what Paul knew was a bullshit charge. Sam, with the eternal optimism of an inexperienced defense counsel, was convinced that Paul's argument was brilliant and that the jury would return a lenient sentence.

Jim took no part in the discussion. He just stood there, looking out the tall windows at the westering sun beyond the post cemetery and behind the ridgeline. As the lawyers fell silent, he broke the temporary lull in their conversation. "I'm going to go crazy sitting here waiting for the sentence," he said. "Listen, I may be behind bars tonight. I think I'd like to get a quick run in while the court's deliberating. I may not get to run freely for some time. I've got my running gear out in my car, and I can change in the latrine."

"I don't think the court members are going to sentence you to confinement," Paul responded, "but if you have to run, go ahead. Just don't go too far. The court could reach a sentence quickly."

About an hour later, the bailiff knocked on Sam's door. The court members had reached a sentence. The two defense counsel huddled together, then asked the bailiff to get Major Morgan and Captain Lewis. When the trial counsel arrived, all four lawyers went into a conference before returning to the courtroom.

Back in front of Judge Savage, Major Morgan preempted the judge's usual procedure. "Your Honor, could we have a hearing out of the presence of the court members?"

"Again? I suppose," Judge Savage replied in an irritated tone, looking at his watch. He was always very conscious of keeping the court members waiting, especially after normal duty hours.

"Your Honor, the bailiff has informed me that the members have reached a sentence, but Lieutenant Colonel David has told me that the accused went running an hour ago and has not returned. Because it's approaching 2100 hours and we can't keep the court members here indefinitely, I propose we have the court announce the sentence in his absence."

"Of course, we can do that," the Judge thought out loud. "We're certainly past arraignment, and if the accused is voluntarily absent, the trial can continue without him. We can have an Article 39a session tomorrow and advise the accused of his appellate rights then. Does the defense object to announcing the sentence now?"

"No, your Honor."

"Who is responsible for the accused?" Judge Savage asked. "Why wasn't the bailiff watching him?"

Both Paul and Ken stood up and started to say, "It's my fault, your Honor," but Judge Savage cut them off, saying he'd figure out whom to hassle about it later.

During their conference before they went back into the courtroom, Paul and Ken had decided what to say about who was at fault for letting the accused go run, but apparently, they would have to answer for it to the staff judge advocate after the trial rather than to the judge.

Lieutenant Colonel David watched as the court members filed in. Again, he couldn't read their expressions. Why did I let Jim go run, he thought. Where the hell is he, anyway? A couple of the members looked at the defense table and frowned, apparently wondering where Major Thomas was. The only sign of his presence was the blank yellow legal tablet on the table in front of his empty seat.

Meg was not in the courtroom. She couldn't trust herself not to attack Ken Morgan if she had to wait around in the courtroom and had gone home to wait for a call from Jim that the members had reached a sentence. The few spectators who had waited this late to learn what the sentence was stirred expectantly as Judge Savage asked the court members whether they had reached a sentence.

"We have, your Honor," the President answered.

Judge Savage instructed the bailiff to bring him the sentence worksheet. After reading the sentence that was written on it to himself, he had the bailiff return it to the President of the Court. "I have examined the sentence worksheet and find no defects in form. You may announce the sentence, Mr. President."

Normally, the judge ordered the accused and counsel to stand during the announcement of the sentence. The President, who was familiar with this procedure, looked at Major Thomas's empty chair at the defense table.

"Major James Thomas, it is my duty, as President of this Court, to inform you that this court sentences you to forfeit one dollar."

The spectators gasped as the two defense lawyers smiled. Judge Savage raised his gavel to silence the spectators, but put it back down as the noise subsided. "Thank you, Mr. President, Members of the Court. You are dismissed. The court is adjourned."

"All rise," the bailiff commanded.

After the judge and the court members had left the courtroom, Ken and Pam came over to congratulate the defense team. As they shook hands, Ken said, "Great sentencing argument. Let's go to the club for a beer. Pam's volunteered to go find Jim. Sam, why don't you go help her, and then you two can join us at the club. We can celebrate the end of this case, if nothing else. That's a fantastic sentence for the defense."

Paul responded, "Thanks. Jim can probably spare a buck."

"He doesn't even need to cough up the money," Pam Lewis said, pointing to the jury box. "Look."

Paul, Sam, and Ken turned their heads in the direction of Pam's pointing finger. There, draped over the bench in front of where the President of the court had sat, was a dollar bill.

CHAPTER 42

The FLOOM—The Fort Leavenworth Officers' Open Mess
Fort Leavenworth, Kansas

JUNE 1986

"Over here, Paul," Ken called out. Paul wound his way through the tables crowded together in the dark, cramped bar in the basement of the club house in the middle of the golf course. Only a few other officers were in the bar this late. Most of them appeared to be CAS-Cubed students relaxing after working late at the Command and General Staff College. Ken was sitting in a corner with a pitcher of beer and two mugs before him on a small, round table. Paul tucked his garrison cap into his belt and sat down as Ken poured him a mug from the pitcher of Coors Light. "Have a diet Coors?" Ken asked.

"Thanks, Ken. So where are Pam and Sam?"

"I have no idea. They must still be out looking for Jim."

"So who congratulates whom, Ken?"

"You've got me. It's too bad that the one time we got to go head to head, it had to be a stupid case like this one. I think everybody lost. Not just Jim Thomas, not just us, but everybody—and the Army, too. Even with the nothing sentence that is, in effect, no punishment, Jim's career is ruined. And the way you raked your senior rater over the coals, you're not going to make full colonel."

"Yeah, but I really don't care. I can retire in a year and try to earn some real money as a civilian lawyer. I won't have to sit here in the middle of nowhere watching all the lawyers who kiss the Judge Advocate General's ass get all the good assignments anymore. But I'm sorry for Jim—all this stress, a federal conviction, and for the court to say, 'Yes, you committed a crime, you disobeyed an order, but you don't deserve punishment for it.' Why didn't they just find him not guilty if he didn't deserve any punishment?"

Ken thought for a moment and then spoke. "I wasn't going to tell you this—I was just going to do it—but you might as well know. Because the sentence was so light, I'm going to recommend that the convening authority disapprove the guilty finding. That way Jim won't have a court-martial conviction on his record." Ken smiled. "That way you won."

Paul stared into his glass of beer. "I appreciate your doing that, but I doubt if you can convince the convening authority. He'll probably ask you whether there's some way he can increase the sentence. Good thing he can't. And believe it or not, I don't give a damn about who won this case anymore. I really wanted to beat the great Ken Morgan when this case started, but it's pretty irrelevant now. I agree with you. We all lost. Sometimes, an officer's future worth to the Army is more important than absolute disclosure of some incident. We've destroyed Jim's future worth to the Army for this obscure incident that didn't harm anyone or impair mission accomplishment. And any publicity that may ultimately result can only hurt the Army. You know, Ken, I really came to like the guy. I'm not sure I ever liked a defense client before, and I certainly disliked a lot of them, but Jim is ok. And I really have a strong sense of loss about his conviction, far beyond any personal feelings about losing a case against you. And I went through the entire trial without ever letting him know that I cared about him as a person rather than just a client."

Paul paused for a moment before continuing. "Look what we've done to him. Even with the light sentence, the rest of his career and his life will probably go spiralling down. What will he be in a few years? A passed-over major, retiring at twenty years with no marketable skills. We can retire and practice law. What skills does he have that civilian employers want? Leading men in combat or planning tactical operations? No, I can see Jim in ten years as an old, embittered, lonely ex-officer trying to sell life insurance or mutual funds to soldiers from a dingy little office from a strip outside a military base. Maybe it would have been better if he'd died in Vietnam rather than have to live to be disgraced like this, for doing what he thought was his duty.

"You know, there doesn't seem to be any statute of limitations on the effects of the Vietnam War. Jim is another casualty, the same as if he had died of his wounds there. Now, he'll have to suffer the embarrassment for the remainder of his career of being the officer who was convicted of disobeying an order during combat. Come on, let's get the hell out of here. I'll leave word with the club manager to tell Pam and Sam that we've left."

As they walked out of the front door of the club, Paul stopped, looking at the orderly rows of tombstones in the national cemetery directly across from the golf course in front of the club. They shone palely under the light of the street lamps. I wonder whether Jim will be buried here at Fort Leavenworth some day, Paul thought. We certainly killed his career here.

Before getting into his little brown Toyota to go home, Paul shook Ken's hand. "Thanks, Ken, for caring," he said. "I just wish a few others had cared." As he drove away toward the back gate of the post, down the dark streets, relieved only sporadically by the soft glow of the street lights, Paul's thoughts became less bitter. Regardless of what they do to Jim, Paul thought, he's got a living memorial in the lives of his platoon members and in the sons and daughters they lived to conceive after returning home. And a living memorial is far better than being nothing more than a name chiseled in black marble in a V-shaped wound in the earth, memorializing the human cost of a lost war.

CHAPTER 43

Ridgeline West of the Cantonement Area
Fort Leavenworth, Kansas

JUNE   1986

After Jim had left the defense office to start his run, he went to his car, got his running gear, and changed quickly. As he laced up his good old, American-made Saucony running shoes, he decided to run up the ridgeline. He had always found running along the top of the ridge-line comforting, worth the climb. He liked to look out over Salt Creek Valley to the rolling hills of eastern Kansas to the west and see the post at his feet to the east. The post always looked so benign with the sun warming the red brick buildings spread out before him like a toy village. From the top of the ridgeline, even the gray walls and dome of the Disciplinary Barracks looked like a castle rather than a bleak penal institution.

Jim walked down the steps of the SJA building and started jogging easily. In a few moments, he was on Doniphan Avenue, running the same route that Lieutenant Colonel Glenn, the Article 32 Investigating Officer, had run the day he decided what he would recommend, but in reverse.

The sun was setting behind the large hill mass west of the cemetery as Jim settled into an easy rhythm. He ran along Hancock Avenue between the older part of the cemetery, where Tom Custer, winner of two Congressional Medals of Honor in the Civil War, was buried, and the newer part, with the graves of the honored dead of later wars. His eye fell on the grave of a lieutenant colonel. The inscription on the simple mar-ble headstone showed he had died in Vietnam.

Maybe he's the lucky one, Jim thought. He died before anyone questioned his role in the war. It's ironic that if I had died from my wound, I would have been a hero. But I lived to be convicted by a court-martial. He felt his eyes tear up again as he thought, damn, all I ever wanted was to make lieutenant colonel and command an infantry battalion. And no matter how light my sentence is, I'll never be promoted or selected for command with a conviction on my record. I'll never lead troops again.

For a few moments, Jim's morbid thoughts subsided as he turned west and started running up the hill. His stride shortened and his breathing quickened as the slope got steeper. He pushed up the hill, punishing himself, letting the pain of the lactic acid buildup in his leg muscles wash away his anger and hurt. But anguish returned again after he had crested the top of the hill and his furiously pumping heart had flushed the lactic acid out of his muscles. So he picked up his pace and concentrated on his running rather than on his problems. He looked up and saw a large bird—a hawk or an eagle—flying high overhead, and for a moment they soared together as his stride smoothed out, and he felt as if he could run—or fly—forever.

He ran past the small monument marking the site of Fort de Cavagnial—an early French outpost overlooking Salt Creek Valley. There must be some symbolism here, he thought. We followed the French to Vietnam and lost, and I followed them to Leavenworth and lost. A loud "moo" from one of the cows in the Disciplinary Barracks farm pasture on his left startled him. He almost laughed, thinking that he couldn't go anywhere on this post without being reminded of the DB.

I've never done things quite right in the Army, he thought. When I was a brand new lieutenant, I was too mission-oriented. Then, according to the court-martial, in Vietnam I cared too much about my men. And Meg was right—recently, I've worried too much about my career and not enough about our personal life. There must be a happy medium. But the military makes it damn hard to find.

The sun was redder and lower behind him as he turned to the east to run down the northern end of the hill. As long as he kept pushing it, he felt fine—almost a runner's high. Maybe it's ok, he thought. Maybe I should have died that day near Quan Loi. Maybe everything's been gravy since then. I'll certainly never top leading American troops in combat, especially now, in the peacetime Army, with a court-martial conviction on my record. The lush foliage of the trees alongside the road made a canopy, reminding Jim of the canopied jungle of Vietnam.

He picked up his pace even more as the downhill slope became steeper. As he ran down the hill, he stole a quick glance at the Disciplinary Barracks graveyard looking quiet and peaceful under the trees in the gathering dusk. He thought about the German POWs who had been buried there after their execution at the end of World War II.

The United States had hung them for doing what they thought was their duty, executing a fellow prisoner of war who had been collaborating with the American camp administration. And I'm going to be punished for doing what I thought was my duty. I wonder whether the German POWs would still have executed the traitor if they had known that they would be hung for it? Probably not. But maybe because I'm not facing execution, or maybe because I saved lives instead of taking one, I'd do it again. In the words of my acting platoon sergeant, SP4 Rivera, I'd do it a goddamn 'gain.

An Army truck was leaving the warehouse at the west side of Sherman Army Airfield as Jim continued downhill. Their paths would intersect at the base of the hill. The sound of gunfire from the skeet range behind the northeast corner of the warehouse reminded Jim of Vietnam. His pace picked up, and as he flew downhill, he saw the faces of his platoon: SP4 Rivera, his RTO, PFC Darnell, Doc Calvin, Sergeant Hamm, and all the rest. He spared a moment from the thoughts of his platoon to think of Margaret. She looked as beautiful to him now as she had during his thirty-day leave before he left for Vietnam, and he realized that he loved her even more now than he had then. Yes, Jim thought, since Vietnam, it's all been gravy.

He flew faster down the hill. Maybe it was the thought that at least he had come back from Vietnam in one piece and had had more time with Meg, or maybe it was a runner's high as his brain released endorphins, but for whatever reason, all of a sudden, he felt better. I'll show those jerks, he thought. I'll look the court members in the eye and take whatever punishment they want to dish out. I'll hang in there and do the best I can in whatever shit job the Army sticks me with. They may take my career, but they can't take my Combat Infantry Badge and the respect of the men I led in combat. What do I care what the wimps who have never led American fighting men in combat think? I'll hang tough and show them how a combat leader deals with adversity. I can even forgive Armstrong. Screw revenge. Meg always said that the best revenge was to live a happy life anyway. After I'm done with this hassle, I'm going to go back and really talk to her and work out our problems and make the best of whatever time we have left.

He held that thought as he approached the intersection at the base of the hill, running all out. He was so pumped up from the run and his raging determination to survive and conquer that he didn't see the Army truck as it headed south toward the Disciplinary Barracks. He ran directly into its path. As he realized the danger, his life flashed before him and for one brief, shining moment, he was twenty-one again and immortal—running through the elephant grass to get smoke grenades to mark friendly lines so gunship fire wouldn't hit his men.

Suddenly, he felt a violent pull on his arm, yanking him out of the truck's path.

Paul kept a tight grip on Jim's sweaty arm and led him over to his car, which he had parked by the side of the road when he saw Jim running towards him. "What are you trying to do, you dumb shit, kill yourself?"

"Sorry. I kind of lost it there for a minute. Has the jury reached a sentence?"

"Yes, almost an hour ago. I don't know how to break this to you, but they fined you a dollar."

"A dollar? That's all?"

"Yes, and they left you a dollar bill, so they paid your fine for you. And before you start feeling depressed that you've still got a conviction, the prosecutor is going to try like hell to get it disapproved. And knowing him, he'll succeed. Let's get you back to your quarters—I thought you'd rather tell Meg the good news yourself. She's worried sick about you. After I got home, I called your quarters to give you the good news, but Meg said you weren't there. We decided you must still be out running, and I knew the best place on post for a good long ball-busting run by a pissed-off client was the ridgeline, so here I am. Obviously, my legal services don't end when the trial's over. Now, let's get you back to Meg."

As Jim got into Paul's car, he gave Paul a long look, held out his hand to shake, and said, "Thanks, man. I guess I owe you my life, as well as my freedom."

Paul favored his client with a rare smile. "Yeah, now according to ancient Chinese tradition, your life's mine. So I'm telling you to go take care of that good wife you have and to continue to take care of your troops, ok?"

"Yes, Sir. You know, you're not too bad for a lawyer."

HEADQUARTERS
U.S. ARMY TRAINING AND DOCTRINE COMMAND
Fort Monroe, Virginia 23651

Court-Martial Promulgating Order   6 July 1986
No. 37

In the case of United States v. Major James N. Thomas,
312-64-3109, U.S. Army, Student Detachment, CGSC, the
findings of guilty and the sentence are disapproved. All rights,
privileges, and property of which the accused has been deprived
by virtue of the findings of guilty and the sentence are hereby
restored.

FOR THE COMMANDER:

LARRY E. REDDICK
CW2
Assistant Adjustant

CHAPTER 44

Garry Owen Task Force Tactical Operations Center
Southeast of Baghdad, Iraq

MARCH 1991

The task force operations officer, Captain Lee, hung up the secure phone to the Brigade TOC and let out a whoop. "Get the CO in here, ASAP!"

The operations NCOs and the RTOs had no idea whom the young captain had addressed the order to, but the troop closest to the door pushed aside the curtain that kept any light from getting out of the S-3 section of the task force TOC and giving away their postion and left to get the commander. A few minutes later, the battalion commander of the First Battalion, Eighth Cavalry Regiment, First Cavalry Division, now named the Garry Owen Task Force because of its augmentation with other units, walked in and asked, "What gives, Three?"

Captain Lee answered quickly, "I wanted you to be the first to know, Six, the President has ordered a cease-fire, effective immediately! We've won!"

A cheer erupted from the TOC's inhabitants as their commander, Lieutenant Colonel Thomas, raised his fists in the air in triumph, making the horses on his Cav patches jump upside down on both shoulders. After a fleeting thought about whether he should disobey the cease-fire and attack, so he wouldn't be court-martialled for lack of aggressiveness this time, the big grin on his face faded as he realized he had to get back to business quickly to avoid unnecessary casualties on either side. "Get the word out to all our units, ASAP. But be sure that they don't start celebrating and fail to keep good security. We can't be certain that the Iraqis have all got the word or that the ones who hear the word will agree to cease firing."

After the S-3 had complied, he sat down next to his commander, who had sunk into a reclining position in the folding chair he sat in while planning tactical operations. Fatigue was etched in the colonel's face, with its two-day-old growth of beard. But he looked happy—or at least relieved. Captain Lee said, "Sir, I've got more news. The Brigade Commander passed along his compliments on a job well done and said that he was putting the battalion in for a distinguished unit citation. Congratulations."

Thomas rubbed the stubby growth on his face, thinking the irrelevant thought that at least it wasn't a Fu Manchu mustache this time, and said, "The award goes to the men who were out there eating sand, not me."

"Don't be so modest, Sir. Your tactical plans were brilliant."

"I don't know about that, but if they were, I suppose I have to thank the Command and General Staff College. At the time, I thought many of the classes were bullshit, but I see their worth now, especially all that AirLand Battle stuff. You can't imagine the complexity of modern warfare, even as low as at the battalion level, unless you try to integrate combined arms tactics, logistics, law of war, and everything else into your operations. The Middle East Exercise certainly was a great preparation for desert warfare, even though we had to transplant the principles from Iran to Iraq. But I guess that's the beauty of the doctrine—you can transplant it from one AO to another. Even the hated writing course was a help because any commander worth his salt must know how to write an operations order that is understandable. Every time I edited your draft OPPLANS, it was with the voice of that unrelenting civilian woman writing instructor ringing in my ears, "The only acceptable writing is writing that your readers can understand the first time through and can come to no other conclusion but the one you want them to." I certainly didn't want the company commanders coming to different conclusions about what they were supposed to do when we went on the attack. Even the leadership courses weren't so bad—although, like every other CGSC student, I thought I knew everything there was to know about leadership and everything else before I got to CGSC. Yeah, I learned a lot at Leavenworth—not all of it in the classroom. I'll tell you about it sometime."

Lieutenant Colonel Thomas turned around in his chair as he heard someone clear his throat behind him, and saw Specialist Four Allen standing there, holding a stack of mail. "What do you have for me, Allen?"

"Looks like mail from home, Sir. Us U.S. mailpersons can't stop delivering just because we kicked Saddam Hussein's ass!"

"Roger that! Thank you much."

Lieutenant Colonel Thomas sorted through the handful of letters Allen had handed him and picked out one that he instantly recognized as from his wife by the robin-egg blue envelope she always used. He tore it open and took out the letter.

Dear Jim,

Hope this letter finds you well. Listening to CNN makes me think that you will be home pretty soon, which is good because I really need you home! Do you remember when you came home to see me the day you had free before returning to the war after you went to the Pre-Command Course at Fort Leavenworth when you were given your command? Well, you weren't firing blanks that day, troop! Yes, I'm pregnant! I know we are both too old and had given up, but I guess all those little soldiers you deposited in me that wonderful day learned that deep attack stuff and finally conquered! So you keep your head down— you've got enough medals—and come home to me and your son or daughter (or both!).

Love, Meg

E P I L O G U E

Jim Thomas retired shortly after Meg gave birth to twins—Jason and Victoria. Along with one of his old Army buddies, he formed Veterans' Development, Inc., which develops residential property in the greater Kansas City area. He runs the ridgeline several times a year when he goes to Fort Leavenworth to shop at the commissary or post exchange.

Paul David was passed over for colonel, retired at twenty years' service, and formed a law firm in Chicago. He occasionally defends a court-martial for old times' sake.

Ken Morgan made full colonel and served thirty years before retiring down to a farm in Louisiana that had been in his family for generations. He spent his last six years in the military as a military judge—often trying cases at Fort Leavenworth.

Colonel Farmer never did make general. He retired and became an administrator of the bar association of a southern state. Following its downsizing, he opened up a one-man law office in a small town.

Lieutenant Colonel Mark Armstrong commanded an infantry battalion in the Gulf War. His brigade commander, Colonel Nesbit, relieved him for lack of aggressiveness, and he retired shortly thereafter. He now sells life insurance to soldiers at Fort Benning from an office in Columbus, Georgia.

Major Lewis and Major Wilson ended up as CGSC students together shortly before their promotions to lieutenant colonel. Like children arguing my dad is better than your dad, each one never failed to take an opportunity to try to convince the other one that the attorney each had worked for during the court-martial many years earlier was the best trial strategist and tactician in the Army JAGC. Both of them were right.

ABOUT THE AUTHOR

Besides having served as an infantry platoon leader with the First Cavalry Division in Vietnam, Lieutenant Colonel (Retired) Jonathan P. Tomes has been a military prosecutor, a military defense counsel, a military judge, the President of a General Court-Martial, the Chief Military Law Instructor at the U.S. Army Command and General Staff College, and the Chief of the Special Claims Branch, Tort Claims Division, U.S. Army Claims Service. He earned the Silver Star, the Legion of Merit, the Bronze Star, the Meritorious Service Medal with Oak Leaf Cluster, the Air Medal, the Army Commendation Medal, various service medals, the Combat Infantry Badge, and Parachutist's Wings.

After his retirement from the Army, Tomes taught evidence, appellate advocacy, military law, legal research and writing, administrative law, professional responsibility, criminal procedure, and hospital law at IIT Chicago-Kent College of Law in Chicago. He won Professor of the Year Award for 1993–94 and the Black Law Students' Harold Washington Award for 1992–93 and 1993–94.

More recently as a partner in a Chicago law firm and now a partner in a Kansas City law firm, Tomes has extensive litigation and transactional experience and is AV rated by Martindale-Hubbell. His practice areas include administrative law, criminal law, health law, medical malpractice, and military law. Recognized nationwide as an expert in information law, health law, and military law, Tomes has given seminars for the American Bar Association, The Business Network, the Lorman Business Center, and Faulkner & Gray and has provided expert commentary for numerous radio and television shows, including *American Justice* on A&E. Since graduating first in his law school class, Tomes has been admitted to practice law in Illinois, Missouri, Kansas, Oklahoma, U.S. District Courts for the Northern District of Illinois (Trial Bar), the District of Kansas, and the Western District of Missouri, and U.S. Courts of Appeals for the Seventh and Federal Circuits. He has also served as an arbitrator for the National Association of Securities Dealers, the Commodity Futures Association, and Illinois Uninsured Motorists. He represents servicemembers in courts-martial and administrative matters around the world.

Tomes is also the author of *The Servicemember's Legal Guide* (Stackpole Books, 3d ed.) and more than two dozen other nonfiction books and another two dozen journal and law review articles primarily in health law and military law. His recent books include compliance guides to electronic and other health records and *Responding to AIDS: The Healthcare Professional's Guide to Legal Issues & Responsibilities*. The U.S. Supreme Court in *United States v. Solorio*, 107 S.Ct. 2924 (1987), cited Tomes's 1985 *Air Force Law Review* article, "The Imagination of the Prosecutor—the Only Limitation on Court-Martial Jurisdiction Now, Fifteen Years After *O'Callahan v. Parker*." His recent use of mitigation experts in criminal, civil, administrative, and court-martial cases for both civilian and military clients led him to write his latest law review article, "Damned If You Do, Damned If You Don't: The Use of Mitigation Experts in Death Penalty Litigation," 24 AM. J. CRIM. L. No. 2, p. 359 (Spring 1997). *Lawful Orders* is his first novel.